TAKE A LEFT AT TOMORROW
A Novel

by

Renée Anduze

ISBN # 978-1-940189-29-1

Library of Congress Control Number: 2021942319

Author's Note

My intention was to write a believable story set during important historic times and events. I made an enormous effort to depict everything accurately. But I'm a novelist, not a historian. There were a great many people at some of the events, and no one's view was exactly the same. President Nixon's quoted words in the Lincoln Memorial scene, based on an actual event, can be found at nixonlibrary.gov and nixonfoundation.org.

Twisted Road Publications

Twisted Road
PUBLICATIONS

For

D. M. H.

— ONE —

All Gone

"Get over it," my boyfriend Tommy would say whenever I tried sneaking my mother into the conversation—which I usually did over cigarettes after a necking session in his baby-blue Thunderbird on the old road behind Johannsen's dairy farm.

"What's the sense in hashing it over?" he'd say as I drew pierced hearts in the backseat window steam, trying not to drop ashes on his white leather upholstery and listening to a whippoorwill share its woe. "You had her for a while. Now you don't. All gone, finito, kaput."

Tommy's dad had left a while back, on the very evening Willie Mays hit his five hundredth homer—called Tommy's mom collect from Reno three nights after failing to come home from his paper-mill shift—and memories, regrets, and what-ifs were not places Tommy liked to park, even when Eric Burdon was singing "House of the Rising Sun" on the radio and making abandonment and misery sound so romantic, so cool.

"If you'd stop gabbing, we'd have time for another beer," he'd say on the nights he was feeling especially talkative, pulling his church key from the pocket that held his bone-handled jackknife.

I liked Tommy for more than his taste in automobiles and his skill with small buttons. I liked his wayward brown curls, which flopped around like little puppy-dog paws, and the wiry tuft that sprang from his V-neck sweater, which he never wore with a turtleneck or shirt. I liked that he preferred Mick Jagger to Paul McCartney and could strike a match and light a Lucky with one hand. I liked that he could take a corner without putting his foot on the brake, could downshift without touching the clutch. I especially liked that when we slow danced, he pulled me tight, pressing his hand on the small of my back till my thigh

1

slid between his legs and my hipbone nestled in that valley along the ridge.

I even liked Tommy's silent streaks and impatience with reminiscences and idle chitchat. I'd been a romantic since Elvis begged me to love him tender from inside a radio that was taller than me. But I was also a north-country girl, accustomed to folks who didn't ramble on. There was something wimpy about a chatty guy, something solid about a fellow who didn't need to prove himself with spoken words. Something deep, poetic, and intense.

I liked a great many things about Tommy, who'd lettered in hockey, was handsomer than most, and never left hickies. And we'd gone steady long enough to reach the snap of my bell-bottom blue jeans. But I knew I had to return his class ring—so heavy and masculine with its blood-red stone, held on my finger by a wad of adhesive tape. A guy who didn't like hearing that my mother could be an owl or a sparrow or even a hummingbird, that she was always watching over me from a treetop, telephone pole, or antenna, just wasn't the right guy for me.

But breaking up—as Neil Sedaka warbled over WLS while *You Only Live Twice* glowed across the drive-in screen—is hard to do. "Talk? Let's crack a Grain Belt in the backseat first," Tommy would say. Or, "What's there to discuss when you look so good?" Other times he'd just laugh and say nothing at all.

And without Tommy, my life was mostly dirty dishes, dirty clothes, and dirty floors. It was wiping Jimmy's runny nose, looking for Jeff's lucky socks, and begging Jack to take out the trash. It was finding the Sears Roebuck catalog in the bathroom when Daddy was too broke for toilet paper, and catching his tipsy "But I'm going to put it right back on in the morning" when I asked him to hang up his coat.

Even if Tommy was mum about my mother, he was a reliably good distraction from my troubles, structuring his social calendar as methodically as he did everything. Once a weekend, if my Bridgeman's schedule allowed and Jimmy didn't have another cold, I could count on a date.

Oh, I *knew* I was going to miss Tommy if I ever managed to call it quits. But as sure as dirt on a granite gravestone, I also knew you only live *once*.

☙

The Saturday night I met Kit Griffith, Tommy was walleye fishing at the shack he'd built with his kid brother Kenny in the woods near Lake Winnibigoshish. I'd been there just once. Tommy didn't have to say it for me to know my sole invite to that manly world was based on my womanly ability to tidy up.

And I didn't mind lending a hand, though cleaning a shack was pretty much my daily life. Tommy, in his common-sense way, had brought a six-pack of malt liquor and a bag of Old Dutch potato chips to sweeten the task. But that little cabin was a quarter mile beyond the overgrown end of a long road, tucked inside a giant cocoon of vegetation I was sure no small creature could penetrate. Its location just sucked up my breath, made me feel smothered by hovering green monsters and looming dark shadows. I needed to view treetops and telephone poles, streetlights and rooftop aerials. Perching places for Mamma. Tommy had never seen me in such a state, gasping and gulping back tears.

"Holy Jesus, what the hell's wrong with you? There's fresh air all around and not a bogeyman in sight." My broom, bucket, and rags never made it to the cabin door. Tommy hated tears.

Walleyed pike—a fish as shy and wily as November sunshine—were the pride of Minnesota's ten thousand lakes. Battered and pan fried, they were fine eating. A few fillets wrapped in butcher's paper was a gift on par with a bottle of chokecherry wine or a hand-knit muffler. I didn't begrudge Tommy his weekend pursuing such a prize, though it left me dateless on a Saturday night I didn't have to scoop ice cream. But Saturday night was couples night, so Tommy couldn't begrudge my going out without him.

It was a late June evening in the summer of 1967—the summer of love, though no one I knew called it that. Nary a hippie lived in Grand

Rapids, Minnesota. Haight-Ashbury was a street corner on some other planet.

Due to the clouds, the evening was darker than usual and not quite summery. Instead of shorts and a halter top, I was wearing my brown pants with leather side laces and my yellow poorboy sweater. I'd sewn the pants on my old Singer and found the sweater in the markdown bin at Ben Franklin five-and-dime. My plastic sandals could almost pass for leather in the low light.

I also had on my best jewelry—gold-plated hoop earrings Dee Dee had given me last summer for my sixteenth birthday. Dee Dee Perpich and I had been friends since second grade, when her folks bought the yellow stucco house six backyards and two alleys away. She'd pierced my ears with an embroidery needle soaked in rubbing alcohol so I could wear her grand gift. Ice cubes had numbed the pain, but the needle's crunch had been freaky. Tommy's mom had told him a girl who pierced her ears would do *anything*, but Tommy, to his dismay, knew better.

I'd washed my hair with lemon juice and dried it in front of the oven to make it less wispy and stuck in that sad place between blonde and brown—a color Miss Clairol planned to change one day. If I didn't look like a girl out of *Seventeen* magazine that night, it wasn't for lack of trying.

Dee Dee and I were sharing a bottle of Coke on the asphalt stretch of the bus depot alley where the long silver beasts rolled up, around the corner from the pool hall, a cellar lair only bad girls set foot in. We were waiting for a booth in the pizza/coffee shop at the back of the depot, wishing it wasn't even worse for a lady to smoke a cigarette standing up than to let it dangle from her mouth. A girl who smoked had to do it right if she wanted to keep her reputation. Really nice girls, of course, didn't smoke at all. Really nice girls had nice families and no reason to be rebels.

Dee Dee and I had learned to smoke two summers back, when I decided we needed more than long bangs and eye shadow to make us sophisticated sophomores. Nightly under the beam of a flashlight, we hacked our way through a bummed pack of charcoal-filtered Tareytons

4

after the boys were in their bunks. We hid our ashtray—the Vikings mug Jimmy had given me for Christmas—under my bed when we'd puffed ourselves sick.

By our junior year, we'd switched to Benson & Hedges menthol—which sported a snazzy metallic-green pack—and could inhale without coughing. And we could now loop smoke between mouth and nose, like the chicest French person or the worldliest senior. We were cigarette pros who, in the right car or at the right party, dared light up in public. Dee Dee kept her pack down the front of her jeans, but I kept mine in a flip-top Band-Aid tin right in my purse. "You're one brave rebel," Dee Dee would say. "Just don't ever forget that bag somewhere."

I was a rebel, all right, but I didn't really want to be. And my cause was no secret to those who knew me well. Which pretty much meant Dee Dee, whose mom spent most of her time caring for Dee Dee's dad, a grumpy man with an ever-changing assortment of illnesses, leaving Dee Dee free to help me concoct the little social mutinies that felt so necessary to being who I'd decided I had to be. When you can't fit in, your only choice is to be an outsider. And if your work ethic is strong, you try to be the very best outsider.

What I really wanted, though, was just plain *out*—a place Tommy could never take me. Out of that shabby house and its never-ending needs, out of that paper-mill and iron-ore town on the west end of the Mesabi Range, out of the clothes that came from my cousin Carla's charity boxes, my garage-sale Singer, and the leftover rack.

Some girls aspired to be a schoolteacher, some a nurse, some a secretary. Most wanted to be a wife and mom—caretaker of the picket fence and maker of the perfect boy-girl-boy-girl family, who'd naturally grow up to be a doctor, nurse, lawyer, and secretary. But me, I just wanted to be something other than a motherless girl stuck with the parts of Mamma's job that Daddy's nameless ladies—who never crossed our doorstep—clearly weren't interested in. To be something *else* with a capital E. Which meant being Elsewhere. Elsewhere by about a million miles.

～

As soon as I saw him, I knew he wasn't from around here. He was wearing a blue polo sweater and corduroys that actually matched. Guys from this neck of the woods wore corduroys only for school, and a sweater of that caliber was strictly church attire. Matching colors, those were reserved for weddings, if ever. And this fellow's hair was longer than northern Minnesota guys dared grow theirs if they didn't want to be called girly. Long but not scruffy, swaying waves saying someone got paid to cut it. And *red*. Strawberry blond, to be fair, but the freckles pegged him. Then there was that silver bracelet on his wrist. Nope, no redheaded guy from here would walk down the alley toward the pool hall on a Saturday night wearing a getup and a haircut like that.

He didn't walk like a local guy either—didn't strut as Tommy tended to, gangle the way Tommy's big brother Ralph did, or lumber like my brother Jack, who loved his meat and potatoes. He strode like a guy who knew where he was going and didn't give a hoot what anyone thought about it. He was plainly no local sight, and all eyes in the alley huddles followed him into the light of the streetlamp and the café's neon sign.

He was an outsider, but he didn't seem a stranger. Several guys gave thumbs-up as he passed, and a nursing student named Becky yelled out, "Hey, Kit. The Cities get too hot for ya?"

He answered Becky with a wink and kept going. Figuring he was headed to the pool hall, I said to Dee Dee, "A guy named Kit who looks like that would be better off drinking coffee than playing pool."

Dee Dee handed me the Coke after a swig. "That one can take care of himself in or out of a pool hall."

Dee Dee could be a smarty-pants, and I was about to say, "How on earth would *you* know?" when the topic of our girl talk stopped in front of us. In front of me, to be exact.

"Hey there, baby. Your mamma must be a knockout to have a girl looks like you."

Dee Dee and I had rehearsed our flirting on many a sleepover night, but every clever comeback deserted me as I stared at this overdressed city slicker who didn't act like the outsider he was.

"My mother is dead."

6

He wasn't as tall as he walked, but I had to look up a fair distance to meet his eyes, which were green and were also blue.

"Then she's a knockout angel," he said. He was no pretty-boy, but his moxie and those maverick eyes made him hard to look away from.

"She wasn't so beautiful after she got sick."

My remark would have made Tommy's eyes roll, and I heard Dee Dee mumble "sheesh" as she slipped mercifully from my side and walked away.

"Now she has wings," he said. "She can fly anywhere you are, like a bird."

All I could do was blink. How could he know such a thing?

"And where you ought to be is a long way from this alley, little girl. This is no place for the likes of you."

He reached out and slid his hand behind my neck. I didn't push it away, though I was pretty sure Dee Dee was looking out the corner of her eye and shaking her head, even if my mother wasn't doing the same from some telephone pole.

"You still miss her," he said.

He smelled like English Leather. Tommy thought cologne was for girls and sissies, but I loved sniffing the English Leather sample bottle at Reed's Drug Store.

"I guess."

"She misses you too. Where's she buried?"

"Greenwood Cemetery in Bemidji."

"Let's go."

He was smiling. You'd have thought we were talking about the A&W drive-in or the Rialto showhouse. But I saw no mockery in his eyes.

"That's over an hour from here." Any local guy would know that.

He pulled a key from his pants pocket without looking down.

"Perfect night for a ride. If we're lucky, the breeze will zap the clouds and uncover the full moon. Crazy things happen when the full moon is out."

I couldn't help smiling back. "Like what?"

He took a step toward me, which was pretty much all there was between us, leaned down, and kissed me right on the lips. Hard, quick, tongue entering on the left and exiting on the right.

"Like that."

I definitely should have pushed him away then or told him to get lost. Any rule I knew about being a nice girl and not being easy said so. No one in that alley who'd noticed his boldness would have expected otherwise, Tommy's ring on my finger or not. But I didn't protest. I just stood there thinking he knew something about kissing that even Tommy didn't know. And something about me that no one did.

And when he took my hand and pulled, I followed him toward the bend at the dark end of the alley. I heard Dee Dee shout my name as we started around to where the trash cans, gas canisters, and stray cats hung out. I shouted back without turning.

"It's okay. I know him." It didn't feel like a lie.

He didn't stop until we got to the far side of the garbage cans, and neither did I. But even then, I was surprised more than scared.

"A motorcycle?"

"Got a scarf for your hair? We're gonna race this wind."

"All the way to Bemidji?"

It was big and purple and said Triumph on the side.

"Her name's Lola. She's not the jealous type, but she's nosey. Before you get on her, you gotta tell her your name."

I took a deep breath. The breeze wasn't yet chilly and didn't cool the flush I felt everywhere.

"Joey. Joey Dean."

He patted the seat of his bike.

"A good name." He was still smiling but not making fun.

"It's short for Josepha. Ugly."

"Nothing ugly about you, baby."

He took the Coke bottle that was still dangling from my hand and tossed it into a trash can.

"Hop on and put your feet here once I get her fired. Don't touch the exhaust pipe, and hold on real tight. Lola's going stir crazy, and we gotta blow outta here right now."

He put one hand on my elbow, tipped his brow with the other.

8

"Kit Griffith. That's short for Christopher."

He undid his saddlebag and pulled out something red.

"Take my bandana. Don't wanna tangle up that pretty hair."

"My mother's hair was black and wavy. A lot prettier than mine." Tommy would have groaned.

"Yours is beautiful," he said. "Angel's daughter's hair."

And so I hopped onto his purple motorcycle—trembling, trying hard not to giggle, unsure of what to hold on to. But the moment I settled into Lola's leather seat, I was ready for the ride, even if Greenwood Cemetery had been as far away as the moon.

— TWO —

Mirror Image

The mirror had made her twice as naked because I could see both sides of her, as she'd stood before the dresser and I'd stood behind her in the doorway, scared as I'd ever been in all my twelve years. Scared too stiff to move.

She'd let her robe crumple to the floor, let it snag on the pine boards that always gave me splinters when I walked on them barefoot. Tidiness and pretty things no longer mattered to her. It was the scar she was interested in. Fresh and crimson, it screamed under her right breast, around her ribs, and up her back.

An arm that looked like a birch branch—pale, papery, ragged—rose from her side, and she touched that thick line slicing her body nearly in half. I could see it throbbing, and she stroked it the way old folks sometimes do old photographs. A sunbeam poking past the dusty blinds landed on a frozen tear, but it refused to melt. She let her arm drop and turned away from the mirror. Her sigh said she'd seen all there was left to see.

"You wanted me, Mamma?" I just couldn't step into her room. It scared me worse than the root cellar at night, worse than the cobwebby place under our porch steps.

She must have heard me because her dark eyes rolled my way. But their gaze settled somewhere beyond me, though nobody else was there, except maybe the ghost of the Mamma she used to be. The frog in my throat felt bigger than my tongue.

"I'm here, Mamma." I needed to swallow, but didn't. It would have come out a gulp or a whimper.

"I wanted you to see this. The boys, they won't understand. But I think it's something you ought to remember."

10

I saw and remembered like a Brownie camera. Forever, I would own the snapshot of what cancer and doctors had turned her into. Burnt-brown skin stretched over a bundle of sticks topped with a clump of ashen string—Mamma, the fairest mother of them all. The queen of the whole wide world.

"My doctor at the hospital in Minneapolis, he says they hung me up to get at my lungs the right way. Sawed open a couple of ribs. Then he took my heart out, set it right on the table and gave it a pat."

Her far-off smile said she was amused by the image. I nodded and tried to smile too, fighting back a shiver. Carcasses, cleavers, and men in white coats were pounding on a door somewhere. I blinked, blinked again, trying to keep that door shut.

"He looks like the dark handsome one in *West Side Story*."

We'd seen the movie together. I said, "Oh. That's nice." Switchblades and stilettos. *Bam. Bam. Chink. Chink.*

"So. What do you think?" she said.

I thought her bosom looked sunken, her nipples oddly black, the knobs of her spine too pointy, and her hipbones really truly like *bones*. I thought her shoulder blades looked like plucked bird wings. I said, "I think you should try to eat something, Mamma. Would you like some cantaloupe?"

Cantaloupe was the only thing I'd seen her eat in months. Aunt Cora cut it into little squares because Mamma didn't have the strength left to scoop.

She didn't bother to pick up the robe, just shuffled back to the bed and sank.

"Not now," she said. "I'll bang the spoon when I'm hungry."

The bedside floor lamp sported an honest-to-goodness silver tray with a curlicue design, set in an iron hoop where a big glass ashtray had once sat. The tray didn't quite fit the hole and was dented on one side, but it was one of Mamma's little touches proving she had good taste. She'd once been so proud of those touches—the philodendron with a hanging planter that looked like a birdcage, the bookcase of real-leather encyclopedias bought on time, the woodsy wallpaper with the golden pinecones. Mamma's glamorous silver tray and her chic long spoon—which I later learned was for iced tea, a beverage most Minnesota coffee

11

folks didn't drink—served as her call bell. Spoon clanged on tray told the household she needed something, usually another hypo, which Aunt Cora knew how to give from practicing on a Sunkist orange.

I hated to see Mamma's chiffon robe lie on the floor that way. It had taken a year of layaway payments to become hers. But I wasn't brave enough to undo something Mamma had done, even now. Especially now. I finally stepped over the puffed sleeves, lace collar, rhinestone buttons, and lavender-and-yellow pansies with just enough courage to sit beside her on the mattress. This made her wince and slide my way. I wasn't very big, but it was an *old* mattress.

I thought of laying a hand on the jagged edge that had once been a knee she loved showing off in summer-white shorts. Her tanned skin had looked so alive in the August sunshine. But I didn't touch her, and I couldn't think of anything else to say.

After a wheezing moment, she said, "Do you have a boyfriend?"

I looked at the wall, which she'd painted *aqua*, not just blue, and said, "Uh huh."

"Is he rich?"

I glanced at the rumpled bedspread, which she'd stove-dyed *taupe*, not just brown, and said, "I don't think so. He's only in eighth grade."

"His parents," she said. "Are *they* rich?"

"Um. I don't know. Maybe. I guess so."

"Rich is better than poor."

"Uh huh. I know, Mamma."

"Find a rich man who won't stick you in a shack. Who'll put *your* dreams first."

"Uh huh."

I wanted her to ask me if I was in love. Then I might have said his name was Kevin, and described the adorable swirl his dark hair made on his princely forehead, or even mentioned the magic kiss in his dad's garage, where there was room for both a car and a boat.

But she didn't ask. After a while she just said, "I'm tired now." And I said, "Okay, Mamma," and left her alone with her fancy tray and her elegant spoon.

I was invited into my mother's room again a few weeks later, on the day I used her eyebrow pencil on my eyelids. Liz Taylor or Audrey

12

Hepburn had made eyeliner a beauty magazine topic, and my one-kiss passion to look doe-eyed gorgeous had anchored me in front of the bathroom mirror for serious artwork, while my aunt rubbed witch hazel on Mamma's back so she could maybe take a nap.

I forced my eyes wide during that rare visit, so hoping Mamma would notice how bewitching they were. I ogled the taupe curtains and the pair of ceramic art-deco cats—drugstore darlings of my mother's bureau top—and batted my eyelashes at each of those tastefully painted walls. Her new oxygen tank, colored what she called *emerald*, got an especially long once-over.

"I know I'm a frightful sight," she finally said. "But you could try not to look terrified when I'm feeling up to a little company."

A minute later I was out the door and never invited back. When Aunt Cora said Mamma was too tired for visitors, I felt guilty but relieved.

Mamma had been tired for so long. Tired and sick since way back when I was ten, her bedroom door closed more than open after a little cough left blood on her good lace handkerchief. Closed for long spells when she went away for the operations and the cobalt treatments, closed on and off for naps when they sent her home. She didn't sleep much, door closed or not. I knew that because, even when my brothers were arguing over who would be the Lone Ranger, Tonto, and the bad guy, the door didn't block out the moans.

Mamma hadn't been herself for so long I sometimes made a list in my head as I lay in the dark on the sofa, listening to Aunt Cora snoring in her cot on the other side of the coffee table. A before list.

The pink dotted-Swiss dress and matching bonnet for Easter . . . Tuna fish sandwiches and grape Kool-Aid on my birthday . . . A yellow puppy named Max one Christmas, who was in Heaven now because he liked chasing cars . . . Oreos and milk on a TV tray when I brought Sandra the new girl home from school . . . Gauze and mercurochrome when I pretended my bicycle was a trick horse . . . Curls and barrettes on school picture day . . . Brand-new PJs for my first slumber party . . . A baby doll that wet its diaper when you gave it a bottle and said "Mamma" when you squeezed it, for no reason at all except I wanted it so bad.

13

Mamma's silver spoon eventually stopped Aunt Cora's snoring every night, and that bedroom door would open and close, open and close, until my list making eventually stopped too.

One night, Aunt Cora never made it to her cot. I heard strange voices replace the moans, heard feet scuffing in the hallway, car doors slamming, people crying, even Daddy. Then silence. And the next time I saw those aqua walls or stared into that dresser mirror, my mother was in a coffin beneath the hard November ground.

She died on a dank and chill northern Minnesota night, and she was buried on a dank and chill northern Minnesota day. They painted her lips with sharp peaks, and even though they gave her some stuffing and put her in her orchid and magenta dress, she looked more like the dead bird I once found on the road and spooned a hole for in the ditch than my mother. My pity for that bird had been bigger than my fear of its shriveled body. I'd touched it with my bare hand. An automobile windshield is probably what killed it. And if the bird saw it coming, it must have been scared, even if all it could see was its own reflection.

I moved from the sofa to Mamma's aqua chamber after three live-in housekeepers came and went in short order, once Aunt Cora had folded up her cot and gone home to Memphis. Daddy, who'd been bunking with my three brothers since Mamma's illness, said of the new arrangement, "The lady of the house needs her privacy."

A railroad station agent, Daddy worked the depots of western Minnesota and eastern North Dakota, only coming home on weekends. After the third housekeeper dumped his Seagram's and trashed Jimmy's sneakers, which had just two holes, he put me and a pillowside butcher knife in charge of the household five days and spooky nights a week.

"You're thirteen now. We don't need some old biddy snooping around and acting snooty."

My mother's ghost visited my new room one night, glowing like a big owl's eye at the foot of the bed, then darting to the ceiling, where it hovered above me. Somehow, I just knew it was Mamma, but after several minutes when she didn't speak, I pulled the covers over my head.

I wouldn't have known what to say anyway, and to be honest, she scared me.

I didn't mind that she never came back to her old room again, though I eventually wondered where her spirit flittered off to, if it found another nesting place. But that night it was enough to know she still existed in some fashion and her essence wasn't stuck in a box in the dirt.

My father, a handsome man with a boyish smile, never mentioned my mother after her death but to say, "Do what she would have wanted you to do." This lone bit of parental advice seemed pretty easy until I tried to follow it.

Then one rare Saturday night that he made it home from his highballs before my bedtime, he said something else. "Your mother and me. I wasn't . . . I didn't . . . Well, if she'd lived, we wouldn't have stayed together anyway."

His hangdog stare confessed what his words only flirted around, making my misunderstood eyeliner experiment, which had banished me from Mamma's last days, especially regrettable. She'd been so alone in her deathbed.

My father initiated my one visit to my mother's grave—probably on a guilty whim—about a year after they put her in the ground. The grave lay in her hometown cemetery a good distance west, but even after I learned to drive, I shunned it. That shiny flat stone in the grass was just too much like a mirror.

I could watch for only a moment as he pulled the weeds from around the stone, brushed dead grass from its surface, dug wet dirt from the etched words with his bare hands. It was another dank day, and the grass left splotches on his normally dapper khakis. Maybe it was just the wind against his jacket that made him look so bowed and so small. I backed away, staring up at the sky. A bird I couldn't see was chirping from the top of a big oak tree, and I stood in the shadows, wishing I knew what it was saying to me.

THREE

Full Moon

Kit got us to Bemidji in less than an hour, even with a slowdown in Cohasset for the famous Highway Patrol speed trap and a stop in Deer River to fill his thermos with coffee. I can only imagine how fast he drove that purple Triumph that night, grain trucks whizzing by just across the centerline, because I kept my eyes closed the whole sixty-nine miles. If Tommy had been driving, I would have yelled for him to slow the heck down so we didn't break our skinny necks. But speed and Kit Griffith seemed to go naturally together, like thunder went with lightning, like rock went with roll, and it didn't occur to me to complain. Somehow, I just knew he'd get us there in one piece. I knew I wasn't meant to die on the blacktop that night.

And he was right about the breeze. By the time we hit the city limits of Bemidji, the full moon had escaped the clouds.

Despite the streetlights, the moon, and the car beams on the highway alongside it, Greenwood Cemetery looked dark and shadowy as we rolled through the Irvine Avenue entrance. The night suddenly seemed cooler, and I began to shiver in spite of my sweater. I was holding on to Kit's waist, and he must have felt a change in my grip because he patted my hand and slowed almost to a stop.

"Which way?"

I looked around to get my bearings. It had been a long time.

"Just beyond and left of that big old spooky oak tree."

His hand was still on mine. "Trees are just branches with leaves, even at night. We'll park right under that one."

And so we parked under the biggest, spookiest tree in the cemetery I'd avoided for years. With the ease of someone who'd had many a rider, Kit whisked me off the seat with one arm after setting his kickstand and angling his handlebars, clearly a guy who knew his machine like an old girlfriend. He pulled something bulky from his saddlebag and stepped toward me as I slipped his bandana from my hair and shoved it into my pants pocket.

"Put this on," he said. "You're too pretty for goosebumps."

I didn't need to see it to know what it was, as he slid it over my shoulders—a leather jacket, supple and smooth from long use, heavy and smelling musky, like a hug from my father when he'd been to the Vets' Club and was in his sentimental mood.

"Feels good."

My shivers had disappeared.

"So do you, baby."

He'd slipped his arms inside the front of the jacket and around me, and I was surrounded by the scent of leather, cologne, tobacco, and skin—a scent that made me feel even fuzzier than one of Tommy's beers on a hot summer day. I was tipsy, and all I'd had to drink was half a Coca-Cola. And when he turned to pull a flask from the other side of his saddlebag, I realized my brassiere was no longer hooked. Everything I'd been taught or figured out on my own said I should head for Irvine Avenue and a phone booth. Even Dee Dee, who was no goody two-shoes, would have said so. But I didn't feel alarmed or the slightest bit shocked by Kit's boldness. I just slipped Tommy's ring into my pocket and took a deep breath.

"Show me where she is," he said. And I did.

Maybe it was only night shadows of tree limbs that made the stone seem dulled, to have lost its mirrorlike shine. It now looked like just an oversized brick sunken in the grass, and I wondered if Mamma could see it from wherever she was, which might have been on a branch of that scary oak tree. I wondered if she felt neglected. Or even forgotten. Her name and the dates of her life were just dark spots in dark patches.

"Her spirit's not there, of course," Kit said. "But it's a good place to pay our respects and show her you remember her."

He unscrewed the cap of the flask and held it out over the stone.

"Here's to you . . ." He put his arm around my shoulder and pulled me close. My head fit right under his chin.

"Marjorie," I said. "Her name was Marjorie."

17

"Here's to you, Marjorie. You did a great job making this little girl." His voice was low and in no rush. "And you are deeply missed, though we know you've got a pad in a better place than this crazy little planet."

He took a swig and handed me the flask. I followed his lead and stifled a cough as the foreign-tasting liquid burned its way to my stomach. I was suddenly toasty inside and out. And happy in the saddest, wildest way.

I took another gulp when he knelt down and began brushing the dirt and dead grass from Mamma's stone in such a familiar way, in this place where memories suddenly enveloped me like liberated moonbeams. And when an owl hooted overhead, I began to cry. And hiccup. And laugh.

By the time the owl stopped hooting, Kit was again standing beside me, his arm tight around my shoulder. I looked up and saw him frown for the first time since we'd met. Somehow, even when he frowned, his eyes were smiling.

"Forgive me, Joey. I should know a chick like you isn't used to brandy."

"Brandy?"

"Christian Brothers. Only brand worth drinking, in my book."

We were walking back to the big oak tree, his arm nudging me along in a way that was firm but not pushy. My tears, hiccups, and laughter had vanished.

And then we were sitting on the ground on top of a sleeping bag he'd retrieved from the back of his bike and unrolled.

"Here. Try to eat a little of this."

He slid something between my lips and I took a bite.

"What is it?"

"Venison jerky. Made it myself."

It was chewy and surprisingly moist, with a tang.

"You shot a deer?"

Even though I was a northern girl, I always got melancholy during deer hunting season. I hated seeing the lifeless creatures lashed to the front of cars, their pretty heads and white tails drooping in defeat and indignity.

"I did. But I made sure he didn't feel a thing. And he was an old buck who'd had his share of antler tussles and fawn making."

He was sitting so close to me, our thighs were touching. "I thought you were a city boy," I said.

"I have family up here I visit sometimes. I like being in the woods once in a while."

I suddenly remembered Tommy, who was in the woods at that very moment, and reached for the flask. I didn't want Tommy in my thoughts right then.

"Just a sip," Kit said. "I think a little of that goes a long way with you."

I took a sip and the burn sent Tommy back to his shack inside the trees. Kit slipped his arm under the jacket and around my shoulder.

"Tough break, a chick losing her mom. That's something she doesn't get over."

I didn't hear pity in his voice, which would have made me cry again. I just heard words that I knew he knew were true. How he knew, when Tommy didn't, I wasn't sure. Maybe he just had a keener imagination, could better pretend to walk in someone else's shoes. I looked down at my sandals, not knowing what to say and suddenly wishing I'd taken the time to paint my toenails the Revlon pink that looked so sunny in the summertime.

"You an orphan now, Joey?"

He took the flask from my hand and drank from it slowly, eyes closed. He'd been pals with brandy for a while.

"I have a dad. Sort of. You?"

"Both folks alive and kicking. Kicking pretty hard, lately."

"They're mean to you?"

"A matter of perspective, I suppose."

He was stroking my back in the spot where my bra was usually hooked. His hand was on top of my sweater, though, and the motion seemed reassuring more than forward. I didn't feel like crying anymore.

"That pretty baby face tells me you're still in high school."

"Gonna be a senior. You?"

"I was enrolled at the U in Minneapolis for a few years."

"Not now?"

"Not now. My curiosities found me a new future."

He passed me the flask.

"Take another bite of the jerky too."

He wasn't bossy. His way of taking charge made it feel as though you were doing him a favor, and I did what he said.

The brandy and the jerky and the hand on my back were somehow making me not mind the idea of having a picnic in the middle of a graveyard in the middle of the night with the full moon staring down and Mamma's ghost probably hovering close by.

I was getting so comfortable with the situation that I began to crave a cigarette. But my purse was in Kit's saddlebag, and I didn't want to move from the hardness of his shoulder, which felt like the safest place in that cemetery. Maybe in the world. He must have read my mind because he pulled a pack of Camels and a Zippo lighter from a pocket of the jacket I was wearing. He tapped out a cigarette.

"This is another girlfriend of mine. Her name's Mary Jane. Know her?"

The cigarette was no Camel.

"Not really."

The closest I'd ever gotten to marijuana was the library magazine articles I'd read about the hippie scene in San Francisco. To my knowledge, no one I knew had ever smoked grass. Not even Tommy, who was no square and who the brandy hadn't fully sent away.

"She's a mellow chick with no meanness in her soul, but she's gotten me in a bit of trouble lately."

"What kind of trouble?"

Even in the tree's shadow, the moonglow caught the reddish glint of his hair. A gust blew it back from his face, revealing that his sideburns were true red, darker and brighter than the rest. And faint freckles dotted even his forehead. He wasn't what I'd call handsome, but his face had strong, straight angles.

"No trouble that matters tonight, little girl."

He flicked the Zippo and lit up. Several seconds later, he exhaled and put the cigarette to my lips.

"Hold it in for a bit. Works better that way."

I couldn't hold it in at all. I started coughing and suddenly felt like crying and laughing again.

"Try it once more. It goes down smoother after the first toke."

He was right. And by the time we finished our shared smoke, the cemetery was a bright cozy place and the oak tree a dear old friend I hadn't seen in far too long. With a bonfire in the field across the highway making a backdrop, Kit looked truly ablaze as he sat beside me. Marijuana lived up to its whispered reputation.

"We need some sounds," he said, maybe a minute or maybe half an hour after pinching out the last of the cigarette, which he called a roach and put back in his Camel pack. "Music goes nice with grass."

He rose and took something else out of his saddlebag. He carefully set it on the ground and sat back down beside me.

"Know what this is?"

It was a small plastic box with dials and a handle.

"A transistor radio?"

"Even better. It's a portable music-tape player."

He gave me a grin that absorbed the distant streetlights and headlamps, and the bonfire too.

"The hip new gear," he said. "Cool, huh?"

"Yeah." I'd never heard of such a device let alone seen one.

"You like Smokey?"

I nodded, thinking he meant the marijuana. He kept smiling as he fiddled with the player.

"There's a song on here sends shivers up my spine, it's so pretty. Smokey Robinson, he just breaks my heart sometimes."

Tommy would never have said such a thing aloud, even if he felt it inside. He'd have viewed an observation like that as sappy and unmanly. But Kit Griffith's admission didn't seem one bit sappy. And not a thing about him was unmanly, even the freckles. Kit clearly didn't feel the need to act tough all the time. He wasn't one to follow social rules that didn't suit him.

He worked the dials of the rocket-age gizmo, then slipped his arm around my waist as it began to play.

"I hope you dig this as much as I do."

21

It was the prettiest song and prettiest voice I'd ever heard. If Kit hadn't said the singer was male, I wouldn't have been sure. Smokey Robinson sang like an angel, and the night went to a magic place as soon as he crooned the opening lyrics, lyrics filled with sensuous passion and urgent desire.

Before the song was over, we were inside the sleeping bag, the leather jacket flung somewhere into the hazy shadows of the tree. It was hard to tell the difference between the music and Kit's kisses, and when I opened my eyes to get my bearings, the ground seemed to have disappeared and the sky and its shining moon were all around us. I sank into the world of Kit's mouth and tongue until another gust found its way into the sleeping bag and made me aware I was missing my sweater and my bra.

I sat up gasping for air as the final notes of the song faded away.

Kit sat up facing me, and the pale skin of his chest glowed in the night. It was hairless except for a small red V, which seemed spellbindingly symmetrical just then.

"Your breasts are beautiful," he said, not gasping in the slightest.

"They're not very big." I crossed my arms to shield them from his frank stare, suddenly aware that I was sitting topless out in the open with an absolute stranger and wondering what on earth I was doing.

With a touch so light I almost didn't feel it, he pulled my arms away. "They're perfect."

I didn't know what to say, but I badly needed to change the subject. "You have a tattoo."

The image inked onto his chest above the V was impossible to miss. "Sure do. I drank a fifth of brandy the night I got it."

The tattoo was a bird whose wings spanned most of Kit's upper torso. Though my dad had a small anchor tattoo on his forearm, which he called a San Juan souvenir of his wartime Navy days, boys my age didn't have tattoos, even small ones. Not the boys I knew anyway.

"It's an eagle about to fly," Kit said.

"Oh," I said.

He fiddled some more with the tape player and pulled me back into the bag. Smokey's voice joined the night again, a violin string pleading for love and surrender.

22

When the song ended the second time, I again sat up for air. By then we were both naked, and the night had definitely grown chilly.

The eagle was in front of me again, and I put my palms on its wings, not sure whether to grasp or push away the smooth skin beneath them. Kit laid his hands over mine and pulled my arms around his neck. He was stroking my breasts, and his fingers were very warm compared to the air. He put his mouth to my ear.

"I want you, Joey." He had a voice like a midnight DJ.

For all my backseat experience on the old road behind Johannsen's dairy farm, I'd never once considered doing what I knew Kit was suggesting. My rebel spirit always ended at the snap on my waistband. I could feel my face getting hot and my chest squeezing in on my lungs. I looked down at the ground, which seemed far below us in a vat of black.

"I haven't." I just couldn't seem to catch my breath. "Done it before."

His whiskers were against my cheek, scratching in a pleasant way. His neck smelled of musky citrus and marijuana and heat.

"I know. And that's good."

He could have been introducing "Moonlight Sonata" or reading the lyrics of a romantic ballad. My mouth was as dry as dead grass on a sunken gravestone.

"How come?"

His hand was under my chin, lifting my face back toward his.

"Cuz that refugee heart of yours hides a pure soul." He glanced at the sky. "And this night is the only thing that's for sure."

His mouth and his hands were everywhere, and I had to emerge from a mile-deep lake to finally reply.

"I can't."

His tongue was a warm ripple on my skin.

"Can't, or don't want to?"

"Can't."

There was a moment of silence, and from very far away, I heard the owl hoot again and a car horn honk.

"Time of the month?"

I shook my head.

"You a Catholic girl then, Joey?"

He scooted closer and pulled my legs around him too.

"Lutheran," I said, feeling another flush come to my face and glad for the dark.

"Believe in Jesus, huh?"

"Don't *you*?"

He looked me in the eyes, smiling slightly, in that way that wasn't laughing, and I searched hard for something bad and couldn't find it.

"I believe there was a pretty cool guy who wandered the countryside trying to help people feel better about their miseries a few thousand years ago," he said in a low voice that was almost a whisper. "But I'm not sure he was much like the cat people hear about in church and read about in the Bible."

Tommy, who'd spent a year at a Catholic seminary before he and his roommate were found drinking communion wine with a couple of girls, would have been appalled, though Tommy would never have initiated a chat, especially about Jesus, once my bra was off.

"What makes you say that?"

Kit's breaths were slow and even. Mine weren't.

"Books I've read by scholars who spent their lives searching for the real person in those New Testament red words. I was curious about this joe from Galilee who sacrificed himself for his cause."

His hands were now well below the sacred line, and they knew exactly what they were doing. This college city boy was in a brand-new category.

"You think the Bible's a lie?"

A crazy notion that seemed brave and fascinating even as I questioned it. I hadn't known other books about Jesus even existed.

"Let's just say I don't take everything it says at face value."

The things he was doing and saying were blending together in a way that left me unable to reply.

"I think the Bible was written by some gloomy guys with good intentions about someone they never met," he said. "I sure don't think Jesus made people feel guilty about their natural desires, or said they'd burn forever in hellfire if they didn't follow a list of rules. And I don't think he meant for a woman to think this was evil."

He was being very bold, and I was feeling confused about intentions and rules and fire, breathless from mixing the heavenly with the earthly.

"Does this feel evil, Joey?"

It didn't feel evil.

"How about this?

He lifted me up, and when he set me back down, he was right up against me, hard and a lot warmer than his fingers and waiting for my answer. I closed my eyes, shook my head, then nodded.

"Say it out loud so I'm sure."

I heard my voice whisper yes just before he pulled me as close to him as he possibly could.

— FOUR —

Just a Mirage

I rounded the jog in the bus depot alley and stood in the dark. The café was long closed by then and so was the pool hall, but a few diehards lingered outside finishing the last of their beer and cigarettes. None of the remaining girls were what I would call nice girls. Nice girls were safely tucked into the front seat of some Chevy or Ford on the old road behind Johannsen's dairy farm. Really nice girls were home in bed. I leaned my head against a telephone pole, careful not to look up. Avoiding those bird eyes.

If I'd been a nice girl with a rebel streak before throwing my leg over the seat of that Triumph, I wasn't any kind of nice girl anymore.

Not being Catholic, I wasn't compelled to confess my sins to anyone, and I had no intention of spilling the secrets of this night. Not even to Dee Dee. But I'd never again be the girl I'd been at sundown, and I wondered if the change would be obvious, something anyone with a few brains and the desire to look would spot in the time it took to say "What's new, Joey?"

I finally headed for the streetlamp side of the alley and turned onto the sidewalk, thinking it was going to be a long walk home. Suddenly, I missed Tommy something fierce. Good old Tommy and his solid T-Bird, which he washed and waxed every Sunday afternoon and never drove above sixty-five. Tommy, who didn't take chances or complicate his kisses with his talking or his tongue. Tommy, who always had his feet on the ground, which he never made seem like the sky.

A passing cloud set the moon free again, and in its glow I saw that Tommy and I had reached the limits of our bond. I'd betrayed him, and even if he never found out, I knew what I'd done. I'd traveled on a one-way road and met my match, found the *one*, if only for a blink in time.

I was so distracted by the realization that my life as I knew it was over, I almost tripped on Dee Dee's penny loafers, which were stretched out in front of her as she sat smoking a Benson & Hedges in the doorway of the pool hall.

"Dee Dee. What in the world are you doing here at this time of night?"

Dee Dee didn't look up.

"Seems to me the wrong one of us is asking that question."

"What do you mean?"

She didn't stand up either, so I sat down next to her on the sidewalk. I was starting to feel sore all over, and a bit sick to my stomach.

"I mean where the hell have you been all night, and with Kit Griffith of all people? Damn it, Joey. I've been worried to death about you. How could you do such a thing?"

"What thing?" Was it so obvious she could tell even in the dark?

Dee Dee sucked hard on her cigarette, then hissed out the smoke.

"Take off with *him*, abandon *me*, and double-cross *Tommy*. That thing."

The fickle clouds once again hid the moon.

"I didn't mean to abandon you. You had plenty of company when I left." The night had gotten way too dark, and I was feeling like a lone dandelion sprung in a sunless gulch. "And you didn't have to stick around. How did you know I'd come back here, anyway?"

Another suck of her cigarette, another hiss.

"A criminal always returns to the scene of the crime."

"Criminal. I didn't break any laws, Dee Dee."

They say the first lie is the easiest. I'd drunk half a flask of brandy, smoked half a joint, exceeded the speed limit on a motorcycle by plenty.

"Well, if you didn't, you were lucky. Cripes, Joey. I thought you said you knew Kit Griffith. And if you knew Kit Griffith, you'd know he's no guy to be fooling around with."

"What are you talking about?"

"He's a very wild, very bad boy, Joey. Way too fast for a babe in the woods like you." She crushed her cigarette out on the sidewalk and

27

flicked it away with her forefinger. "Rumors say he belongs to a Minneapolis gang, like the Sharks or the Jets. I heard that some of the members even file their front teeth into points."

I shivered. "I don't believe it."

"Joey, Kit Griffith is famous all the way to the Canadian border for being wild. He's wild and spoiled rotten, with folks as rich as the king and queen of England. Dad's a top dog at 3M, mom's from big bucks, and every scrape Kit gets into they save his hide with their moola and hoity-toity social contacts."

I still didn't believe her. "He didn't strike me as spoiled rotten, or say a thing about any gang."

Even in the dark, I couldn't miss Dee Dee's smirk.

"Well, he's a real charmer. Every girl who's ever met him knows he's a love-em-and-leave-em guy. Which tells me you spent half the night with an absolute stranger."

"Not really." It was impossible to explain, even to myself.

"Yes, really. Because if you knew Kit Griffith, your jaw wouldn't be dangling the way it is now."

I closed my mouth so hard my teeth snapped. I wanted to curl up on that sidewalk and die.

"I see you at least had the decency to take off Tommy's ring."

I touched my pocket surreptitiously, defensively.

Dee Dee rose to her feet and turned her back to me, hands on hips, head shaking. "I have to sleep at your house tonight or my mom will kill me for getting in so late. Let's go, huh? Your crazy stunt has worn me out."

Dee Dee had taken off ahead of me, and, feeling even sicker and sorer after rising from the cold concrete, I trailed her down the sidewalk like a bad dog. She clearly had no words left to condemn me, and I had none left to defend myself. At the corner we turned in the direction of my house. As I stepped from curb to street, I realized that my underwear was wet. About the only thing I knew for sure at that moment was I hadn't peed my pants, and a quiver of reality rippled up my spine.

Dee Dee wouldn't talk when we got home. She just smoked a cigarette, got into my bed, and scooted over close to the wall. She didn't reply when I said I was going to take a bath.

28

I brought my little transistor with me to the bathroom, and turned it on low so I wouldn't wake anyone. I twisted the dial to WLS, which came through like a bell on Saturday night, even on that little portable.

The song wasn't the one he'd sung on Kit's player, but I immediately recognized his voice—all violins and teardrops and leather-scented smoke, crooning of false love and heartbreak all the way from Chicago.

Clutching the sturdy links of the other item I'd brought to the bathroom, I stared down at the thick silver nameplate. Boldly engraved letters—KIT—winked at me from above the pink bath water as I sobbed.

"Oh Mamma, what did I do?"

Movie love scenes and that special day in health class don't let a girl know about the part of lovemaking that comes first, the part that feels like a burning knife and makes you gasp. Tears had filled my eyes the moment Kit had pulled us together, and I'd wanted to push it all away, to pull apart from the piercing pain that had badly tricked me. I'd wanted to slap him like I should have back in that alley by the bus depot. And maybe kick him too.

But before I could do either, Kit whispered, "I'm sorry, Joey. There's just no way I know to keep it from hurting the first time. Take a deep breath and let's just rest a second." He didn't sound a bit sneaky or mean, and I inhaled, trying hard to swallow my moment of panic.

"Okay."

In one seamless, connected maneuver, Kit had us lying in that sleeping bag, with him propped on his elbows above me, looking down. The moon was high, and I saw that his eyelashes grew from light to dark, in that kooky redhead way, which was maybe the reason he always seemed to be smiling. The pale part of his lashes made little halos around his eyes, which were already a bit daredevil in their zigzag between blue and green. I liked being under him and looking up. The lack of motion helped. I finally exhaled.

"I'm going to move now, real slow at first," he said. "I'm pretty sure it'll get better for you as we go along."

I refused to let the tears have their way. Then I suddenly remembered something.

"But what about, shouldn't you—"

Kit kissed my forehead, then my chin. "I don't believe in wearing a raincoat in the shower, Joey. Trust me, I'll be very careful."

It did get better. Kit's mouth and hands and easy pace made me pretty much forget about the soreness, eventually. Made me relax enough to respond to the things he was doing. New things. Sensual and racy things. It was a pleasant interlude all in all. Not too long, not too short, with most of the sensations rising above my awkwardness and my embarrassment. If I didn't see fireworks, I somehow knew it wasn't Kit's fault. His sleeping bag was a moonbeam away from the backseat of the Thunderbird.

When it was over—ended by a shudder, a moan, and a long sigh— he ran his thumb across my eyelids and said, "I hope this will be a memory you won't mind having."

I knew he wasn't angling for reassurance. He was clearly not a newcomer to lovemaking or someone who needed praise to buck up his self-confidence. What he was doing, I realized as I opened my eyes to the night, was soothing any doubts, regrets, or fears I might have about the over-the-speed-limit ride we'd taken since getting off his Triumph.

And I should have had them. Whatever safety measure Kit had used, it wasn't the one Tommy, optimistically, always kept in his pants pocket—a silver dollar from a machine in the men's room of the Mileage gas station. And though Kit had said some very nice things in the minutes or hours since he'd so deftly removed both his clothes and mine, "I love you" wasn't among them. It was as true as the nagging pebble under my right shoulder blade that I'd just done the riskiest thing a girl could do, a thing that would ruin her reputation if people found out, and her whole life if she got caught by Mother Nature. None of the options for a girl in trouble were good. A secret trip to a home for unwed mothers and adoption. Eternal shame and spinsterhood if she kept the proof of her mistake. A lifetime of people counting months behind her back if a shotgun wedding took place.

But none of those potential consequences entered my mind as I lay there looking up at Kit Griffith. Looking at the freckles I wanted to lick from his face and swallow so they would be part of me forever. Looking at the half-smile that lit the air I was breathing with an invisible match. Looking at the backward eyelashes that made a little sleeping creature inside my chest want to jump up and dance.

The only concern I had as I studied the bright stubble on Kit's chin and the slender bridge of his nose and the absence of a worry notch between his brows was that the night might be coming to an end. My focus was too narrow to take in anything outside the brandy smell of his breath and the tickle of his hair and the stair-step straightness of his spine as I ran my shaking fingers up and down it. Anything outside the archway of his shoulders and arms, which blocked all that scared or hurt me from view. Anything beyond the weight of his belly against mine, holding me hard in a place I could never voluntarily leave. I wrapped my trembling legs around his hips without a thought in any direction but now. Without a desire from the life I'd been given but *more*.

"I wish you wouldn't stop," I wanted to whisper.

And he didn't.

"I'm sorry, baby," Kit said, apologizing for the third time that full-moon night, fishing a pocket watch from the pants he'd pulled from the bottom of the sleeping bag we'd been in for hours or maybe eons. "But I have a promise to keep and we gotta be on the road."

The face of Kit's watch looked like a tiny full moon. It was half past midnight.

"A promise?"

Kit snapped the watch shut and slid it back into his pocket.

"Not the kind you're thinking."

He slipped out of the bag and stood up.

"You have another girlfriend besides Lola and Mary Jane?" I asked, knowing I shouldn't.

He handed me my own pants and tossed my underpants on top of my head with a wink. He seemed a lot more comfortable with his nakedness than I was with mine, even after all we'd done in that sleeping bag. Still inside the bag, I put my underpants on backwards and left them that way, yanking my pants up over thighs I thought were too chubby and a bottom I thought was too curvy.

"Not anymore."

He stepped into his corduroys and when he zipped them, they settled just below his navel and his narrow hipbones. He had the palest skin I'd ever seen, even in Nordic northern Minnesota. It made me momentarily think of a ghost, and I wanted to touch him to make sure he was still real.

"She break it up?"

He pulled his sweater over his head and ran a hand through his hair.

"You could say that."

"What's her name?"

"Her name is Peggy."

He was collecting all that was strewn about us on the grass, and something in the way he said her name told me he didn't want to talk about Peggy, though he clearly was no man of few words. I didn't want to talk about Peggy either. She was a cloud in the sky threatening to cover the moon, a shadow in the graveyard that temporarily hid my mother's gravestone and the hovering truth of the night. Suddenly, I wanted to get on that bike and fly to somewhere else.

I stood up, turning away from him as I put on my bra and sweater.

"A promise is a promise," I said when I turned back.

Kit blew a strand of hair from my face. He pulled his bandana from my pants pocket and tucked it down the front of my sweater with a grin. "If I could break it, little girl, I'd break it for you."

It was the wee hours when Kit pulled into his former spot in the bus depot alley, where I'd asked him to drop me, knowing a motorcycle in Daddy's driveway might not go unnoticed. Who could predict my father's whereabouts on a Saturday night? Kit set his kickstand without shutting off the bike and swooped me to the ground. I slid the bandana from my hair and hung it on his handlebars. He turned me toward him and gripped my arms, playfully running his tongue across my upper lip before giving me a quick kiss.

"Take good care of yourself, Joey. I won't forget you."

The lingering glow from the brandy and the marijuana, which had begun to seem part of me, suddenly died. The night, I realized in that moment, was now truly cold.

"But, but when will I see you again?"

Even so far from the streetlamp, I could see he was looking me straight in the eye.

"I really don't know."

It was hard to look back.

"*Will* I see you again?"

He exhaled what was maybe a sigh.

"I don't know that either."

My ears were ringing and my knees felt mushy.

"Why not?"

He took my hand and held it tight to his chest, still looking at me in a way that made me shake.

"I just don't. But I do know one thing."

His hands felt so warm and mine felt so cold.

"What?"

He was stroking my palm. "I *want* to see you again."

I stared into his stare, too stunned to be appropriately coy.

"I don't get it, Kit."

He shrugged. "I really want to."

"You're giving me the brush-off." Bile slithered toward my gizzard when I gulped. "This is a one-night stand."

He shook his head, then pulled me so close and kissed me so hard the air left my lungs in a gasp.

"Take this," he said when he finally let me go. "You don't have to wear it or anything. Just keep it so you know what I said is true."

He unclipped his bracelet and slipped it into my pocket, where Tommy's ring hid.

"Good night, Joey Dean. If there's a next time, we'll ride west all the way to the ocean."

And then he was gone, just gas fumes and a rolling rumble melting into the muffled chug of a passing train, after the Triumph turned onto

33

the street. He was so gone, he might never have been there at all. So gone, he might merely have been an illusion of deranged, desperate hope.

— FIVE —

Needles and Pins

"What do you mean, you need to figure yourself out? I swear, Joey, you make things complicated sometimes. Let's just drink our brew and slide into the backseat like we always do."

Tommy was looking down at his palm, where I'd placed his class ring. The dashboard lights of the T-Bird made the red stone flicker when he tried to hand it back to me.

"I can't wear it anymore."

He balled his hand into a fist.

"Why the hell not?"

I gulped a big swig of beer and spun the radio dial from "You've Lost That Loving Feeling" to "I Think We're Alone Now." This wasn't going to be quick or easy.

"Is it another guy?" he said as if asking for a light. Tommy would never admit to jealousy, an emotion for wimps.

"I just need to be on my own for a while."

Tommy stared at the steering wheel as I held my nose and took another swig. I liked beer's effect but not its taste, smell, or pesky bubbles. But I would have downed a bottle of cod liver oil to get through this conversation.

Tommy had been in good spirits after the picture show. Once we'd settled into our spot behind Johannsen's, he'd cracked his church key into a beer with a happy flick of the wrist, ignoring the flimsy pull tab. Just as Tommy was a Ford man, not a Chevy guy, he preferred Grain Belt to Hamm's. Somehow, he'd scored a whole six-pack. Between the movie, popcorn, Raisinets, and beer, Tommy'd shelled out plenty on this

Saturday night, which had taken forever to get here and come too soon. I suddenly felt sadder than I already had.

I was glad, at least, for the film—*The Dirty Dozen*, a real shoot-em-up I'd mostly watched through my fingers. Tommy loved war flicks. The only time I'd seen him get emotional was the day he learned his flat feet and inability to tell green from red would keep him from ever enlisting. Tommy collected pictures of Patton and MacArthur the way some guys collected baseball cards. He'd read *The Thin Red Line* twice, seen *PT 109* three times, and thought anyone against the war in Vietnam should be hanged as a traitor.

"On your own for how long?" he finally said.

"Long enough for you to ask someone else to our senior prom."

"Did someone else ask you to the prom?" He turned my way. "Who?"

"No one asked me to the prom."

He drained his beer and crunched the empty can. Tommy was a can guy, not a bottle guy. He liked crunching things with one hand, and even he couldn't do that with a bottle. He shoved the mangled container into an open slot in the carton on the floor and cracked another. His Adam's apple rose and fell as he took a deep chug. Tommy could drink a whole can without burping.

"Are you mad about something, Joey? Did you want to go fishing with me and Kenny last weekend?" He opened his ashtray, where ashes were forbidden, and set the ring inside. The stone looked up at me like a very bloody eye. "You always feel sorry for dead things, and didn't seem to like our fishing place. All we caught were three walleye, a few wormy perch, and an old northern that'll likely taste strong."

"I'm not mad."

"You get upset just putting a minnow on a hook."

"I'm not upset."

"The boat would have been too crowded anyway, after my cousin showed up."

"It's not about fishing."

I covered my mouth before letting some of the yeast escape. I wanted to jump out the car door and run someplace far from that notch in the bushes behind Johannsen's.

36

"I would have come back Sunday night, Joey, but we got pretty soused out on the lake, and I didn't want to risk it. There's almost always a cop at the Cohasset speed trap."

His explanations were so logical. So decent. I wished he would yell. And burp.

"I'd never want you to drive when you might get pulled over, Tommy."

He unrolled his pack of Luckies from his shirtsleeve, shook one up to his mouth, and lit it. He flicked out the match with his thumb, blew the smoke sideways to avoid my face and his upholstery.

"It was sort of a special occasion. Kit drove all the way from Minneapolis—"

"Kit?"

"—to say goodbye."

"Goodbye? Where's he going?" All of a sudden, there was a sink stopper in my throat.

"I didn't know you knew my cousin Kit. He usually only comes up for hunting season." Tommy took another gulp and another drag.

"I don't. Know him." My heart was hammering on my eardrums.

Tommy shook his head, nostrils spewing smoke like a drag racer hot off the line.

"He's one of a kind, that guy." The look on his face was either wounded disbelief or baffled surprise, and I wasn't sure who it was meant for.

"How's that?"

My brain and my mouth just weren't reading from the same book.

"His dad pulls strings to save his college deferment, and then he loses it over weed."

"Weeds?"

"Grass. More than a little. And something about a girl whose folks brought a statutory rape charge."

My ears felt hot and my face felt cold.

"Peggy."

"Huh?" Tommy was opening and closing his fist over the cellophane from his cigarette pack, crunching it into a little ball.

"Nothing."

37

It was my voice talking to Tommy, and it was my hand slapping a mosquito on my arm. But I had left that Thunderbird.

"The judge gave him a choice. Vietnam or jail."

"No."

"True story. And nobody who knows Kit would ever call him a coward. He left on Monday for MCRD San Diego."

"MCR what?"

"Marine Corps Recruit Depot.

Tommy tossed the cellophane ball into the ashtray, where it covered the red stone with a plastic twinkle.

"That crazy sonofabitch stopped for a game of pool and didn't make it to the cabin till nearly dawn on Sunday. On his motorcycle yet. He's something else, my cousin Kit. He once ditched his brand-new Mustang for a joyride in a beat-up Rambler, which he returned with a full tank of gas and a wash job."

"But your cabin is halfway back to Bemidji from here."

"That's another reason I didn't think you'd want to go fishing."

My head was spinning so fast that I'd left the night behind, and tomorrow wasn't there to greet me.

"Jesus, Joey. What's the matter with you tonight? You're spilling beer all over my seat."

༄

I managed not to throw up in Tommy's car, making it all the way home before losing half a bag of popcorn and a box of Raisinets. I threw up again after replaying our conversation as I sat trembling in bed, and again at three thirty after waking up with the shakes. Come morning, the urge seized me again, but there was nothing left in my stomach, and I just shuddered over the toilet bowl and staggered back to bed.

I didn't understand enough about body mechanics to be sure what had brought on my internal revolt. A lot of things could make you throw up, maybe even shame and humiliation. I didn't know what was wrong with me, and that made me even queasier. One day in health class just wasn't enough to overcome ignorance, especially for a girl who'd never had the mother-daughter talk. But even I knew vomiting was a *sign*. I called in sick at Bridgeman's, donned my favorite nightgown—the too-long ruffled pink flannel one that had been Mamma's—crawled into my saggy bed, and tried to sleep my life away.

Day after day, I stayed in bed, shade drawn to block any view of treetops, telephone poles, and antennas. I let my brothers eat peanut butter and jelly for supper, ignored the ironing, the bathtub ring, the sand on the hallway floor, and the dirty dishes in the kitchen sink.

Tommy called every night for almost two weeks. I paid Jimmy six bits and my ten-foot gum wrapper chain to man the telephone and say I was sick, which wasn't a lie. Even Daddy noticed my ailment when he found his dress pants without freshly starched creases. But the crease in his brow seemed genuine when he rapped on my bedroom door and poked in his head.

"You're looking awfully peaked, young lady. Before I leave for the club, I'll send Jeff to Gianelli's for a some liver and a can of spinach. You're not getting enough iron."

The waiting and wondering were beyond agony. As I flipped between July sunflowers, June lilacs, and May tulips on a calendar I'd never bothered to make monthly notations on—counting backward to a date I couldn't pinpoint and forward to a date I couldn't calculate—every minute was a lifetime ruined, every second, a heart ripped in two. Sliding the calendar under my pillow near my butcher knife, knees ignoring the floor's splinters, I prayed for the pitchforks and whips of hell. For the second time in my life, death held no fear, as I contemplated a girl's worst fate.

Dee Dee also eventually called. Her stretch of silence had been her way of saying I'd betrayed our friendship by not asking her advice about hopping onto Kit's motorcycle. And her way of opining that I'd done wrong by Tommy, a boy everyone liked and a hockey player entitled to respect. Dee Dee was no angel when it came to boys and zippers, and she hadn't pried about my night with Kit Griffith. Her disapproval was about etiquette.

Posted near the phone, which hung on the kitchen wall by the radio, Jimmy also recited the script when Dee Dee rang. Another quarter and a whole book of S&H green stamps saw to that. But Dee Dee wasn't a dumped boyfriend who finally got the message and had his pride to think of. I knew that sooner or later she'd come pounding on my door, just as she had last summer, the *first* time I'd faced The End.

— SIX —

Pincherry Jam

"Open up, Joey."

"Beat it, Dee Dee. I'm in no mood for company."

The day before my sixteenth birthday had been an August cooker, especially in our windowless bathroom, but I hadn't broken a sweat when Dee Dee kept twisting the knob. In fact, I'd felt cold all the way down to my spine. Cold and weary.

"Open this door right now, and I mean it."

"Buzz off."

I looked into the medicine chest mirror, long ago cracked by Jack's bony elbow. Speckled with soap splatters and rust spots, my face was that of an old hag with two moods—blue and black.

"I'm counting to three and calling the cops."

I knew she could actually do such a thing, and I didn't want to scare the boys.

"You're a real pain, Dee Dee." I opened the door, pulled her in, and relocked it. "What're you doing here?"

I sat on the bathtub rim. She sat on the toilet lid. Avoiding her eyes, I began counting the worn spots in the linoleum, which was meant to look like a gray carpet but never had.

"I phoned to drop a hint about your birthday present. Jimmy said you'd been in the john for over an hour and he had to pee. I told him to go in the pincherry bush behind the house."

"My bedroom door doesn't lock. I wanted to be alone."

"You could go for a walk to do that."

I didn't see any reason to lie about the situation. I didn't see any reason to do anything but wait. And I guess I didn't mind doing that with Dee Dee's company. What did it matter now?

41

"I was feeling sick," I said.

"What kind of sick? Headache? Cramps?"

"Sick of it all." An ant was scurrying for the curled-up edge of the linoleum, trying to escape to where he came from. I understood his desperation and let him keep going. Someone would step on him soon enough. "God keeps punishing me for my screw-ups and I'm ready to face hell."

I didn't cry as I made my admission. I didn't even blink. Crying didn't change anything. I'd learned that. Crying was just a form of whining. Crying was a coward's way of avoiding the inevitable. I'd cried all I ever intended to.

Dee Dee finally spotted the aspirin bottle in the sink. She snatched it up and started trembling.

"What the hell have you done, Joey?"

I didn't answer because the answer was obvious.

"How many were in here?" she said, her voice rising to nearly a shriek.

I still didn't look at her. What was the point? The empty bottle clinked onto the linoleum without breaking, covering one of the worn spots. What was done was done.

Dee Dee yanked me from the bathtub and began shaking me. I was feeling sort of sleepy, and my head and arms flopped like they belonged to Raggedy Ann. "Damn it, Joey. How many?"

She was shouting now, and I was wishing I hadn't let her in, cops or no. Dying was a solitary business. I'd learned that too.

"Sixteen. I took sixteen." Dee Dee let me go and I plopped back onto the tub rim. "Isn't that a coincidence? I'll be sixteen tomorrow and there were sixteen aspirins in the bottle. I just hope it's enough."

"How long ago?"

The room was too small for Dee Dee's voice. I covered my ears, which had begun ringing. Letting her in had been a bad mistake. I added it to my list.

"A while."

Dee Dee had thrown open the door of the medicine chest and was pushing aside bottles and tins, scanning labels. The Ipecac Syrup was on

42

the top shelf where I always kept it, in the corner behind the Phillips' Milk of Magnesia.

I shook my head. "Not on your life. I'm not drinking that."

Dee Dee twisted off the cap, shoved the bottle toward me.

"You have two choices, Joey. Drink this or get your stomach pumped. The ambulance, of course, will make a big racket. So sooner or later everyone in town will know, including that cute Tommy you hanker for. Think he'll give you his ring after he finds out about this?"

I certainly coveted Tommy's red-stone ring, which others wanted yet I was close to acquiring. But I'd finally realized it was a foolish trinket to wish for. It was a booby prize in a bingo game I was playing with no card—another thing I'd learned. Tommy's ring was a trick. Misery with a red sparkle was still misery. In the scheme of the existence I'd been given, Tommy's ring was a piece of penny candy, a temporary diversion from the mean prank of my life, which I'd had enough of.

But stomach pumping. *That* was a complication I hadn't counted on when I'd finally made up my mind to outsmart doom, a snag I hadn't considered when I'd let Dee Dee into my last afternoon. If Dee Dee called the ambulance, I was in for it. Men in white coats would pound on the door and haul me away. They would strap me down, muzzle me to a machine, and suck out my insides. I would be in the very movie I couldn't stand to remember. Stomach pumping scared me worse than hell.

Dee Dee's hand was shaking and she was sniveling. I stared at her nasty offering, playing out the next hour of my life if I stuck with my plan. Stomach pumping. I was going to have to postpone my little victory over fate.

I drank the awful stuff and sat down on the floor by the toilet. Dee Dee sat beside me and lifted the lid. The boys were splashers and the bowl needed cleaning, as usual.

"Take a deep breath and try to relax," she said, patting my back with one hand, chewing the already-chewed thumbnail of the other. Gnawed fingernails, at least, was one failing I'd managed to overcome. "It shouldn't take long," she said.

It didn't. After flushing the toilet, Dee Dee wiped my face with a washcloth. I suddenly felt too warm and very empty. Now I truly felt weary. I wanted to lay my head down right next to the ant passage and take a nap, but she was waiting for the answer to the question she hadn't asked out loud. Waiting and wiping her nose with her sleeve.

"Sweet sixteen, ha ha," I finally said. "I'd rather skip out on tomorrow's sick joke." My eyelids felt like sandbags when I met her stare. "I hate my life."

She blinked. "No you don't, Joey. You just hate your situation."

"Same thing."

"This won't be forever. You can marry Tommy once you graduate."

I leaned back against the faded fake-lace wallpaper and closed my eyes. I was so tired. "But you don't know the mistakes I've made. All the horrible things I've done since Mamma left."

"She didn't leave, Joey. She got sick and died."

"Same thing."

"She'll always be with you in spirit."

I shrugged. "Her spirit is mostly staring bird eyes and my own guilty conscience trying to guess what they're saying."

Dee Dee waited for an explanation, but all I gave her was a scowl. What a mess I'd made of my attempt at bravery. Another screw-up.

"I thought we told each other everything," she said. I could hear the hurt in her voice.

"I've told you a lot, but not the worst. Even you wouldn't want to know the worst."

"Give me an example. Just one."

I shook my head. It felt like a bowling ball ready to fall off my neck. You'll be disgusted."

"Hell, Joey. I'm your best friend."

I gave up, pulling the last Band-Aid from my pride. "I wore a white skirt to school the day I got my first period."

Dee Dee scoffed. "No girl knows when that day will come."

I scoffed right back. "But every girl with a mom knows to keep a Modess in her purse, that a wad of toilet paper won't do. People saw the stain. Boys saw."

Dee Dee's sniff said she'd flipped her hair over her shoulder. "Trust me, they weren't shocked."

"It was my cousin Carla's castoff, but I loved that skirt. I washed it in hot water. Any girl with a mom knows hot water sets the stain."

The shames rolled out faster than Dee Dee could comment. I confessed the time Buster Jones made fun of my armpits and I removed the hair with a match, like chicken pin feathers, blistering my armpits. The time I didn't know what silverware to use on the school trip and faked a stomachache to avoid eating. The time I smiled when someone's mother smirked at my homemade clothes. The time I said, "At the Moose, Elks, Eagles, VFW, or American Legion," when someone else's mother asked where my father was, thinking his club memberships were a social achievement.

I opened my eyes. Another ant was searching for the exit, sorry fellow. There was no sense stopping. I blabbed how I agreed to model my uniform for Mr. Pliska when I was hired at Bridgeman's, though the uniform was shorter than my slip. How I said, "All the way to where?" when my first date asked if I'd gone all the way. How I stuffed cousin Carla's too-large brassiere with toilet paper that fell out in gym class.

My voice was a ragged rasp when I finally ran out of proofs of my failure.

After a silent moment that added to my shame, Dee Dee said, "You just didn't know stuff, Joey. You were ten when your mom first went away to the hospital."

Sometimes it was hard to believe she'd flown her rickety coop that long ago. Sometimes it wasn't.

"That's what I've been *saying*, Dee Dee. I didn't *know*. But I should have been smart enough to figure things out. God's been testing me and I keep messing up."

"Some things you can only learn by making mistakes."

I was glaring at Dee Dee now, fed up with her dopey remarks. "*That's* what I've been trying to tell you. I keep making mistakes. I haven't been *sweet* in years, so what's the point? Hell can't be worse than this."

I sighed, suddenly feeling all alone in that tiny room. No one on earth would understand if Dee Dee couldn't. "I'm not feeling sorry for myself, mind you. I'm just ready to move on."

45

The leak under the sink was plinking into the coffee can I'd put there to catch it. I wanted to dump the can over Dee Dee's head when my glare didn't shut her up.

"Do me a favor," she said, voice cracking. "Can you at least stick around until our first prom?"

I spied a cobweb on the ceiling. I detested those sneaky, clingy things. "Junior prom. Whoopee. I'll be the girl in the Simplicity-pattern dress."

Dee Dee slumped against the toilet bowl. "But you're the wiz with brush rollers and rattail comb, Joey. I need you to fix my hair. French twist with top curls and a half-bang."

She had me there. Dee Dee was hopeless with hair, her plain pageboy the only do she could manage on her own.

I took a deep breath, wondering if the spider had gotten caught in his own web and died, or if he was merely taking a nap. One way or another, he was a goner. Poor dumb creature.

"You should wear it partly down," I finally said. Dee Dee's hair was almost as dark as Mamma's, and there was a small piece of me that still cared if my best friend's prom do was a dud. "I'll make curls on top and a feathered flip on the bottom. Maybe sprinkle in glitter and fix a bow that matches your dress."

Dee Dee was sobbing outright.

"I don't know what I'd do without you, Joey."

I handed her the roll of toilet paper, biting back tears of disappointment. Then I tossed the aspirin bottle into the wastebasket. Today was not my day to escape destiny. "You'd figure it out sooner or later."

I rose from the floor, brushed the dust and aspirin crumbs from my clothes, flipped the door lock. I'd already pressed Daddy's dress pants and sent him off to happy hour. It was time to make supper. To hear Jack say, "Why can't you cook porterhouse steak like Billy Hekkola's mom?" To hear Jeff say, "Drying dishes is girls' work." To hear Jimmy say, "I ripped my school pants on home plate."

"Listen, Dee Dee." My breath was rancid, my stomach moaning. "We gotta get out of here before the boys poison Mamma's prized pincherry bush."

46

SEVEN

Cold Sweat

Jimmy knew the Dee Dee telephone script, but he switched allegiance when she showed up at the door with her charming way, a dollar bill, and a pack of Chiclets.

"What gives, Joey? I've been calling for days and days."

She was standing beside my bed, looking down with a frown.

"I think I have a touch of the flu."

"Nobody gets the flu in July."

"Or maybe mono."

She shook her head. "You gotta be in college to get mono. I'd bet my entire collection of silver charms that you don't have mono."

I tried another course. "I broke up with Tommy."

Her sigh was immediate. "For godsake, why? What he doesn't know won't hurt him. I think Bob Dylan wrote that, and they're wise words."

"Because it's over."

She looked me in the eye and laid her hand on my forehead. "Tommy has nothing to do with this."

I looked away. "I just don't feel good, that's all."

"Hmm."

She sat on the edge of the mattress. I rolled toward the wall.

"When's the last time you ate something?"

Even the aqua color of Mamma's wall, which I'd always thought was pretty, made me feel nauseated. I closed my eyes.

"I had a bowl of shredded wheat on Wednesday or Thursday."

"Today's Sunday, Joey."

"Maybe it was Friday."

"Hmm."

I opened my eyes and turned my head. Dee Dee was studying me and blinking, looking an awful lot like an owl. I shivered, even as I felt my face grow hot with humiliation.

"You need to get up," she finally said.

"Not right now, thanks." I pulled my pillow over my head, pushed the calendar well under the covers.

"Yes, right now. Come."

There was just no saying no to Dee Dee. I got up, put my robe over my nightgown, and padded behind her, thinking we were heading for the kitchen.

"I'm really not hungry."

"That's fine." She walked right by the kitchen, opened the basement door, and stepped back.

"After you."

Thinking she was offering to help with my chores, I turned on my heels and shuffled back toward the bedroom. "Thanks, but I'm not up to doing laundry."

She was right behind me, hand on my elbow.

"Josepha Dean, you need to *do* something about this, and that's all there is to it."

"Maybe I'm just tired."

"Maybe so. But you're not helpless."

"Not much to do for the flu but sleep."

"Flu schmu. There are tried-and-true ways to fix your... ahem. . . situation, and if you had a mother to tell you female stuff, you'd know them."

So down the stairs we went, the scent of damp concrete, furnace oil, and dirty laundry doing nothing for my nausea. I leaned against the cool basement wall, attempting to sleep while standing up.

Dee Dee was rummaging in the old barrel that served as a catchall for Daddy's household tools, my brothers' sports equipment, and old toys. She pulled out a jump rope.

"You need some vigorous exercise to help you get back to your old self. Gimme a hundred. Fifty two-footers, fifty one-footers." She handed me the rope.

"Are you nuts?"

48

"No. And neither are you, my friend. Get going."

She settled on the smooth spot in the center of the wooden steps and slapped her hands together.

"One."

I just stood there, rope dangling between my bare feet. "I can't."

"Yes, you can."

I looked down at the dragging ruffle of my nightgown. "I'll fall on my bottom."

"Not a bad idea," she said. "One."

Every time I stopped, she clapped and called out a number.

"Thirty-three, keep going … Fifty-four, get those knees up … Seventy-six, we're on the downhill now."

By the time she reached a hundred, my head and stomach resided inside a thundercloud and my knees had turned to rubber. I moved to sit beside her, but she sprang to her feet, shaking her finger.

"When's the last time you had a bath?"

I could actually smell the wet dirt under the cellar floor.

I shrugged.

"In all the years I've known you, Joey, you've never been stinky."

"Woozy. Gotta eat something."

"Not smelling like that."

Up the stairs we went, bypassing the kitchen, Dee Dee clutching my elbow as if she owned it.

She left me leaning against the wall outside the bathroom, struggling to catch my breath. But she was back in no time, jerking me through the bathroom door.

"Are you kidding? I can't step in *there*, Dee Dee."

"It's not that hot. Get in."

"My skin will peel."

"Take it an inch at a time."

"But there's steam rising."

"Steam's good for the complexion. You can get out when I knock on the door."

By the time her knock came, the bathroom walls were dripping and my big toes were scarlet prunes.

The towel she gave me didn't keep me from shivering.

49

"I gotta go back to bed, Dee Dee. Please."

"Not till you get something in your stomach. Like a pot of strong coffee.

"Coffee! What are you trying to do to me?"

"Save you from desperation, Joey."

The patch of red on my sheet the next morning put an end to my affliction. It cost me another quarter to get Jimmy to run the block to Gianelli's for a box of Modess, but I hugged both him and the box when he returned, tears rolling down my face as he said, "Jeepers, Joey. You been in a goofy mood lately."

In the bathroom, the tears continued, dotting the snow-white pad I attached to my sanitary belt, spattering the toothpaste sludge in the sink, damping the fresh nightgown Dee Dee had yanked over my wilted body the day before. The mixture of relief, regret, and renewal I felt was too potent to hold in. I thought of the day I'd tried to die in this windowless room, of the night that had made me feel more alive than I'd known possible, of a child I would have kept and loved no matter what, had the worst-case scenario been my problem and Dee Dee's remedies failed. I wept for what was and what wasn't and what I would never know for sure, until every tear I owned that day was gone. Then I returned to the world I knew.

By nightfall, I'd caught up on the laundry, done the dishes, cleaned the bathroom, and made a phone call that put me back on Bridgeman's waitress schedule. My life went on.

— EIGHT —

Paint It Black

And the summer of '67 went on. But it didn't take long for my relief to plunk to the bottom like Alka Seltzer in a water glass, for my deeper feelings to rise like released fizz. As fall and my senior year approached—my birthday passing while I scooped ice cream, washed dishes, and ate seventeen Fig Newtons in bed with *Return of the Native*—my blue mood eventually became the color of Daddy's navy peacoat, which hung on a porch hook even in summer to prove he could still get it buttoned. It became so dark you could mistake it for black.

Nothing in the windshield of the coming year seemed worth looking at. Up ahead was only work—chores, homework, job. I saw no Saturday night dates, in or out of a graveyard. No picture shows. No homecoming games. No prom dress. No beer and potato chips. Without Tommy, all I had were memories of people who'd made me love them and then left.

My hand-me-down aqua room became my cloister when I wasn't busy. I no longer chatted on the kitchen phone with Dee Dee until Jimmy began shooting his Johnny Eagle cap gun to get my attention. I didn't watch the living room TV while folding clothes and sewing on buttons. Ed Sullivan's rock stars and the Smothers Brothers' jokes no longer interested me, and even though Walter Cronkite was the main father figure in my life, *That's the way it is* wasn't something I wanted to know anymore. His nightly war clips just made me afraid I'd recognize one particular soldier's face. I hunkered down in gloom.

I sat next to my record player on Mamma's beige loop rug, which had taken her a whole winter to make, and sank into the saddest songs in my box of LPs and forty-fives—"Tears on My Pillow," "As Tears Go By," "Tracks of My Tears," "Letter Full of Tears," "96 Tears," "Crying."

51

Well into every night, I aimed my phonograph needle for the vinyl tracks that understood me.

☙

"Well, if it isn't Miss Stuck-up, too good for her old friends."

Dee Dee had found my secret lunch spot at the window table in Miss Eickstadt's empty classroom, where I was staring out at the blacks and grays of November.

"Not true. Even if I had something to be stuck-up about, I'm not, and you of all people know it."

"Miss Mope, then."

Dee Dee hovered behind me like a mugger's shadow. I looked down at the carved initials and ink stains of the old oak table, feeling twelve instead of seventeen.

"I'm not moping either. I'm just thinking." I was wishing the bell would ring, longing for my back-row desk in geography class where I never had to say anything.

She grunted. "Too much thinking isn't healthy. Too much thinking can make a person start feeling sorry for herself. And when you start feeling sorry for yourself, you start feeling sorry for people you know. And then you start feeling sorry for strangers, then for the whole world. The next thing you know, you're feeling sorry for everyone who ever was and ever will be. Too much thinking just gets a person in a feeling-sorry-for jumble."

Dee Dee's logic was making me feel sleepy, which was how I felt most of the time these days.

A featureless two-story stack of bricks, Grand Rapids High School had reopened its doors on a bright Indian summer morning. On the first day of school, I'd worn my mood in homemade high style—my black A-line minidress, black patterned tights, and black pilgrim pumps looking like part of a Mod funeral. My locker was by the water fountain where the jocks and cheerleaders hung out before first bell, including Tommy, so I'd gone directly to my homeroom, where I'd sat in the back corner playing the Everly Brothers in my mind. "Crying in the Rain."

I'd picked art class for my elective. Miss Eickstadt, a spinster whose too-yellow finger waves had earned her the name Goldilocks, was a teacher we respected, even though she didn't teach a real subject and her classroom was in the school attic. Her oil paintings and clay sculptures won blue ribbons every year at the county fair.

Miss Eickstadt had us start with ink drawings, which we eventually developed into watercolors. I realized I had a knack for the medium the day she matted two of my paintings and hung them in her artist-of-the-week corner.

"Your sense of composition is strong, and you have an eye for color," she'd said. "But you might consider putting leaves on your trees and people on your benches. And perhaps some flowers in that field and some sun in that sky."

These days, I avoided the lunchroom as well as my locker, even when I had cash for hot lunch and they were serving sloppy joes and fruit cocktail—everyone's favorite. I'd eat my baloney sandwich in Miss Eickstadt's empty classroom and stare at the sky. I was so lost in clouds the day Dee Dee found me, I didn't even jump when she touched my shoulder.

"I'm not feeling sorry either," I replied, sliding my elbow over a page of doodles—a page covered with the name engraved on the silver bracelet now stowed in my cigar box of treasures.

But Dee Dee was nothing if not observant. She whipped the page from the table and crumpled it. My artwork thudded to the bottom of Miss Eickstadt's wastebasket.

"Too much thinking also gets you thinking about things that are best to forget ever happened."

I sighed. A bird was flying across the sky heading south. It looked like a jagged scar in the clouds.

A chair scraped the floor. Dee Dee had finally sat down.

"Nothing has to change, Joey. Tommy's a damn good catch, a good-looking hockey player with all his front teeth and a nice car, and he'd take you back in a minute."

I just stared out the window, wishing the bird was me.

"And he's already set for a job in his uncle's lumber mill when he graduates."

"I'm tired, Dee Dee. Let's talk later."

"How can you be tired? It's only noon and you're the most energetic person I know."

I bit my lip, trying to reconjure the Everly Brothers.

"I just am."

"You've been reading Thomas Hardy again. And I'm not sure those gloomy love stories are good for you right now. I mean, there's no one on earth with worse luck than Tess of the d'Urbervilles. And Eustacia Vye, well, that girl was doomed from the start, stuck like she was on that heath."

I'd never seen one, but I didn't think a heath and the colorless field before me were that much different. I sighed again, remembering that Tess had gotten five whole days with Angel Clare before she died.

"You're not tired, Joey. You're bored."

I shrugged, accepting Dee Dee's diagnosis as a partial possibility.

"What would be so wrong with going back to Tommy?" she said. "If you wait too long, some other girl's gonna snag him. I saw Mary Beth Anderson passing him notes in history class, and Joanne Schwartz has been camping out by his locker every morning."

The bird was flapping hard, trying to get where it should have gone long ago, trying to outfly winter.

"Go away, Dee Dee."

She had no answer for that.

"Please."

The chair scraped the floor again, and by the time the footsteps faded, the bird had vanished over the horizon.

On Thanksgiving, I baked the turkey Daddy had won in a raffle at the Moose Club, though Daddy didn't plan to drive all the way from North Dakota just for a meal, and Jack was spending the day at Billy Hekkola's house, where Billy's mom had baked two pumpkin pies, one apple, and one lemon meringue. I skipped the stuffing, cranberries, and candied yams, knowing Jeff and Jimmy would want to move straight to turkey sandwiches. Turkey sandwiches with Miracle Whip, which I'd bought with my tip money.

After dinner, Jimmy agreed to dry the dishes for only a dime and my promise to make red Jell-O with maraschino cherries soon. Jeff was in the basement punching on the punching bag, which Daddy thought was more important for a boy to do than housework. Dishes done, I went back to my room, placed a carefully selected stack on the phonograph spindle, and sat on the rug with my new library book.

It was one of those big books teachers call an anthology, the kind you always end up needing for a special homework project, which in this case involved memorizing a poem to recite in Mr. Ingersoll's English class. *A Treasury of Great Poems* weighed practically as much as a frozen turkey. With Mick Jagger crooning "Cry to Me" and Keith Richards making his guitar strings sound like teardrops, I thumbed through the book, looking for a short poem by a poet with a long, poetic-sounding name. I didn't fear memorization, but stage fright truly terrified me. Freezing in front of thirty kids who were just waiting for something to giggle about.

I finally found a poem that fit the bill. "The Desire of the Moth," two stanzas, sixteen short lines, written by a guy named Percy Bysshe Shelley. Now *there* was a poetic name.

After reading the poem, I knew I'd found a kindred spirit. Sniffling but not yielding to tears, I suddenly felt better about my life. Over a century ago, someone had understood me. In less than a page, he'd explained—in rhyme no less—what it was like to want someone impossible to have, to long for what existed in an unreachable place.

Mr. Ingersoll—who wore a goatee and a beret, smoked clove cigarettes, and was rumored to have once been a bongo-banging beatnik—gave me an A for my recitation, and I didn't return that book to the library. I'd never swiped so much as a Life Saver from Jack's secret jacket pocket. But our town had no bookstore, and neither the Sears Roebuck nor the Montgomery Ward catalog sold poetry books. Percy Bysshe Shelley understood me better than I understood myself, and I couldn't give him back just yet.

Dee Dee slept over the night before Christmas Eve, a tradition I couldn't break no matter how much I wanted to be alone with my daydreams. We exchanged gifts—mine to her a genuine sterling silver shamrock charm and hers to me a lipstick called Ballerina Pink in a red velvet case. Then I rolled and teased her thick dark hair into a Jean Shrimpton do. Jean Shrimpton was the British fashion model Dee Dee wished she looked like. Mine was Patti Boyd, George Harrison's wife, whose hair, makeup, and wide-eyed pout I copied with care, but whose bust would always be bigger than mine and whose hips would always be smaller.

I spent the rest of Christmas break deep in Shelley, Tess, Smokey, and Mick. Daddy's annual bonus was another turkey, which I baked with all the trimmings on Christmas Day.

Christmas was also the day I sank into another Shelley poem—*I weep for Adonais–he is dead! Oh, weep for Adonais! Though our tears thaw not the frost which binds so dear a head!* By the time I pulled myself out, the turkey was burnt. Daddy was sleeping off one of his "headaches" and didn't notice, but Jack said I'd never be the cook Mrs. Hekkola was, and Jimmy said no amount of Miracle Whip was going to save his turkey sandwich.

The January day that school resumed, Dee Dee searched me out in my homeroom hideout, where I was again reading snitched Shelley.

"Guess what, Joey."

Percy was at his most passionate—*Oh, lift me as a wave, a leaf, a cloud! I fall upon the thorns of life! I bleed!*—and I really hated losing my place.

"What?"

She sat down right on the arm of my desk, her skirt covering my book.

"Mr. Ingersoll's added a drama class to twelfth grade curriculum. Want to sign up with me?"

I pushed her skirt away, wanting to finish "Ode to the West Wind" before the bell.

"You can't take two nonacademic classes," I said, "and I like Miss Eickstadt's art class."

Dee Dee leaned in.

"Ah, come on, Joey. It sounds like fun. How many more glum watercolors do you have in you?"

I looked at the clock above the blackboard. It's fat face was grinning at me. The door to out *there*, high above everything I knew and wished to get away from, was closing any second now.

"But I'm getting an A in art. It's my only one, and offsets my C-minus in biology. You know how I am about worms and frogs."

Dee Dee snorted, her penny loafers swinging.

"How hard can it be to get an A in *drama*. Seems right up your alley."

I yanked my book from beneath her skirt and closed it, careful not to crease the pages.

"But you have to get up in front of people, Dee Dee. I'd probably freeze, forget the words, and make a fool of myself."

I hugged the book, a friend who never asked anything of me.

"You did fine with that love poem in English class. You didn't miss a line."

My irritation was sliding into gloom, and I gazed off into my mind, where I saw dead leaves fleeing the west wind like ghosts. "It was only sixteen lines long."

Dee Dee hopped to her feet, hung her head.

"Joey, you've been treating me like I have leprosy for months now, and I haven't complained. Can't you do me this one small favor? Mickey Sweeney is taking the class, and I don't want to be obvious. Sign up with me, and I'll pretend you haven't been acting like you're too good for me since you took a ride on a purple motorcycle."

Mr. Ingersoll gave each student a pick of three textbooks—*Best American Plays,* third, fourth, and fifth series. Thumbing pages, I noticed that a playwright named Tennessee Williams was in each volume. I liked the faraway flavor of the name, male or female. I chose series three, dated farthest from the here and now.

Our assignment was simple. Assemble a cast from students with the same textbook, cut and block a scene, and present it with costumes and props to the class in a month. The grade would count as a midterm exam, and Mr. Ingersoll was available for advice in the meantime.

Naturally, Dee Dee and Mickey Sweeney became my fellow cast members. Dee Dee's breathlessness in Mickey's presence and Mickey's bewilderment in hers gave me the job of picking the play. *Death of a Salesman* sounded too morbid, *The Iceman Cometh* too cold and biblical. But Tennessee Williams, who turned out to be a man, had written a play with a name as exotic as his own. *A Streetcar Named Desire*. Naturally, Dee Dee wanted to be married to Mickey, and an elbow in my ribs gave me the part of Blanche Dubois.

We didn't know what we'd gotten ourselves into. In our workshop corner by the drafty well-window of our basement classroom, the more we read, the more Mickey twitched, Dee Dee giggled, and I shivered. But I knew I'd found another melancholy rebel spirit in Tennessee Williams.

Any girl who read *Photoplay* had seen Marlon Brando's sultry T-shirt pose from the movie of the play. But that film hadn't been in theatres since Dee Dee and I were in diapers, and we didn't know the story. We soon realized that, despite its title, our pick wasn't exactly romantic.

Dee Dee pushed for the Stell-lah scene, but we were short on players. When we read the rape scene, she begged to swap parts, but Mickey turned the color of a geranium and threatened to drop the class. We finally chose the scene where Stanley rifles through Blanche's things, after Mickey remembered the trunk in his attic that we could use for the prop.

Performance order was decided by drawing numbers from Mr. Ingersoll's beret. With Dee Dee nuzzling his ear, Mickey drew the highest number, making us last. The second week of February would be our acting debut.

For Minnesota bleakness, the only month that exceeded January was February. In the few hours the sun was up in those early days of 1968, it shone from the farthest edge of its route, beam dimmer than Daddy's old flashlight. Dee Dee didn't sew, so she volunteered to paint the backdrop for our seedy New Orleans bedroom, which Mickey was building in his dad's garage. Costume design became my job by default, and for those dreariest of winter days, I spent my spare time creating an aging southern belle and a 1940s wardrobe, sometimes forgetting to turn on my record player, open my poetry book, or doodle a certain name.

Terrified of flubbing my lines, I practiced myself hoarse before Mamma's mirror, drawing my southern accent from memories of old movies. None of Hardy's heroines provided inspiration for a character more than twice my age, so I just imagined how I'd look and feel in twenty years if I were still standing in front of that mirror. It wasn't hard to do.

✂

Dee Dee, Mickey, and I took to rehearsing during lunch hour, using Miss Eickstadt's classroom to keep our project secret from our competition. I'd often skip my baloney sandwich as I urged Mickey to put some oomph into his Stanley Kowalski. Mickey looked nicely brawny in a T-shirt, and he acquired a pretty good swagger after I told him to pretend he was John Wayne. But it just wasn't in Mickey's nature to toss around furs and fake pearls with pizzazz. I worked hard concocting images he could get mad at. A missed field goal during a tied homecoming game. A flat tire on a below-zero night. That crack in the sidewalk you always stubbed your toe on. But none of them did it for Mickey.

What finally brought out Mickey's inner rage was my reminder that his mom had pushed him into taking drama class as a cure for his shyness and tendency to stammer. Stanley's Napoleonic code made good sense to him after that. I had to restring our dime-store props once Mickey got the hang of being Brando with braces and a crew cut. Actually, the braces didn't mar Mickey's characterization, since there wasn't a line that required him to smile. As our performance date approached, I started to feel we might pull off a decent grade. I started to look forward to one day in my life.

— NINE —

I Can See for Miles

Without using a prop, Mr. Ingersoll caused an explosion the day drama performances began. Duluth's public television channel had called our principal in search of educational material. Recruited to fill part of a program, Mr. Ingersoll was turning our assignment into a contest. The best scene would be replayed in the gymnasium, in front of the whole school and a TV camera.

I wouldn't have had to rack my brain for ways to get Mickey Sweeney steamed for his role if we'd known about the contest beforehand. Mickey didn't much want to get up in front of the classroom in a T-shirt, saying and doing things that weren't natural for him to say or do, and the prospect of a thousand live spectators and a cameraman had him ready to quit school and join the merchant marines. Luckily, we were last on Mr. Ingersoll's list, because it took me days to convince Mickey we didn't have a chance of winning. His braces were what clinched it.

"All you gotta do is give a surly grin when you ask Stella if she's ever heard of the Napoleonic code," I told him. "Believe me, Mickey, not even Mr. Ingersoll will want to see a silver-toothed Stanley Kowalski on Channel 13."

I was wrong about that. We beat out *Inherit the Wind*, *The Seven Year Itch*, and *Who's Afraid of Virginia Woolf?* We even outdid *Oh Dad, Poor Dad, Mamma's Hung You in the Closet and I'm Feelin' So Sad*.

I'm not sure what won us the contest. Our scene didn't seem to get more applause, hoots, and snickers than the others. But I must admit we were in fine form the day of our performance. Nobody missed a line, cue, or movement. After weeks of being tugged on and pulled off,

60

Mickey's T-shirt had acquired a dramatic rip in the sleeve, and Dee Dee had slept on bobby pins to create her 1940s curls. Mickey's backdrop turned the front of Mr. Ingersoll's classroom into a decent replica of a low-rent bedroom—Dee Dee having painted twelve rows of identical roses for the wallpaper—and Mickey's mom's trunk and Daddy's old navy cot were the most realistic props of the bunch. And, not to brag, my costumes looked great. I'm sure no white dress was ever more mothlike than the one I sewed my Blanche, and Dee Dee looked truly housewifely in the blue shirtwaist frock I made for her Stella.

It might have been the spray of spit that accidentally flew from Mickey's mouth when he said, "And what have we here? The treasure chest of a pirate!" that tilted the scales in our favor. Or Dee Dee's impromptu sigh of indignation when she said, "Those are inexpensive summer furs that Blanche has had a long time," right in Mickey's face. Maybe the tear that fell when I said, "These are love-letters, yellowing with antiquity, all from one boy," conjuring Mamma's gravestone to make me weepy, helped put us on top in Mr. Ingersoll's grade book. Whatever it was, it was enough to overcome the fact that Mickey's teeth twinkled when he gave his sneering leer, Dee Dee stood three inches taller than her virile costar, and my crow's feet were drawn with Maybelline eyebrow pencil.

Mickey didn't quit school and join the merchant marines, but Dee Dee's hopes for romance had hit the skids by the time Mr. Ingersoll opened the maroon velvet curtain of the gymnasium stage, the TV camera looking like a big eye or a booing mouth. The pressure proved too much for Mickey, and by our final rehearsal he'd become as brooding as a Brando magazine photo. On the big day, he blew his very first line, blurting out, "What is this monkey doing?" instead of "What's all this monkey doings?" as he glared at Dee Dee. The audience giggled, and Dee Dee's look of horror and mismatched reply didn't help matters.

Things went downhill from there, and when the string of fake pearls broke when Mickey yanked it from the trunk, beads flying across the stage and raining onto the front row where all the teachers sat, our drama had turned into a comedy. Everything we did after that got a laugh.

61

When my big teardrop line came, I gave it my Smokey-Shelley-Tess best. The laughter didn't stop, but it paused for a moment, and I felt the heat in my cheeks cool just a bit, believing I'd touched someone in the way I'd meant to. Facing the audience full on, I saw smiles momentarily freeze in place, and one frown—Tommy's—rise into what looked, for a few hammering heartbeats, like rapt attention.

For all the wrong reasons, our performance got plenty of applause. We were a smash hit for making fourth period as much fun as a pep rally. But somehow, it didn't matter to me that our moment in the limelight wasn't quite what we'd hoped and worked so hard to make it. Shelley had been misunderstood too, had been unappreciated for his art all his life. Rebel spirits weren't rebel spirits because they fit in. And I had achieved that pause. I'd made Tommy listen one time to my reminiscences, even though they belonged to someone who wasn't real.

Dee Dee and I watched the Channel 13 airing a week later, my first view of Daddy's RCA Victor in months. Our TV debut came right after Walter Cronkite—who knew the truth about everything—reported that the Vietnam War wasn't winnable. That didn't seem like news to me, who'd avoided the shooting and shouting that Jack turned the knob to every night at six, so my imagination wouldn't wander to a certain Marine.

Dee Dee and I sat up close on the rag rug Mamma had braided to give the front room a touch of class. Watching ourselves be somebody else, we both agreed that the microphone had captured the applause more than it had the hoots of laughter.

A month later, Mr. Ingersoll suggested I try out for the school's very first stage play. *Pygmalion.* I won the role of Eliza Doolittle. In a few weeks, I was living in London, speaking cockney, and sewing myself a ragged shawl.

🕊

"Tommy's going steady with Mary Beth now," Dee Dee said, blowing a smoke ring as she set the book with the play I'd been reading on the bed. *Cat on a Hot Tin Roof.*

"Mary Beth sits by me in biology, and I haven't seen a ring on her hand," I said. Talking about Tommy made me want to bite my fingernails, a habit I'd cured back in seventh grade.

"She wears it on a chain around her neck."

"Good for her." We were sharing a cigarette on the floor by my record player, but I lit my own, inhaling the sulfur after shaking the match. "And good for him."

"If you say so."

"I say let's drop it, smart aleck. Tommy and I are done. And none of your little digs are going to change my mind about that."

"If you say so."

The only thing to do when Dee Dee was on a sassy streak was change the subject.

"More Tang?"

It was Easter weekend, and Daddy must have been feeling flush. He hadn't crossed the Tang off my grocery list, or the jellybeans I planned to hide, along with colored eggs, in the yard after church for Jimmy and his pals. Our usual household drink was Carnation powdered milk, and Daddy's cupboard rarely held sweets.

"Not right now, thanks."

Tommy was lingering in the room like Dee Dee's last smoke ring, which grew bigger and bigger as it floated toward the cracks in the ceiling plaster. To my way of thinking, blowing smoke rings was a guy's thing to do, and I'd never learned the trick. Dee Dee and I didn't always agree on what constituted appropriate feminine behavior. She often didn't bother to shave her legs for a month, and thought nothing of wearing nylon stockings in the meantime. I shaved my legs every other bath, even in winter when I wore knee-highs or tights with my skirts. Dee Dee thought it was okay to wear rollers when she ran to Gianelli's for a can of tomato sauce for her mom's casserole. I wouldn't step out the door without my hair styled and glued in place with Aqua Net. Dee Dee saw nothing wrong with necking at a picture show if you and your date sat in the last row. Holding hands in the middle row once the lights were down was my movie limit.

Dee Dee wasn't giving up on the subject of Tommy. "So, what are you going to do about the prom?"

"What do you mean?"

I'd made my special popcorn, half a stick of melted oleo on top, and Dee Dee tossed three oily kernels into her mouth as she stubbed her cigarette in my Vikings mug. "I mean, has anyone asked you?"

"It's only the middle of April, Dee Dee."

Her smirk was ready. "Well, Curtis Gleason has already asked *me*. Lots of girls have been asked by now."

She was studying the lipstick print on her glass. Dee Dee always sealed her notes to boys with a Revlon kiss.

"You *know* I don't have a boyfriend. I've been too busy with rehearsals for that." I mashed my cigarette butt on top of Dee Dee's. "Besides, I don't know any guy I'd want to go to the prom with who doesn't already have a girl."

My admission had me picking at the pink nail polish on my thumbnail. Nothing was more unladylike than chipped nail polish. And nothing was more pitiful than a girl who missed her senior prom because she didn't have a date.

"Hmm."

"Where is it written that I have to go to the prom, anyway?"

Dee Dee scoffed so hard a kernel of popcorn hit her knee.

"Joey, every girl who's anybody goes to her senior prom. What will you have to look back on when you're old if you don't go to your last prom?"

I could feel my face getting hot. I was starting to wish Dee Dee was home in her bed and I was in mine with Percy Shelley.

"Something more important than a dumb dance in the high school gym, I hope."

"Like what?"

"Like playing the lead in the school play."

Dee Dee rolled her eyes. "That's a line in the yearbook, not the biggest night of your life."

She had me there. I took the Who off the record player and put on the Bee Gees. I needed more harmony.

"I'll remember what I did with myself *after* high school, that's what."

Album cover atop her lap, Dee Dee was drawing a moustache on Barry Gibb with eyebrow pencil. I pretended to ignore her mutilation of the cutest guy in the band.

"*After* high school? Most girls just do something useful until they get married and have kids."

After-graduation options was an old topic. Dee Dee still wavered between nursing school and secretarial school. Sick people made me sad, and I wouldn't cut my fingernails short enough to type fast, so those were options I'd never considered. And I'd basically been a housewife and mom for years. Stewardess was the woman's job that appealed to me—soaring above the earth in a chic uniform to faraway destinations. I'd been crushed when I'd learned that, at five feet one, I was too short for airline regulations, something about reaching overhead compartments. I could thank Daddy for my lack of stature. Mamma had been taller than her husband when wearing spike heels.

"I've been useful long enough," I said. "I want to do something glamorous and exciting, something that makes me feel the way I do when I hear Smokey Robinson sing, or read a Shelley poem."

Dee Dee jabbed Barry with the pencil. "Don't tell me you've taken up writing poetry. I swear, if you get any gloomier, I'm bringing you to the nurse's office. Maybe she has a pill."

She was now giving Barry a goatee. ·

"I don't think I can put together words well enough to be a poet," I said.

"Thank God."

Dee Dee saw nothing wrong with using strong words. Though I was the rebel, I couldn't bring myself to curse.

"I think I can *say* words well, though. I think I have a flair for conveying the meaning of others people's words."

"Lord above. What the hell are you talking about, Joey?"

She was now drawing Barry's private body parts, and I yanked away the album cover and slid it under the bed.

"I went to visit Mrs. Wilson," I said.

"The school counselor?"

I nodded.

"So? Every senior gets an appointment with her before the year's out."

"I went there on my own last week. Mr. Ingersoll suggested I see her."

"What for?"

Now she was drawing daisies on her palm.

"For guidance in picking a school. Mr. Ingersoll thinks I should continue my education."

Dee Dee tossed the eyebrow pencil to the floor. "I thought you said your dad couldn't afford that. What kind of a school are you talking about, anyway? Secretarial? Beauty? Nursing?"

"Drama."

"Drama school? What's that?"

Her frown said I was getting too serious for a Saturday night on a holiday weekend.

"I went to see Mrs. Wilson to find out where I can learn to be an actress."

Dee Dee swiveled away from me and hunched over my record collection, which was filed in a cardboard box I'd covered in polka-dot contact paper, the thirty-threes behind the forty-fives.

"You don't go to school to be an actress, Joey. You dye your hair blonde, go to Hollywood, and sit in a drugstore wearing a tight sweater, or on a casting couch wearing your birthday suit."

She was flipping through my albums. I knew she was looking for something perkier than "I Can't See Nobody."

"That's how you become Lana Turner or Marilyn Monroe." I was hurt by her lack of interest in my big announcement. "But I don't want to be a movie star. I want to be a *real* actress."

"What's the difference?"

With a screech of the needle, "Let's Spend the Night Together" blasted into the room.

"Plenty. I want to be a respectable actress, not a starlet."

Dee Dee turned to me and sniffed. "You don't look like an actress, Joey. You need brighter hair, bigger boobs."

I really wanted her to understand. To care about my new dream.

"Stage actresses don't need big boobs. I found a picture of Jessica Tandy in a library magazine, and she doesn't have big ones."

"Who's Jessica Tandy?"

"The actress who played Blanche Dubois on Broadway."

"Broadway. No wonder I've never heard of her. Hollywood is where actresses go."

The walls of Mamma's little aqua room were thin and the boys were sleeping. I reached across Dee Dee and turned down the volume, but not enough to belittle her song choice.

"Movie actresses don't say their lines to real audiences. They say them to cameramen, lighting guys, and makeup girls. They never know if they did their job well until months later. And they never get to hear applause or take a bow."

"Hmm." Dee Dee got up, plopped onto the bed. Her protruding bottom lip was playing tug-of-war with her frown. "Sounds like you've been thinking about this actress idea for a while. You used to talk to me about things the minute they popped into your head. You've been mighty secretive since last summer."

She was right, but there was nothing left to say about last summer.

"Well, I'm talking to you now."

"Aren't I the lucky one."

I got up, straddled my rummage-sale sewing chair, faced the bed.

"I'm just learning my new part, Dee Dee. But I loved being Blanche Dubois. She's somebody I'm not, and I got to be her for almost six weeks. I got to live in New Orleans, talk with a southern accent, and have a sister. I got to see the world through someone else's eyes. And when I said my lines, people listened. Even Tommy."

"You expect too much from a guy, Joey. Talking is what girlfriends are for. Tommy's quieter than most guys, but most guys aren't talkers."

"How do you know what most guys are like, Dee Dee? You've only been to Minneapolis twice, and you've never once been out of the state."

Dee Dee punched a pillow, and I knew another curse word was coming.

"Hell, Joey. I don't need to go somewhere different or dress up like someone else to figure that out. Or to make my life okay. People are people and things are what they are, and I don't feel I have to escape this town to know the score or be happy."

How I craved her understanding, or at least her acceptance.

"Well, I do," I said, reining in the quaver in my voice.

"But what's happening somewhere else that isn't happening right here, Joey?"

"Plenty."

"Like what?"

"Important things that matter."

"Name a few."

"Artistic developments. Political movements. War protests. Race riots. Sheesh, Dee Dee. When I told you Martin Luther King had been shot, you didn't even know who he was."

She scowled at the dent she'd made in the pillow.

"Joey, I feel real bad about Dr. King, and I surely agree with the idea of everyone being treated the same. But I doubt there's even one black person in all of northern Minnesota."

"My point exactly. There's more out there."

She was in no mood to be bested. "Seems to me, you should have learned your lesson about the thrills of the big bad world last summer, back when you had the flu for two weeks."

She had pushed the pillow under her blouse, making her look PG, patting it as if it were alive.

I was feeling confused. Ignorance could get you in trouble. But how could you overcome ignorance without seeking knowledge? How could I get out of this nowhere house without walking out the door? From the corner of my eye, I saw a reflection in the dresser mirror. And from somewhere beyond the ceiling, I heard a voice saying my dreams mattered.

"I want a different life, that's all."

Dee Dee shook her head. "Different how?"

"Different in a lot of ways."

"Like?"

She was still patting the pillow, and her cattiness suddenly made me more angry than ashamed. More than anyone on earth, Dee Dee knew the things I hated about my life. "Don't patronize me, damn it."

I ignored Dee Dee's gasp.

"If Jessica Tandy can cross an ocean and land on Broadway, why can't I hope to get there from here?"

One swear word hadn't scared her off. "The annual Showboat musical is held every summer right here on the world-famous Mississippi River. There's a community group that puts on plays in the Presbyterian Church basement. North Country Players, I think they're called. And once you turn eighteen, you don't have to live with your dad and brothers. You can get a better job and an apartment. Or, if it's not too late, you can marry Tommy."

There was no getting through to her.

"I want to be a real actress, Dee Dee. And that means going where there's a real playhouse and a real audience. But first I have to learn the craft."

She snorted. "Sounds like you're planning to take up knitting this time. I have enough of your embroidered handkerchiefs to get me to my grave."

"You know what I mean. I need to attend a school that can teach me how to do the thing I'd like to do with my life."

"And what school would that be, pray tell? Fantasy College? The University of Never Never Land?"

She'd lit another cigarette, and the smoke rings floated between me and the mirror.

"The school Mrs. Wilson recommended is called Pasadena Playhouse College of Theatre Arts. Mr. Ingersoll and the producer from Channel 13 wrote letters of recommendation for me. I sent in my application last week. If they take me, I'm going to California. Aren't you happy for me, Dee Dee?"

Her stunned look told me it wasn't a matter of happiness or sadness. Her sagging shoulders said it wasn't that she didn't *want* to understand.

"If you say so."

TEN

Reporting Live

I didn't attend my senior prom, even though Denzel Granger invited me just after homeroom bell the Thursday before the biggest dance of my life. I suppose it took him that long to get up the nerve. His hands were shaky and his smile crooked, like Daddy's when he'd try to sneak in the back door on Sunday morning. But my rebel streak was in high gear the day of Denzel's invite. Sewing a formal dress by Saturday was more effort than I wanted to give my current world, now that I knew I was leaving it, now that my life had a purpose that couldn't vanish in the night.

Only thirty-six people came to see *Pygmalion*, which we performed the night before the prom. They'd been mostly teachers and parents—not Daddy, of course—but they'd all sat near the stage, not in the bleachers, and that was good enough for me. I now had two well-known roles under my acting belt.

Dee Dee had hugged me with all the enthusiasm a best friend should have when I handed her the letter from Pasadena Playhouse College.

"Well, if it's what you want, kiddo, it's what I want for you," she'd said, no fakery in her smile. "I mean that, Joey. Way to go, hip hip hurray, rah rah. And you can call me collect anytime you get homesick. I'll give you the skinny on everything you're missing out on."

Daddy hadn't been quite as gracious, reading the letter as I pressed his evening's white shirt.

"Pasadena. Now, Joey, this letter's a very nice thing to get in the mail all the way from California. But whatcha going to pay for this acting college with, sweetheart? You know I don't have that kind of money."

I didn't know what kind of money Daddy did or didn't have. I'd been footing my own bill for years, earning cash by tossing *Duluth News Tribune*s for Jack and babysitting the Schmidt twins long before my ice cream parlor job. I'd hated explaining my monthly need for thirty-five cents, especially when Daddy's pockets were empty, which had left me to search under sofa cushions, mooch from Dee Dee, or improvise sanitary napkins from strips of an old bed sheet. I'd stopped asking Daddy for money long ago.

"I got a scholarship, Daddy. And I've saved some of my waitress money."

Pasadena Playhouse had given me a scholarship of a thousand dollars. A letter on linen stationery and $1,482 at First National Bank of Grand Rapids were my ticket out of northern Minnesota.

"And I've been promoted to grill girl, which will give me forty hours a week when school's out, plus a split of the tips. I have the whole summer to save even more."

"I'll worry about you being way out West," he'd said as I focused on his collar. Daddy was particular about his collars. "That's where all the kooks and goofballs live."

"I'll be fine, Daddy. They have a dormitory."

I'd heard Daddy slapping his face in the bathroom, and I could smell his Old Spice aftershave, which he preferred to Aqua Velva. I loved the smell. It made me think of the long-ago day he took just me for a Dairy Queen and a stroll across the bridge, set me right on the parapet to watch the Mississippi gush over the dam.

"Why do you want to go to college, anyway, young lady? Why don't you just marry some nice local boy with a job at the mill or the mines and have some kids? In that order, of course."

I flipped the collar over. For good measure, I always pressed the side that didn't show.

"I want to give this a try, Daddy. I'm only seventeen. There's plenty of time to get married if this doesn't work out."

There was no sense explaining how prestigious a theatre school Pasadena Playhouse was or how fortunate I'd been to get accepted, to get a recommendation from a television producer. Or how much I wanted to be an actress.

"Your mother was eighteen when she had you."

Mamma. I wondered where she was perching right now. Maybe just outside the window.

"I think Mamma would want me to do this."

"Your little brothers will be lost without you."

What Daddy really meant was *he* would be lost without me.

"They're not so little anymore, and they'll manage. I promise I'll write often and call when I can afford to."

"Your room will be waiting for you anytime you decide to come home, sweetheart."

I buttoned his shirt onto a hanger and handed it to him, kissing his forehead the way I did Jimmy's whenever he had a cold. To me, Daddy was one of the boys, and I didn't expect him to understand.

"I know that, Daddy."

Most of my classmates spent the spring and summer of '68 celebrating their high school graduation. According to Dee Dee—who dutifully kept me informed—plenty of beer kegs were tapped and bottle seals broken in honor of new freedom and new choices. Beach parties, hangovers, romances, and drive-in movies jam-packed those weeks of passage into adulthood for my peers. But while the Beatles sang "All you need is love" and reporters shouted "Live from Khe Sanh" and Rod McKuen crooned "Listen to the warm" and college kids chanted "Make love not war" and President Johnson announced "I will not accept the nomination" and protestors screamed "Black is beautiful" and "Burn your bra" and Bobby Kennedy proclaimed "And now it's on to Chicago" but never got there, I was flipping burgers, shaking grease from a french fry basket, and decoratively placing parsley and pickles next to coleslaw and cottage cheese whenever I wasn't sitting at my sewing machine creating a California wardrobe out of marked-down fabric from Ben Franklin. The day I learned about Pasadena Playhouse was the day I'd stopped caring if Paul Newman was handsomer than Steve McQueen or vinyl sounded better than eight-track or a one-piece was more flattering than a bikini. Even Shelley and Tess got short shrift after I'd decided on my life's goal. I actually returned the poetry book to the library and paid the late fee.

My airplane ticket was tucked into my cigar box. My new miniskirts and bell-bottoms were hemmed. My blue American Tourister with the price tag still on it was packed. Come the end of August, I was heading out, just a few weeks after my eighteenth birthday.

Bridgeman's lunch rush was over, and Judy Benson was on her break. This left me to cover the cone counter as best I could between sandwich and burger orders. Out of the corner of my eye, I saw a customer slip in the side door and march up to the counter, straw hat, sunglasses, and beard saying he was probably a tourist on the way to the lake.

"Be right there," I said, poking green frilled toothpicks into tuna salad and egg salad sandwiches. I tapped the pickup bell by the cutting board and butter bowl, wiped the mayo and crumbs onto my apron, and darted around the partition that separated the grill area and counter.

Bridgeman's was essentially two stainless steel islands of ice cream bins circled by bar stools, red vinyl booths, and a walk-up counter. Between orders, three white-clad waitresses and one white-clad grill girl per shift were expected to keep that stainless steel spotless with Ajax, seltzer water, and a dishtowel.

"May I help you?" I pulled the scoop from its water-filled holder.

"I'll have a triple decker," the man said in a gruff voice, jingling his keys, glancing back at the door. He was in a hurry. "Strawberry, chocolate, and vanilla."

"Sugar cone or regular?"

"Regular."

The vat of vanilla always ran out faster than the other flavors, and I had to lean deep into the bin for the first scoop. The vanilla vat was why some guys bought ice cream cones. A chunk of chocolate wound up on the front of my uniform after the second scoop. After the third scoop, I raised my head, smile ready, arm outstretched.

"Here you go. A dollar five."

The customer shook his head.

"Can't pay that."

We were definitely more expensive than Dairy Queen.

"A dollar's okay," I said. "I'll toss in the nickel."

"I asked for strawberry, chocolate, and vanilla."

Someone bellowed, "Order." I was needed at the grill.

"Right."

"This is vanilla, chocolate, and strawberry."

"Right."

"That's not what I ordered."

He was clearly a tourist. Probably an uppity city slicker in summer mode.

"Um."

The vanilla was already dripping. Someone yelled out another grill order, and I looked around, hoping Mr. Pliska was back from the bank. He wasn't. I knew what I was expected to do now, even for a jerk.

"Sorry about that. No charge."

I was mentally subtracting a dollar five from my tip cup when the jerk smiled. The cone fell from my hand into the strawberry vat. Trembling, I reached across the counter and pulled the sunglasses from his face, leaving a pink smear on his cheek. The sunglasses bounced off the counter and plopped into the scoop holder with a splash.

"Is it really you?"

He had more freckles than I remembered and a new crease between his eyebrows. His eyelashes still looked like little halos.

"Lola asked the same thing when I tried to start her."

"You rode your motorcycle?"

"Nah. She thinks I have another girl in Da Nang. Wouldn't fire."

"You grew your hair."

"Our barber liked to use a machete."

"Beard too."

"Shaving mirror was always foggy."

"How did you know where to find me?"

"I found the Ho Chi Minh Trail without a map."

He leaned over the counter and ran a finger across the stain on my dress. I was too shocked to move.

"What time do you get off?" he said, licking his finger.

"Four-thirty."

His eyes rose from the stain to my face. I gripped the counter edge to stay upright.

"See you then. And don't forget. I always save the best for last."

 ❧

"Wow. Some wheels."

Minus the straw hat and sunglasses, he'd pulled up in a blue Corvette. No one in town drove such a car. I stifled something between a yelp and a warble. Still clearly not a local, Kit Griffith was offering me another cool ride to Elsewhere.

"I was drunk when I bought it," he said, after helping me into the low passenger's seat and sliding into his side with practiced ease. He cranked the key as he closed the door.

"When was that?"

He toed the gas pedal until the engine gave a little roar, shifted, and turned west onto Highway 2.

"Day before yesterday."

His hair, sun-bleached to a burnished gold, now fell past his shoulders. His beard, as flaming as his sideburns, was full and thick. He looked like a Nordic version of Jesus.

He smiled at me when he hit a stoplight, and put his hand on my thigh. I didn't mind his hand or his silence. The electricity they both exuded was transfixing.

"How long have you been home?" I said when the light changed and he turned back to the road, leaving a scorched place where his hand had been.

"You mean home when the Golden Gate Bridge came into view? Or home when the house by Edina Country Club opened its door?"

"Home with your folks."

"A few weeks."

At the next light, he looked at me again but kept his hand on the shifter.

"You're not wearing my bracelet."

I'd held that bracelet in my hand a thousand times since I'd last seen Kit. But I'd never put it on.

"There's no one else," I said.

75

Two seconds after the light changed, he was shifting into third gear. "Someone else wouldn't stop me, Joey Dean."

We crossed town with no further talk, the low rumble of the Corvette motor and the thumping in my chest filling the silence. There was no one behind us when he pulled into the parking lot of the Rainbow Inn without using his turn signal and shut off the car.

"You're staying *here*?" The Rainbow Inn was the nicest hotel in town.

Kit turned toward me and reached across the console. His hand slid into my dress and across my breasts. The hotel key made a jangling sound when he dropped it inside my slip.

"*We* are."

I'd never stayed in a hotel room, with or without a man, and I wasn't sure what to do with myself as Kit latched the door chain, laid the key on the dresser, drew the drapes, and switched on the bedside lamp. So I just stood at the entrance to the room—a ritzy mix of scarlet plush, floral brocade, and knotty pine—watching him, trying to catch my breath and slow it down at the same time.

There was an ice bucket on a small table, and Kit gave the green bottle inside it a turn, but didn't make a move to open it. He reached for the knob of the fancy bedside radio, then, apparently changing his mind about music, let his hand drop. He walked over to me and put his hands on my shoulders, leaning down. But if he had planned to kiss me, he changed his mind about that too, running his palms down my arms, taking my hands in his, and pulling me into the room.

My hands were shaking and clammy. I could feel the blood rush to my face as I realized just how shaky and clammy they were. I was having trouble swallowing. I was having trouble even breathing. Instead of looking at Kit, I glanced over at the bottle in the ice, knowing that willpower alone wasn't going to stop my hands from trembling, or stop my ears from roaring as if a train were passing through the hallway.

Kit put a finger under my chin and turned my face back toward him. I just couldn't help the tears that came into my eyes when I looked up at him.

"What is it, Joey?" His voice was so low, almost a whisper, and I leaned forward to catch his words.

Even through the tears, I could see the little haloes that gave his eyes their constant gleam. But I couldn't find enough air to answer him.

"It's been a long time since that night in the graveyard," he said.

I nodded, and he smiled, still holding my hands.

The bottle made a sharp whooshing sound as it shifted in the melting ice. I jumped, then tried to cover my jitters by clearing my throat. The train had finally passed, and I could hear the clock on the bedside table ticking. It sounded like a bass drum. The crevice between my breasts felt damp.

"Maybe it's been *too* long," Kit said.

I tried to return his smile but failed. All those months of not knowing, of wondering and feeling forlorn. Of feeling lost and forgotten. Of remembering the night that had exploded the world and blown open the future. Of finally finding a way to move on.

"It was lousy timing, Joey. Me on the way to boot camp."

A tear rolled down my face, and I could see his gaze follow it past my chin and down my neck to the point where it slipped beneath my collar. Then he looked me in the eye again.

"I didn't think it was fair to you, trying to hang on to a few hours with letters."

The common sense of what he was saying shrank those months by only seconds.

"Those few hours," he went on. "I didn't want to spoil them. I couldn't mix you with where I was going."

Those few hours had been the only thing that mattered to me for most of those long months—the memory of them, my reason for living.

He shook his head and sighed. "It was just a night without a tomorrow."

It seemed so reasonable. Even kind. But there was a hidden little cave in my heart where the notion that I'd been a last-chance lay would always reside. I stared at him, blame in my eyes, anger in my frown.

He looked at the floor. "I should have told you, Joey."

He looked back up. "But I needed you so much that night."

I nodded, because I actually understood. And because deep in that cave crouched the awareness that I wouldn't have done differently in that cemetery no matter what I'd known.

"Would you like to wait, Joey? . . . I can take you home if you want."

I simply couldn't find enough breath to speak. And that was probably good. Heaven knows what might have tumbled out after all that time of silence and despair. I blinked, mentally scanning the female calendar I'd learned the hard way to keep. I shook my head.

"Then I think we should take this slow and easy, little girl."

All I could do was nod.

He pulled me to the far side of the bed near the table and chairs.

"Don't move a muscle." He gave me a wink, blew my hair away from my face.

"I'll handle everything," he said, releasing my hands. They fell to my sides, and I just stood there, letting him take charge of the moment I hadn't dared even dream of. The truth of that moment was, I couldn't have moved a muscle if a siren had gone off and the room had burst into flames.

He unbuttoned my uniform dress—smelling a bit of sour ice cream and hamburger grease—all the way down, and slipped it off my shoulders. I shivered, though his breath was warm on my skin. After folding the dress rather neatly, he reached behind him and set it on the chair nearest the bed, eyes never leaving my face. Then he unbuttoned his shirt, took it off, tossed it to the floor.

He was still slender, but broader in the chest than I remembered, and he had a new tattoo—of a tiger fighting a dragon—on his bicep. His chest hair was thicker now, partially covering the spread wings of his eagle tattoo, and it now joined a thin line of hair that went down as far as I could see. He slid the straps of my slip from my shoulders, then pulled the slip down to my waist. I felt suddenly too exposed, as if he were peeling layers from my heart.

His skin was still remarkably pale, though the added freckles on his face made it look ruddy in the light of the lamp. He bent and kissed the side of my neck as he unbuckled his belt. He pulled it through the loops of his jeans, let it drop from his hand to the floor. The little clink of the buckle made me gasp. He seemed taller than I recalled. And much older.

78

He knelt on one knee, pulling my slip down as he went. I wanted to run my fingers across his brow. He kissed my stomach as he lifted one foot, then the other, removing my shoes and pushing them aside, gathering up my slip with one hand. He stood, folded it, and set it on the chair. In the moment his back was turned, I saw a thick white scar spanning the distance between his shoulder blades.

I reached to touch it, but he was already facing me again.

"I told you to stay put, little girl." It was more of a caress than a reprimand, and the look in his eyes seemed warm and sad at the same time, soft but also hard.

My voice found itself and didn't wait for my permission.

"What happened?" I wanted to touch the raised ridges of the scar.

His shrug was almost imperceptible.

"Our bunker got hit. We'd made the roof from sandbags and steel runway matting, and it mostly stayed up."

He kissed my shoulder, then unbuttoned and unzipped his jeans. His hands were longish and slender and freckled. Beautiful hands, for a man. He slipped off his shoes, then slid his pants to the floor and stepped out of them in what seemed like a single movement.

He was narrower in the hips and more muscular in the legs than I remembered. And there was a deep, puckered red scar on his left thigh that hadn't been there before.

I pointed. "What happened there?"

Another hint of a shrug. "The NVA sniper was having an off day and missed the body part he was aiming for." He winked again. "It was also his last day."

I stifled another shiver as a cold draft entered the room, swirling through my excitement and longing. I didn't like the implication of Kit's remark. And I didn't like thinking there was a foreign jungle full of information about him I didn't know.

Kit reached behind my back with one hand, and my bra—which I wished wasn't the one with the safety pin—was no longer hooked. He pulled the straps over my shoulders and down my arms. Without looking away, he tossed the bra onto the chair. I tried to lift my hands in an automatic move to cover myself, but he was holding them at my sides.

"Too small," I said.

79

"Perfect," he said.

In that magical graveyard, he'd said the same thing. And both times, though my own eyes told me otherwise, I almost believed him.

He was kneeling again, and my underpants, the elastic frayed only at one leg, wound up on top of my bra. He rose, leaving my garter belt and nylon stockings in place. He slipped off his briefs. The hair below his waist was the same color as his beard, bright against the almost translucent whiteness of him. He sat in the empty chair and took off his left sock.

His feet were narrow, freckle-free, and high-arched, with blue veins running close to the surface. Nice feet, as feet go. He put his right foot on his left knee and pulled off the other sock.

He looked up at me.

Of course I saw it, but a moment passed before it registered. This foot didn't match the other one. Humped in the middle as if the arch had a tumor and the tumor had lumps. Skin stretched shiny and red, crisscrossed in places by thin purple scars. Big toe mangled and partly missing, as if something had taken a bite out of its side. The toe next to it had lost its top and was shorter than its neighbors by half. The little toe was gone altogether. When God had formed Adam's feet out of a clump of clay, this foot must have been his rough draft.

A heavy door slammed somewhere, and I heard voices on the other side of it shouting. It took me a moment to realize they were all saying the same thing and they all sounded like me. No. No. No. No. No. Something was pouring into my lungs, making it hard for me to inhale, even in the shallowest of ways.

I knew I couldn't keep staring at it, but I was afraid to look him in the face. I finally lifted my gaze, which weighed so much I groaned. His eyes were smiling. And something else. Something I'd never seen them do before and couldn't name. Something that made my chest hurt.

"I took shrapnel from a mortar round at Khe Sanh."

I wasn't really sure what shrapnel was, let alone a mortar round. I remained silent.

"Hill 881 South was a little crowded at the time." I couldn't tell if he was making a joke or being serious, or both.

"I can imagine."

Of course, I couldn't. Did Khe Sanh have nearly nine hundred hills? And if it had all those hills, why would number 881 be so crowded?

"The foot was number three."

"Three?"

"You get to cut out after your third Purple Heart."

"Cut out?"

"Leave Vietnam."

"For a hospital?"

"Several. I fought the saw. Hard."

"Saw."

Sawed open a couple of ribs. Then he took my heart out, set it right on the table . . .

Oh my god. I'd done this all before, in another bedroom where the hush of death had drifted. I was looking into a mirror, and the reflection was just too naked.

The smile had left Kit's eyes. "Screws and K-wires, debridement, traction, physical therapy. The works," he said. "But no saw."

Carcasses, cleavers, and men in white coats. I was watching it all again. The horror of human suffering.

I nodded. "Uh huh.

"It's not pretty but it's mine."

Switchblades and stilettos. It was that same old movie, blades slashing away at what had been a perfect image, my eyes glued open by shock.

"Does it hurt?"

Bam. Bam. Sharks on one side.

"Some days more than others. They couldn't get to all of the shrapnel and it says hello now and then."

Chink. Chink. Jets on the other.

"Oh."

"When it does, I use a little help from my friends."

The bottle in the ice shifted again, and I looked at it with true longing. I wanted to drink a potion that would blur the scary parts of this scene.

Kit glanced at the bottle, then looked back at me through the stone soberness he clearly preferred just then.

"I almost never use my crutches anymore." I heard pride in his voice, a touch of defensiveness, a bit of chagrin. "And I only limp when I'm tired and don't concentrate."

I swallowed.

"I didn't even notice."

It was time for me to move, despite his decree, despite my shock. I stepped in front of his chair and reached out my hand, mentally begging it not to shake, my question in my eyes. If Kit flinched, it was a hair's breadth movement camouflaged by a blink. He nodded. And as lightly as I could, I laid my hand over the hump of bones and skin. The ankle that held it onto his leg was slender and white, the palest flesh of his whole body.

"It's the most beautiful foot I've ever seen," I said.

A long moment passed before Kit set his foot on the floor and broke the silence, looking up at me with more seriousness than I'd ever been witness to and shaking his head.

"Joey Dean, there's something else I have to tell you." He cleared his throat and I stopped breathing. "It's hard for me to talk about, but all things considered, I think you have a right to know."

I waited, suspended in fear.

He slipped a finger under a garter and slid his hand down the inside of my thigh. He bit his lip and frowned. Then he snapped the elastic, giving me a little smack.

"There's a run in your stocking that's longer than the Mekong River."

Before I could answer, he stood up, gripping my bottom and taking me with him. Reflexively, I wrapped my arms around his neck and my legs around his hips. And he was inside me before he reached the bed, even before I exhaled.

☙

We didn't get out of bed for four days. Sometime deep into the first night, I fell down on the way to the bathroom, and Kit was beside me before I hit the red-shag carpet.

"Tell me what's wrong, Joey."

"I think my legs gave out."

"Hmm. You look very tasty in red. Almost as good as you do in chocolate."

"But Kit, I'll wet my pants.

"I hate to tell you this, baby, but you aren't wearing any."

My eighteenth birthday passed in a haze of champagne, sex, catnaps, and whispers about nothing beyond that slightly squeaky hotel mattress. We finally ate something other than salted peanuts in the shell on the third morning—eggs, toast, and coffee in bed—which Kit ordered by phone and had them leave outside the door. Then he opened another bottle of champagne. Somewhere in those four days, I called home and work from the nightstand phone. I think it was Sunday afternoon when we finally got up. Kit took a short shower while I used the phone again. Then I had a long bath, breathing the steam he'd created deep into my lungs, reluctant to wash away the smells of him, trying to make them part of me.

Wearing only half-zipped jeans, Kit pulled a shirt from his big Marine-green seabag and tossed it to me. He watched as I unwrapped my towel and donned the shirt, then sat down and fired two cigarettes with his Zippo. He handed me one. The floral brocade of the other chair felt scratchy against my bare legs. Kit leaned back, crossing his legs in that loose guy way, and took a long drag.

"I think I should get you a real meal, little girl," he finally said. I liked watching the smoke drift from his nostrils and lips when he exhaled.

I would have been content never to leave that room. But we were out of champagne, and a beam of sunshine was snooping through a crack in the curtains.

"I suppose so." I picked a piece of tobacco from my lip. The Camels Kit smoked didn't have filters and made me a bit dizzy.

"And then I should probably bring you home. I don't want the police or your father to come knocking."

I watched the piece of tobacco disappear into the scarlet depths of the rug. Kit's last goodbye and its aftermath were still sore spots just behind my breastbone.

"I'm past the age of consent, Kit."

He wagged his finger playfully in the air. "I've heard that one before."

His jest made my chest throb. For whatever part his former girlfriend had played in his departure for Vietnam, I hated her.

"How old was Peggy, anyway?"

Kit glanced at the nightstand and then patted his pants pockets.

"I told you about Peggy?"

"Sort of."

He pulled his pocket watch from his jeans.

"At the time I knew her, she was fifteen going on thirty, and I was twenty going on twelve. The few months she fibbed about definitely had a maturing effect on me, though. I think the judge would have believed the three pounds of marijuana really were for a Lake Minnetonka beach party, not customers, if Peggy hadn't washed off her makeup and worn a ponytail and turtleneck to court. But what else could a poor girl do when her mom found a diaphragm underneath her Barbie doll?"

"Hmm."

I'd had a lot of time to think about Kit's reason for going to Vietnam. And between Dee Dee and Tommy, I'd heard plenty about his wild reputation. But I was a girl who wore eye shadow and kept her cigarettes right in her purse. And I was a girl who'd slept with Kit Griffith. I didn't want Kit any less because of his rebellious side. Maybe I wanted him partly because of it.

As for Peggy, my pride overrode my curiosity, and I let her dissolve in the pesky sunbeam that kept reminding me there was another world outside the ritzy red room I was so reluctant to leave. I picked up Kit's lighter, flipping it over in my palm. It had a dent in the flip top and was heavily scratched. USMC was engraved on one side, CCG on the other.

"What's the second C stand for?"

Kit emitted a sharp scoff.

"My mother's father didn't get the son he wanted, so she did what she could to keep his name and money going. Christopher Callaghan, he was, chieftain of a dying Irish branch."

"Oh."

Kit looked at his watch and I felt a shiver dash down my spine.

"You may be past the age of consent, little girl, but there are kidnapping charges to worry about. It's time for this chick to eat some decent food and return to the coop."

"You're probably right," I said in the airiest voice I could manage. "I've missed two shifts, and the laundry is sure to be piling up at home."

But I didn't make a move to rise. I just looked at him, wondering for an eerie moment if he was really in that hotel room, suddenly scared he might vanish into the sunlight if we walked out the door. I was afraid to take my eyes off him. He was so much more solid than my memories, so alive and in control of each moment. He owned the space he occupied and everything he looked at or touched. Within his universe, Kit Griffith was the director of the movie, the leader of the band, the person who put the paintbrush to the canvas. Like his crazy eyelashes, there was a sort of glow about him, a bright energy I couldn't see but knew was there, the way I knew when there was a bird at the top of a tree so full of leaves you could only see green when you looked up. Four days with Kit was more life than I'd lived in eighteen years. Four days with Kit was a streetcar I'd gotten on and prayed would never stop.

In those four days, I'd seen every inch of his body. In the shadows of lamplight, draperies, and cigarette smoke, between the hazy tangle of blankets, sheets, pillows, and clothing, I'd studied it, memorized parts of it. I'd watched every gesture he made, every facial expression, listened to every nuance of his voice, taken note of his speech patterns. I'd analyzed his words and reactions, trying to know his mind, trying to absorb the essence of him. He was now burned into my brain so deeply, no amount of time would allow him to fade should he disappear from my life again. To lose the reality of him again would be to spend forever facing the intensity of that loss every time I let my mind wander.

My forgotten cigarette was burning my fingers, but I still didn't move.

Kit slipped the watch back into his pocket, met my stare, and nodded.

"I won't be gone fourteen months this time, Joey. I promise."

He'd counted the months, though maybe for different reasons than I had. I crushed the cigarette stub in the ashtray when the ash finally fell onto my bare leg. Then I stood up and slipped off Kit's shirt, dropping

85

it into the triangle between his legs before picking my uniform up off the floor, where it had somehow landed despite Kit's care.

"I need a bacon cheeseburger, CCG of the USMC, and you'd better feed me before I tell a judge you kidnapped, raped, and starved me."

He stood up, and the sunbeam turned his smile into the core of the universe.

"If a bacon cheeseburger is what will sate your appetite, little girl, I know just the place."

— ELEVEN —

To Love Somebody

Just the place turned out to be the dining room of the Rainbow Inn, as fancy a restaurant as you could find in town. I had to laugh when Kit gave me his elbow and escorted me straight down the hall and through the open doorway. Before we left our room, he slipped his fringed suede vest over my wrinkled uniform, hiding the chocolate stain if not the fact that I was an off-duty waitress/grill girl. He also took the do-not-disturb sign off the doorknob.

Bacon cheeseburgers weren't on the menu, but the waitress said the cook had all the ingredients and wouldn't mind. Kit ordered spaghetti with tomato sauce and the vegetable medley. I watched the waitress pocket her pad and walk away, envying her clean uniform and confident stride. When I turned back to the table, lighted so softly it might have been evening, vase of carnations and red cloth napkins so elegant, Kit was staring at me.

"You're a pretty girl, Joey Dean."

I was glad the lights were low. I could feel a blush coming on.

"So you keep saying."

I didn't think Kit was lying. I just didn't believe his standard for pretty matched mine. And any makeup I'd once worn was days gone, except for my Ballerina Pink lipstick, which had doubled as rouge, which my blush was now making too bold. Tommy had never answered the how-do-I-look question with more than a nod, and Kit's ease with compliments ruffled me. He had a way of looking at me that literally sped up my heartbeats.

"Even prettier than I remembered," he said.

He reached across the table and ran a thumb across my lower lip. His hands smelled of Camay, the hotel soap. Daddy never bought anything but Dial.

"You thought about me?"

"Maybe too much, considering. Vietnam's not a place for day-dreaming."

I didn't ask him to explain. Kit was the opposite of Tommy in terms of saying what was on his mind. If he held something back, it wasn't because he didn't like chatting or felt awkward expressing himself in words. And though I shunned Walter Cronkite, Vietnam was unavoidable these days, a place you didn't ask to hear about like you might a trip to Yellowstone Park or the zoo. And that's why I knew any talk of what had happened to Kit between a midnight motorcycle ride and a triple-decker ice cream cone had to be his idea. What had happened to me, in a little aqua bedroom, well, that would stay locked in my secret heart-cave. I was glad when our food arrived and Kit turned his gaze to his plate.

My cheeseburger was divine, though my hunger and happiness probably assisted the cook's efforts. But three bites into my meal, I realized Kit was only fiddling with his food. When he set down his fork and lit a cigarette, I held out my sandwich.

"This is terrific. Have a bite."

He blew a smoke ring, which made me realize I hadn't called Dee Dee.

"And risk getting girl germs?"

His smile was fleeting, but it lit up my day. I wanted to paint the sky the color of his eyes, and also the grass and the trees. But I knew I'd never capture the subtleties of that maverick hue.

"Bacon and girl germs. Definitely delish," I said.

"No thanks, baby. I don't eat animals anymore."

I took another bite, trying not to laugh with food in my mouth.

"Why on earth not?"

Chewing happily, I waited for his flirty comeback.

"Because their faces show pain and they moan when they die."

I swallowed, not quite ready to.

"Oh."

I set the burger on my plate, grabbed the saltshaker, and shook it over my fries. Pepper fell from the holes. Kit didn't seem inclined to elaborate, so I stuttered into another subject.

"So—so—when are you heading back to Minneapolis?"

That was the subject I least wanted to talk about.

"Not for a while."

"Gonna visit your north-woods family?"

The thought of Tommy, who was part of that family, didn't cause even a twinge. The thought of Kit leaving town had my heart now beating twice its normal speed.

He raised a finger toward our waitress.

"Eventually," he said. "But I want to get moved in first."

"Moved in?"

The waitress stepped our way, and Kit ordered Christian Brothers on the rocks, and another Coke for me. He turned back to the conversation, and his eyes on mine made me want to sing.

"I bought a little place just outside of town. It's not quite ready for habitation." He winked. "No shag carpet and no room service."

I drained my Coke in one loud gurgle of my straw.

"*What?*"

"I'm going back to school."

Everything I knew about Kit was in its own little encyclopedia in my brain. I hadn't forgotten that he'd attended the University of Minnesota before joining the Marines.

"But the only school here is a tiny junior college."

Kit's drink arrived, and he gave up the pretense of eating. The ice cubes in his glass tinkled like little bells when he downed half the brandy.

"I didn't manage to earn many credits in my two years at the U," he said as he set down the glass. "But they all transferred."

It was impossible to hide my shock. Shock and something awfully close to fear.

"But *why* would you want to live and go to school in this one-horse town?" The carnations suddenly smelled oversweet. The napkins suddenly looked garish.

His hair swayed when he shrugged. Girls I knew slept on orange juice cans to achieve those loose waves. "I've always liked this town. The lakes. The woods. The girls." He cocked an eyebrow, clearly teasing. "I'll probably like the one horse too, once I meet him."

It was more than I could absorb. I stared at him.

He had taken my hand in his and was studying my palm as if trying to read my fortune. His fingers felt so smooth, so strong.

"I realize this is relatively sudden, Joey. And I don't know what post-graduation plans you've made. But I was hoping you might like to be with me."

"Huh?" It was just too much to follow.

He looked up.

"Go to school with me. Share my pad. Be my old lady."

Hard as my rebel spirit tried, I wasn't especially hip, and what he was suggesting didn't immediately register. In this small town I'd grown up in, we called it shacking up. And even in 1968, that was a scandalous thing to do here.

I pulled my Band-Aid tin from my purse. Kit held out his Zippo as I flipped the lid of my makeshift case, but I couldn't retrieve a cigarette for the shaking of my hands.

"Times have changed," Kit said as he removed and lit one for me. "Mature people get to know each other before getting serious these days. Living together is no big deal."

My Band-Aid tin suddenly looked silly instead of rebellious, my half-eaten burger like leftover kids' food.

"But I was accepted at a college in California, Kit."

He leaned back in his chair.

"California," he repeated, his tone sounding as if he'd said Siberia or Timbuktu.

"Well, yes. Pasadena, actually."

Kit was studying my face with an intensity that alarmed me. In the dim light, the crease between his eyebrows looked like a gash.

"Couldn't this college defer your enrollment for a few terms? First year is generally core courses anyway."

My heart shattered silently on the floor. He wouldn't ask such a thing if he understood.

"A drama college. A famous one."

The crease eased into a raised brow as Kit flashed a smile that made me sigh in relief.

"Drama, is it? Well, Itasca Junior College must offer a few drama classes and put on a play now and then," he said. "And there's probably a local theatre group you could join."

How could I admit all the tears I'd shed for him? How acting had saved me from drowning in them? The room had become a high-speed carousel.

"But I got a scholarship to Pasadena Playhouse, Kit. A very prestigious school. We could both go to college in California."

He took a sip of his brandy, ran his hand down his beard—which looked the same color as his drink in the low light. His smile was gone.

"Scholarship. You're one smart chick, Joey Dean. But I was spit on and booed in San Francisco, crutches and all."

A stunning image. The room kept spinning.

"Baby killer, they called me." His laugh wasn't really a laugh, and I flinched, too horrified and confused to reply.

"But hey, that was nothing compared to some jungle greetings I've received," he said.

He took another sip of his brandy and his body visibly relaxed.

I stubbed out my cigarette, never having taken a drag.

"It's a big chance for me, Kit." The pitch of my voice had risen, and I knew I sounded whiny. But I couldn't help it. The choice before me was too cruel. Blood seeping from the heart of my cheeseburger had become an open red wound on my plate.

"I'm proud of you, Joey. But couldn't you postpone this college of yours? I've waited so long to see you."

My mouth just kept going.

"But Pasadena is nowhere near San Francisco, Kit. And you said we'd ride west all the way to the ocean." I'd memorized those words.

He blinked, as if taken aback.

"That was before, Joey."

I shifted in my seat to steady myself and kicked something under the table. Kit's grimace told me what it was as my face began to burn.

He tipped his glass once again, and the ice cubes were now chiming.

91

"All things considered, I didn't expect to come home to a ticker-tape parade," he said. "But I'm fresh out of one war and not quite ready for another. I need a little peace, Joey. And I was hoping to find it here. With you."

His eyes sought mine, and I saw pride, resignation, and weariness in their ocean-colored depths. I looked away, only to catch his profile in a mirror on the wall, jaw clenched, as if from pain.

"California's not an option right now, Joey." He set his glass down slowly. "For me."

Silent moments passed as my mind scrambled to rearrange the future, as I tried to pull a mask down over my devastation.

"Then how about Minneapolis? We could both take classes at the U for a term, and you'd be close to your parents." I was a blind beggar groping for tossed change, thoughts grasping for a way to keep my acting dream and this man I loved together. The University of Minnesota was light years from Pasadena Playhouse, a scholarship, and the ocean. But anywhere was better than here.

He ran a long freckled finger around the edge of his glass.

"I've made an agreement with my parents to live away from them."

What little I knew about Kit's parents hadn't come from him.

"Your parents don't want you near them?"

His cracked laugh held no humor.

"My parents acknowledge my failings as a son and are trying to accept the consequences. From a distance."

The look on his face told me not to pry.

"One year, Joey. That's all I'm asking of you."

I closed my eyes right there in the restaurant, conjuring up the library photos I'd studied like a script, seeing the palm trees and flowers and pretty streets, picturing the ocean, oh so close by. I could hear wind whistling, waves crashing, seagulls screeching, see an endless white stretch of sand. I could feel sunshine on my shoulders.

"I need you so much, little girl." The plea in his voice was softer than sea mist.

I looked into his eyes and saw something more captivating than that faraway daydream. Something I couldn't forsake.

"A year," I said. "I guess I could use it to catch up on my Shakespeare." My emotions just then were too mixed to sort out. I swallowed them whole. "But come next fall term, it's Pasadena, California."

Kit had lit a Camel, so his sigh might have been just so much cigarette smoke, the quaver in his voice merely a remnant of the brandy he'd been drinking. And the shine in his eyes, that could have been simply a reflection of the lamp above our table.

"We have a deal."

Kit picked me up the next morning and drove me to work. I cashed in my ticket to California on the way there. The following morning, I wrote a letter to Pasadena Playhouse College before going to see old Dr. Wexroth. When I asked him for birth control pills—the second most daring thing I'd ever done—Doc congratulated me on my marriage.

— TWELVE —

If Winter Comes

"Honestly, Joey, it's just a little farther. Five hundred yards at most. Do you think you're going to make it or should I turn back?"

"You'll hit a tree if you try to turn around," I mumbled into the black leather upholstery of Kit's Corvette. My head was between my knees, and I was trying not to faint, or worse.

"Reverse gear's my specialty. Saved me more than a few times. Tell me what to do, baby."

"Just keep going."

"Hold on. We're almost there."

I glanced up at the shadowy green tunnel Kit was driving through and moaned without meaning to.

"Carsick? Is it the ruts? I'm going as slow as I can."

Another moan slipped out. "It's the trees."

"Trees are just branches with leaves."

I took a deep breath, which smelled of new leather and wet vegetation. "Not when there are so many so close together."

"Poor little girl, you're claustrophobic."

Kit stroked my hair with his free hand.

"No I'm not. I just need to see the tops."

"Makes sense to me, if it does to you."

Fighting my urge to open the door and jump out, I could only say, "Uh huh."

"I didn't know about this road when I bought this car," Kit said. "I've scraped bottom twice."

At this point in our journey, I didn't dare open my mouth.

"Close your eyes, Joey. It's just around this little bend."

My eyes were already closed.

The Corvette came to a stop, and I heard Kit pocket his keys.

"And here we are. Home sweet home."

I stumbled out of the car before Kit could reach my door, and scrambled into the clearing at the end of the road. I looked up, took another deep breath, and felt the nausea and panic ebbing. There were treetops galore and plenty of sky. Kit's arm was suddenly around my shoulder and the sun was shining.

"The Corvette was rather impetuous." His sigh was full of chagrin. He ran a hand through his hair and it caught fire in a sunbeam. "Old habits die hard."

I saw a bird flying far above the trees. A hawk, maybe a crow. Maybe Mamma.

"I like the Corvette," I said.

Kit's car was a flashy choice that appealed to me yet made me curious. I didn't know anyone else who could afford a Corvette. And I didn't know anyone, myself included, who would buy a Corvette even if they could afford it. I momentarily wondered where the money for such a car had come from.

Kit squeezed my shoulder, and my head slid nicely under his chin.

"I'm glad you approve of my overpriced fiberglass whim. But today's question is, what do you think of our new pad?" He turned me to the right, an eager look on his face.

New pad. Bigger than a cabin. Tidier than a shanty, despite peeling paint and bald spots in the shingles. The porch—leaning eastward, siding bare, stacked concrete blocks for steps—was an obvious afterthought. Knee-high weeds composed the yard, and the driveway was simply the end of the road, a meander of dirt ruts through the trees. Frog croaks said there was a pond or swamp nearby.

"It's far out," I said, not daring to look at him.

Kit laughed and kissed my neck, making me shiver despite the sunshine and the hot irony burning in my chest. This place made Daddy's house look positively swanky.

"A pithy appraisal, dear roommate. Think of it as a wilderness retreat. A rustic nature sanctuary."

Kit had a way of making down look like up, moonglow like daylight. I attempted a smile. A year was only twelve months long.

"I thought you might like to pick the color, so I didn't paint the outside yet," he said. "And I haven't had a chance to build steps or get a mower. But let me show you where I was thinking we might plant a little vegetable garden come spring."

He'd taken my hand and was pulling me through the weeds.

"But I don't know anything about growing vegetables," I said, batting away the overgrowth, wondering what I might be stepping on.

He looked back and winked. "No sweat, baby. I'll buy a gardening book."

Perhaps an acre of wild vegetation stretched behind the house to the woods. Two sheds and a rickety outhouse poked above the weeds like overfed offspring. Kit stopped in the middle of the field and pointed at an especially sunny spot.

"Voilà. Our own backyard pantry."

"Kit, please tell me this pioneer outpost has an indoor toilet."

He wrapped an arm around my waist, slipped a hand under my blouse.

"A fully flushing john. The outhouse is just a little relic from the past." He pointed with his free hand. "That building to the east is our toolshed, the one to the west, our laundry room."

"A washer. What a relief."

"A washtub. So it's the laundromat for now. But there's a clothesline on the far side of the house."

A garter snake slithered in front of Kit's right boot. I jumped back, but Kit just shrugged. He'd cut the tongue from the boot, left the laces loose to accommodate his damaged foot, and it looked so exposed, so vulnerable.

"It's been a while since I've seen a snake I was sure couldn't do me in," he said.

I was now behind him, eyes glued to the clump of weeds the snake had disappeared into.

"Any snake is a scary snake."

Kit tucked my hand in his. "Trust me, little girl, some snakes are scarier than others." He turned and gave my hand a sturdy tug. "Let's step into our humble abode."

Kit had clearly been busy. The room we entered smelled of fresh paint.

"I thought this was a pleasant color," he said. "Reminded me of your hair."

He'd painted the room beige. I would have chosen Lady Clairol pale gold, but the color *was* rather pleasant. I took a step and surveyed the place.

An old heating stove hulked in the far corner of the room, a fat pipe connecting it to the wall. A field-rock fireplace dominated the opposite wall, a thick board serving as its mantel. Two side-by-side windows, clearly a makeshift picture window, offered a broad view of the weed field. A small television—its metal cabinet painted to look like wood— and a broken pair of rabbit ears sat on the floor under the windows. An old twenties-style brown sofa and a wooden rocker with a hole in the caned seat made up the rest of the room's contents.

"I was thinking you'd like to choose the furniture too," Kit said, looking pensive. "After the car and this place, bread will be tight for a while, though. But there's a used store in town that looks decent."

"I'm used to used furniture," I said.

Kit's worried tone and my dismay made me say, "I have some money, Kit."

His head shake was firm, almost angry. "No. It's just temporary."

He was looking out the window, and bitterness had seeped into his voice. "My folks are considerably more generous than Uncle Sam and his GI bill, as long as I stay in school, stay away, and don't do anything that gets into the *Minneapolis Tribune*. My ending up in Vietnam like some ghetto kid, and coming home with permanent proof of my folly, is an embarrassment they're willing to pay well to hide."

I didn't know what to say, so I didn't say anything.

Kit's gaze reentered the room. "I mopped the floor three times, so it's good and clean," he said with a touch of pride. "Those dark spots are just worn places."

In Daddy's house, no one ever mopped the floor but me. I tried to focus on that as I stared at the old gray linoleum, curled at the edges, so similar to the linoleum I'd been mopping for years. A colorful mix of throw rugs had been strategically placed around the room. I followed them into the kitchen.

The kitchen had also been painted beige, except for the cabinets, whose white doors and drawers yawned open to let the paint dry. The cabinets sported antiquated latches instead of handles. The icebox was the old motor-on-top kind, and the stove was gas, not electric. A chipped porcelain sink jutted from the wall, no cabinet built beneath it. A wooden table and four chairs, also newly white, sat under the lone window, which faced the trees smothering all but the end of the road. A yellow phone hung on the wall near the table, looking defiantly modern. Looking like something Mamma would have chosen, if there'd been money for the colored-phone fee. The kitchen was smaller than Daddy's, but big enough, since I'd now be cooking for only two.

"I also decided to let the dishes and cooking utensils wait for your input," Kit said. "I didn't want to screw up something so important to a woman."

I just nodded. How could he know my true feelings about dishes and cooking utensils, how sick I was of producing meals for a small tribe?

"With no mom in the house, you've probably done plenty of cooking and dish washing," he went on. "I can't say I'm handy with much more than a can opener when it comes to food preparation. But I'll spell you with Chef Boyardee. And I'm an ace with a dishtowel."

"Really?" No one had ever willingly helped me in the kitchen.

"True fact. My mother's idea of child rearing was turning me over to the maid while she played bridge and drank sherry. Lizzie was a good teacher, and I eventually worked my way up to the crystal."

The bathroom was another afterthought, popping from the side of the hallway like a pimple on school picture day. I had to duck to look out the window, a piece of semi-clear plastic thumb-tacked to a wood frame. The bathtub was the old claw-foot kind, the sink about the size of my poetry book from the library. Beige walls, a small white cabinet, gray linoleum with more worn spots, a little red rug.

"I hope to install a real window before long. Curtains are something else I thought you'd like to buy. Or sew, if you know how."

"I know how to sew," I said.

Kit nodded. "I could tell you were artistic."

"How's that?"

"By your slightly sassy sway and your flair with clothes. You're stylish with a rebel streak. That sunshine sweater and those leather laces said a lot about you the night I spied you in that alley."

Dee Dee had sometimes remarked on my ability with a needle and thread, but no man in my life had ever praised my mostly homemade apparel.

The two rooms across the hallway were small, beige, empty.

"I was thinking we could make a library in one of these," Kit said. "You like books, Joey?"

"I like books," I said. How could he know how much I liked them, how long they'd been a refuge?

Yet he somehow did know. "Books are a good way to escape. You've probably felt like doing that sometimes since your mom died."

He slid his arm around my shoulder and pulled me into the last room. "And if you like, we could make a sewing room here." Sweeping my bangs aside, he kissed my forehead. "Sound good?"

"I guess."

Kit had clearly put considerable thought and effort into making our new home feel homey, but my heart was brawling with my head. What Kit saw as a rustic sanctuary, I saw as a shack.

"This house is as much yours as mine," he said, stroking my face. "I want you to feel comfortable here. I know it's not fancy, Joey, but it's peaceful and it's paid for. As long as the taxes are met, this is a place where we can be free."

"From what?" A mass of green was the only thing I could see outside the window.

"From heartless authority."

Authority. That was something I didn't have much experience with. In fact, I'd often felt abandoned and alone for lack of it. For having to figure out so many things on my own. On the other hand, no one had ever forced me to choose between jail and war. No one had sent me halfway around the world to get ripped apart by flying metal. This house represented something to Kit that I could only imagine.

He led me back to the main room and up a narrow staircase.

"Our bedroom."

It was an attic room the size of the bottom floor, with a window at each end and a peaked ceiling. A double bed stood in the middle, its spindle headboard and white chenille bedspread clearly new. Folded upon it was a red blanket with oriental designs, and Kit's big green seabag lay on the floor at its foot, his crutches set neatly on top.

I'd yet to see Kit use his crutches, and the sight of them startled me. They were strangely primitive and technical at the same time, geometrical mini-trees cloned in a scientist's lab. I immediately hated them, a clumsy manmade fix for a delicate God-made part.

Blinking, I looked away. My gaze fell on two black carvings sitting on a bedside table. One was an elephant, the other an animal I couldn't name.

"Water buffalo," Kit said. "Ebony."

In terms of the exotic, the figures definitely outdid Mamma's art-deco cats. I looked at the table on the other side of the bed, noting a lamp, an alarm clock, and a fat volume of Shakespeare, hard cover, gilded pages. Tapping the book, Kit said, "Your side, if that's okay."

I couldn't guess where he'd found such a book in a town with no bookstore. It was now the grandest thing I owned.

There was a makeshift board-and-brick stereo stand by the far window, a stack of albums on the floor beside it. Kit crossed the room and turned on his hi-fi.

"You know CCR?" he said.

I shook my head, remembering the magic first song he'd introduced me to.

"John Fogerty, he finds a great groove."

An earthy male voice and a driving bluesy beat filled the room as Kit walked back to me.

"I hope you like this color," he said. "I was going for something easy on the eyes. Something peaceful."

I looked at the wall behind the stereo, and the color finally registered.

"What do you think, little girl?" He unzipped my jeans and slid his hands inside them, his tour clearly over.

I glanced from wall to wall, getting a bit dizzy in the process. Kit had painted the room aqua, the color Mamma had used to spruce up a dump.

The neighborhood loon chose that moment to mute the music with its warble, and I took it as advice to look for the big view. Pasadena Playhouse and all it promised was just a few hundred days away. And I had Kit all to myself for a year.

I wrapped my arms around his neck. His beard felt smooth on my skin as he nuzzled my ear, his fingers like a new frontier. No doubt about it, he'd put a spell on me.

"It's peaceful, Kit."

— THIRTEEN —

Coming Up Rosie

"Why can't this Kit fellow call for you at your own door the way Tommy did? Crazy Californians might practice marriage before the fact, but it's not the northern Minnesota way, young lady. You could lose your job."

Daddy was pleased that Pasadena Playhouse was out of my near future, but not at all pleased that Kit's dwelling in the woods—which Kit, with a twinkle in his eye, had named the Homestead—was in it. But Daddy didn't face me when he voiced his protest, an uncharacteristic bit of preaching he technically followed by always pulling into his own driveway before dawn.

"Kit is from Minnesota and hates California," I replied. "As for my job, I don't plan to announce my new living arrangement. I'm eighteen now, Daddy, and you need to let me make my own decisions."

I'd been making plenty of decisions for years, but I didn't like to hurt Daddy's feelings by reminding him.

"Then why can't you live in town near your brothers instead of out in the sticks? I didn't even know there was a house on that old road."

In my opinion, our town was out in the sticks.

"It's not that far away, Daddy. And Kit has a car."

"Well, it's not going to be the same around here without you."

That, of course, was his real concern. Though I'd delayed California, he was still losing his babysitter, cook, and housekeeper in one fell swoop. And I felt bad about that. He depended on me. But the boys were five years older than when Mamma had died, and between them they'd manage. There was no point in telling my father what I felt sure he'd eventually learn, though, so I just kissed his cheek and left the room.

Daddy returned Kit's handshake and said a proper "How do you do?" when Kit came for me, but he didn't help with my suitcase, sewing machine, or three cardboard boxes, and he didn't come out to the driveway to say goodbye, the way northerners usually did. He just gave my forehead a peck at the doorstep and said, "You know where your home is, Joey," as Kit and I headed for the car.

Dee Dee had been a bit tetchier than Daddy when I told her my news.

"Jesus Christ, Joey! Your reputation will be ruined. Shredded. Who'll ever date you again after you've shacked up? Who'll marry you? Why don't you just wear a sign around your neck that says I've been had? You're dooming yourself to old-maidhood if you do this mad thing."

We were in our old sparring spots—Dee Dee on my bed facing me in my sewing chair.

"Don't be dramatic, Dee Dee. This is 1968."

"The year doesn't matter, kiddo. Men don't buy the cow when the milk is free."

I rolled my eyes. "I'm not a cow and I don't plan on belonging to anyone."

"Who are you kidding?" she sputtered. "Can you honestly tell me you don't want Kit Griffith to marry you? Hell, you've given up your precious acting school for him."

I couldn't tell her that any more than I could broach the subject of marriage with Kit. Or allow myself to even daydream about it just now. He was back in my life, and we'd made a deal.

"It's not an *acting* school. It's a college of theatre arts. And I'm only postponing it."

"You deserve better than this, Joey."

"How can you say that? You've never even met Kit."

"Don't need to. His reputation precedes him."

I studied the scuffs on my white sandals. "He makes me happy."

Dee Dee grunted. "This isn't the life you said you wanted."

I counted three chips in my toenail polish. "It's just temporary."

"You're going to get burned by this guy."

I shot her a frown.

"Kit makes me feel alive, that great adventures lay out there for us. But he needs a rest after what he's been through."

Dee Dee crossed her arms, stare unwavering.

"Don't say I didn't warn you."

The subject of loyalty had been a landmine between us ever since my motorcycle escapade. Dee Dee continued to treat my feelings for Kit as a betrayal of our friendship and her better judgment. But Dee Dee was a fellow rebel, someone I'd stood by right or wrong, and I was tired of feeling guilty about Kit. The order of my loyalties was now as plain as Dee Dee's disapproval. I held her stare.

"I won't say that. But the next time you warn me about Kit Griffith is the last time we ever speak."

It took me less than an hour to unpack and become a resident of the Homestead. I'd left Mamma's bedroom intact—fancy floor lamp, taupe curtains, loop rug, ceramic cats—removing only my personal belongings —clothes, books, records, cigar box, Singer—after presenting my old phonograph to Jack.

And it took only part of the afternoon and part of my savings to become a student at Itasca Junior College. Kit tried to pay my tuition, but I said no. We had a deal, and I had my own college money.

We visited Piggly Wiggly after that, where Kit tossed Tang, real milk, and even butter into our shopping cart, and insisted on paying for it all.

I made fried chicken, mashed potatoes, and corn on the cob for our first meal, serving sliced tomatoes, cucumbers, and radishes on the side, the way Minnesota folks did in the summer. I felt pretty sure of my menu, having cooked many a meal for a houseful of guys. Still, I was nervous when I announced dinner. Kit was the first man I'd cooked for who wasn't family.

He ate enough to make me feel good, praising everything I'd set on the table, even the radishes. Everything but the chicken, that is, which he didn't even put on his plate. I could feel my face glow when I realized my mistake.

"You don't eat chicken either?"

He set down his fork before gazing out the window, whose only view was a bunch of leaves.

"I just can't, Joey. Every village in Vietnam had them, and the way they shrieked when the flames went up is a sound I don't like to remember."

He took a long sip of the lemonade I'd made from fresh lemons, not a mix, and I wondered what he saw in those trees.

"It's okay," I said. I rose and slipped the platter of chicken into the icebox. When I returned to the table, he was back in the room with me.

"I'm not surprised you're a good cook," he said. "You move easily around a kitchen. I like watching you."

Another blush. What I knew of cooking had come from Mamma's *Encyclopedia of Cookery*, eighth grade Home Ec class, and the fact that there'd been no one else to do it. My skill was enough to stave off complaints from three hungry boys, most of the time. I wasn't used to praise.

"I'm no stranger to a kitchen, I guess."

Kit helped with the dishes after our meal, proving he really was an ace with a dishtowel. Jimmy had always charged at least a dime for dish drying, and Jack and Jeff couldn't be bought at any price.

Kitchen clean, we moved out to the porch with our lemonade glasses. We had no TV antenna or radio, but a breeze kept the mosquitoes from landing, and the crickets, frogs, and lone loon were more than enough entertainment. Sitting on the concrete block below Kit's, I leaned back between his legs, head on his chest. He opened his flask and poured something into his lemonade. Christian Brothers. He'd been on his feet a lot that day. I lifted my glass.

"Just a little," Kit said. "Brandy makes you hiccup."

"You remember that?" It seemed a lifetime ago.

"I remember."

He lowered his cigarette to my mouth and I inhaled, liking the idea of putting my lips where his had been. Something close to a sigh came out when I exhaled, and I peered into the night, trying to find where the stars and the tree branches met, hoping to spot an owl or even a nighthawk.

"I got a postcard from an old hospital mate of mine," Kit said when the cigarette was gone. "Buzzy Sempser. He says there's a big picnic in the works. A gathering of groovy folks and peaceful vibes. Maybe some live music and a beach party. Interested?"

"Sure." A *picnic*. I was already trying to decide whether to add celery to my potato salad. Jack and Jeff liked the crunch. Jimmy didn't. "Gunn Park?"

Gunn Park was the place locals used for big picnics, like family reunions, wedding receptions, and employee appreciation days.

"Lincoln Park," Kit said.

"Don't know that one. Which lake?" Every park was on a lake, and I was wishing my swimsuit wasn't two years old and homemade.

"Lake Michigan."

The brandy suddenly made me cough, and Kit's laughter made my head bobble. He leaned down and gave me a loud smooch.

"Ever been to the windy city, baby?"

"Nope." I'd been to exactly two cities—Duluth and Minneapolis—though some people classified Duluth as merely a big town.

Kit was nibbling my neck, and I couldn't tell if his lips or the brandy was making me feel warm.

"The Democratic National Convention is being held there." He pulled me into his lap, slid a hand between my thighs. I let my head fall onto his shoulder, reveling in his touch and his suggestion. Elsewhere here we come, in a Corvette. The night suddenly seemed to have more stars.

"I didn't know you were interested in politics, Kit." The loon emitted a warble, which could sound a lot like a wailing woman if you didn't know your bird calls.

"I'm not interested in politics."

He wasn't laughing now, and I wondered if the picnic was connected to the convention. I wondered why his body suddenly felt tense. But I let those thoughts join the breeze and slip away.

"I'm sure Judy Benson will cover my shifts. She'll probably think I'm nuts to dump shifts for a picnic two states away, though."

He removed his hand from my leg.

"I'm interested in mortars and bombs that blow up human beings for no good reason."

The stars suddenly looked like searchlights, and Kit's tone made me wish I'd put on a sweater. Something had shifted the evening's mood, and I did what most good cooks would do.

"How about dessert? We've got strawberries."

"Conventions pick the man with the big say about mortars and bombs. What happens in Chicago could decide the fate of folks still stuck in that jungle I was so lucky to get out of."

Kit didn't sound angry, exactly, but he was clearly no longer in the mood for romance. After setting me back on my concrete block, he began rubbing his right foot, which he'd slipped into a sheepskin slipper after supper. I wasn't interested in politics or things that exploded. I was interested in Kit's kisses.

"Or I could make coffee."

Kit carefully lowered his foot. "Ever see what napalm does to a person's flesh?"

He was topping off his lemonade again, and I was feeling downright cold.

"Of course not."

"How about what Agent Orange does to a grove of live trees?"

I didn't answer because we were no longer engaged in a conversation.

"Ever see a headless man still wiggling toward his trench?" His question echoed through the trees.

I wrapped my arms around me, wondering how our first supper had gone so awry. Kit set his flask between his legs.

"Well, neither has the president of the United States," he said.

He downed half his drink in one long pull, and I could feel his tension recede. "A good turnout at a gathering about peace might get our future leader thinking, whoever he ends up being."

On my list of things to avoid, I ranked politics right up there with war flicks and the six o'clock news. Chicago clearly meant something more to Kit than a good time at the lake. But I was game if it meant being with him.

"A picnic by Lake Michigan sounds like a blast," I said. "A last hurrah before classes start."

He polished off his drink with a sigh.

"There might be some antiwar stuff, but we'll stay away from that." He smiled as if we'd been discussing potato salad. "We need to take off first thing in the morning."

First thing. I wouldn't be cooking for this picnic. I closed my eyes, trying to sweep away the evening's odd vibe like sand from the steps, remembering the other trip we'd taken. I was momentarily beneath a full moon, wind racing by, Kit's back hard and sure against my face.

"Won't all the Chicago hotels be full?"

He'd slipped an arm around my shoulder, and the present was again solidly beside me.

"Don't worry, baby. I've already arranged our accommodations."

I tried to outlast Kit's flask, but it had been a long day, and I finally gave in to weariness. Kit didn't protest. "You need your beauty sleep, baby. I'll be up soon as I check our route on the map."

I didn't like being in that strange new bed without Kit, and sleep didn't come. The bedside clock said two thirty when I heard Kit climbing the stairs. The tap-tap-thumps told me he was using his crutches.

We arrived in downtown Chicago sixteen hours after Kit swapped his Corvette for a Volkswagen bus and a cashier's check at the car lot where he'd made a deal for practicality over beauty. Part of the deal was a set of new tires, which the mechanic had come in early to put on.

The tires were new but the van—bold red in color—was not. Its scrapes, nicks, rust spots, and well-worn fold-down bed said it had done fair duty as a camper for its former owner. If I didn't cross America's dairyland for my first time in sports-car style, I did cross it in some comfort. We bought groceries and a small cooler in Eau Claire, then ate lunch—bread, cheese, apples—at a pretty rest stop near the Dells. The van's radio didn't work, but the scenery, Kit's discussion of our spring garden, and his portable tape player made the hours whiz by like passing cars. Though Kit was unpredictable, I was still surprised to hear Frank

Sinatra, Ella Fitzgerald, and Dr. Zhivago mixed in with Smokey Robinson, Jimi Hendrix, and Arlo Guthrie.

"Besides regular vegetables, we could plant miniature pumpkins, squashes, and gourds," he said as he slipped Ol' Blue Eyes—Daddy's favorite singer—into the player. "We could sell them as autumn decorations to stores like Dayton's and Donaldson's. This bus will come in handy for transport."

Frankie was singing "Come Fly with Me."

"But we'll be in Pasadena next autumn, Kit." The rolling hills of Wisconsin didn't have a crag or sharp edge among them, but I felt something jagged poke into my view.

Kit patted my knee and ran his hand up my thigh before returning it to the steering wheel.

"Of course. I got caught up in an Old MacDonald game I used to play in my head in Nam. It got me through times much less pleasant than sitting next to you."

By the time we found a parking spot not exactly near Lincoln Park, Kit had named his new vehicle Rosie and I'd studied the Chicago map and street signs until my eyes crossed. Chicago made Minneapolis seem like a whistle-stop along the tracks. The closer we got to the circle I'd inked onto the map's paper maze, the more the streets began to feel like dark ravines at the base of concrete cliffs. I wanted to feel only excitement as we drove ever deeper into the famous old city. After all, we were a long way from the town I wanted to be a long way from. No doubt about it, Chicago was the big time—not a forest, field, or farm in sight. Trouble was, the taller and denser the buildings got, the more they reminded me of trees. Lots and lots of them, blocking the sky, tops impossible to find amid the towering profusion of walls, glass, and shadows. I fought back mounting panic with simple logic. We were in a city, not a forest. Period. Pasadena was bound to have tall buildings, as would any city with playhouses and a theatre district. I kept my eyes on the map and the street signs, and eventually my panic faded, like a puff of car exhaust—something black and foul, but only temporary.

Kit didn't seem a bit intimidated by the streets of Chicago. And as he'd assured me, a place to stay wasn't a problem, since all we needed was a short length of curb on one of those streets. The late-night air was perfect for sleeping, a light wind blowing off the unseen lake, and we cracked Rosie's curtained windows before making very nice use of her fold-down bed.

Kit was still above me, in no hurry to end our interlude, his chest rising and falling in sync with my breaths, when I felt his right foot shudder and his right leg stiffen. He'd been pressing a gas pedal for most of those sixteen hours since we'd left Minnesota.

And so I sat on the floor of the van, cradling his foot in my hands, somehow knowing it was too fragile to massage, stroking it like a baby's cheek until we both fell asleep.

— FOURTEEN —

A Walk in the Park

Something not very groovy or peaceful was in the air the next morning, floating alongside the protest signs and flags we passed on our way through Lincoln Park after peanut butter sandwiches inside Rosie. The weather was picnic perfect, but the roaming jumble of park visitors— many sporting headbands, love beads, sunglasses, sandals, and peace signs—contrasted jarringly with the solid walls of police—all sporting baby-blue uniforms, baby-blue helmets, and rifles. Kit's hand was tight on mine as we walked to meet Buzzy Sempser at the south end of the park, a summery green stretch of rolling hills and open grass.

Kit had warned me his friend was "a rather flamboyant character," and even in that big mix of people, Buzzy Sempser stood out. Well over six feet, he wore a buzz cut on top, a ponytail in back, and a Fu Manchu moustache up front. Not to mention his red and yellow tied-dyed shirt, camouflage-print pants, and rainbow shades.

Introductions were short and sweet. Buzzy had stories to tell.

"Hiya, Joey. Not surprised to find Redbeard of Khe Sanh hooked up with a true foxy lady."

Kit shrugged, smiling wryly my way. "That's the least colorful of my Nam nicknames."

I laughed. In the noonday sun, Kit's beard was fairly flaming.

Buzzy turned to Kit, his handshake a quick downward clasp. "Last time we met, bro, you were trying to avoid the tag Peg Leg, and I was hoping this metal plate in my bean wouldn't magnetize my gray matter."

"Those were the days," Kit said, slapping Buzzy's back, an edge to his laugh. "As I recall, the main thing you were hoping for was the little brunette nurse who worked the night shift." He scanned the park's

111

cluttered sprawl. "Haven't seen so many uniforms since boot camp. What gives?"

Buzzy snorted. "Man, it's been all over the news. You just fly in from the moon?"

"More or less, and no airwaves on the flight." Kit's glance at me said he'd enjoyed our little holiday from society. "I thought you said this was a peace thing. Those blue shirts aren't my idea of good karma."

Buzzy gave Kit a quizzical look. "Yeah, when I wrote, it looked like this was gonna be a cool scene. Folk singers and a peace march maybe. Dave Dellinger rapping about nonviolence and everybody crashing in the park."

Two shirtless fellows wearing head bandanas passed us, one carrying a black flag, the other carrying a red one. I wasn't sure I wanted to know why.

Buzzy twisted the tips of his facial hair as he shook his head. "But you really been MIA, man. Mayor Daley's nixed permits and closed the park every night at eleven, leaving a parkful of pissed-off folks, who've been creative in expressing their displeasure."

He curled his lip toward a nearby group of police. "To which the pigs have been less than hip. Three nights of billy clubs and tear gas, man. Things are a bit tense, you might say. Besides a shitload of cops, Daley brought in the Army and National Guard. There's barbed wire around the convention hall, for fuck's sake."

Buzzy gave me a little bow. "Scuse my French."

Kit frowned. "Land of the free, huh?" He slid an arm around my shoulder and pulled me close, silently saying Buzzy was okay despite his language. I'd flinched at the bad name and worse word, a word most guys didn't use in mixed company. I wasn't sure I liked Buzzy.

Buzzy grunted. "Oink, oink."

"Billy clubs." Kit sounded skeptical. "That's heavy."

Buzzy squinted and curled his other lip.

"And not just for show. Even the press got bashed. The gas ain't been sweet either. The pigs wore gas masks like they was flushing out a VC bunker."

Kit's freckles had disappeared into his spreading flush. "That so?"

Buzzy nodded so hard his ponytail began to swing. "Fucking affirmative. Positively no shit." He stabbed a finger skyward. "They also brought in choppers, man. Made me want to hit the dirt, that sound."

A quiet moment passed as a sign saying DUMP THE HUMP floated by. Kit finally said, "What's the score with the Minnesotans?"

Glad of the topic switch, I chimed in. "Guess we're not the only ones who drove this far."

"Probably Humphrey," Buzzy said, sucking his teeth as Kit scanned the park, clearly sizing up the situation for himself. "Which don't thrill the peaceniks and McCarthy kids."

"That's unfortunate," Kit said, his tone making me realize they were discussing the two presidential candidates from our state. I rearranged my bangs to cover my chagrin.

"Things look pretty calm right now," Kit said.

"Temperature rises when the sun goes down." Buzzy was spinning one end of his moustache with amazing speed. "Today's the peace march. Grant Park at four. Don't know why that should freak out the Man."

"Sounds low-key enough." Kit was studying the people milling about, more and more of them as the minutes passed. Mostly young, but ranging from babes in arms to downright old.

"Abbie Hoffman's Yippie pranks with Jerry Rubin ain't helped," Buzzy said. "He talks of pulling down Humphrey's pants, and Daley's ready for World War fucking III. And that crackpot shit about lacing the water with LSD. Where would anyone score enough acid to turn on a whole fucking city?"

Buzzy rolled his eyes, said "Scuse my French," and kept jabbering. "Allen Ginsberg's doing his own fruitcake thing. Phil Ochs, Dick Gregory, Tom Hayden, Rennie Davis, they all showed. A real mixed bag."

Kit nodded, listening intently, clearly impressed. "Big peace cats, SDS folks."

"What's SDS?" I said, not recognizing a single name, desperately trying to keep up.

"Students for a Democratic Society," Kit replied without glancing my way.

113

He raised an eyebrow at a passing boy of about fifteen who was waving a makeshift flag tied to a broomstick. Red and blue with a yellow star in the middle. He shook his head. "Christ. Never thought I'd see one of those in the heartland of America."

"How come?"

"That's a Viet Cong flag, baby."

I looked down at the ruffled pink blouse I'd thought was picnic kicky and suddenly felt like a country bumpkin. All I needed was a bowl of potato salad and a straw hat. But Kit didn't seem to notice my embarrassment.

"Flaky way of making the point," Buzzy said, working on the other end of his moustache. "But point taken."

Kit laughed in that edgy way again. "I think that kid has completely *missed* the point. In a couple of years, when he's in-country trying to guess which little Asian guy wants him dead and which one just wants him the hell out of his rice paddy, he'll figure that out."

"Can't tell one gook from another, that's a fact," Buzzy said. "Scary little bastards, all of 'em."

Kit scoffed, turning to Buzzy with a look that seemed more disappointed than perturbed. "Gonna do the march?" he finally said.

Buzzy rubbed his flattop, swaying from one leather thong to the other as he watched three braless girls with flowers in their hair stroll by. Two were wearing white pants, which seemed a wildly optimistic color for a picnic, to my way of thinking. With three brothers to do laundry for, I'd developed strong opinions about grass stains. About bralessness, I felt less dogmatic. I was too insecure about my chest to make it my thing, but I saw the appeal of no hooks and straps for girls who were stacked.

"March? Why not?" Buzzy said. " If they don't forbid that too, this is where it's at. Tonight's the nomination."

Kit squeezed my shoulder, running his thumb up and down my arm and making my insides purr.

"Want to check out the Chicago scene while promoting peace, little girl?"

114

I saw excitement and curiosity as well as indecision and wariness in his eyes. This didn't look like much of a picnic, but it looked lively and far from northern Minnesota.

"Why not?" I said, parroting Buzzy.

"We'll scope things out and split for the bus if they don't look cool," Kit said, his little kiss sealing the deal for me, his smile sparking the air. "Okay?"

"Okay."

Kit was looking at his pocket watch when my stomach grumbled so loudly both men laughed. "Hungry, baby?"

"Starving." I brushed back my hair again. "And waterlogged."

"Well, we can't have you blowing away in the windy city or drowning." Kit glanced at his friend. "Partner, let's round up an establishment with food, drink, and facilities."

"I'm down with that," Buzzy said, ogling a beflowered female duo off to our right.

Kit's hand slid into the crook of my elbow. "Relief coming up."

The crowd and its distractions kept us from getting close to a restaurant or a restroom, so our lunch wound up being the Snickers bar and Ritz crackers I'd stashed in my bag. When we finally reached Grant Park, south of Lincoln Park along the lake, it was aswarm with folks bent on marching to the International Amphitheatre where the convention was underway—though there was still no parade permit. Dozens or even hundreds didn't come close to their numbers. There were thousands upon thousands of would-be marchers. And in every direction around them were lines upon lines of helmeted policemen with handguns and billy clubs, lines upon lines of helmeted National Guardsmen with rifles and bayonets and other weapons of war—all bent on stopping them. What kept me from feeling overwhelmed was our position on the edge of the throng, Kit's nearness to my side, and the tall form of the Conrad Hilton Hotel off to one side of the park, its top visible and a fine perching spot.

We wandered the fringe of the crowd for hours—changing positions to take it all in, listening to voices over loudspeakers and the chatter and chanting of those around us, watching bystanders wave their signs and pass their fliers, waiting for whatever the mingling of people and opinions might bring. The signs said things like END THE WAR, PEACE NOW, and SANITY PLEASE. One especially colorful one said FIGHTING FOR PEACE IS LIKE FUCKING FOR CHASTITY. Chanters shouted things like "Hell no we won't go," "Let us march," and "Hey, hey, LBJ, how many kids did you kill today?" Some people held transistors to their ears, conveying the convention proceedings to those nearby. It was the wildest scene of my life. Pure theatre.

The crowd grew as we continued to mosey, watch, and wait—though I wasn't exactly sure what for. Kit and Buzzy joked about their shared hospital days, compared notes on musicians and sports figures, smoked every cigarette we had, sipped from Kit's flask, eyeballed the police line. Buzzy sneaked tokes of marijuana when it occasionally passed our way, but Kit and I didn't. To Buzzy's raised eyebrow, Kit shrugged. "Mary Jane's a girl I don't talk to in public these days, especially with badges around."

I'd vaguely wondered where that particular old girlfriend now stood in Kit's life, since they'd clearly once been close. But he'd paid dearly for that relationship, and I didn't blame him for keeping his distance.

The crowd thrashed, chanted, and chattered, some taunting the cops, as the guys passed the time in their old-buddy way and I picked up more tidbits about the man who'd brought me there. Their back-and-forth eventually hit again on politics, which was gibberish to my ear.

"McCarthy's star seems to be fading," Buzzy said. "We're probably stuck with the old guard that got us into this fucking mess."

"Johnson's happy warrior isn't likely to end it if he gets in," Kit said, kicking a clump of grass as if it were a chunk of carrion.

In deference to my unemptied bladder, I didn't sip any of the brandy. And I didn't smoke anything, not wanting to break the lady's standing-up-while-smoking rule in the middle of downtown Chicago. I should have done both.

My craving for a cigarette eventually began to fray my mood, and as the sun slowly headed for Chicago's skyline, my legs grew heavy. I wanted to plop down on the grass, stains be damned, and take a nap, but I refused to be a killjoy. Though it seemed clear this lakeside picnic had never really been one, I was still eager to be part of what was clearly Kit's idea of an interesting day. But a sense of unease settled into the spot in my stomach where lunch should have gone. I couldn't help but wonder about Kit's bad foot as my own feet began to ache.

But when I said, "Isn't your foot getting sore?" he batted my words away with the flick of a wrist.

"I'm not focused on that right now."

The convention was the opportunity, politics the logical topic. But the gathering was clearly about ending the war. And my feelings about the Vietnam conflict began and ended with Kit. My father was too old and my brothers too young for the war to hurt them. But it had hurt Kit. It had mangled his foot and left him with memories he didn't like having. It caused him to laugh in an odd way sometimes, at other times to gaze off and leave the room while still in it. The war had wounded Kit, and that was enough for me to be against it. To hate it like the work of Satan. But ending the war was not something I actually thought much about, and it definitely wasn't my cause.

At some point as the day meandered on, Kit stroked my back and said, "Since we're already here, baby, do you mind if we hang tight and see what happens?" His hand felt so good. "I don't mind," I replied.

The crowd kept growing, and as it grew, so did the volume and sense of frustration. The crowd wanted to do what they'd come to do, and the cops weren't going along with the plan. Somewhere in the strained hours of late afternoon, a transistor listener with an Arlo Guthrie twang yelled out, "The peace platform got inspected, infected, neglected, and rejected. Johnson's war goes on."

"Fuck" was Kit's response to the announcement, and "Fucking aye" was Buzzy's reply.

Famous antiwar folks took turns speaking to the crowd, but we weren't standing near them. Despite loudspeakers, they were hard to hear above the general rumpus and the police directives. But when I occasionally caught what they were saying, they took my mind off my physical woes.

As Buzzy had noted, they were a real hodgepodge. Jerry Rubin turned out to be a little guy with a big pig named Pigasus, which he'd nominated for president. Allen Ginsberg, a bespectacled black bear of a bloke, got the crowd to chant "Om," apparently to keep them calm. David Dellinger, a balding gent, introduced Tom Hayden, a mop-haired guy who rambled on about the military machine, flowing blood, and tear gas.

Somewhere in the evening, when I'd settled into a state of semicurious zombiehood, we suddenly began moving en masse. In one moment, we became a dense fraternity of like mind, all heading in the same direction, though I wasn't sure which direction that was, or why we were going there.

"Hold on, baby." Kit gripped my wrist, long fingers making a tight circle, and I went where he pulled.

We were moving and then we weren't and then we were. I was an attachment to Kit's arm, welded on by his protective insistence, following, trying to keep up. The surge of communal energy had zapped my discomforts in an instant, and I was as awake as a bolt of lightning. Through a momentary break in the swarm, I glimpsed a row of what looked like snowplows made of barbed wire rolling down Michigan Avenue. I was so lightheaded from lack of food, I was hallucinating.

Then someone shouted, "Gas! Gas!" and the noise grew and the speed increased. Kit yelled, "Pull your top over your nose right now," just as a thick fog rolled in, blurring the world. I plunged through the haze, almost tripping, but Kit's arm jerked me away from the ground. Then I was running again, eyes scalded by the steam that had once been the air.

Someone shouted, "They're attacking," and Kit yelled, "Stay behind me, Joey, and keep your head down." He yanked my arm for emphasis. "*Down!*"

🕊

We were moving, moving. Madness whizzed by us like a macabre parade we were caught in the middle of. I stumbled, but Kit's handcuff hand flouted gravity, and the steel of his grasp stopped me from shrieking like most of those around me. Looking like medieval weapons, rifle butts rammed and billy clubs swung down as a blur of bedlam rolled by like a horror film on wheels.

To my right, a tangle of summer-clad bodies running, some toppling like hacked-down saplings. To my left, a shirtless youth in jeans crawling on elbows and knees, hair mopping the ground each time he tried to duck a black-booted foot. To my right, three teenagers dashing into the onslaught, bare fists and curse words punching at whatever they met. To my left, a girl in a blue sunsuit wilting into a heap from the frenzy of savagery unleashed. To my right, a cigar-smoking policeman dragging a boy by the feet toward a paddy wagon. The boy's head bumped up and down, and I wondered in a crazed moment if hair could get grass stains.

The shouting became a single great voice above all the racket as the crowd took up a new chant. Over and over they screamed at the television cameras the police hadn't been able to stop from rolling.

"The whole world is watching! The whole world is watching!"

Eyes and skin afire, nose running, I peered at the sky, searching for something that might be looking down on me, though I wouldn't have seen it through the acid mist even if it were hovering right above my head.

"I'm scared, Kit," I wanted to say, but Kit wouldn't have heard me. And I knew he already knew how I felt by the way my free hand clutched his shirt collar. Instead, I just whispered into the night, "Mamma, are you there?"

We weren't in the park anymore. I could tell by the feel of the ground beneath my feet—harder, flatter, grassless—and by lights so bright I could no longer see ahead. I stepped on a bump in the street that moved and sent me tumbling until the relentless grip again halted my fall. My head whipped around and down as I scrambled to keep up with Kit's arm, squinting to see. I'd stepped on the leg of a girl about my age. She'd wrapped her arms around her head and blood—oh my god, blood—ran down her face.

I wanted to stop and say I was sorry, for stepping on her and for this insane night, but torsos thrust me forward, and Kit wrenched me onward. Bodies crisscrossing the pavement quickly took her place and my attention.

We ran and ran, heads down—helmets above us, bodies below, billy clubs in the middle. A new volley of gas billowed toward us, and my eyes gushed like burst spigots, burned as if lit by a torch. I swiped my free hand across them and blinked uncontrollably, coughing so hard I retched, staggering on. I glanced in the direction that might have been up, trying to catch my bearings as I stumbled once again, and spied two glimmering electric words that seemed, just then, to be a divine promise of salvation from the flames of Hades: THE HAYMARKET. And below them, two smaller words assured me the universe still contained a whit of hospitality: COCKTAILS *** RESTAURANT. Kit pulled me, faster yet, toward that lovely sign, and I followed, eyes latched onto the bright words, no regard for the rolling fumes and flailing sticks that were everywhere.

Suddenly, Kit gave my arm a great yank, and I whirled through space. Just as suddenly, I came to a stop, my back tight against something hard, smooth, and cool. A metal wall maybe, maybe a slab of stone. Kit was now facing me, one hand clutching my neck, his mouth against my ear.

"Here are the keys to Rosie," he yelled. "If we get separated, go back to the bus." His other hand shoved the keys into my front jeans pocket. "Do you remember where it is?"

I gasped for air and nodded, too dazed and breathless to absorb what he was saying. He gripped my neck tighter, moved even closer. "Run from any uniform you see and go north around the park."

He wasn't making sense. I shouted back, panting between words. "But Kit, if we stay together, we won't get separated."

His brow hit mine when he shook his head. "We might."

Being on my own in that pandemonium was something I couldn't consider. And it shocked me that Kit could. "We can't get separated," I said. "How will you get in the bus without keys?"

His hands were now pressed against the solid surface at my back, his arms straddling my shoulders, his body shielding me from everything out there behind him.

"I'll get in, Joey."

I heard impatience in his voice. And excitement, even now.

"But Kit, we won't . . . I don't—"

He glanced over his shoulder, and I suddenly felt alone. Someone had made a bonfire in the street, and it glowed in the night behind him, making his hair shimmer and his body look as if it were pulsing. From somewhere in the chaos came a refrain that made my scalp tighten. "*Seig heil! Seig heil!*" I wanted to pull Kit to the ground, have him lie on top of me again, his breaths matching mine, until this night gone berserk went away.

He turned back to me. "*Listen* to me, Joey. If we get split up, go around the park, not through it." He shouted even louder. "Repeat what I just said."

"Around the park not through it." Shouting was the only way to be heard.

"Okay, good."

Relief flashed across his face, but not through his body. His arms, encasing me, felt tense, straining. I saw bodies crushed tight against his back, crushed and pushing, pushing to get away from the billy clubs and the gas.

"But Kit, we're not going to get—

That's when the solid surface behind me disappeared.

We went down and down, falling for what seemed a mile, and suddenly Kit really was on top of me, the sound of crashing glass and screaming people surrounding us. Everyone who'd been behind Kit was now on top of him, and somehow, he was keeping them from crushing me, from grinding me into the glass shards I could feel through my blouse. And the clubs kept rising and falling.

Kit was now crawling and pushing me at the same time, squeezing us out of the human pileup in the room we'd fallen into. With one great heave, he lifted me to my feet, leaving something wet on my arms. He grasped my wrist again, pulling me along once more. I glanced back. Tables overturned, their contents smashing onto the floor. Some of the clubs followed us, some landed on crouching people. We passed an elderly lady huddled against a wall, clutching the top of her head. We sidestepped a pretty girl in a skimpy black uniform, who looked as though she'd seen a ghost, and I wondered if that ghost was me.

Kit pulled, and we wound through furniture and bleeding people. I realized we were in a hotel lobby, but Kit kept running, around and through. He seemed to know where he was headed, and I wondered if he'd managed to rent us a room after all. Knowing Kit, there'd be a

121

bottle of champagne waiting in a bucket of ice. He'd make this a picnic after all. I struggled to keep up with his arm. We ran and ran . . .

Until Kit stopped, chest heaving, at a door. He turned toward me. This must be our room, I thought, hoping I was presentable, looking down at my attire. That's when I realized I'd wet my pants and lost my handbag.

"Go in here," Kit said. "Lock yourself in a stall, stay there an hour, then go back to the bus the way I said."

I'd lost my handbag and Kit had lost his mind.

"You're *leaving* me?"

Kit was looking over his shoulder, clearly anxious about the nearing mayhem.

"Joey, this is the safest place I can think of."

"But—"

"One *hour*. You can find Rosie if you just remember the map. Then wait with the doors locked until I show up, however long that takes."

Tears were rolling down my face, probably from the gas, whose peppery odor I could still smell.

"But why are—"

His eyes were steady on mine, rimmed red and no twinkle in sight. He put his hands on my shoulders and gave me a little shake.

"Because I *have* to, Joey. Now go."

The little shake was very little, but it might as well have been a slug in the teeth for how much it jolted me. As assertive as Kit could be, his touch was always gentle. "But Kit—"

He pecked my forehead with something far short of a kiss, swung me toward the door, shoved it open, and pushed me so hard the air left my lungs.

"Go!"

Gasping, I turned back to plead my case. But he was gone, disappeared into a churn of arms, legs, clubs, blood, and manmade tears before the door had enough time to swing shut.

ॐ

My pants were long dry by the time I unlocked Rosie's door, crawled inside, and locked the door again, pulling her curtains against the war zone I'd skirted by following Kit's directions. And by hugging shadows, darting from doorway to parked car to trash bin, avoiding noises and light and humans like some feral cat. My watch had stopped shortly after my hour in the Conrad Hilton ladies' room, and I didn't have any idea what time it was and didn't care.

By the streetlight beam peeking past the curtain blocking Rosie's windshield, I stripped off my clothes, stuffing them and their acrid smell into a grocery bag, then washed myself as best I could with paper napkins and a bottle of club soda. Dried tears, dried snot, dried urine, tear gas residue, and something dark that was all over my arms. I yanked my nightgown—a frilly rosebud print affair—from my overnight bag and slipped it over my head. I curled up on the fold-down bed, using Kit's extra shirt for a blanket, listening to the sounds of raging mankind a few blocks to the east as I waited for Kit's footsteps. I fell asleep before the raging ended or the footsteps arrived.

I dreamed I was running alone in a field of wild red roses, which turned into a grove of orange-colored trees that dropped their leaves and turned black when I tried to pick a flower. Little blue men were crossing the field toward me, smiling and carrying bowls of potato salad, which exploded in my face and set me afire when I reached out my hand. I woke to the sound of my own howl. "Don't *leave* me."

The lowering sun said it was late afternoon, and I'd smoked every cigarette butt in Rosie's ashtray, even the Camel ones without filters, when Kit finally rapped on the bus door. I fell into his arms sobbing as we both sank to the bus floor after he locked the door behind him.

"Where have you been?" At that moment I was so glad Kit was alive, the shrill in my voice startled me. And the blame. "I've been terrified something horrible happened to you."

I wanted him to smile and look me in the eye in that way that said don't worry, baby, but he didn't.

"They finally let me out of jail to go to the hospital." His voice was hoarse and half gone. "And the hospital took a while."

He was rocking me, and I held on as though the Grand Canyon lay below me.

"Jail? Hospital? Jesus." For some reason, swear words no longer bothered me.

He kept rocking, arms tight around me, breathing heavily. He gave a little laugh that might also have been a cough.

"Yeah, but I made those child-and-old-lady beaters earn their pay before they caught me."

Kit finally let me go with a quick kiss and began searching through the bags of supplies we'd bought, which didn't include cigarettes, since you could get them from a machine in any café, gas station, or corner market when the world was sane. That's when I noticed the bandages.

"What happened to your hands?"

"Glass from that window. Stitches."

He pulled out a fifth of Christian Brothers, unscrewed the cap, and drank straight from the bottle.

He moaned as the brandy went down his throat. His clothes were torn, his face and arms filthy, and he looked about ready to collapse. He sank to the bed, head near his knees, and I knew it wasn't the time for anything but essentials.

"Do they hurt?"

"They?"

"Your hands."

"Not as much as my foot."

He pulled off his right shoe and sock. Another bandage.

"Oh no. How bad?"

"Split open. Someone stepped on it when they were dragging me."

I, more than anyone but his doctor, knew how much that must have hurt. The skin that had healed over Kit's reclaimed foot was onionskin paper stretched across a cauldron that was always close to boiling over.

He took another swig of brandy, pulled off his other shoe and his clothes. The rest of him looked bruised and scraped but in one piece, the purple and red places contrasting sharply with his pale skin.

He emitted a little shudder as he lay down on the bed and closed his eyes.

"Christ, I could use a joint," he said, sounding far away. Sounding truly gone. I wanted to hold him again, pull him back into my life and lock the door to the outside world forever.

"What can I do, Kit?"

With another shudder he sat up and vomited into his ruined shirt, then lay back down, throwing an arm up over his eyes.

"Drive us home, baby."

His mouth was half open, and I could hear his ragged breaths. I wanted to curl around him and kiss him until he opened his eyes and smiled at me.

"But it's a stick shift, Kit."

I glanced over at the foot-long rod jutting from the bus floor, its white knob looking like a pierced eyeball. Guys drove cars with stick shifts. Girls did not.

His voice was already in Wisconsin.

"Just remember to push in the clutch when you start up and change gears."

And then I was alone in a city I didn't know with a vehicle I couldn't drive and five hundred miles to go.

FIFTEEN

Back at the Homestead

Whatever makes a soldier go forward into battle when bullets and mortars are flying his way is maybe what got me through that concrete gorge stretching for miles and miles of Illinois—no glimpse of the sky or chirp of a bird to lift the thick, entrapping darkness. Somehow, with the help of the map, I found the route. Somehow, I drove that bus and kept it heading west.

I pulled through the tunnel of trees and into the Homestead some twenty hours later, my worst wrong turn having put me in the South Side of Chicago—a place that Kit, while we were driving so merrily to a picnic, had said was best to avoid. In a neighborhood that looked as if it had been bombed during World War II and never rebuilt, I'd stalled Rosie's engine at a stop sign. Two burly men with stony eyes had strutted over to assess my situation. But they ultimately gave me a driving lesson and directions when I told them I'd lost my purse in last night's riot and my husband was in the back, sick from being beaten by police.

"Welcome to Chicago," the burliest one said.

Kit woke up only twice on the trip home, to pee on the shoulder side of Rosie and to swig more brandy.

Kit took to his crutches and then the bed when we got home, and I served dinner on a tray to keep him there. The newspaper I'd bought at a Wisconsin gas station lay next to him. It had plenty to say about the Chicago Convention Police Riot, but Kit didn't.

I'd made vegetable soup and rarebit for our second Homestead meal. Our bowls were still steaming when I said, "That's one picnic I won't forget."

"Definitely memorable, baby," Kit said, chewing his toast.

I looked at him through the steam, which was eerily reminiscent. "I felt scared when you left me, Kit." There was no holding back. My anger had festered for five hundred miles.

Kit set his soup back on the tray, without trying it. "You were in a safe place and others weren't." His eyes were bloodshot, his face drawn.

"It was a long way back to the van."

He held my gaze. "I told you what to do, and I knew you'd make it."

That wasn't what I wanted to hear. "But how could you know that?"

He ran his napkin down his beard, tossed it on the bed. "You're a resourceful girl, Joey. I had faith in you." His voice was so matter of fact, he could have been stating the time of day.

"I was frightened, being alone."

He cocked his head, eyes unswerving.

"They were beating on kids and old ladies, Joey." He was frowning now.

"You abandoned me in the middle of a riot."

An eyebrow shot up. "That's not how I saw it. Nobody was going to swing a billy club at you in that locked bathroom stall."

I lifted my bowl, blowing on it as I matched his stare.

"They were screaming, Joey. Screaming. That's a sound I can't bear to hear. I was a fool not to realize what might happen there, but once we were in the thick of it, how could I ignore such brutality and abuse of power? I had to *do* something. Something meaningful."

I didn't blink. "I think you knew damn well what might happen there, Kit. Did you believe a confrontation with authority would bring you peace?"

Kit made a sound like a man who'd been sucker-punched, then picked up his own bowl and hurled it across the room. It crashed against the wall, shards and soup flying wildly before hitting the floor.

He swung his legs off the bed and reached for his crutches.

"I'm going for a walk until the soup cools down."

Before settling myself on the old front-room sofa, where I lay wondering how long my walk to town in the morning would take, I set a bucket and rag outside the porch and locked the door. It was a message the boys always understood when they evaded a chore. Kit must have hidden a spare key somewhere. I heard him laugh before unlocking the door, climbing the stairs, and cleaning the mess.

We resolved our Chicago differences later that night when he slid next to me and said three words that allowed me to sleep for the first time in a full spin of the earth.

"I'm sorry, baby."

ॐ

We spent the next day in bed healing our Chicago wounds, eating little and talking less, putting a troubled interlude behind us through sleep, matched breaths, and entwined flesh.

But a complete day's rest wasn't to be ours. Sometime past the starless misty hour we'd said good night, as a wolf howled for his mate north of the dark, I woke to the sound of hard smacking. Too startled to be afraid, knowing in my semiconscious state that Kit was nearby, I sat up and switched on the lamp.

Standing naked at the foot of the bed, Kit was slamming one of his crutches against the floor.

I yanked the blanket up to my face, wrapped it behind my neck and over my hair in a makeshift hood. "What is it? A bat?" That old fireplace chimney probably didn't have a screen.

Kit was now peering under the bed, crutch poised above his head, narrow end gripped in his fists like a baseball bat.

"Goddamn rats. One sonofabitch was chomping on my toe." He lifted his bandaged right foot, which indeed looked as if something had chewed it.

Rats. They rarely bothered with houses. They were landfill dwellers with a steady source of warmth and sustenance. But this was northern Minnesota, we lived right next to an open field, and it was now early autumn, when field mice went searching for a warmer home. I wasn't surprised that a mouse was in our bedroom, or that a city boy like Kit would think a mouse was a rat.

"I saw some mousetraps out in the toolshed," I said, much preferring a mouse to a bat, trying to be helpful without leaving my cozy spot.

I let the blanket fall from my head, pulled my knees to my chin. I wasn't overly squeamish about mice, which were kind of cute if you ignored their slithery tails, but setting mousetraps was a male duty. In Daddy's house, Jack had been the mouse trapper.

"There's a flashlight in the drawer by the stove," I said.

But Kit didn't reply, and the crutch crashed again to the floor.

"Goddamn rats. There are more fucking rats on this fucking hill than there are men."

That's when I knew Kit was having what they called a flashback, that there was no rodent under our bed. And I didn't have the faintest idea what to do. But when the crutch hit the floor once more, tossing splinters into the air as Kit shouted, "This isn't your goddamn hill, buddy," I knew I had to do something. Freaking out or gently leading him into reality were the only two things I could think of. Spinning like a roulette ball, my mind landed on the latter.

"Whose hill is it?" I managed to say, sounding strangely like someone chatting over a cup of coffee, watching him raise the crutch above his head again as I began to tremble.

The crutch crashed to the floor one more time. Kit answered me as he bent low, searching the floor, the surprise in his voice nearing anger.

"What do you mean, whose hill? It's *our* fucking hill, the one we've been burrowed into for seventy-seven fucking days."

The name had been branded onto my heart by an iron straight out of a blue flame, the first and only time Kit had said it. "Hill 881 South," I murmured, feeling much too close to that infamous place on the other side of the world.

"It's them or us on this fucking hill," Kit said. "Rats with tails or rats with rifles. That's the situation. No fucking room for us both."

Though I'd made my peace with swear words, Kit rarely used them, and the change in his demeanor took my breath away. Indeed, we were both panting. I didn't know what to say, so I just said, "Of course there isn't."

Kit was now poking under the bed with the narrow end of the crutch. "Get the hell out of here, you motherfucker. I dug this hole in the red muck for me, not you."

The scrape of the rubber tip against the floorboards went on for a moment, giving me a chance to grab onto my swirling thoughts. As much as I felt I knew Kit, having had him in my mind for so long and analyzed him so much, I suddenly realized there was a great crater in my knowledge. Although I'd seen Kit lose his temper, I'd never felt afraid of him. *This* Kit, however, was downright scary. I found myself jerking with each shove of his crutch.

Kit suddenly whirled away from the bed, as if whatever he was attacking had attacked him back.

"Jesus, I hate these goddamn rats. Give me lice and leeches any day," he said, crouching and searching the floor again. "Give me spiders. Give me snakes, even."

The next blow broke the top off the crutch, and Kit lost his balance as it went flying. I jumped right there in the bed when he fell to the floor with a crack of bone against wood.

As scary as Kit was acting, he was the man I loved. Reflexively, I scrambled out of bed to help him. But he was now punching the air, and I huddled by the wall, shaking so hard I banged my head.

The punching stopped, and Kit grabbed his wounded hipbone and began swaying in obvious pain. And weeping.

I tiptoed toward him the way you would a wounded dog drooling foam, unable to stop myself from wanting to comfort him, gripping my middle for balance, thoughts tumbling. Would he think I was a rat and try to strike me? Would he be afraid or embarrassed or shocked? Would he stay in this strange state, forever seeing what I couldn't see?

"But it's not their fault," he said. "They're just doing what comes natural, just trying to hide from the incoming same as us." He kept swaying and sobbing, and I halted, too stunned for a moment to move. "They're just hungry and thirsty, same as us," he said. "Scared to die, same as us."

Tears were running down his cheeks now, and after kicking the damaged crutch to the far side of the room, I uttered the only words I could pluck from my skull, stepping deeper into his illusion.

130

"Poor little things."

Sniffling, he nodded, both nostrils leaking. "Right."

I sank to the floor and embraced him, swaying too, pity overcoming fear.

"Poor little things," he said. "They fought goddamn hard for that fucking hill. Seventy-seven days of pounding shells, flying blood, overflowing shit, stinking C-ration cans, and blinding fog. Seventy-seven fucking days they fought for that fucking hill."

"That's an awfully long time," I said, trembling as I stroked his hair.

"Right," he said. His croak was part fury, part anguish. "Seventy-seven days, and the brass let it go."

I forgot my strategy. "What do you mean?"

"I mean they let it *go*." He was growling now, tears and nose still flowing. I kept stroking his hair. "Seventy-seven days of godforsaken hellfire and they just abandoned it. Gave it back to the enemy."

"Really?" What I knew about Khe Sanh didn't even include a sure spelling of the name.

"That's what they did. Gave it back."

Kit's heart seemed to have left his words, and they sounded hollow. He leaned forward and peered under the bed again, then shrugged, apparently resigned to whatever he saw there.

He let go of his hipbone and finally stopped swaying. Closing his eyes, he circled his head, shaking and nodding it at the same time.

"So what was the fucking point?" His voice was now a whisper.

I said the only thing there was to say. "I don't know."

He wiped his eyes and nose with his hand, wiped his hand on his leg. Wrenching away from my arms, he laid his head on the floor, slipped the hand under his cheek, and closed his eyes.

"I'll wonder till the day I die," he mumbled, to me or maybe just the night. "What was the fucking point?"

I covered him with his red blanket with the oriental designs and put his crutches in the closet. When I turned off the light, the room was as black as a rathole in a dirt trench.

131

Kit slept late the next morning, having returned to our bed somewhere in the night, and I set both the broken and the good crutch atop his seabag before going down to make breakfast. When he finally came down himself, he was using the good crutch and carrying the broken one, which he took out to the toolshed after eggs and pancakes and morning pleasantries. When he came back, he was using both crutches and carrying two mousetraps. He baited them with cheese and peanut butter—exactly the way Jack would have—and set them behind the stove and the icebox as I drank my coffee and watched.

"It's the time of year for field mice," he said as he slid the jar of peanut butter back into the cupboard.

"What would a city boy like you know about field mice?" I said, trying for levity. I poured him another cup of coffee.

He leaned his crutches against the wall and took his chair, sliding a flirty hand across my breasts as he passed me.

"You might be surprised, what this city boy knows."

I looked at him and dropped the pretense of banter.

"Do you want to talk about last night?"

His answer was instant.

"Last night? Thanks to my old friends the Brothers, I slept like a log."

He was studying his coffee as if it contained the reasons for his lie.

"I'd like to hear about what happened in Vietnam, Kit. If you'd like to tell me."

He lit a Camel, closed his Zippo with a flick of the wrist.

"No you wouldn't."

"Yes, I—"

"Trust me on that," he said, cutting me off. His voice had turned icy.

"But maybe I could help."

He set his cigarette on the edge of his saucer. "The only thing that would help, is if I got amnesia and lost my memory."

"But . . ."

He turned toward the window and covered his face with his hands.

"For godsake, Joey. Let it go."

132

I began putting Kit's crutches in the closet after he was asleep. It probably wasn't necessary, though. That night was the only night he physically fought the demons only he could see. After that—maybe once a week, maybe twice if he'd been staring out the window a lot—he fought his battles in his sleep, thrashing and gasping, or merely moaning and whimpering, as I lay beside him in the dark and tried to talk his dreams away.

Kit was still on his crutches when we started school in September, the threadbare skin of his bad foot in no hurry to heal. His hands had recovered much faster, small red marks on his palms soon the only visible reminder of the day I learned he was something more than a rebel with a purple motorcycle, bold kisses, and daring thoughts about Jesus. That Vietnam had left scars that didn't show in the light of day. That he was a man I might never fully know.

— SIXTEEN —

Up, Up, and Away

"Wavy bacon. What does that mean, anyway?" The waitress had just left with our order—BLTs on toast, extra mayonnaise, my bacon crispy, Dee Dee's wavy.

"Wavy as in wavy," Dee Dee said, tossing back her pageboy. "Not floppy and soggy, not flat and crunchy. Any short-order cook knows what wavy bacon is."

Dee Dee and I had chatted on the phone a few times since my move to the Homestead, but I knew I'd been neglecting—or avoiding—her since she'd expressed her disapproval of that move. I invited her to lunch at Mickey's Café the day before the start of classes—a blustery Sunday, fallen leaves and fire smoke slashing the sodden air in long strokes. Bacon was a pretty lame conversation starter, but there was an invisible wall between my side of the booth and Dee Dee's that seemed my job to pull down.

"I was a short-order cook until a week ago, and wavy bacon is a new one on me."

Dee Dee was quick with her pistol. "So you dumped your job for him too?"

Kit had indeed asked me to quit my job, arguing that we lived so far from town, didn't need the money, and would have more homework than I was used to.

"Cream?" I pushed the pitcher toward Dee Dee, changing the subject.

She rolled her eyes, and I knew I'd said something dumb just to say something.

134

"Joey Dean, when in all the years you've known me have I ever put cream in my coffee? I've been a straight-black girl since my first set of play dishes, if you can remember back that far, distracted as you've been lately."

I chose surrender over conflict. "I remember those dishes, Dee Dee. Real china, lavender with blue flowers, complete with a teapot. Mine were painted tin. I was always jealous."

Dee Dee's smile said I'd made the right choice.

"Really? You were jealous of me?"

"Green as painted ivy."

She handed me the sugar jar, and I knew I'd lowered the wall a bit. I nodded as she nudged the cream pitcher back my way. She flipped through the tabletop jukebox and I sipped coffee until the waitress brought our sandwiches, layered thick and held together with little plastic arrows.

Dee Dee dropped a quarter in the slot and punched her picks. "I Can't Get No Satisfaction" boomed from the speaker, and with great ceremony, she removed an arrow, lifted the top of her sandwich, peered at the perfectly undulating first layer. "Wavy bacon," she said, sniffing in triumph. My laugh brought down the wall.

We ate in silence until Dee Dee had finished half her sandwich and inspected the other half.

"So, tomorrow's your big first day at IJC."

Itasca Junior College. Kit would be there with me, and that was the payoff of our bargain. But I wasn't exactly looking forward to my first day of higher education, which I'd expected to take place two thousand miles from autumn wind and rain. Maybe my disinterest made me hear sarcasm in Dee Dee's statement.

"Yup. First day. Freshman Communication, Modern Literature I, General Biology I."

Dee Dee raised an eyebrow.

"Biology? The way you feel about pickled frogs?"

I dabbed mayo from my chin "I need a science, and everything less creepy was full. But Kit's in the same class, so maybe I'll earn a decent grade."

"I'll give the guy credit if he can get you past your frog hang-up."

135

Dee Dee's comment was clearly a concession. I refilled her cup from the plastic pot the waitress had left.

"How's beauty school going?" I said. "What's it been now, two weeks?"

Never having decided between nursing school and secretarial school, Dee Dee had enrolled in Hibbing Beauty College, a small cosmetology trade school one county seat down the road, which offered a nine-month course in hairdressing, manicures, and facials.

Dee Dee popped a pickle slice into her mouth. "Yup, two weeks." She took a sip of her coffee. "But I quit a week in, right after mastering the art of holding a scissors and a comb in one hand."

Dee Dee was no career girl. A houseful of kids was her biggest dream, a dream my firsthand experience hadn't discouraged her from. Studying bassinets and baby buggies in the Sears Roebuck catalog was a top Dee Dee pastime. She'd enrolled in the cosmetology course on a whim, after reading three *Modern Beauty Shop* magazines in one day. Still, I was surprised. Dee Dee was also no quitter. She usually finished what she started, out of stubbornness if nothing else.

"You didn't like it?"

Too impatient for dipping, Dee Dee was squirting ketchup down the length of a french fry.

"Something more interesting cropped up when I was in Minneapolis with Curtis last weekend."

"Minneapolis. Ooh la la. Things must be getting serious."

The ketchup bottle sputtered, and Dee Dee reached over her seat, switched bottles with the empty booth behind her, pulled her sweater back down. I'd have flagged down a waitress and let my food get cold rather than make a move like that.

"Nah. We just drove down for a ballgame and a steak dinner. But Curtis ate a bad hotdog in the first quarter, and we ended up at the Radisson Hotel for two days."

"The Radisson. Romantic."

"Nothing romantic about it. Curtis was either shut in the bathroom or groaning in the bed. I sat in the lobby most of the time, bored stiff, trying to be genteel." She snorted. "Curtis is a little shyer than I wish he'd be."

"Lousy way to spend a weekend," I said, ladling on the girl-sympathy. "But surely you strolled down Nicollet and through Dayton's." Nicollet Avenue was the shopping mecca of Minnesota, Dayton's its biggest, most glamorous department store.

"Of course. But wandering through stores when you don't have bucks is a bummer."

I nodded, familiar with the experience.

Dee Dee was doctoring another french fry. "But, turns out there was a Northwest Orient recruitment going on in one of the Radisson conference rooms, and just for the hell of it, I put on the dress and heels I'd brought for our steak dinner and invited myself in." Tipping her head back, she dropped her handiwork into her mouth. "And they took me."

I set down my sandwich. "Are you saying you were hired as a stewardess by Northwest Orient Airlines?"

"Well, I have to get through the training, of course."

"Of course. Then what?"

"Then I'll probably be flying out of Minneapolis."

My appetite had gone the way of an autumn leaf on a windy day.

"You're moving to Minneapolis?" Except for a few years I could barely remember, Dee Dee had always been part of my life.

"Most likely. Minneapolis is a main Northwest hub. They fly from there to cities like Boston, New York, and Seattle. And overseas to places like Honolulu, Hong Kong, and Manila."

My mouth fell open, and I didn't think to cover it with my napkin.

"But I thought you didn't feel the need to escape this town."

Another snort. "I'm not escaping anything, Joey. I'm just leaving here for there for the time being. Curtis is starting to bore me, and the Northwest stewardess uniforms are just too cute for words. They have the most adorable green hats."

She patted her hair, which was a lovely dark brunette. "I think I look especially good in green, don't you?"

"Green." I was staring at my restaurant-beige plate, feeling my insides change hue. "Yes, green's definitely your color."

— SEVENTEEN —

With a Little Help from My Friends

"Here we are," Kit said. Rosie's wheels crunched into the gravel parking lot and splashed through a puddle.

"Yup, here we are." I pushed the sunny white beach from my thoughts and buttoned my coat.

Itasca Junior College wasn't a glamorous place, and probably wasn't meant to be. Set in a scatter of tall pines, alongside the agricultural school fields, and across from a graveyard, the small cluster of nondescript buildings served as a steppingstone to higher education that let serious students save funds on core courses, and less serious students discover their lack of long-term scholarly commitment on the cheap.

IJC didn't feel like a college, or even a high school. The spare and casual essence of the place affirmed the budgetary limitations of both the school and its students. Stately elegance just wasn't to be found in the small rooms with desks, large room with bookshelves, and other large room with cafeteria tables.

When I walked into Freshman Communication class at five before eight—college-ruled paper in my new blue canvas binder, fresh cartridge and nib in my old Parker fountain pen—three-quarters of the faces I saw were familiar. It was my old homeroom cloned.

I was too late for my favorite classroom seat—off to the side in the back. The only open desk was front row middle. I swallowed the lump in my throat as I sat down, feeling like a newbie trying to brown-nose the teacher. The lump returned when the professor walked in, heels clicking, papers rustling, throat clearing. It was Mrs. Pringlehoff, who'd taught me to diagram a sentence and construct a three-point, five-paragraph essay in seventh grade. Her academic position had clearly risen, but she was wearing the mauve worsted suit and pearl circle pin she'd worn every Monday when I was twelve. The sudden rush in my ears sounded exactly the way I imagined the Pacific Ocean would sound on a cloudless day, and I blinked back tears.

When Mrs. Pringlehoff leaned toward me on her march to the lectern, I tried to smile, hoping I had become unrecognizably mature and self-possessed. But her eyes said otherwise, and I could have run into the hallway, blubbering like a kindergartener. This wasn't where I was supposed to be.

Mrs. Pringlehoff's Evening in Paris cologne reached me before her whisper. Evening in Paris was the priciest scent you could buy at Ben Franklin, and I'd always considered it too refined for my rebel image. But today it smelled cloying and cheap.

"Good morning, Joey." The timbre of her voice revealed she still had sinus problems, the odor of her breath, that she still used licorice lozenges. "I've had a dropout in the Beginning Acting course you're waitlisted for. If you're still interested, I'll put your name at the top." She touched my arm. She was still wearing the chipped star sapphire on her wedding-ring finger. "I caught your performance on television. You did a fine job with your Blanche Dubois."

A beam of sunshine entered the day, a waft of sea breeze hit my mood. IJC had moved a mile closer to California.

Kit and I had agreed to meet for lunch. A bathroom detour for my period had me running late and remembering Kit's pre-breakfast words with a blush.

"It's natural, Joey. I want you every day of the month."

By the time I entered the basement room of Wilson Hall that served as the cafeteria/student union, Kit was at a table, deep in conversation with a spindly dark-haired fellow with droopy eyes and a scrawny beard. I hesitated, knowing from experience that interrupting guy talk could make a girl feel as popular as a mosquito in a sauna.

But Kit spotted me when he tossed back his head to laugh, and waved me over. I wound through the coffee drinkers and card players, feeling self-conscious in my paisley bell-sleeved minidress, stitched for

139

Pasadena. Most girls were wearing sweaters and jeans, and I was no leggy *Vogue* girl like Veruschka or Wilhelmina. For the second time that day, I felt late, out of place, and conspicuous.

I slid next to Kit, careful not to disturb his crutches under the table, and reached for his Camel. Taking a deep drag, I leaned against him.

"Tough first class?"

"Could have been worse." I was saving my acting class news for dinnertime, when we'd be alone. "How was yours?"

"Piece of cake. Public Speaking." He slipped a hand around my waist and passed me a cup of coffee. "Last time I did that, I was trying to explain to a judge why I was worthy of his mercy. Didn't get my point across, but I got over being shy in front of an audience."

I laughed along with the dark-haired fellow across from Kit.

"This is Doc DiAngelo," Kit said. "From Duluth. Biology major on a premed track."

A bony hand reached over the table to shake mine. "Hey there, Joey. Pleasure."

"Premed," I said, trying not to be obvious as I wiped the sweat from his limp fingers onto my dress. Though the guy was polite, he gave me the creeps. "Obviously the source of your nickname."

His wispy beard swayed when he shook his head. "Actually, Kit here just made that up. My real name's Arturo, or just Artie."

Range towns were full of Italian surnames. Waves of European immigrants had settled on Minnesota's Mesabi Range when iron ore was discovered there, and Duluth was where loaded railroad cars rolled onto docks to drop their red cargo into steel-mill-bound freighters. A little local history explained why a guy named Arturo DiAngelo hailed from Duluth.

"You do look rather doctorly," I said.

"Hey, then Doc it is," he said with a lazy nod I found irritating. I wondered what a premed student from Duluth—where there was a respectable branch of the University of Minnesota—was doing at IJC. Then it occurred to me that everyone in that hall had a reason for attending this little school in the sticks, including me—a reason based on their own totem pole of priorities. I was in no position to judge.

It was well past noon, and I'd pushed hard to complete Mrs. Pringlehoff's homework assignment in the school's no-frills library. I pulled two wax-papered tuna sandwiches from my book bag, set one before Kit, then looked at Doc. "Sandwich?"

"Hey, thanks." His thin lips stretched into his version of a smile. I handed him my lunch, and for the second time that day felt like crying. I was hungry, crampy, and wearing a California dress. I hid my mood by rummaging in my purse for a stray piece of candy.

"I overindulged on your scrambled eggs and hash browns this morning," Kit said, sliding his sandwich back to me. "Joey's one helluva of a cook, Doc."

"Lots of practice," I said, wadding the wax paper into a ball I wanted to throw at Doc. I wasn't especially proud of the skill I'd learned by default of my gender, but I liked Kit's praise. Each bite lifted my spirits.

"Speaking of food, I invited Doc for supper," Kit said, stroking my knee under the table. "We're going to play a little cribbage as he enlightens me on the allure of the North Shore and the mysteries of the spring smelt run. I was thinking we might have that fish you brought home."

That fish was a package of walleye Jack had slipped from Daddy's freezer when I'd stopped by to make sure the place wasn't falling apart, though I called nightly to solve problems and settle squabbles. Daddy had already left for his clubs, and the boys were dining on Spaghettios, boloney sandwiches, and potato chips. We'd had a nice catch-up while I cleaned the stove, noting three starches but no vegetable, Jimmy's shaggy hair, Jeff's striped shirt with plaid pants, and the fact that they seemed to be managing without me. Jack's gift, coming in the gap between summer boat fishing and winter ice fishing, was a treat I'd been saving, along with two red candles, for Kit's and my Saturday night.

"It needs thawing," I said, raising an eyebrow. "I'll make a meatloaf so supper isn't late."

"Late supper is fine," Kit said, ignoring or missing my signal. "No early class tomorrow."

He turned to Doc. "You like walleye, don't you, Doc?"

"Hey, yeah. Who doesn't?" He was licking his fingers after polishing off my sandwich, and I wanted to pluck them from his mouth with pliers. No doubt about it, the guy bugged me.

"What do you use for breading?" he asked me, crumbs bouncing in his facial hair. "Crushed soda crackers and buttermilk are my mom's trick."

I used flour and egg—flour first, egg second—and wasn't a cook to hide her fish-frying method. But his question struck me as presumptuous. "Family secret," I said, wondering if his droopy eyes would open if I yanked that sorry beard.

Biology class was next, and all three of us were in it. Kit started the conversation about trout smoking that made us late, but I blamed Doc's slow drone for landing me again front row center.

Front row center in *biology* class. But I sat between Kit and Doc, and their raised hands during the discussion on dissection—frogs again— kept me out of the line of fire. The professor's diagram began to blur as my lunch settled, and I found myself wondering if Blanche Dubois would change from a paisley dress to something more casual when frying fish, which vegetable she'd serve, and whether she'd choose mashed potatoes or rice pilaf. By end of class, I'd decided on the patchwork granny dress I'd sewed from a five-year collection of cloth scraps, julienne carrots, and the pilaf with peas. Short notice ruled out cake or pie, so canned peaches dressed up with brown sugar and coffee cream would have to be dessert.

🕊

Raised in a male household, I knew plenty of card games, but cribbage wasn't among them. My touchy mood sank when I found Kit and Doc hunched over brandy and a holey board after I'd done the dishes, by myself. Jealousy, plain and simple, made me want to toss the board into the fire and pour the brandy over Doc's head.

Not that Kit didn't try to include me in the evening. He pulled me near him on the sofa I'd resurrected with leaf-print slipcovers and orange corduroy pillows after mending the rocking chair's seat with twine. He offered me the flask whenever he offered it to Doc—though I turned it down, hoping to be sharp for tomorrow's acting class. He

142

praised my dinner, kissed my cheek, said my dress was pretty. But we were a threesome, and I wanted to be a duo. I'd agreed to live in this rustic hideout, but I wasn't ready to share the hearth I'd scrubbed shiny with anyone but Kit. And Doc was in no hurry to leave.

Sometime well past our usual bedtime, when I'd felt cranky for too long, I decided to join the guy talk, which had turned to Rosie's vehicular assets.

"She handles great," I ventured. "Even I can drive her."

Kit gave me an odd look. "Right. Joey drove her all the way home from Chicago last month."

His hair glowed in the lamplight, and I would have nuzzled his neck if we'd been alone.

"I was in Chicago last month too," Doc said. "The convention."

Kit just nodded, a rueful expression on his face.

"Guess you were at the police riot," Doc said. "Brutal scene, hey?"

Kit set down his cards. I'd clearly flubbed, but any actress will tell you, once you've begun your lines, you can't start over. "Brutal was certainly the operative word for that bit of American history," Kit said, absently rubbing his right foot through his slipper. "You go alone?"

Doc set his cards down too, and I knew I was about to be upstaged.

"I went with a friend of a friend of Tom Hayden. Tagged along to increase numbers. We expected some tense moments but, hey, we never figured on billy clubs and tear gas."

"Tom Hayden, eh? That's one cat I'd like to meet," Kit said. "Dellinger too."

"Antiwar honchos," Doc said. "I actually chatted with Hayden before I got arrested. Intense guy. Dedicated and a bit radical."

"You were arrested?" Kit said.

"Poked a flower into the wrong baby-blue helmet. That cop had absolutely no sense of humor. I was on the sidewalk outside the Hilton when I got nabbed and hauled off to the slammer."

"That's where they tackled me too, man. Ended up on crutches."

Kit was telling the truth, if not all the details. He didn't advertise his war wounds.

"Hey, bummer. Like I said, brutal scene."

Kit was leaning forward, looking nowhere near as tired as I felt. "So, what's the dope on Hayden?"

I didn't know Tom Hayden, and I hadn't been arrested in Chicago. My hour in a Hilton bathroom stall, where I'd blotted my underwear with toilet paper and tried not to rewet my pants when I heard footsteps, just couldn't compete with Doc's recollections. I went up to bed half an hour later. I'm not sure what time Kit finally slipped into bed, pulling me close, tucking my head under his chin. They say that once you've smelled marijuana, you never forget its odor. I'd smelled it twice, smoked it once—sharing its mystique with Kit on the magical night we'd met. I pulled away from his embrace, feeling somehow betrayed.

I could hear the wind snapping the plastic window as I dashed for the bathroom the next morning, the linoleum nipping my toes when I glanced into our would-be library and missed the rug. Doc DiAngelo was curled in a sleeping bag on the floor, ragged beard fluttering with each snore. A black leather satchel sat beside him, looking like no student book bag.

֍

Doc stayed for the next meal and the next cribbage game. And the next. The morning the bathroom window frosted over, a canvas cot appeared under his sleeping bag.

I finally confronted Kit as we headed in Rosie for early class.

"What the hell, Kit. Has Doc moved in?"

Kit's eyes held the road, which was dotted with ice patches.

"He's in a bit of a fix right now. It's just temporary."

His right hand slid over my knee but I set it back on the wheel.

"You didn't ask me? I thought it was my house too."

My glance in the rearview mirror said Kit was surprised. "I guess I didn't think you'd mind, Joey. We have two empty rooms."

We passed a car overturned in the ditch.

"How long is temporary?"

The patches had become a solid sheet of ice, and Kit's gaze didn't stray.

"Hey, little girl. Where's your spirit of brotherly love?"

"With my own three brothers, Kit."

He had reduced his speed to a crawl. "Doc's a good guy, and I'm just helping him out."

"What makes him good? I asked. "His black leather bag?"

Rosie began to skid, and Kit lifted his foot from the gas, pumped the brakes, and cranked the wheel to keep her on the road. "Christ, what a way to start the day."

When we finally turned onto the highway, which the state crews had salted and sanded, Kit gave me a look that melted some of the ice.

"Be a sport, Joey. I offered a bit of kindness. He'll be gone before you know it."

EIGHTEEN

Trick or Treat

"We've only been together three weeks, Doc and me, but it's a love for the ages. We're meant to be. He's my soul mate."

Doc's girlfriend was swishing her way around the table, gushing her life story and placing the silverware just so, as I sliced the meatloaf and strained lumps from the gravy.

"How can you tell?" I asked.

"Our synchronized eternal particles. His spirit slides right through my pores. It's destiny. You believe in destiny, don't you, Joey?"

I set the gravy bowl next to the potatoes.

"Well, I believe some feelings are beyond our control," I said. "And I believe some circumstances are too."

"If those feelings and circumstances make you happy, then there you have it. That's destiny."

She was now rearranging the plates.

"I'm not sure destiny and happiness are one and the same, Tink."

Tinkerbell Jaworski. She wasn't actually the Homestead's fourth resident, since she never stayed overnight. But as the leaves segued from yellow and gold into amber and red, flitting down the wind into restless mounds on the ground, she surely became part of the autumn scenery.

Though she'd finished high school a few years back, Tink still lived with her parents in Hill City—a highway step-on-the-brakes twenty miles south—which had a gas station, grocery store, bar, and ambitious name. She'd dropped out of IJC after one term and moved to Minneapolis, where she'd worked at Dayton's, rising from gift wrapping to jewelry showcasing to window dressing in just weeks. Tink had a decorative flair.

And that flair might have taken her to art school or her own decorating business, but Tink just wasn't a city girl. She'd come home to hear the loons on Hill Lake and feed the chipmunks, raccoons, and deer that wandered into her parents' backyard, where she loved to sit on the low branch of the maple tree she made syrup from every spring. Her little silver Falcon allowed her to be the window dresser at J. C. Penney, where she worked daily ten to three with weekends off—which was less free time than she preferred, but more than she'd gotten at Dayton's. Doc DiAngelo had spied her in the store window, pincushion in hand, trying to make a size fourteen dress fit a size six mannequin. He'd knocked on the glass until she'd agreed to lunch at Mack's Hamburger Shack.

Doc brought her to the Homestead that very night. "Please join us for dinner, Tink," Kit had said, cropping her nickname on the spot.

If Tink had seemed phony, I probably couldn't have tolerated her. Especially her tendency to arrive at suppertime, disappear with Doc during cleanup, and sip too much of the Boone's Farm apple wine I kept in the icebox.

But I didn't think Tink could help the pixie airiness that almost made her see-through. In my close-up appraisal, her spiderweb skirts, gauzy hair, patchouli haze, and spacey brain seemed completely genuine. And with my mother in the treetops, and Dee Dee off earning her own wings, Tink helped fill the female gap in my life. And she kept Doc's mind off cribbage. Kit welcomed Tink into our home, and I went along for my own reasons.

September and October trudged toward winter, leaving a routine in their muddy tracks. Days were classes, homework, cafeteria lunches, campus walks in rain and wind, cigarette breaks. Kit and I shared those activities whenever our schedules jibed. Nights were suppers prepared by me, Kit helping on cleanup, then card games, phono records, more cigarettes, wine or brandy, popcorn, and discussions about anything but the war, a topic Kit invariably deflected with a black joke or acerbic quip. Sometimes there was grass.

Kit had clearly calculated the odds of being busted for weed in his own home deep in the woods. Once or twice a week, neatly rolled joints of apparently good quality slid from Doc's pocket. "In my somewhat worldly opinion, this is fine shit," Kit said one evening after a long toke.

Doc's languid laugh didn't stir the haze surrounding the sofa. "I guess you smoked pot in Nam."

The pause before Kit's reply squelched the subject. "Everyone smoked pot in Nam. It was the sanest thing you could do."

I turned down Doc's offering, those autumn Homestead nights, wondering how such a moocher had money for grass. For me, marijuana was sacred, because it had opened my heart to Kit. It was an experience made mystical through the passage of time, burnished by memory. In retrospect, it didn't smell bad, make me wonder who was outside the window, put secret messages in Beatles songs, or cause me to crave a whole box of Vanilla Wafers. Nobody seemed to mind when I passed it on. Then again, maybe nobody noticed.

୫

It was probably inevitable that Kit's local family and my local history would eventually collide. Why it took so long, I might even have wondered, had I not felt so removed from civilization inside those trees, which still crowded too close on the drive home. Kit didn't mention his northern kin, and I didn't inquire. I wanted him to myself. I wanted to be his family of one.

November was only a thunderstorm away the night Kit decided to throw a Halloween party. We were playing Monopoly, and Tink had just lost all her money—which she'd arranged in little fans on her violet gauze skirt—and Doc was consoling her.

"Hey there, Tink, it's only fake dough. You were never really loaded. All you lost was colored paper."

Tink reached for the Boone's Farm. "But it felt so good to be rich."

"Come to our Halloween party as Cleopatra," Kit said. "She was rich as Croesus, and I won't tell a soul it's really you." And the party was on.

Tink made a knockout Cleo, sporting a headdress, eye shadow, and purple gown any Nile queen would have envied. I dressed up as Huck

148

Finn, my shirt and overalls nabbed from Kit's side of the closet, freckles and missing tooth fashioned from eyebrow pencil. Doc chose to be a hippie, which wasn't much of a stretch, Tink supplying his beads, headband, and peace sign. And Kit turned up as Redbeard the pirate, bandana knotted above his ponytail, brandy in a rum bottle dangling from his belt, patch not hiding the twinkle in his eyes. His gold hoop was attached with string because I'd refused to pierce his ear.

Kit was a fine pirate, but I have to admit, his cousin was a better one. Tommy didn't arrive at our door with a beard or ponytail, and he certainly wasn't wearing an earring, but he aced the role with just a bandana and his swagger.

During our last year of high school, I'd avoided Tommy like a sore tooth, steering clear of his locker, sitting on the opposite side of any classroom we wound up in together, inspecting my shoe whenever he passed me in the hall.

And knowing Tommy as well as I did, I'm sure he'd avoided me just as carefully. I hadn't talked to—or even looked at—my old backseat partner in a year and a half. I'd surmised he'd won a hockey scholarship to a middling Minnesota college where grades weren't too important, and good hunting and fishing were nearby. Or he'd taken the lumbermill job his uncle had offered. First cousins were bound to eventually cross paths. I just didn't think they'd do it while I was holding a bowl of Fritos and looking like a boy lacking a front tooth.

I beelined for the kitchen the second I saw Tommy walk in with his brothers, Kit heading for the door with a grin. And the kitchen was where I might have gone unnoticed the entire night, refilling snacks and drinks for Tink to artfully place about the front room. But Tommy never opened his beer with the girly pull tab, and I'd neglected to set out a church key.

I was opening a bag of pretzels with my teeth when he strutted in. Broken bits and salt granules flew across the room when the bag hit the floor.

"Holy Jesus, Joey. Give a guy a heart attack, will ya."

149

Except for a few new pounds, which suited his swagger, he was the same old Tommy.

"How's things?" I said, once my composure returned.

Tommy had his own question. "What are you doing way out here in the woods, considering your thing about leaves and all?"

If there was a way to reach the truth from an angle, I didn't have time to think of it.

"I live here."

I give Tommy credit. He didn't bat an eyelash.

"With your cousin Kit."

That didn't faze him either. It made him smile.

"Good one, Joey. You had me there for a second."

I really didn't want to do this. Especially here. Especially now. I backed up, bits and granules cackling as I bumped into a chair. "True fact."

A moment passed, but Tommy's smile stayed put. "Well now, haven't you gotten wild and crazy in your old age."

Tommy wasn't one to complicate his conversation with cynicism or sarcasm, even when he was being this talkative. I took his remark as a straight shot.

"That's one way of looking at it," I said.

"What's the other?" He cocked his head without mockery. He was really on a roll.

"I found the right guy."

Maybe I expected him to be jealous. Maybe I even wanted him to be. But his smile didn't waver, and I finally had to accept it as genuine.

"Geez, that's great, Joey. If you're happy, I'm happy for you."

I, for once, was the one short on words. "Um. So, what's happening with *you*?"

Tommy glanced around the kitchen, making me wish I'd had time to sew curtains. I retrieved the pretzel bag, brushed the mess under a rug.

"College. Hockey scholarship," he said.

As I'd surmised. Tommy was a first-rate hockey player, a guy born to wear skates, a skater who could slam a puck through a goalie's kneepads with his eyes closed. "Good for you," I said. "Which school?"

Tommy's gaze shifted from the old icebox to the old sink and back to my face. "Boston University."

I resisted the urge to sit down. "You mean Boston University in Boston, Massachusetts?"

He brushed a wayward curl from his brow. "Same one. I buckled down in class last year."

I nodded, words slow to the rescue.

"Gee that's great, Tommy. Really great." And I meant it. I'm sure I did.

He shoved his hands into his back pockets in that old way of his. "Kit's phone call was a nice coincidence. I just flew in for a family visit. Mom's finally marrying that plumber she started seeing after Pop hit the road."

I groped for my manners. "Super news. Give her my best."

"I'll do that." Tommy finally remembered what he'd come for. "Say, Joey. Would you happen to have a church key? Mine's in the car."

I was rooting through drawers when a girl came up behind him. He pulled her into the room with one hand, grabbed the church key I tossed him with the other. She was a small girl—about my size, actually. But there the similarity ended. Big breasts, slim hips, and blonde hair were features I only wished for.

"Joey, Angela Crawford. Angela, Joey Dean."

She was wearing calico cat ears, hand-drawn whiskers, and a white sweater dress that showed off her slender legs. She extended a hand, something I should have done first.

"Hi, Joey. Great party." Her manicure, done in baby-doll pink, was perfect.

"Thanks for coming." I shook her hand and leaned on a role I knew the lines to. "Can I get you something?"

"Not a thing," she said, giving Tommy a sugary look. "I found what I was looking for."

That was when Kit poked his head through the doorway.

"Hey, baby. How's the ice situation? Do I need to drive to town for more?"

"No, no." I was blushing for too many reasons and no reason at all. "Plenty of ice, darling." I never called Kit darling.

Not one to miss the vibes, Kit glanced from me to Tommy.

"Haven't had a chance to introduce my old cuz to my old lady," he said. "But it looks like you might already be acquainted."

Kit was now leaning against the door frame and scratching his beard. Angela was looking at Tommy. I was looking at the floor. Tommy, of all people, filled the gap in the conversation.

"You bet. Joey and I were in the same high school class, and she always got better grades than me. When we were kids, we saw a few flicks together."

Gliding into the room without a scrape of his skates, Kit snatched the puck.

"Even as a kid, you could spot the cream of the crop," he said, slapping Tommy on the back and touching my arm. "I never once got first dibs on the prettiest girl or the biggest pork chop." He gave Angela a little bow and pulled a bottle of wine from the icebox. "I think this is the perfect time for a toast to cousins and pretty girls," he said, ushering us all back to the party with a sweep of his hand.

We faced off again on the porch at the end of the night when Tommy and Angela took their leave.

Tommy was snapping up the letter jacket I knew so well. "Shot any birds or whitetail this fall?" he asked Kit.

"Not a one," Kit said, slipping a pink cashmere coat over Angela's shoulders.

"Kenny spied a fourteen-point buck up at the shack, and we're hoping to nail him before I head back to Boston. How about joining us?"

Kit shook his head. "Not this time, man."

Tommy clapped Kit on the shoulder with clear deference. "We could use your eagle eye. You're hands down the best shot of us all."

Maybe I imagined the bite in Kit's laugh. "Let's just say my eagle eye is on leave."

Tommy wasn't one to press a subject. "Catch you next time then. Nice place you have here, Kit. And nice friends."

The men shook hands, I gave Angela a girlfriend hug, and then they were gone, the Thunderbird's taillights disappearing into the tunnel of trees on its way to Elsewhere before I could close the door on my conflicted heart.

— NINETEEN —

No Pun Intended

"Mrs. Pringlehoff assigned our term projects yesterday. Excerpts of plays."

"Don't keep me in suspense," Kit said, warming his feet on my thigh. "What role did the old hen give my little chickadee?"

He'd just returned from coddling the cranky cast-iron contraption downstairs—which never quite warmed our room through the floor grate—and we were cocooned in covers, waiting for the alarm clock to ring, listening to a November thunderstorm rattle the windows. He hadn't used his crutches to take the stairs, which warmed my heart if nothing else. I'd goaded him into seeing old Doc Wexroth, whose penicillin and salve had finally healed Kit's nasty Chicago gash.

"Not Juliet," I said with a shiver. "That's the role every girl in class was dying for."

"No pun intended." Kit was nuzzling my neck with a nose as cold as his feet.

"Aren't you witty for a guy with a frozen schnoz. A sophomore snagged Juliet. I was hoping for *Cat on a Hot Tin Roof* or *Bus Stop*, and praying I wouldn't get *Desire Under the Elms*, when Mrs. Pringlehoff added Ophelia's mad scene. Because of the singing, I was the only girl who raised her hand."

"You were the only one brave enough for the hey-nonny-naughtiness, huh?" His hand was heading south from my breasts. I grabbed it.

"You know that scene?"

"I do. The drama department produced *Hamlet* twice during my stint at the U."

"And you *watched* it?"

"Theatre-major girls are usually pretty. I sat through all those soliloquies just to see who showed up."

Sometimes I couldn't tell when Kit was kidding.

"Considering you only went for the scenery, your recall is impressive."

"I'm not a total savage, Joey." Kit was now chewing my earlobe, and when he growled, I had to laugh.

"Be serious, Kit. I know it's just a little scene for a junior college course, but this part matters to me." I liked how Kit smelled in the morning, even his breath.

"Of course it does." He pulled his hand from mine and slid it onto my belly. "And I'm certain you'll get an A-plus or an Academy Award or whatever your professor gives for flawless performances."

I recaptured his hand and held on tight. "Academy Awards are for film stars. I want to be a serious stage actress."

Kit snarled into my neck. "Celluloid is for sissies. My girl wants to tread the boards."

I laughed, noting Kit's theatrical vernacular. He was a man of surprises. "You're making fun of my aspirations."

His beard felt pleasantly scratchy when he shook his head. "I am not. I'm aspiring to have a little fun with my old lady before we have to rise and face this cold and blustery morn."

Old lady. Though better than shack-up, live-in, or roommate, it was a term I didn't care for. "Bet it's not cold and blustery in Pasadena."

Pasadena had been settled last summer. Kit had asked for a year, and I now understood why, still believed he was worth the wait. But this was the third thunderstorm in a week.

"I didn't say cold and blustery was bad," he said.

"But you implied it."

He pushed his knee between mine.

"What I'm implying is that you turn me on and I want to make love to the best Ophelia that Itasca Junior College will ever have the good fortune to witness. You'll be great in the part, Joey. You're great at everything. Cooking, sewing, running a house, doctoring an old vet's war wounds." He licked my shoulder. "Sex."

155

Praise from a man was still a novelty. But this morning I was feeling touchy about my so-called talents. "I want to be better at acting than I am at things like . . . sewing."

"You will be. On a serious stage." The sincerity in his voice felt like a summer day.

"Speaking of sewing, now that you've managed to change the subject," he said. "I ripped my favorite jeans out in the toolshed. Could you rig me a patch?"

I knew the jeans he meant. Skin-tight faded hip-huggers, they were my favorite pair too. "Sure. I'm an A-plus hole-patcher."

His knee had forged its way to the mattress, where it stopped. "Don't belittle the skills you learned the hard way, Joey. That's why they're so admirable."

"Hmm."

He had a way of smoothing my feathers, but I was still feeling ruffled. This was as good a time as any to broach a pesky subject.

"Kit, why does Doc have to live with us?"

If there was a pause before his reply, it was too short to be obvious. But he quit nibbling my shoulder.

"Doc doesn't *have* to live with us. I invited him."

"How come?"

"Joey, why do you hate Doc?"

The storm was abating, and the windows had stopped their chatter.

"I don't hate him." A fib for the sake of the real issue. "I just miss our privacy."

Kit's breaths were steady, a sound I listened for at night, a sound that said he wasn't being shelled on some hill. Except for the weather, last night had been calm.

"We have a whole floor of privacy, little girl. What's wrong with sharing the rest?"

"I know all about sharing a house, Kit. I just liked it better when we were alone."

Kit was stroking my thigh with a hand that was now nicely warm.

"Doc's had some bad luck," he said. "I'm just helping him out a bit. Same as I'd do for you if you were in hard times. Same as I hope someone would do for me."

156

"What kind of bad luck?"

He was up on an elbow now, looking me in the face. I didn't look back. "Doc's dad gambled away his college fund, and his mom's been zigzagging the country with his two sisters, trying to recapture her youth. He's broke and pretty much alone."

That was indeed a tough break, but Doc wasn't a kid. "He could get a job," I said. I just couldn't relate to a parent-bestowed college fund.

Kit, of course, could.

"It's damn hard to get the kind of grades you need for med school when you have to work a job too. You of all people should realize that, Joey. High school couldn't have been easy, waitressing every night like you did. You could say Doc has aspirations."

"Hmm." I usually avoided snooping in Kit's thoughts, knowing how deep and dark they could run. But the foul weather had made me feisty. "How about you?"

Kit's sigh said he was tired of conversation but not offended. He flopped onto his back.

"Do I have aspirations beyond banging the beauteous woman in my bed before breakfast?"

"Yes."

"Let's see, now." He was rumpling his hair, which was already nicely rumpled. "That's a tricky one for a guy who has yet to choose a college major. Aspirations. Aspirations. Let me concentrate. Hang on there, it's coming to me. Wait . . . wait . . ."

He crossed his arms, squinting as if searching through fog. "Okay, I think I've got one. One aspiration on this blustery day that I can't seem to get any nooky."

"Let's hear it."

The pause this time was undeniable.

"I aspire for peace of mind."

The change in Kit's tone said don't pry, but I ignored it.

"And what would give you that? I mean, besides living in this . . . place?" The rain had subsided, a slow drip from the eaves all that remained of the storm. I waited as he rubbed the sleep from his eyes, scratched his chin. He opened his mouth to speak, and I held my breath.

157

Then the alarm clock rang, and he was on top of me, laughing, both knees between mine. "I've been trying to tell you that ever since we woke up, little girl."

I didn't make breakfast that morning or get inside Kit's head. The sun eventually graced the day, but gray clouds to the west said we weren't done with storms.

— TWENTY —

Northern Hospitality

"Happy turkey day, foxy lady. Something tells me a certain tom ain't gobbling no more."

Minnesota folks can smell snow before it falls. Even in the predawn darkness—tossing leftover stuffing bread outside for the blue jays and cardinals—I knew it was going to snow. And sure enough, by the time Buzzy Sempser pulled in—as Kit was pulling the turkey from the oven—several inches of winter newness shimmered beneath the porch light. Buzzy's bald tires told me he'd be sleeping in my sewing room until the snowfall stopped and the plows cleared the roads. Maybe Buzzy had smelled the snow all the way from Chicago. He walked in carrying two suitcases and a sleeping bag.

"Guess I don't have to tell you to make yourself at home," I said, heading for the kitchen without returning his greeting.

I served my turkey that year with all the fixings—sage stuffing, candied yams, wild rice, baking powder biscuits, cranberry sauce. And a salmon loaf to accommodate Kit. Daddy hadn't made it to town, so Kit fetched my brothers, making us a party of eight. Nine if you counted the owl I heard shortly after nightfall. My brothers wore their Sunday best, didn't argue with each other, and didn't put their elbows on the table. Which made me feel better about leaving them, though Jimmy still needed a haircut and Jack had outgrown his sweater.

Kit had turned our kitchen table into a banquet table by placing it under the front room windows and setting the wash shed door on top. I'd covered it with a bed sheet, which Tink had decorated with spruce boughs, pinecones, and birch bark fashioned into little tepees. Kit lit my red candles with his Zippo before bringing out the turkey.

Thanksgiving was a day for gathering, but I would rather have spent it with Kit and a bag of salted peanuts. I craved time alone with him the way a drunkard does his bottle. Our guests seemed an odd mishmash of folks, a combination sure to yield awkward silences and stilted conversation. That assumption shortchanged Kit, though. He was a natural host who, without apparent effort, set people at ease and kept the laughs coming—even from Tink, who tended to miss punch lines, and my brothers, who weren't used to eating "out."

Kit launched the fun by setting the turkey in front of Jimmy and handing him the carving tools. No yellowbelly cowpoke about popguns and rubber Bowie knives, Jimmy accepted the challenge with only a slight blush.

"Hold her steady with the fork and saw off the drumsticks," Kit said over Jimmy's shoulder. "The cavemen at the table can arm wrestle for those."

Jimmy did as told and Kit patted his shoulder. "Good job. Now to the serious business. Start right here, aim for here, and let the knife do the work. You can trust this old leatherneck, it's sharp. Just follow the line of the bone and keep the slices thin."

The first slice slid thin as a turkey plume onto the platter, and Kit led the applause. "Way to go, man."

Jimmy grinned like the cocky clown he was when Kit clapped him on the back.

"Now we need a wine steward," Kit said, nodding man-to-man at Jack, who at fifteen was the elder brother.

He set a bottle of Boone's Farm and a small towel in front of middle brother, Jeff.

"No corkscrew needed for this fine vintage, my friend. We'll just focus on getting the libation into the vessel." Boone's Farm with its screw cap was notoriously cheap, and a spatter of snickers followed. "The towel is to prevent warming the wine or spilling it on your sister's best tablecloth."

Tink's artwork couldn't hide the truth of the table covering. More laughter.

"Try to leave a gap at the top so the wine can catch its breath and the company doesn't get sloshed before dessert."

"Good advice," Doc said, who was already intoxicated on something.

Jeff followed Kit's directives, and Kit passed everyone a glass. To my raised eyebrow he replied, "Barely more than a communion sip and entirely appropriate at a private family meal." He lifted his glass. "To fellowship."

"Hear, hear," Buzzy said, clinking glasses down the length of the table.

Kit was clearly in his element that day, bounteous king and irreverent jester to a court of his assemblage, the simplicity of his castle both defiant and grand, his happiness suspended in the air like an exotic spice everyone inhaled. His brandy flask didn't appear that evening, and I would have cooked another turkey dinner to prolong his high mood, even if it meant sharing him with a crowd.

☞

"Uh oh," Kit said from the doorway. "Looks like you've been nabbed for a game of barber shop, partner."

Kit and Jimmy's help had made quick work of the cleanup, and with everyone settled around the fireplace for pie and coffee, I'd cornered my kid brother in the kitchen, sewing shears in hand. He was now in a chair, towel tied around his neck, pout pointed at the floor.

"Guess so," Jimmy said.

I leaned in to prove my kid brother possessed ears and a collar.

"Wait." Kit entered the room. "We haven't set the rules of this game."

I glared at him, not lowering my weapon. "What rules? It's a haircut. I'm the cutter and he's the cuttee."

Kit raised a finger, a gleam in his eye. "But there must be a quid pro quo."

"What do you mean? He's in grade school and needs to look presentable."

Kit brushed my bangs aside before kissing my forehead. "I mean, presentable is in the eyes of the beholder. One haircut deserves another."

He tugged a wayward strand of my hair. "She's looking a bit scruffy, wouldn't you say, Jim?"

Jimmy nodded. "You're starting to look like a vagabond, Joey."

That, of course, was what I'd said to Jimmy three minutes back.

I shot Kit a scowl, but he just shrugged. "Goose and gander, one good deed. Fair is fair, big sister."

The owl hooted in the moment it took me to reply. I jumped, then burst out laughing. Kit now topped John Wayne on Jimmy's list of heroes. "Take off, you twerp." I yanked the towel from Jimmy's neck, tossed my shears onto the counter. Kit somehow turned my slug to his arm into an embrace.

The snow kept falling, and Buzzy Sempser stayed on through the weekend—during which he complained loudly about the long drive back to Chicago, and how weary he was of the accounting-firm "gig" that forced him to wear a jacket and tie, tuck his ponytail down his collar, and find tax loopholes for people whose monthly profits exceeded his yearly salary.

I'd figured on a weekend with Buzzy in my sewing room, but not on the bunk bed he and Kit hauled in Sunday night, after shoving aside my sewing table.

"Buzzy needs a little break," Kit said when we were alone in our room. "The plate in his head's been giving him trouble since that night in the park."

He didn't reply when I said, "What's wrong with a goddamn hotel?"

Kit moved my sewing table and its contents to our bedroom the day Buzzy got word he'd lost his job.

"I couldn't say no," he said, pushing the table by the window. "I owe him."

I scoffed. "What could you possibly owe the guy who said Chicago would be a picnic? Who disappeared when things got rough?"

Kit looked at me. "My right foot."

I looked back at him.

"Buzzy talked the doctor out of sawing it off when I was in no shape to speak for myself."

Carcasses, cleavers, and men in white coats.

He set my Singer dead center on the table and left the room.

My sewing basket fell on the floor when I sank to the bed, sending a dozen sewing machine bobbins helter-skelter, like a pinball game gone mad.

TWENTY-ONE

You Must Wear Your Rue with a Difference

Kit's torn blue jeans hung on the bedpost until the Saturday morning I skipped breakfast to run Ophelia's lines. The toolshed's garden rake had probably caused the slices in the right leg. Though Kit hid it well, his right foot just wasn't as agile as his left one, and I wanted to erase the proof. In my view, embroidery was just fancy darning—another skill I'd acquired by default. I decided on an outdoor theme, pulled out my embroidery hoop.

Ophelia's brokenhearted jibber-jabber was tough stuff to memorize, much harder than my previous roles. I let my needle wander as I tried to make her seventeenth-century laments my own.

"There's rosemary, that's for remembrance; pray you, love, remember. And there is pansies; that's for thoughts."

Wildflowers, herbs, and greenery began to sprout in a denim field.

"There's fennel for you, and columbines . . ."

Somewhere in time, I heard Kit's slightly halting steps on our stairs, heard him rummaging through a drawer. I kept reciting as he kissed my neck.

"You must wear your rue with a difference. There's a daisy. I would give you violets . . ."

"How about dandelions, my pretty maid? As wildflowers go, they're highly unappreciated. They make very nice wine, and even nicer belly ticklers."

"Hmm. You'll have to wait for spring for that, randy prince."

Spring. Just one season away from Pasadena.

164

By Monday, I knew my lines cold for first rehearsal, and the right leg of Kit's jeans was a spring meadow just outside Elsinore Castle, complete with birds, squirrels, and dandelions.

"Let's take it from the top of Ophelia's first song. In your places, everyone. Willard, please dispose of that chewing gum forthwith. And everyone *hush*."

Arms raised like an orchestra conductor, Mrs. Pringlehoff nodded at me and I scrambled to the entrance of our improvised stage, clearing my throat. I didn't consider myself much of a singer, but any shyness about my rather reedy soprano had been obliterated by repetition. If Mrs. Pringlehoff had been a nitpicker about nouns, verbs, adjectives, and adverbs, she was a demon about scene blocking, voice projection, dialogue inflection, and stage business.

"Once again, Joey," she said, arms swooping down like raptors as I stepped forward. "With *feeling*. Every rehearsal should be worthy of a first-night audience."

And that was the puzzle about Ophelia. What was she *feeling* as she wandered like a lost spirit into madness? What were the emotions she could express only in suggestive ditties and double entendres? Grief for the death of a beloved parent? Shame at being used and rejected by the man she'd given herself to? Confusion because he was now a different man? Despair over unfulfilled expectations and altered dreams? All of them, I believed after my hours of donning Ophelia's self. Each emotion wove through her torn mind like colored threads through faded cloth, until the threads became the whole picture.

I maundered over to Queen Gertrude, who was Jenny Fitzsimmons offstage, and began.

"How should I your true love know . . ."

And all I had to do for *feeling* was picture Mamma naked before a mirror or Kit bashing phantom rats. Then my voice began to quaver, my eyes to fill with tears, and I became Ophelia.

When King Claudius greeted me, I knew just what to say.

"Lord, we know what we are, but know not what we may be . . ."

There was such logic and mystery in that statement. There was the here and now, and there was the whole universe up ahead.

Weeping with sorrow, I made my first exit at the appropriate time and place intuitively.

"*Good night, ladies, good night . . .*"

On my next entrance, my brother Laertes was there, looking shocked. I sang songs and gave flowers all around because I realized *acceptance* was the only way.

"*And of all Christian souls, I pray God. God b' wi' you . . .*"

Then I left the stage at the tape-strip doorway, pulling my hanky from my pocket. I blew my nose, waiting for Mrs. Pringlehoff's judgment.

Her bad sinuses had her sniffling, and she slid a lozenge into her mouth.

"Well done," she said, wiping her eyes with her sleeve. "Next time, use that handkerchief onstage."

🕊

"Sorry I missed your performance, Joey." Casper LeBlanc set his coffee on the lunchroom table and patted his pockets. Casper was a cigarette bum who always forgot his pack at home. If there was actually a pack to forget. "Public Speaking class was mandatory today, and I couldn't cut. How'd it go?"

I tossed Casper my Band-Aid tin, knowing he wouldn't find a smoke in any of his pockets. Casper lived with his folks and nine siblings in a rusty trailer house between the railroad tracks and the river. "I messed up a line."

Mrs. Pringlehoff had docked me for a flub that turned "columbines" into "concubines" and a nervous giggle. Only two people had snickered, but I was disappointed. B-plus. I'd wanted my first performance on IJC's little stage to be perfect.

I'd been replaying my mistake over coffee and a cigarette in the cafeteria, wishing I'd chosen Eugene O'Neill or Tennessee Williams instead of Shakespeare, when Casper sat beside me.

"That's no big deal, playwright considered," Casper said, savoring my gift with a deep drag. "I mean, the Bard's stuff, beautiful as it sounds,

166

just isn't written in the language we know. Speaking it 'trippingly on the tongue' ain't easy."

"Nope. Not easy." I shook out two more cigs, grateful for his sympathy. Kit had worn his mended jeans to school, and the only praise I'd received so far that day was for my needlework. Three students had tried to place orders for jeans just like Kit's.

Casper had been a year ahead of me in high school, so I'd only known him through the grapevine. His long pale hair had caused "fairy" talk among the jocks. But we were now classmates in Modern Literature and members of the college's artsy set. An aspiring poet, Casper revered Jack Kerouac, Allen Ginsberg, and especially Bob Dylan—verse writers nowhere to be found in *A Treasury of Great Poems*. He thought our Modern Lit professor, a rookie with a Mia Farrow haircut and an armload of turquoise jewelry, had wrongly named Rod McKuen as the definitive poet of our times.

"McKuen's hawking sex, and there's not an intellectual or inspired thought in any of his gooey pages," Casper would say, adjusting his John Lennon glasses with ink-stained fingers. "Only teenyboppers are into his lovelorn drivel. Poetry schmoetry. The guy writes backseat bushwah."

Casper stowed the spare cigarettes in his shirt pocket. "In case you haven't heard, let me be the one to tell you. A star was born today at IJC."

My smile at Casper's praise was halfhearted, since he hadn't even seen my performance.

"No kidding, Joey. It was the most thrilling thing I've witnessed since the summer my cousin Maynard took me to the Newport Folk Festival and Dylan plugged in."

Casper clearly wasn't talking about my Ophelia.

"Say what?"

"Your old man's speech this morning. He just blew everyone's mind."

"Kit gave a speech?" Leave it to Kit not to mention his own presentation when I was busy fretting and babbling over mine.

Casper was stroking his brow the way he did when dissecting Dylan song lyrics, his favorite being "It's Alright, Ma, I'm Only Bleeding."

"He brought the house down. Honest to God, even the professor stood and clapped."

"Kit got a standing ovation?" For all his intelligence and general curiosity, Kit didn't spend much time on homework or seem to take his studies very seriously. "What did he talk about?"

Casper sucked in the last quarter inch of his cig.

"Nam."

That, of course, didn't mean the geography, natural resources, or history of the Southeast Asian country. It meant the war.

I stared at Casper, dumbfounded. Except for a caustic quip, Kit never voluntarily talked about the war.

"What did he say?"

Casper was now smoking the filter.

"He said the government is hiding the truth about the war. He said the war's a crime. He said plenty."

Casper might as well have slammed a crutch to the floor. He finally stubbed out the butt. "Kit's one fine wordsmith. A street messenger in his own right. I almost started bawling."

Though Casper LeBlanc was artsy and intense, he was no crybaby. "But why?"

He removed his specs and rubbed them on his shirtsleeve. "The people he talked about. People suffering and dying for a lie."

I found a vase of roses on the kitchen counter when we got home from school. In the icebox, a bottle of champagne sat next to the casserole I'd put together for supper.

I'd drunk champagne once, on that blissful weekend of Kit's return. Champagne was for special occasions. Tink's birthday, I guessed. Doc had somehow scored the price of flowers and bubbly. I frowned. Macaroni and tomato sauce wasn't going to cut it for a birthday dinner, which Doc certainly wouldn't be cooking.

Kit had slipped into the doorway.

"Roses for the fairest actress to ever pass out wildflowers. I thought they might be better than columbine for celebrating your Ophelia."

"You heard about that? Great. I'm famous for a flub."

I hadn't mentioned my performance on the way home, and Kit hadn't asked about it.

"I ducked out of class after my speech, rules be damned. Peeked in and caught your whole performance. It was brilliant."

I closed the icebox. The roses were red.

"I mean it, Joey. You were wonderful."

Jimmy's clover posies were the only flowers I'd ever received. Red roses for a blue lady, the song went. I couldn't help the tremble in my chin. "I wanted an A."

Kit moved to my side. "It was a cute slip, Joey. One that Ophelia, ashamed as she was, might have made."

"Mrs. Pringlehoff didn't think it was cute."

"Mrs. Pringlehoff is a fool. I felt very bad for her."

"For Mrs. Pringlehoff?"

"For Ophelia. You brought her to life, Joey. Her anguish was there for all to feel. She made me want to cry."

"Really?"

"Really."

He lifted his hand and shook a bag of peanuts.

"Want to replay a different scene tonight?"

That was a scene I'd also memorized.

"But what about—" I nodded toward the hallway.

"The other cast members? They're spending the evening offstage."

"*All* of them?" Buzzy already had a steady, a grocery clerk named Rita who stopped by most nights. "How did that miracle come about?"

Kit ignored my sarcasm.

"A bribe. Movie tickets and pizza. They're banished until midnight."

"That must have wiped out your allowance."

Kit tossed the bag of peanuts and I managed to catch it. "We're not quite destitute." He kissed my hair, which I'd skipped washing that morning to keep the bathroom line moving. "A night with Ophelia is worth it," he said.

Kit made an ice bucket out of a Nabisco saltine tin, and we brought the roses, champagne, and peanuts upstairs, where our dinner didn't end until the rusted muffler of Buzzy's Buick boomed up the road.

I was pulling up the covers, readying the bed for sleep, when I finally broached the day's other subject. "So. Tell me about your speech."

Kit's eyes were closed, and they stayed that way. "Nothing to tell. We had an assignment. In Public Speaking class, that's usually a speech."

"Casper LeBlanc said you brought down the house."

I had to wait for Kit's reply. "Casper LeBlanc has quite a way with words."

"That's what he said about *you*."

"Hmm."

His breaths were slowing. A student of his habits, I knew he was moments away from sleep. But I wasn't.

"I want to hear about your speech, Kit."

A twitch of his eyelids said he was still awake.

"It wasn't a big deal, Joey."

"I heard otherwise."

His eyes were now open, but just barely, and not looking my way. "Current events was the topic. I hadn't prepared anything, so I just winged it. I might have gotten carried away."

I jumped on that.

"How so?"

He sighed. "You did me in, baby. Forgive me, but I'm ready for some shut-eye."

"The class didn't think you got carried away. They thought you were great."

Kit turned ever so slightly away from me. "Vietnam's not something I like to talk about, Joey."

No revelation there. Whatever he'd said to the classroom, he'd never said to me. My jealousy made me keep going.

"So what made you talk about it today?"

Kit's eyes were again closed, and a puff from his lips said his today was done. "Dunno, baby. Guilt maybe. Maybe guilt . . ."

Kit invited Casper LeBlanc to supper the next night, and over a four-man hand of cribbage, it was decided that Buzzy would take the top bunk, Casper the bottom.

Once we were in bed, Kit said, "Casper has to crash in a room with five other people." My back was to him, and he was stroking it, clearly trying to keep the peace. "It's not right, Joey."

I tried to channel Ophelia's gentle spirit and failed. "How right is it that there'll be five people waiting for the john in the morning?"

Kit didn't answer.

"Do you need to save *every* stray out there to feel okay?"

Kit reached for his flask, always nearby.

"I don't know."

Kit swabbed the old outhouse with Pine-Sol the next morning. Each night thereafter, the men of the Tribe—as Kit called his collection of Homestead souls—drew cards for morning exile to the latrine.

Casper—soon dubbed Boo by Kit—brought a rickety chest of drawers and an old pullout sofa along with him. Which gave everyone a place for their things and a place to sit.

— TWENTY-TWO —

There Is a Season

"A blue spruce would be pretty." I wrapped the muffler I'd knitted for Kit around his neck. "A nice big one. We have plenty of trimmings."

"Trust me and my trusty hatchet, little girl." Kit gave my bottom lip a playful nip. "A nice big one it shall be."

In the northland, when snow falls by Thanksgiving, it sometimes melts before Christmas, leaving mere humans to make the season look festive. I was glad that didn't happen for the Christmas of 1968. Two feet of snow lay heavy and glistening across our field, gently mounded where the weed clusters crouched, the night-blown drifts rising window high on the weather side of the house. The rest of the decorating fell to the Tribe's creative troop—Tink, Boo, and me.

We split the task. Tink strung popcorn and cranberries. I baked gingerbread and spritz cookies. Boo cut paper snowflakes and stars. And as master of the house and its sylvan grounds, Kit chopped the tree. Every male had offered to help him, even Doc—which made me snicker—but Kit demurred. On a Sunday afternoon when the sun was struggling to push its pale face through the gunmetal clouds, he headed out alone.

Given that we lived in the middle of the woods, he returned surprisingly late. The gloaming was nudging the day below the treetops when I heard him stomping the snow from his boots. Tink had stayed home that day, and a football game on Buzzy's radio had emptied the front room, where the tree stand was now waiting in the alcove I'd cleared for Kit's prize.

He entered ahead of the tree, looking mighty serious for a self-appointed St. Nick.

172

"I hope you like it."

I rose from the rocker, wondering how many needles I'd soon be sweeping. "Don't worry about the mess. Just bring it on in."

It took him but a moment to pull the tree across the room, and the needles it left behind amounted to exactly five. He set the tree in the stand, gave the bolts a few turns, and we both stood back. The festive side of me wanted to laugh. The sober side wasn't sure what to do. Instead of a lush six-foot blue spruce, Kit's prize was the scraggliest jack pine in the state of Minnesota, topping out at four feet, two of its branches broken and gone, the rest looking as if they'd been beaten with a bat and deprived of water, the lower needles a rusty orange.

I was speechless.

"I couldn't leave it." Kit leaned on his left foot, tucked his hands into his pockets. "It's fought a hard battle. It deserves to go out with respect."

He was staring at the tree, seeing something I couldn't, feeling something I didn't understand.

"It's a fine tree," I said, kneeling to straighten the skinny trunk and pour water in the stand. "It just needs a little TLC."

Kit nodded. "Your kindness and green hair are what I love about you." He plucked a dab of frosting from my bangs and put it into his mouth.

He was ambling toward the kitchen, his gait saying he was in search of brandy, his remark hanging in the air like a partridge feather caught in a cobweb.

I trimmed that jack pine until it was more decoration than tree, until a blaze of tinsel, ornaments, and lights fully concealed its war wounds. At dinner the next night, Kit made a rule. Every gift placed under it must be homemade. No store-bought presents allowed.

All the Tribe members but Kit had poverty in common, so it was a thoughtful rule. Though Kit bore our household expenses, my brothers often had needs I paid for because Daddy didn't or couldn't. My savings had dwindled in my months without a paycheck, and my Christmas shopping list had been heavy on my mind.

Come Christmas Eve around our spruced-up jack pine, I gave out vouchers—one chit worth one date with my needle and thread. Kit's blue jeans had advertised my supposed talent, and everyone seemed happy with my gift, though the spiked eggnog might have helped.

Craftwork abounded that night. There were little peace-sign wreaths from Tink, personalized poems from Boo, tie-dyed bandanas from Buzzy, beaded key rings from Doc, decorated packs of wild rice from the boys—who'd been fetched by Kit after Daddy left for his own festivities.

The only one who broke Kit's rule was Kit. He gave everyone a red sock with a fifty-dollar bill in the toe.

"I knitted those socks myself," he said. "And make sure the ink is dry before you put that paper in your pocket."

I'd been hoping to find something more romantic in my sock, something more personal, but the actress in me just smiled as everyone thanked Kit.

"Cool key ring," Boo said, studying Doc's gift. "Now all I need is a key to something. Door. Car. Treasure chest."

Everyone laughed, and blinking through his haze, Doc said, "It doubles as a roach clip."

"What's a roach clip?" Jimmy piped up, ever curious.

"It's—"

"Something like a mousetrap," Kit said, cutting off Doc.

"Made by nitwits who don't know when to keep their trap shut," I said, glaring at Doc.

"Hey now, Joey. No need to blow the Christmas spirit," Doc countered.

"Peace, sister," Buzzy said, holding up his wreath."

"No sister of yours," I snapped.

"Yeah, peace be with you," Tink said with an airy giggle, clearly missing the gist.

My glare had Doc squirming.

"Joey's right," Kit said, shutting down the exchange. "Let's be cool about certain things. Christmas is a time when grown adults should let kids be kids."

"I'm not a kid. I'm ten," Jimmy said, getting a laugh that made him grin, the attention right back where he liked it.

I lit my red candles when it began to snow again. And after passing around the nut bowl and nutcracker, I sat on the floor, leaning on Kit and watching through the window as heaven created its own tinsel. Despite everything that confused me about my life with Kit, I still felt safer than I had in all the years since Mamma had sprouted wings and gone her way.

Most of the household was heading out early in the morning to spend Christmas Day with family, so I followed Kit upstairs after a last round of eggnog, hoping the boys wouldn't squabble over sofas and blankets. A rare current of heat rose through the grate by the bed that night, and I dreamed I was running barefoot on the warm sand of an ocean beach.

❧

It was nearly noon when I woke to the smell of cooking food. Kit handed me a glass when I entered the kitchen, uncombed and hastily dressed. I took a sip. Pineapple juice doctored with brandy and maraschino cherries.

"A little tropical elixir for a less than tropical day," he said. "The mercury already reads twenty-two below. When the sun sets tonight, it's going to be a bit chilly."

"Whatever you've been up to, it smells good."

Kit wrapped his arms around my neck. "The ham is parched, mashed potatoes lumpy, and gravy burnt." He kissed my shoulder. "But the green beans are still a bit green, and the pineapple rings are as round as they ever were."

"Sounds delectable," I said, looking down at the gold heart that now hung from my neck.

A gust shook the window when he kissed me again. "Have another sip of that liquid sunshine."

❧

The mercury meandered between twenty and forty below zero all through the holiday week, lack of moisture giving the snow an iridescence only a wind straight from a polar icecap can beget. Truly cold snow squeaks when you walk on it, shifts like a spooked deer in the slightest breeze, its crystals too dry to cling together.

175

You can't make snowmen with such snow, and wouldn't want to. On those coldest of days, you ran the car for half an hour before getting inside, held your breath on the way to the mailbox so you didn't freeze your lungs, rubbed ice from your lashes once back inside, and shoved a rug in the crack between door and floor. On those days, fantastical ice webs grew thick over windowpanes, and wind wailed through walls like a zombie in search of its soul. On those days, no quantity of burning fuel or wool covering could overcome the drafts that sliced like wanton blades through every room.

Whatever wildlife had failed to head south in the fall now hid in the deepest cavities they could find, leaving the wasteland of white totally without life. Tink chose that week to officially make the Homestead her residence, and I didn't protest. Going anywhere in that weather could literally kill you.

Kit had wanted to throw another party on New Year's Eve, but put off invitation calls, waiting in vain for warmer weather. When the thirty-first dawned with a minus temperature matching the date, he scratched even his alternate plan—dinner and dancing at the Rainbow Inn. The Tribe spent the night huddled under blankets between stove and fireplace, playing Monopoly with gloves on, trying to warm ourselves with Pink Floyd and hot toddies, no one daring to leave the fold even for bed.

The boys called at midnight with New Year's wishes, and I acted shocked that they were still up. Daddy had braved the elements for some holiday cheer, and I tried not to worry about his foolhardiness as I curled up against Kit, pretending the fireplace sparks were shooting stars in the sky above the Pacific.

Kit nixed my plans for a New Year's Day roast beef.

"The Tribe can fend for themselves today. Why don't you and I spend the first day of 1969 trying to improve the weather? If we stay under the covers long enough, I have a feeling the temperature will rise."

I ventured out to our mailbox before heading upstairs, dressed in my best version of Eskimo gear. A postcard from Dee Dee lay atop the neglected pile, and I slipped it inside my parka. Back in the house, I sat right on our bedroom grate, parka still on, to read it.

Dee Dee wrote the way she talked, straight as a gun barrel, blunt as a bullet.

This is a frequent layover of mine. I'm currently fending off a married pilot who could be Marlon Brando's brother. Stay cool and out of trouble, kiddo, if you know what I mean.

I turned the card over and looked at the picture. It was a photo of Times Square at night, the lights of Broadway shining so brightly through the glossed paper, my eyes watered.

"What's up, little girl?" Kit said when he entered the room. I was still sitting on the grate, trying to remember when I'd last seen or heard a bird, and crying my eyes out.

"Oh Kit. I wish the birds would sing again. And I wish our Christmas tree hadn't been through such a hard battle."

Kit sat down beside me and took my hand. "Me too," he said as a tear ran down his face. "Me too."

— TWENTY-THREE —

And a Time to Every Purpose

"I really hate being mean to a blind person, especially a blind *chick*. They're going to boo and throw rotten tomatoes at me, Joey."

My costar Gordon O'Toole scooted closer to the candle lighting our corner of the room.

"Just keep in mind that I douse you with gasoline, try to burn you alive, and finally stab you with a knife," I said.

Gordon flipped to our script's last scene, a violent showdown between his evil conman and my sightless housewife. "Right. I almost end up dead."

The shadow of his nod looked like a bobbing black ghost. It was a heebie-jeebies kind of night. "And when you put out the lights out, it's even-steven between us."

"Not hardly," I said. "*I* know how to be blind."

The ghost bobbed again. "True. You're an ace at using your other senses, and I'm a defenseless schmuck."

"Worse than that. I've got matches and want to barbecue you."

"Oh my god, you're really a *bitch*, Joey. Don't let me forget that."

Classes had resumed in January, and snow had fallen again when the temperature finally rose above zero. By the first day of school, our field was four feet under, and the snowplow border around the school parking lot was taller than Rosie.

Although IJC's schedule didn't list any acting classes that term, Mrs. Pringlehoff was directing the school's annual spring play. On a cloudless Friday that looked like summer from the treetops up, I'd been first in the audition line. *Wait Until Dark* was the play, a thriller by Frederick Knott with a blind woman as female lead. I think I got the part when I tripped over a chair and kept reading my lines. Opening night was in March.

Though Suzy Hendrix wasn't as plum a part as Blanche, Liza, or Ophelia, she'd been played by Lee Remick and Audrey Hepburn, and I wanted to do her justice. I'd pored over her lines trying to understand her world. With great purpose, I'd begun doing things with my eyes closed. The morning I salted the pancakes and poured orange juice into the sugar bowl, Kit spilled his coffee laughing.

"Bravo, baby. You've nailed the part before first rehearsal."

The Homestead's lights went out for forty-eight hours when a February blizzard blasted in from Canada. The timing couldn't have been worse or better. Gordon, a gangly and rather nervous journalism major, had stopped by to run lines just before the wind kicked up. Some men might have resented such a visit, but Kit offered Gordon a glass of wine at the door.

Candles, Kit's kerosene lantern, and the fireplace kept us from total darkness the two nights we practiced our roles in a corner of the front room.

"Yes, I'm the bitch who wants to make you a human blowtorch," I said, rattling a matchbox behind Gordon's head.

Gordon gasped, and Kit, who'd been studying by flashlight across the room, burst out laughing.

"Ahem," I said, pointing a finger Kit couldn't miss even in the dim light. "Do you know what happens to men who eavesdrop on desperate blind ladies?"

"Uh oh. Caught in the act." Kit threw up his hands. "But you can't blame me for getting wrapped up in your thespian aspirations, Joey."

My thespian aspirations were a sore with only a thin scab. "If you keep your nose in that book, maybe you'll discover an aspiration of your own."

If Kit minded my rebuke, he didn't show it. "I should definitely take a page from your script."

During a practice break the second night of the blackout, Gordon and I joined the scariest-thing-that-ever-happened-to-you huddle in the front room's darkest corner. My story was naturally about trees and tree shadows. Running out of gas on a date with the pastor's daughter was

Boo's scariest experience, and sneaking into a creaky abandoned house was Tink's. I was more than curious when Kit's turn came. Would he tell a funny childhood story, or actually talk about the things that gave him nightmares? But he chose his moment in the candlelight to notice the log bin was low and slip out to the woodpile.

I tried to be grateful that our cooking and heating stoves weren't electric. But our water pump was. So we melted snow for drinking, washing, cooking, and flushing during our power-less days, and I tried to be grateful for our bucket and ample supply of snow.

When the county plows finally opened our road three days after the lights came back on, Kit went to town for another bed. Gordon hailed from Bigfork, a forty-mile drive to campus on a narrow road notorious for ice. Gordon was a nice fellow, and Kit's offer was kind, even logical. "Supper at six, clean towels on Saturday," I muttered.

Gordon became Pancho Villa the night he translated the preamble of the Declaration of Independence into Spanish on a ten-dollar bet with Kit, who paid up with two fives and a nickname.

March finally arrived, but I was too sick of winter to notice if it came in like a lamb or a lion, too sick of life at the Homestead to care. I'd made an agreement for love, but I didn't love the agreement.

Not that Kit didn't lend a hand or try to make things easier. He'd rigged an old washer and dryer in our laundry shed, decreed that suppers be one-pot help-yourself affairs. And all the Tribe members—except Doc the weasel—chipped in with chores. But dispensing those chores naturally fell to me, the lady of the house. Approaching meal, muddy entryway, dirty laundry, iced-up icebox. I was the one who noticed and did it myself or tried not to sound bossy when appointing a doer. Like an endless TV rerun—first played when Mamma had left for other roosts—full bellies and household tidiness were my job by default. By the end of March, though a stretch of sunny days had melted even the deepest ditches and highest banks, I was ready to head west with only one roommate. But there were still five months to go.

Our play was a big hit. We received standing ovations at our three standing-room-only performances on a rainy March weekend. Though

Mrs. Pringlehoff allowed only full-cast bows at curtain call, I felt sure my Suzy had stood out. But our lighting man was probably the true star of the show. The final scene called for the stage lights to go black—a crowd pleaser I couldn't take credit for, though I'd flipped the fake switch.

Kit attended two performances, missing the matinee for a long-distance phone call, probably from his parents. I was actually glad he didn't see that one. Our dusty prop sofa made me sneeze in the tensest scene, causing Pancho to gasp and flub his lines.

As always, I wasn't sure if Kit was serious when he said, "Not even Helen Keller could have topped your performance, baby." But as always, his praise felt good.

⌇

"Does Lennon really think sitting in bed all day with a camera pointed at him and Yoko Ono will end the war?" Boo was cleaning his Lennon specs on his shirt sleeve, bummed smoke dangling from his lips. "Does he actually believe our commander-in-chief took that bit of circus seriously?"

Buzzy's mouthful didn't hinder his reply. "Bed-In. And who says our fucking head honcho even watched it?"

"Scuse your French," Tink said, raising a cloud of patchouli as she tucked her skirt under her knees.

Buzzy chomped into a second drumstick. "Fucking affirmative."

Kit raised a finger. "Ah, cut the poor guy some slack. He's on his honeymoon and not thinking with his brain right now." As always, Kit sidetracked any talk that touched on the war.

Pancho's girlfriend, Kate, piped in. "Do men usually think with their brain?"

"Good point," Kit said, winking at me.

When Easter arrived pretty as a Sunday bonnet and actually warm, Kit had called for a picnic in our field, which he'd recently scythed clear. Though the hard labor hadn't pleased his foot, it had given his face and mood a healthy glow. I'd fried chicken and fish for our feast, and Tink had made the most colorful potato salad this side of Oz, chopping up every vegetable in our kitchen.

By full bloom of afternoon, the Tribe and followers were sprawled on every blanket and mat they could scrounge. My brothers hadn't made it to Easter service, but a jaybird chattering in the big Norway beside the field said fresh air and sunshine were acceptable substitutes for the stuffy interior of a church.

Kit was now pouring apple wine with a free hand, having paid my well-fed brothers a good fee to paint the new porch steps. As usual, the talk went where the wine took it.

Doc brushed crumbs from his wispy beard, which now met his second shirt button. "Hey, Morrison wasn't thinking with anything when he got arrested in Miami last month."

Boo considered The Doors' front man a street poet of high caliber. "The booze and little helpers that give an artist an edge can push him over it if he isn't careful. Jimbo can fill any auditorium and score any chick, but maybe he's so far gone now, he can only get his kicks by exposing his ... his ..."

"Drumstick," Buzzy said, tossing a bone into the paper bag I'd set out for trash.

"Well put." Pancho tossed in an apple core.

"The cops certainly aren't backing down," Kit said. "Which means old Jim will probably be a rider on the storm for a while, unless he drowns in the downpour."

Boo tipped his glass to Kit's musical allusion, and Buzzy said, "Freaky thought, man," staring into his second or third refill. "Morrison's on some mystery trip."

Tink, who didn't need much wine to slip into a gossamer zone, had been intermittently studying the clouds and weaving clover on her skirt. Twirling a four-leafer, she emitted a sigh. "Speaking of mystery trips, I've been wondering about something. Maybe it's wicked to ask, especially on Easter, but do you all think Jesus really rose from the dead? Or is that resurrection stuff just a way to say folks haven't forgotten him, is it just a ... a ..."

"Metaphor for the endurance of his message?" Boo said.

"Yeah."

The leap from earthly to heavenly cast a short pall over our lively forum. Kit, always the savior of a social lull, flipped another tape into his player, uncapped another bottle. He held it out as Hendrix's lightning-and-thunder version of "All Along the Watchtower" blasted toward the passing clouds, immediately spinning images of chaos and entrapment.

"That's a deep question, Tinkerbell," Kit said, voice blending with Jimi's. "And maybe the best answer is another question."

Empty glasses were reaching for Kit's bottle, and he poured as he spoke.

"What difference does it make?" He filled his own glass and took a swig. "People can blame whichever bully they want to for his death, but truth is, the guy got killed and remembered for exposing lies, oppression, and injustices suffered by the nobodies of this world. He knew the risk when he rocked the boat. His honesty was literally suicide."

A sunbeam was doing a spry jig in Kit's hair, and Jimi was singing of false talk and fate. As his guitar whined and moaned, I could almost see the notes rising into the sky.

Kit twirled his glass and his wine did a little shimmy. He bent down to fiddle with the laces of his right boot, and I knew he was trying to relieve the pressure on his foot. When he sat up, he gazed at the trees edging the field, which was aswirl with spring scents and small flying creatures. In a day that felt warm and safe, Jimi was howling about the howling wind, about a wildcat growling in the cold.

"You might say, Tink, that self-sacrifice for a better world was a type of resurrection, because his beliefs and his cause lived on."

Jimi's closing wail joined a sudden gust from the north, and I shivered. Kit clicked off the tape after the final note, and the rustle of leaves in the distance was the only sound for a long moment that felt rather ghostly.

Then Boo clinked his glass with a fingernail. "Hear, hear."

Buzzy tapped his own glass, and Tink giggled at the chorus of chimes that quickly followed, accepting it as praise for her question. Leaning forward with a swish of gauze, she placed a clover garland over Kit's head.

"You're such a smart guy." Her glance at his foot was unmissable. "I'll never understand why you let them send you to Vietnam. Especially with Canada so close by."

The cessation of chimes boomed like a gong. Clearly not realizing her weighty faux pas, Tink turned back to her weaving, her pursed lips perhaps a comment on Kit's choice.

Among our group, no one but Kit and Buzzy had been in the service, let alone to Vietnam. And though everyone there disapproved of the war, no one had ever faulted Kit's involvement in it. He was the chieftain of our little Tribe—respected and admired beyond criticism for his kindness and generosity—and the price he'd paid for his tour of duty was obvious to anyone who spent time with him. Kit had gone to Vietnam, and he'd been punished forever.

The silence didn't lift. Everybody but Tink was waiting for Kit's reply, and his sigh said he knew he had to give one. But as much as I liked hearing Kit speak his mind, I didn't like seeing him cornered. For all the loveliness of that Sunday, I wanted to go into the house where the light wasn't so bright, where the breeze didn't reveal the parchment-pale skin at the edges of his brow.

Kit shrugged in that flip-yet-humble way of his.

"Well, God knows I didn't go to Vietnam because I was a great believer in some cause," he finally said. "I didn't go there to fight for freedom or democracy or any highbrow concepts like that. I knew guys who did, but that definitely wasn't my reason." His laugh—halfway between a snort and a chuckle—had no smile attached to it. I needed to change the subject.

"Hey, who wants more—"

But Kit cut me off with a squeeze of my wrist.

"Mostly I went to Nam because I didn't feel proud of myself, and I wanted to." He set his glass on the ground. "I'd made a mess of things. Pissed people off, embarrassed myself, lived for the here and now." He shrugged again. "Done what felt good at any given moment because the given moment seemed more important than every other moment." He scratched his beard. "I'm not so sure I've changed my mind on that one, but what the hell."

He tapped a Camel from his pack and lit it. By now everyone had leaned in, but perhaps only I noticed his shaking hands. I closed my eyes, unable to watch.

"Anyway, I'd screwed up royally, in the opinion of some. And I thought maybe I could redeem myself by doing something most guys my age were trying damned hard not to do. Maybe I might eventually even be appreciated for not taking the easy way out. Tink's right. Canada would have been a cinch. Hop the border and find a little shack in the woods, live off the land hunting and fishing. No sweat, man. A long camping trip. Even jail would have been easy, to my way of thinking back then. What's so hard about letting time pass you by for a while when you've got a whole lifetime to waste?" I heard him take a deep drag. "I went to Vietnam to do a good thing."

When he exhaled, I heard regret and resignation in his breath. I heard chagrin.

"And when I was there, I didn't try to be a hero." He spit a piece of tobacco from his tongue. "Heroism wasn't my bag. I just wanted to prove I could do something worthy, to those who needed proving to. I wasn't bucking for stripes and chest candy. I just wanted to make it out of there and back home to get the approval I hoped for.

"The do-good part got tricky right away, though. The bad guys, well, they weren't so easy to pick out in those rice paddies and straw huts. They weren't wearing black hats and spouting communist doctrine, and every Vietnamese, no matter which side, screamed when they died. The good guys, well, they were your buddies getting blown to bloody bits just trying not to let you down. Trying not to show the fear that sank to your bones. John Wayne, he was nowhere to be found in that wet maze of death where nothing you did felt like a good thing.

"But I did what I was told to do to, and did it to the best of my ability. We all did. What we were told to do . . ."

He was back there now, gone from our newly shorn and fragrant field and halfway around the world. Maybe at the siege of Khe Sanh, maybe in the jungle along the Ho Chi Minh Trail, maybe near the banks of the Mekong River. He was at one of the places he dreamed about.

"And some of the things we were told to do . . . and did," he said. "Some of them . . . well, I'm not sure even the guy from Galilee could forgive them. Things I can't . . . ."

He swallowed, and I wanted to jump up and shoo everyone away. This was what I'd wanted to hear him talk about for so long, but not in the glare of the sun, not in the presence of others.

Barely audible, he kept going.

"I did my job thinking there were people waiting for my return, people who'd appreciate what I'd done ... who'd care about what I'd lost ... but the people I'd tried to please, by Christ, they weren't waiting and happy to see me. Us. Huh uh. They weren't remotely proud when we made it back home. They certainly weren't waving any flags or throwing any parades. As a matter of fact, they were angry and embarrassed. They booed us, came right up close, looked us in the eye, and spit on us. We'd done wrong, they said. Been fools, been duped. We'd betrayed the spirit of our country.

"And those who didn't boo just looked away, didn't like seeing the wheelchairs, crutches, and stumps. Cripples are not what freedom and democracy are about, not here in squeaky clean Jesus-loves-me America, where the truth is supposed to be pure and simple. Dear God, who wants to see gimps hanging around the home of the brave?"

My eyes shot open. Cripple? Gimp? Who was he talking about? Surely not himself. Never once had I thought of Kit Griffith as less than whole. Changed, yes. Altered. Different than he'd once been. But not diminished, not ruined. Though I'd heard far more than I wanted to, he wasn't finished.

"Nah, we weren't appreciated when we got home. Oh, I admit it took a while for that hard fact to sink in. I was a little distracted when I first got back, you see. A little out of the mainstream, you might say. But it eventually became as clear as tracers on a moonless night. And then I knew I'd done it all ... *all* of it ... for a lie. I'd done unholy things for a false prophet who didn't give a goddamn about the nobodies in this world. I'd been a whore that no savior was ever going to rescue from the flying stones."

The bitterness in his voice and the bare honesty of it was more than I could stand. I jumped to my feet.

"Who's up for ice cream?" I looked down at the stunned crowd, forcing a grin. "I have it on good authority the Easter bunny hid a carton

186

at the back of the icebox." I took a step toward the house. "Chocolate sauce, anyone? Sliced peaches?"

But Kit grabbed the bottom of my jeans and pulled me back to a sitting position. Pulled me so hard I hit the ground with a thud.

"You're absolutely right, Tink," he continued. "I wasn't very smart about Vietnam. But I got some new IQ points pounded into me in that torn little country where life is cheap—especially if it's Asian life or comes from the poor side of town—and where the body-count numbers don't add up to the truth. Where one day a hill is worth the bravest men you know, and the next day it's worth nothing and tossed back to the enemy like a football in a game where the rules keep changing and the goalpost keeps disappearing."

He removed Tink's garland and set it back in her lap.

"I'm not a smart man. But I'm capable of learning when the truth sheds blood and makes people scream. When tear gas can't hide it from those with open eyes. This older, slightly wiser crip from the rice paddies can tell you two things for sure. Killing will never yield peace, and this war is wrong. Anyone who knows those two things has an obligation to speak out and a duty to end this ungodly mistake in any way he can."

Kit turned and patted my knee. "You wanted an aspiration, little girl? Well, there you have it."

He tried to wink before he rose to his feet, and maybe only I saw that he failed. Then he headed across the field, slow enough to camouflage his limp, and kept walking until the trees and their shadows swallowed him whole.

TWENTY-FOUR

Summertime Blues

"I'm going out tonight, if you don't mind."

Kit was tying back his hair with a leather cord, having changed from jeans and flannel shirt into his best pants and sweater.

"You mean without me?" I asked. In our time as a couple, Kit had never gone out at night alone.

"That's what I mean."

"It's a free country and you're almost old enough to be out after dark," I said, trying to be funny. Trying not to be alarmed.

He smoothed a stray hair from his brow. "I'm going to the VFW club."

"Say hi to Daddy if he gets that far." I wasn't trying to be funny anymore.

"I'm going to crash a chapter meeting. Not your cup of tea, little girl."

"Doesn't sound like your cup of tea either, Kit."

"It is now." He slipped on his good suede jacket. "Now it is."

If Kit had been a sparrow gliding on an aimless airstream in the last eight months, he'd suddenly become an eagle circling below the currents, his sight fixed on one specific prey.

At the VFW meeting, two days after Easter, Kit asked to speak about the war and they let him. Ever nonchalant about speeches, he was vague about his reception. Given his audience and his Purple Hearts, I guessed he hadn't gotten a standing ovation but hadn't gotten heckled.

Somehow, Kit also arranged with IJC's American History professor to give a guest lecture, which earned him plenty of lunchroom chatter, mostly positive. And he cut class three afternoons the next week to coach the high school debate team for a statewide competition on the pros and cons of the war. He shrugged off that effort as well, but when the team took second place, he broke out a bottle of wine with a real cork.

Long-distance phone calls had been a Homestead rarity, usually two-minute person-to-person notifications from Kit's parents about their travels. But now the operator rang almost every night and always for Kit. Though he didn't hide the calls, I didn't pry. But the initials VVAW sometimes carried from the kitchen to the front room, and eventually the whole name—Vietnam Veterans Against the War.

Letters and parcels, also for Kit, now filled our mailbox, bearing out-of-state return addresses with male names. Kit had acquired an aspiration, and he was pursuing it wings wide.

Kit also received a thousand-page tome called *How to Grow Vegetables and Fruits by the Organic Method* in the mail. He'd ordered it from *Whole Earth Catalog*, a publication the Tribe members passed around with reverence. From then on, his schoolbooks lay unopened on the floor by his reading spot.

In May, Kit organized a local pancake feed to raise funds for disabled vets, and visited the Toastmasters and Rotary clubs. He also tilled our field, using only a hoe and shovel, refusing any help. As spring sauntered toward summer, the growing plot of upturned earth began to look like an unplanted garden. A big one.

On a Friday night when the Tribe was well into its usual Friday night activities—a little wine, a little pot, a few card games, a couple of record albums, and every topic an assortment of slightly altered minds could contemplate—Kit hijacked the conversation.

"Does anyone have special plans for tomorrow?" he said, slipping a snuffed-out roach into his pocket after a final toke.

He lit a Camel during the languid huh-uhs and nahs that followed.

"I'm thinking of planting a garden," he said. "And I'm looking for long-term paid assistants."

Heads perked up.

"Tomorrow's job is planting. Long-range tasks will be weeding, watering, building a fence to keep out wildlife, and picking the produce.

Anyone who helps from now through harvest time earns an equal share of the profit."

Despite the wine, weed, and late hour, all faces looked alert, curious.

"Organically grown vegetables is the crop," Kit continued. "My research says there's a burgeoning market for them. And that we'll find an outlet in the farmers' markets, especially near the Cities, and possibly some of the bigger grocery stores." He leaned back and stretched his legs, clearly comfortable with his subject. "I also have a business plan for selling decorative gourds."

Positive comments meandered the room as Kit flicked his ashes into our shared ashtray and gave me a smile I didn't return. He began flipping through a stack of albums like someone who'd just mentioned the weather. James Taylor, Blind Faith, and Crosby, Stills, & Nash were his current favorites. And always Dylan, rebel bard from just down the road.

"How about a show of hands, brothers and sisters of the Homestead," he said, laying his selection on his lap.

Everyone's hand but mine went up. If Kit noticed my lack of response, he didn't let on. He pulled a paper from his pocket and unfolded it.

"Here's my list." He passed the paper to Buzzy. "Every vegetable I think we can successfully grow on this land. Suggestions are welcome."

He slipped the album from its cover, placed it on the turntable, deftly set the needle in the gap before his chosen track. Steve Winwood's high tenor, anchored by Eric Clapton's dancing acoustic strings, floated upward as he proclaimed the need for change after waiting so long.

Kit had barely reached the top step when I switched on our bedroom lamp, whirled toward him, and gave my opinion of his plan.

"What the fuck is all this shit about a garden? We've got to be in California before fall term."

He looked surprised, but walked to the bed at his normal pace, unbuttoning his shirt as he went. He sat and began unlacing his boots.

"I was just brainstorming, Joey."

"Research? Burgeoning market? Business plan? Sounds like a helluva lot more than brainstorming." I was trembling and didn't care if he noticed.

"It's just a business venture, an investment." His boots hit the floor one by one. "Nothing says I have to be here on a full-time basis for it to succeed. Onsite managers aren't a new concept."

I threw up my hands, knocking the lampshade cockeyed.

"Don't bullshit me, Kit Griffith. It's obvious you have no intention of leaving this tumbledown shack in the middle of your personal Sherwood Forest. Christ, you've actually been doing market research on organic vegetables? What about Pasadena Playhouse? What about our agreement?"

Kit gave his right foot a rub before donning his slippers and removing his shirt.

"I didn't realize you felt so negatively about our home," he said, tone even, voice low. "It's no mansion, I'll admit, but I've tried to make it habitable. Tell me how I can improve—"

"You're digressing, and insulting my intelligence. The topic of this discussion isn't the Homestead. The topic is California."

Kit lay back on the bed, hands under head. A long moment passed as he studied the ceiling. "Forgive me, Joey. Although I'm starting to put the pieces of myself back together, I still don't think I'm ready for California. And, frankly, I don't understand the big rush to go there. Aren't we getting along pretty well here?"

I suddenly felt invisible, as if Kit had never seen me, never heard me. As if I didn't exist to him. Big rush? Getting along pretty well? Who the hell was he talking about?

I stomped to the end of the bed. The red of his beard looked so regal in the lamplight, the paleness of his skin so vulnerable. That face was my weakness.

"The big *rush* is that Pasadena Playhouse has been holding a place and a scholarship for me for months. They won't do that forever, Kit. They made an accommodation for me so I could accommodate *you*. We have a goddamn agreement. One year, quid pro quo, goose and gander. Remember?" I was shouting now, and didn't care if the whole house heard me.

191

He sat up and shrugged, palms up.

"But you don't need that scholarship, Joey. I can always pay your tuition, anytime, anywhere, and you know it. You also know there are plenty of ways and places to get acting experience without up and moving two thousand miles." There was bewilderment in his tone, and dismay. "We have a home here. We have friends here. We have stability and peace here. Can't you look at it from my perspective? It's a big change, and it just seems rather unreasonable, all things considered. And rather selfish."

"Selfish!" Any sympathy for what had made his perspective different from mine dropped dead into a dirt hole. I stared at him, the truth taking my breath away. "Oh Jesus, you're fucking blind. And you've been leading me on all this time."

His hands fell to the bed with a thud. "Not true, little girl."

"It's been a fucking con. Just like that night in the cemetery."

He was instantly on his feet.

"It's not like that, Joey. That night—"

"Then tell me how it *is*, goddamn it. Tell me that, after riding off with my virginity and leaving me wondering for fourteen months, you didn't deceive me."

He was in front of me now, shaking his head.

"And tell me what makes your needs matter, but not mine," I said, still shouting.

"Ah, come on, baby . . ."

I shoved his hands away when he reached for me.

"No, *you* come on, Kit. It's been your way all along. And you can just fucking *keep* it that way, for all I care. I won't play the bitch who comes between you and your precious peace of mind. You do what you goddamn want, same as always. But come next term, *I'm* going to be in California."

His hesitation lasted only a moment, but it filled the room like a foghorn.

"All right, then. California it is." His sigh might as well have been a police whistle. "If that's the only alternative. If that's your ultimatum." He combed his fingers through his hair, and it fell back onto his shoulders like amber neon threads. I wanted to shear them with a dull blade.

"Just give me a date, Joey, and I'll have Rosie packed, gassed, and ready to roll."

I snorted. "I don't fucking believe you." My jaw dropped. I'd just called Kit a liar.

"I mean it, Joey." His face was so close to mine, his eyes so like the sea of my dreams.

"Believe me."

"Give me one fucking reason I should."

No hesitation this time. "I need you."

I scoffed, wrenched myself backward. "Fleas need dogs. Gardens need manure. Weeds need pulling."

He blinked, revealing the scatter of freckles on his eyelids, and another look of surprise. "I care about you, Joey. I really do."

"How nice." I slapped him in the face and headed for the stairs. "I'll be outta here as soon as I collect my things."

As much as Kit was able to run, he ran after me. He grabbed my shoulders, whipped me around, and in half a heartbeat had me up against the wall. "You can't leave me."

I fought his grip, but his thighs were between mine, his tongue deep in my mouth. In one movement, my sweater was gone and my arms pinned to the wall above my head. Except for the persistent rise and fall of my ribcage, I was literally trapped.

"I love you," he said in a low groan, allowing me one breath before sucking the air from my rage. "I would move all the way to Hanoi for you, Joey Dean."

I didn't think he was lying.

The radishes and cucumbers had already sprouted the day Jimmy dropped the letter in my lap. He was on his way out the door after an afternoon of holding fence posts for Kit's sledgehammer.

"Hey, sis. This came in the mail for you." The envelope was folded in half and bent at the corners, its postmark and my name smudged by grimy prints. But the return address was clear enough—Pasadena Playhouse College of Theatre Arts, Pasadena, California.

Night had long fallen when Kit found me in the toolshed, his flashlight forcing my eyes shut.

"What the hell are you doing in here, Joey? I've been worried sick. The whole Tribe is looking for you."

"I wanted to be alone."

"In the toolshed?"

"The other option for privacy was the outhouse."

In my hours of isolation, my initial emotions had been carried away by tears, and my tears were now just crusty salt pathways to my chin. I rose from my seat on the upturned wheelbarrow and threw the letter at Kit as I passed him.

"Fuck you and this stupid farm. Fuck all these trees and the sunshine they hide. And fuck your freeloader friends, who all matter to you more than I do. This is on your head, Kit Griffith. You have ruined my life."

Once inside the house, I went straight to bed. When Kit eventually turned on our lamp, I covered my face with a pillow and screamed until he turned it back off.

Even the potatoes had sprouted when I finally let Kit look me in the eye and say what he'd been trying to since the letter had come. Two weeks after planting day, I didn't walk out when he found me alone in the kitchen.

"Joey, I'm really sorry your acting school has closed. That's a lousy break, and a letter's a shitty way to get the info. I can imagine how disappointed you are."

I was staring at the bottom of my coffee cup.

"It was *not* an *acting* school. It was a renowned college of theatre arts, and your imagination won't get you close to how I feel about losing my chance to study at the same place as William Holden and Dustin Hoffman."

The coffee grounds looked like tiny dead bugs.

"But the college must have been having troubles for a while, Joey." It was a frustrated, almost weary, plea. "Things like that don't just happen overnight."

"I could have attended there for a whole school year."

194

"Joey, there are other—"

"No there aren't. Not like that." I swallowed the coffee, grounds and all, and left the room.

I was inconsolable. I sulked for half the summer of '69, hiding out on the porch, where I slept and read Shakespeare—even the comedies, which I liked less than the tragedies, histories, and sonnets. But none of Will's clowns, fools, and sprites—or Kit's ardent pleas—lifted my gloom. Even when Boo and Pancho kidnapped me for Franco Zeffirelli's *Romeo and Juliet* at the Rialto, despair clung to me like wet gauze. The moon landing—turned into a Homestead happening by Kit's purchase of a TV antenna and deemed outasight by the Tribe—couldn't pull me from my hermitage.

And after a while, Kit quit trying to cheer me up and get me upstairs, and I quit crying. I moved back to Daddy's house then, sleeping on the couch so the boys could stay put, assuming my old household role, unable to aim my thoughts forward, to find a hole in the mental wall I'd hit. I just nodded when Daddy said, "Welcome home, sweetheart." The boys knew better than to say anything at all.

I refused Kit's calls and attempted visits until the muggy August day he learned that Jimmy could be bribed. He was carrying a manila envelope when he stepped into the living room and motioned for Jimmy to step out.

"I read about an event called the Woodstock Music and Art Fair, probably in *Rolling Stone*," he said. "I asked a friend in New York to see if he could get us tickets. They came today."

He pulled a large piece of paper from the envelope, unfolded it. It was a red poster, with an image of a dove perched on the neck of a guitar above the words 3 DAYS of PEACE & MUSIC. He laid it on the sofa beside me, and I looked down.

There were at least two dozen musicians listed on the poster, many of them ones we listened to on Kit's stereo. Joan Baez, the Who, Jimi Hendrix. It was an impressive lineup by any musical standard.

Kit was holding a letter. "Oscar wants to meet us at the festival. In the Catskills. Pretty country, I hear."

I sighed. "Trees, I suppose."

"Not as many as Sherwood Forest."

"Who's Oscar?"

"A Nam vet I correspond with. Journalist. He wants to write a story about my . . . new aspiration."

I kept my eyes on the poster.

"The first day of the festival is your nineteenth birthday."

He'd remembered.

"Sunshine, music, and the two of us in the back of Rosie. Give us another chance, Joey. It's only three days."

I was afraid to look at him. I'd been so lonely and so blue.

"Oscar says they think Bob Dylan might show up." He leaned down and slid a hand behind my neck. It felt so cool and so warm.

"Dylan, huh?"

☙

The New York state line wasn't far behind us when Kit pulled onto a side road and shut off Rosie's motor. It was shortly after midnight, and we'd barely gotten settled in the back of the van when he pulled a stout leather case from his duffel bag and set it in my lap.

"Happy birthday, little girl. How does it feel to be pushing twenty?"

"Like five minutes past eighteen. What's this?"

I'd agreed to the trip, but words between us, as one state rolled into another, had been stilted, impersonal, and few.

"It's an Argus Autronic 2 camera with all the accessories and plenty of film," he said, clearly proud of his offering. "Automatic rangefinder, so you should get sharp images with minimal effort. There's a manual."

I opened the case and removed the camera. Though not large, it felt heavy in my hands. Solid, sturdy, full of future moments.

Guessing it wasn't loaded, I aimed it at Kit. He was barely visible under Rosie's dome light. I pushed the shutter button, wondering if I could ever forget that face.

I lowered Kit's gift and set it on my lap. "What use do I have for a camera?"

— TWENTY-FIVE —

Home of the Brave

"Gosh. What could it be? Fender bender? Stray cow?"

The first photograph I took with my birthday camera was of traffic. Looking like a madras-plaid sash gone mad, it stretched as far as my lens could view, both lanes plus the shoulders crawling in one direction.

"Maybe we're closer than we thought," Kit said. "Maybe we should park."

By Kit's map and my calculations, we weren't anywhere near the Woodstock festival site—which wasn't actually at the town of Woodstock—when the vehicle jam finally halted. Only the pedestrians kept moving, trudging onward between the cars, spilling far over the boundaries of the road, adding a jagged fringe to the picture.

"Whatever the problem, it's gotta clear up eventually." I prized my white poet's shirt and the flock of bluebirds I'd embroidered on my jeans. I wasn't anxious to step into the red dust billowing from the road on that humid and hot day.

Looking out at the alfalfa fields, grain silos, barns, and cows that said we were in farm country, I wondered if we'd hit a dead end. I shot more pictures to pass the time, trying for artsy compositions.

Forty-five minutes later and only a few yards farther down the road, Kit pulled Rosie into a meadow and parked, as many vehicles in front of us were doing. "We're burning gas for nothing. We might as well hoof it."

Kit gave me a tentative smile when he slung the strap of our sleeping bag over his shoulder and pulled the picnic basket from Rosie. Heat, dust, and our wounded relationship couldn't hide that it was a pretty summer day.

"Would you mind grabbing my jacket, little girl? And don't forget your camera. You might get a picture of Dylan."

On foot, we followed the parade of jeans-clad, long-haired people ahead of us, road scorching my sandals, sun searing my red polka-dot kerchief. I glanced at Kit, who'd wisely put on his leather hat. His tunic, which I'd sewn from a floral cotton remnant I'd found at Itasca Dry Goods Store, was probably as cool as anything he might have worn, and the holes in his jeans provided some ventilation. But his lace-up boots, which protected his foot, had to be warm at best.

We hiked for perhaps ten miles, passing a mosaic of cars, trucks, vans, psychedelically painted school buses, motorcycles, tents, teepees, farmhouses, and barns before the angle of the plodding throng said we were near our destination. I felt hungry, thirsty, ready for a nap, almost ready for a U-turn. And worried about Kit's foot. But his good humor and steady pace told me he was either not in pain or not about to admit it.

We stepped over a trampled chain-link fence as we neared the top of a rise. "This crowd could fill our whole town," I said, trying to hook onto his mood.

He took my hand as we crested the ridge, where we stopped to look down at the cow pasture chosen for the festival. Basically a big bowl of knee-high grass, it was filled with enough souls to populate the Twin Cities.

"Wow," Kit said.

I nodded, stunned. The Woodstock gathering sprawled literally out of sight. And in the glare of the sun, it sported more moving colors than a kaleidoscope. At that distance, it looked like a great jungle of rainbow-hued vegetation.

"Oh my god. What should we do, Kit?"

Leaning on his left leg and repositioning his hat, now sopped at the brow, Kit surveyed the scene, far left to far right. "No one's taking tickets. I suggest we just plunge in and aim for the left side of the stage. That's where Oscar's going to meet us." He patted his pocket. "He sent a picture."

There was indeed a stage at the bottom of the bowl, white tarp stretched and waving in the breeze above it. Two sky-high yellow speaker towers stood on one side of it, three on the other. It looked another ten miles away.

Kit headed into the expanse of bodies, giving my hand a tug. He was limping, something he didn't do if he could help it. I stayed put.

"I can't."

He stopped, looked back, face bright with anticipation. I glanced at our immediate neighbors. They were all smiling. No doubt about it, the air was fairly electric, as if half a million good moods had plugged into each other. "What do you mean, baby?"

I swallowed. "I mean I can't possibly go through there." I was already feeling dizzy, my breaths matching the speed of my heartbeats. Though the sky was clearly visible, bonny as a field of cornflowers, clouds casting only the softest of shadows, I couldn't distinguish a single perching place in that forest of humanity below.

I inhaled deeply, trying to rein in panic, but the smell of manure, marijuana, cigarette smoke, sweat, incense, and patchouli had taken up weapons and turned on my stomach. I leaned over, palms to thighs, fending off vomit with gasps. "All those people so close together. I can't . . . I won't make it, Kit."

His response was instant. He dropped the basket to the ground, set me atop it, pushed my head between my knees. I hated being a wimp, on this trip meant to mend what was so torn, but my tears had a mind of their own and fell faster than I could wipe them away. At the gates of carefree merriment—not a roommate or chore for fifteen hundred miles—I fell to pieces.

Kit sank to his knees, brandy flask and hanky in hand. "Take a good swig," he said and I did.

"Take another." He pulled a joint from his Camel pack, lit it with his Zippo, handed it to me. "Now take two hits of this. And don't fake it, Joey."

He swabbed my face as I complied, coughing and sputtering. Suddenly a bird swooped down from the sky and flew across the stage, just inches above the people swarmed in front of it. People, not trees.

"We'll stay along the perimeter as long as possible, then head in at the shortest angle." Kit pulled me to my feet, brushed the sweat from my upper lip, and hoisted the picnic basket. "Ready, little girl?"

My first step was shaky, my second a bit surer. "I guess so."

We didn't make it all the way to the stage. But Kit, sharing his joint with strangers along our route, found a gap in the throng big enough for our sleeping bag, about thirty feet back and to the left. I kept my eyes on the ground during the journey, counting my breaths to stay calm, trying not to step on anyone.

Kit unrolled the sleeping bag in our patch of grass, set the picnic basket in front of it like a table. Half stoned and totally exhausted, I sighed as I lowered myself to firm ground. In the moment before oblivion, I noted that my shirt was soaked from neck to hem and my bluebirds were now red.

☙

The roar of the crowd and the flapping wings of a giant bird were what woke me. The bird turned into a helicopter when I blinked. Groggy, sticky, parched, I sat up to see a brown-skinned man—tall, bearded, garbed in pajamas and robe—dash onto the stage, acoustic guitar in hand. Strumming with a frenzy even before he sat on his stool, he had a pleasantly raspy singing voice. I glanced at Kit, whose heavy eyelids said he'd had more to drink or smoke in the hours or minutes I'd been napping. He handed me a half-empty wine bottle.

"Take a sip and pass this on to Coco and Roxy."

He nodded to two girls sitting on my left. The one with waist-length red hair flashed me the peace sign. The one with stars painted on her face tossed me an orange section. "Welcome back to our music meadow," she said in a thick southern accent. "Don't you just dig it?"

I popped the fruit into my mouth and bit down. Tangy and warm, the juice slid over my tongue and down my throat, its scent joining all the others around me.

She handed me the rest of the orange. "Take what you need and give the rest to Hank and Jerome and your old man."

Coco and Roxy, I soon learned, had driven a VW bug all the way from Little Rock—where they owned a secondhand clothing boutique with a head shop in the back—just to hear Jimi Hendrix play "Purple Haze."

And Hank and Jerome, to my right, were twin brothers from Maine. They'd climbed out their bedroom window a few nights back, having been locked in by a father who didn't think prep-school boys had any business at a hippie orgy masquerading as an outdoor concert.

It was almost sunset when Richie Havens left the stage—pouring sweat and clearly sung out—after a song consisting of frenetic strumming and the word *freedom* cried over and over. The intensity of his effort had left the air feeling explosive.

By then I'd met Babs, Bennie, and Dwight—NYU students just behind us who'd hitchhiked from the city without tickets, money, or food. And I'd learned that the New York State Thruway had been closed because of the hordes trying to reach our field, which was owned by a dairy farmer named Max Yasgur.

I stretched my legs as far as they'd go without hitting someone's backside, Max's grass stroking my ankles, and wondered if marijuana or group spirit had caused my high. Struggling to stay grounded, I studied the sprawl before me, spotting a German shepherd, a horse, a clown, two nude toddlers, and three nuns in full habit. A fellow on one side of the stage, looking official and self-conscious at the same time, wore a T-shirt with the words PLEASE FORCE on it. A fellow on the opposite side wore a toga fashioned from a faded American flag and a hank of rope. To make them all real, I slipped my camera from the picnic basket and took their pictures.

Somewhere in the sense-swamping dusk of my nineteenth birthday, I found myself musing that shared enthusiasm had created a city, if only for a single summer day, that belonged to anyone brave enough to sit this close together. I kept shooting whatever caught my eye, trying to capture, for later proof, the immensity of this particular happening, feeling free but rather lost, like a motherless child far from home.

The nearing of night brought a breeze that raised goosebumps on my sun-cooked skin. By then, Country Joe McDonald was onstage raising a raunchy cheer that led to a rollicking antiwar rag, and expressed the crowd's opinion of Vietnam. "Give me an F," he shouted. "Give me a U . . ."

Kit wrapped his jacket over my shoulders when I started to shiver, and I should have thanked him but didn't. When he loosened the laces of his boots, I pretended not to notice, hating the war for what it had done to him. And to us. And to me. The goddamn war. For a few minutes, Joe McDonald let us just sing it away.

The cicadas took up for the guitars after Country Joe left the stage. In the buzzing, rambling calm between performers, I realized I'd eaten only an orange section and the tail end of someone's candy bar since Kit and I'd lunched on cheese sandwiches and ginger snaps in Rosie. Planning to camp in the comfort of the bus each night of the festival, we'd left behind our cooler, Sterno stove, and most of our food. But, along with my camera, I'd stashed two sandwiches, two apples, the remaining cookies, a thermos of Kool-Aid, a bottle of wine, and cigarettes in our basket. During a break between songs, I turned to Kit.

"Sandwich? There's peanut butter and jelly or jelly and peanut butter."

He gave me an odd look. "The food concessions ran out a while back."

I shrugged. "Too far to walk for a hotdog anyway."

"A mother and two kids passed by when you were asleep. And other people looking for food, something to drink. It was so hot."

A moment passed before I grasped what he was saying. "What's left?"

He lifted the basket lid, flicked his Zippo, peered inside. He held up the remains of our feast, one ginger snap and half an apple. "My jackknife was clean," he said. If a look could be defiant and sheepish at the same time, his was.

Going back to Rosie for more food, or anything else, was out of the question. We'd lose our precious place in Mr. Yasgur's field. And more important, though I'd never say so, I didn't think Kit's foot could weather the hike.

I took a bite of the apple, one of the cookie, and handed the rest back. Resigned for at least three days to Kit's ways, I said, "Pass it on."

The night grew darker, damper, cooler, and the mood of the crowd grew higher, as the helicopters kept whirring and the drums kept pounding and the music kept rolling and the crowd kept cheering, clapping, dancing, stomping. In the spirit of sharing that permeated the pungent air, the crowd passed wine, beer, joints, hash pipes, and LSD tabs along with whatever food they'd brought. One swig, toke, tab, bite. No one took more, and everyone said thanks.

Kit rarely skipped his share except for the acid, having lost a Nam buddy to an orange-sunshine hallucination during incoming. Me, I took nothing but a sip of wine whenever my thirst became greater than my fear of what it might be laced with. But between the smoke fumes and mass euphoria, sobriety was impossible in that packed pasture.

Somewhere in the starless evening, the MC suggested we all light matches. I'd stuck a box of blue tips in my pocket, and passed them out to every upturned hand within reach. On countdown, we lifted our lit matches, and for a few moments, the night simply vanished. I glanced at Kit. Under that matchlight sun, his smile looked like a brand-new day. And I knew, in that moment, that no matter what happened between us, he would always glow brighter than anyone else.

The rain began when Ravi Shankar was onstage. The whine of his sitar snaked through the falling water and into the dark undeterred. Ravi remained onstage, and we remained on the grass, letting the sky wash the dust and heat from our bodies.

The rain brought cold, wind, and cow-dung mud as it grew from a drizzle to a downpour. Before long, wet had soaked our clothes and our sleeping bag, turned the air as fetid as a neglected barn. Kit and I made a tent from his jacket and the plastic tablecloth I'd tucked in our basket with a picnic for two in mind. My teeth were chattering by then, but the wine, music, and fumes kept flowing, and somehow, I felt just fine.

Arlo Guthrie ended his set with a jazzy, wailing version of "Amazing Grace," which seemed the perfect song to precede Joan Baez, who came onstage deep in the night—stately, pregnant, angelic of voice. Her husband was behind bars for refusing to go to war, and she sang a Dylan song about shining light and imminent release. By now the hillside behind us was dotted with small campfires, lit to shoo away the darkness and the chill, looking like flickering stars we could walk up to and warm our hands over, if we had the inclination to leave the cocoon of semi-familiar bodies around us.

Joan closed the night with "We Shall Overcome," and arms linked, bodies swaying, we all sang of freedom and peace. I blinked back tears. In a flash as bright as a field of matches, I suddenly understood what

Kit was trying to create in the woods of northern Minnesota, in his shabby house with room for all, in his eclectic collection of souls in need.

Despite Kit's Zippo and my matches, we had nothing to burn for our own campfire except the picnic basket, the only dry place for cigarettes, camera, and film. Our solution to the cold was a neighborly huddle, the nine of us scooting even closer together, a plastic garbage bag, my tablecloth, three jackets, and a poncho forming a roof above us. In that pileup that could have felt claustrophobic, we all finally fell asleep, my head on Kit's shoulder, Roxy's head on mine, and someone's feet in my lap.

ॐ

"I need a bathroom," I said through gritted teeth.

My shake didn't ease Kit gently into the day. Groaning, he opened his eyes, becoming aware of his own physical reality.

"Right." He brushed the hair from his eyes and looked around. "Supposed to be facilities somewhere."

Our tribe of nine—created by chance, mutual need, music, and mud—had woken before Saturday's dawn to find gaps in the crowd. Together, we'd slid our sopping bodies and belongings to close-up range of the stage and settled back into unconsciousness.

The morning now greeted us from behind a soggy curtain. Steam rose from our mud-sunken huddle like fog from a marsh, blending with the gray drizzle at some invisible place. We'd literally become part of the environment.

But my body insisted I was still a separate entity. I couldn't swallow for the moss on my tongue, my head pounded like Ravi Shankar's drummer, and I had to pee so badly my ears throbbed. Avoiding a trip through the throng, I'd ignored my bladder for too long.

Of all the smells at Woodstock, the portable toilets were the smelliest. It wasn't hard to find them.

On our zigzag route toward the stench and relief, my focus on not wetting my pants or crushing someone's bones probably saved me from another panic attack. Though I stepped on more than a few arms and legs, for every "Excuse me," I received a smile, peace sign, or "It's cool."

Like most things at Woodstock except music, good vibes, and rain, there weren't enough toilets to go around. I crossed my legs one way, then the other as the line inched forward. Kit offered to find me a private spot in the woods. Trees again. I declined. I'd brought my camera and kept clicking as a diversion from my misery, using it as a buffer between myself and the encircling mass. Almost as much as Kit's presence, my rangefinder made me feel safe at Woodstock.

Naturally there was no toilet paper. Hovering above the rank black hole, I considered using my kerchief, but between the slime underfoot and the smell below, a wet spot in my underwear suddenly seemed laughable. Grateful for yesterday's dearth of food, I swore off edibles for the duration.

Back on our squishy sleeping bag, I was feeling almost alive when an announcer in a mangled cowboy hat greeted us.

"What we have in mind is breakfast in bed for four hundred thousand." The surge of group energy that followed his words was palpable, and he quickly dialed down the mood. "Now, it's not gonna be steak and eggs or anything, but it's gonna be good food, and we're gonna get it to ya."

The organizers of the festival—now declared a free event—had opened kitchens with volunteer workers who were attempting to feed us. For the third time in hours, tears filled my eyes. Stuck in the mud far from home, we weren't on our own. Kit touched my hand, unwashed since the day before yesterday, and said, "Whatever it is, try to eat a little. No telling when anything else will pass our way." I just nodded, his tenderness adding confusion to my crazy mix of emotions and discomforts.

Flashing a toothless grin, the announcer—called Wavy Gravy for a reason I never learned—summed up the situation of day two at Woodstock. "We're all feeding each other," he said. "We must be in heaven, man. There is always a little bit of heaven in a disaster area."

When we received our Dixie cup of what looked like toasted raw oats, I took Kit's advice despite my dread of toilet row. The food was crunchy, tasty, filling.

The morning grew warmer as the sun rose, and wine and pot began to flow. Helicopters came and went, the whack-whack of their rotors both intrusive and reassuring. Because of jammed roads, performers and supplies could only reach our field by air. "God, I hate that sound," Kit said. "When the birds come in, it usually means you're in trouble."

My unhealed heart withheld the sympathy I might have offered him about helicopters.

Woodstock's MCs tried hard to make light of our predicament and prevent us from feeling uptight or freaked out. One named Chip Monck had a voice like cool water when the day was hot, like sunrays when it was cold. The announcers became our news anchors and camp counselors, kept us informed about anything that mattered in our field, urging calm in the face of physical hardships—both natural and manmade. Keep cool, stay groovy, be patient, share what you have, feed each other, watch out for the brown acid, we were told. Don't climb on the speaker towers. Don't step on the water lines. Pick up your medicine at the medical tent. Call your mother. We can get through this. We're in this together. We're now the third largest city in the state of New York. We have something to prove to the world. And don't take the brown acid.

A one-page newspaper began circulating, printed by Abbie Hoffman of Chicago Eight fame, according to rumor. Headlined by the word SURVIVE printed six times, the little rag chimed in with specifics on primal survival: Food is being airlifted in. Don't be piggish. Don't drink the water it if it isn't clear. Bag your trash or burn it. There are two medical stations, a freakout tent, and doctors on the way. Avoid strong drugs and sunburn. We took those printed words to heart. Though Woodstock was a giant party, it was also a kind of war zone, where one person's actions affected many. Maybe it was the pot that let Kit admit, "This reminds me of Hill 881 South, minus the mortars and blood."

The mercurial sun was straight above us when the music began that day. A Latin lightning bolt called Santana blazed the stage with a ten-minute instrumental, drum solo and stringwork so hot they exploded. Our tribe fell on each other laughing.

"What just happened?" I asked.

"Aural orgasm," Kit said, trying to pull me close but not succeeding.

The sky split open sometime that afternoon, wind so high the speaker towers swayed like plastic toys. Coco, Roxy, Hank, Jerome, Babs, Bennie, Dwight, Kit, and I again formed a body hut and stayed put, choosing proximity to the stage over comfort. Some Woodstockers surrendered to the gods, running naked through the rain and making mud slides. Others headed for the trees at the field's perimeter or for their tents in the camping area. But the nine of us implicitly agreed that our view was worth whatever Mother Nature made us pay for it, that this was a once-in-a-lifetime show.

Friday had been the day for folkies and acoustic players. Saturday was totally electric, and the plugged-in heavy hitters took their turn at home plate as daylight faded. Pot smoke rose, rain and dark fell, as the performers began to swirl around each other. I lost track of the time, the band, the song. But I kept clicking my shutter button, and individual impressions became as set in my head as on my camera's film.

Peacock bold in his bright blue shirt, John Fogerty sang as if his vocal chords and his soul lived in a bottomless bayou. Barefoot, beaded, and bangled, Janis Joplin sang like a keening banshee who'd known more misery than anyone else for all of history. Sly & the Family Stone got everyone clapping and stomping so hard, the vibrations hijacked my heartbeat and rattled my skull. When Pete Townshend bashed his guitar to a howling death, it seemed a perfectly appropriate focus of collective energy. I froze each experience with just one finger.

Kit decided to defy the weather when the cold returned, stuffing his pockets with cigs and camera gear before smashing our picnic basket to smithereens, which he then lit with his Zippo. Most everyone had abandoned their shoes and sandals hours back due to the mud—ankle deep in places—and we merrily tossed them into the flickering coals when the picnic basket was gone. And when our shoes were gone, Kit did the thing his long swig from a passing wine bottle warned me he might do. His boots and socks kept us almost warm until almost dawn.

Somewhere deep into the night or early into the morning, depending on one's perspective in those primeval hours between sunset and dawn, Kit and I settled into a horizontal position. Babs and Bennie had been a couple before the festival, and by now Jerome and Coco had found enough in common to form an obvious physical bond. Neither couple had been acting very shy in the company of others. Kit and I, however, hadn't had sex since the arrival of the infamous letter from California. In the darkness of our huddle and soggy depths of our sleeping bag, his mouth tight against my ear, Kit tried to change that.

"Don't be cruel, little girl."

"Forget it, Elvis."

"But it's been so long, Joey. You're killing me."

"I'm pretty sure lack of coitus isn't fatal."

"But everyone's stoned and no one will care, or even notice."

"I don't care if they don't care when they notice, which they will. I don't want to."

"But Joey, you feel so warm and I feel so cold."

"It's just an illusion."

"Can I at least take your hand in mine?"

He'd already done that and was pulling it persistently toward the waistband of his jeans.

"Absolutely not. Go to sleep."

And that's what we did as daybreak slowly burned away yesterday.

Sometime later, I returned to consciousness long enough to hear Grace Slick tell everyone, "It's a new dawn." In her white ensemble, she looked like the queen of light, and I managed to click the image onto film before drifting off into that half-here, half-there place as Jefferson Airplane became airborne.

🕊

Same as Saturday, Sunday met us garbed in gray mist, and we woke with very basic desires. I had to pee again. Kit wanted other relief.

"I need you, baby. Real bad."

"Wrong time, wrong place," I said, shrugging off his forlorn face and bedraggled demeanor.

Clear as a cloudless day, his eyes latched onto mine. "The here and now is all we really have, little girl. Trust me, this world can be gone in a flash."

I couldn't help my smirk. "Now there's a hip rationale for sex."

"Maybe so, but I'm weary of being pushed away. It's been months, Joey, and it feels like I'm in another unwinnable war."

I shook my head, matching his unwavering stare.

He pulled Rosie's keys from his pocket and placed them in my hand. "If there's no hope for us then, I'll just head out and hitch my way home."

He didn't sound angry, just defeated.

"So you'd abandon me again in the middle of bedlam?"

He sighed. "As always, our perspectives differ. I regret that. I really do." He tipped his brow, the way he had the night we met. "Take a picture of Dylan if he shows."

And then he was walking away, shoeless, hat hanging from one hand.

Our perspectives differed, but I knew intuitively I'd never see him again if I let him leave that field. That our relationship would be forever severed. It was a future I couldn't imagine.

"But where can we go?" I yelled through the throng.

He stopped, turned around.

"If you want privacy, there's only one place."

And so we made love in a shadowy thicket of trees, where the sky was beyond sight and the birds couldn't see in. Where pine needles, fallen leaves, and damp grass were our bed. Where his exhale became my inhale. Where I realized I couldn't live without him and couldn't not love him.

As we floated back into that shady copse, Kit lit a cigarette and handed it to me. "I'm sorry about Pasadena Playhouse, Joey."

I took a drag and handed it back. "There are other acting schools, Kit."

"Pick one and I'll drive us there."

When we emerged from the trees, a big olive-green helicopter was hovering above, dropping items from its belly. Confusion, even fear, swept over Kit's face. He looked ready to hit the ground, and I pulled him close, wishing I could zap the flapping contraption. But the big bird wasn't dropping anything Kit was used to seeing fall from the sky. Clothes, oranges, flowers descended upon us. The National Guard, we learned, was dispensing daisies. It occurred to me just then that Woodstock had actually altered my life.

209

We took the long way back to our seat, trusting our tribe to hold our place and our share of communal food. We wandered Hippie Lane and Drug Alley, where beads, tie-dyed clothing, scarves, leather goods, and drugs were on display. Kit bought me a new white shirt and a strand of red seed beads, with soggy bills.

We eventually came upon a pond, where people were bathing, some nude, some not. It looked cleaner than mud.

"How about a wash-up?" Kit said.

"I dare step in there if you do."

The murky water somehow grew clear as dew on a mountaintop as we bathed, I in my underwear, Kit in the buff, and I felt like a soul who'd been baptized and reborn.

Maybe it was a Celtic rain dance Joe Cocker did as he got the crowd moving to his quirky gyrations, because another rainstorm fell. Hard wind, hard rain, and more rain blew again that Sunday. But we now had the routine down, remembered it in any state of consciousness. Up went the jackets, tablecloth, garbage bag, poncho. Up went the chant across the Woodstock nation. "No rain. No rain. No rain. No rain."

But our efforts to control the elements and keep wet from getting wetter were in vain. We grew roots in the mud, became one with the spilling waters.

All through the night the music gods defied the sky gods, lighting the dark like electrified moonlight. Camera now a part of me, I aimed for the brightest of the bright spots, always clicking to the downbeat, careful to wipe my lens with the kerchief I kept in my pocket, tucking the camera under my new shirt during lapses in the music or my energy.

Among the jubilee of joys I felt that night was the knowledge that Jimi was yet to come. And maybe even Dylan. After all, in that pastoral place of meadows and cows, the greatest music god was simply a neighbor. I said a little prayer, that third night of Woodstock, that he might hear the music, see the light, and lead us to that magical jingling morning we still believed in.

It was another soaked, shivery night, but cold and wet no longer felt like an enemy we could outsmart. We either accepted it or walked up the hill, down the road, and away from a spiritual warmth we knew we might never find again.

I slept with Kit's feet in my lap, trying to warm them and soothe the one I knew was hurting no matter how many swigs or tokes he accepted. My own feet rested on Dwight's shins, my head on Roxy's thigh. I let slumber and music, leading inexorably toward dawn, twine together in a long plait of colored strands. Which band followed which? What song came before the one that was still playing in my head two songs after the one I'd never forget? It was impossible to tell, and there was no reason to try. The night went on and on, until it slipped in the mud and fell over the horizon.

We'd waited three days and nights to hear Jimi Hendrix perform miracles with six metal strings, ten fingers, a whammy bar, and a wah-wah pedal. And possibly with his teeth if we were lucky. Though Dylan was the wild hope, Jimi was the lunar pull that had kept Kit and me rooted to our seats in the middle of a declared disaster zone. He was the greatest guitar player of them all.

I experienced much of his set in a dream state, finally waking to a song I hadn't heard on his records. He didn't need to sing the lyrics.

Oh say, can you see, by the dawn's early light . . .

I sat up in the gray mist of that chill morning and looked at the stage.

He was resplendent in red hair sash, funky jewelry, and white leather. Between his opening notes, he held up the peace sign like a beckoning torch, and I snapped the image. He was all the sunshine we needed.

I closed my eyes to listen. *What so proudly we hailed at the twilight's last gleaming . . .* A rousing song for people who believed in hard work, honesty, and goodwill. *Whose broad stripes and bright stars . . .* But the familiar melody seemed to grow sad as Jimi stretched and bent it for the huddled mass before him, so sad it seemed to weep. *Were so gallantly streaming . . .* Then a strange thing happened as we sat waiting for him to lift our hearts to electric heights. *And the rockets' red glare . . .* The melody turned into the sounds of war. Bombs soared down, crashing to the ground. Then chaos. *The bombs bursting in air . . .* Buildings exploded. Glass and debris flew. People ran, children screamed, animals shrieked, mothers wailed, sirens howled, bullets pounded. With his magic guitar, Jimi created what most of us had never experienced. As we sat frozen

211

by shock, our national anthem became our country's journey through years of war. Jet planes, chopper blades, machinegun fire, more bombs—we heard them all. Looking pensive, fingers straining, body crouched, Jimi revealed the reality, the horror of Nam. *Gave proof through the night that our flag was still there* . . . The melody returned, then a bit of "Taps." *Day is done, gone the sun* . . . We knew who that was for. *Oh say, does that star-spangled banner yet wave* . . . Still more bombs, screams, sirens. *O'er the land of the free* . . . That seemed the saddest word Jimi didn't sing . . . *And the home of the brave* . . . Then, having said his piece, he slid like gray morning mist into "Purple Haze."

I sat unmoving for a moment, riveted by emotion. Then I looked at Kit, who'd awakened when I had. Cross-legged on the remains of our bed, he was sobbing into his hat, face hidden by warped leather and muddy hair. When I touched his shoulder, he turned away. And I knew I'd just witnessed a bit of what he could never share in words.

Most of the Woodstock Nation missed Jimi's performance. It was Monday morning, after all, and the world couldn't stop forever for music and peace. When I finally pulled my eyes from the stage, I was surprised at how few haggard stragglers remained of the proud nation that had once graced Max's meadow. But Kit and I were among them. We'd gone the distance at Woodstock. Together.

And what that nation left behind was almost as astonishing as what it had brought together. Acres and acres of trash—sleeping bags, blankets, clothing, plastic bags—sunk deep in the mud as far as the eye could see. How poor Max's cows would ever make a home here again, I couldn't begin to imagine. Kit, however, could.

"Have a good life" were the announcer's last words to the attendees of Woodstock. But before he closed the event, he asked for volunteers to help clean up. And nothing I said could change Kit's mind about being one of them.

"But you have no shoes," I pleaded.

"Shoes would only get stuck in the mud. Barefoot is better."

"But Kit . . ."

"This isn't how we found it, Joey. It's not right to leave it this way."

212

So barefoot and muddy we remained for another day as we dragged garbage across the acres of dead alfalfa. And maybe it was the "fourth" day of Woodstock that really epitomized the meaning of what we'd experienced, that let me see the world through Kit's camera lens and understand the magnificence of his dream, the selflessness of his heart, the reason I sometimes felt lost in the crowd around him. After that grimiest day, I somehow loved Kit more for not loving me to the exclusion of all others. I'd come to believe that his calling had great merit, that his Elsewhere offered as much promise as mine.

Bob Dylan never showed up at Woodstock, and we never found Kit's friend Oscar, who'd mailed us the tickets we never had to use.

When we finally reached Rosie, Kit didn't dither.

"I can't push the gas pedal."

Kit didn't own a second pair of boots, but I'd brought my other sandals. And I'd driven Rosie across much of the upper Midwest already, so getting us home was relatively easy.

We spent our first night after Woodstock in a small roadside motel, where we each took a shower before sharing a bath. Even then, I could see mud under my toenails. And even then, it made me smile.

Though we discussed the music and events of the festival all the way to Minnesota, Kit never asked me what I thought of our little vacation, and I never asked him. It went without saying we'd just shared the four best days of our lives.

— TWENTY-SIX —

Soldier Boy

The whole Tribe was tending the garden the afternoon I returned from researching drama schools and college theatre departments at the public library. Woodstock had revived both my relationship with Kit and my sense of possibility—which included a long bath when I found the bathroom door miraculously unlocked.

But Kit had beat me to it. He was perched on the rim of the tub, pant legs rolled high, right foot in water so steamy the new glass window had fogged. The stricken look on his face punctured my good mood.

"What's up?" I said, pretending nonchalance.

"Not much." He looked away from me. "Foot's a little sore, that's all."

I closed the door behind me, took a step, looked down. The swelling and the gash didn't alarm me as much as the colors. Red, green, a hint of black.

"I'm calling Doc Wexroth. He needs to look at that."

Kit swung his left foot into the tub, swished the water.

"He already has."

I blinked. Kit didn't like doctors much better than he did cops.

"And?" I didn't mean to stare, but at that point I felt his right foot belonged to both of us.

"He wants me to see some specialist at the VA hospital in Minneapolis."

I stepped back, grabbed the doorknob. "What's his name? I'm calling right now."

Kit gave the hot water faucet a crank, further steaming the room. "Appointment's tomorrow. Wanna take Rosie for another spin?"

I released the doorknob, truly frightened.

"I'll get the keys. We can be there before dark."

The mirror was also fogged, but I could see acres of cow mud and rotting garbage, miles of road not meant for bare feet, when I looked into it.

"Maybe we shouldn't have gone to . . ."

Kit stepped gingerly out of the water, a hard look on his face.

"That's *not* what did this, Joey."

୫

Kit somehow talked the specialist out of hospitalizing him. Gangrene was the sly invader the doctor was on the lookout for, and his compromise was a daily office visit. For two weeks, we rented a motel room on University Avenue near Dinkytown, the artsy village by the campus where students and young folks hung out. We missed IJC class registration in those weeks.

The doctor had forbidden any activity involving walking, and during our long breakfasts at a nearby diner, I began circling for-rent apartments in the *Minneapolis Tribune* want ads. One crisp September morning when the sky held just a memory of summer's azure, I laid my handiwork next to Kit's coffee cup.

"My parents won't like it," he said. Kit always frowned when he spoke of his parents.

"Minneapolis is a pretty big place. Your parents don't have to know." My tone shut out debate. The VA doctor had ordered Kit back on crutches, and Kit had been complying. But I knew the Homestead's outdoor distractions and male influence would change that. Kit felt his crutches conveyed weakness.

I held firm. "The Tribe can forward their letters."

Kit thumbed through the newspaper, set the sports section atop the want ads. "My parents rarely include a letter." Evasion was his favorite tactic when he didn't like the subject.

"The Tribe can forward their envelopes, then."

Kit's laugh was bitter, full of contempt. "Let's call them what they are. Monthly bribes to keep me at a respectable distance."

I stood my ground. "Forward whatever you want to call them."

I expected another diversion but it didn't come.

"I suppose we could rent a furnished efficiency by the week and go home on weekends." His quick, if reluctant, surrender said I was right to press the issue. Kit was worried about his foot. Which meant his doctor was worried.

"Home on weekends." I was willing to yield on the details.

The furnished efficiency lasted only a few weeks, which didn't include a trip to the Homestead. By then even Kit, who hadn't been fazed by Woodstock's crowd, and who'd endured seventy-seven days crammed onto Hill 881 South, began pacing our tight quarters.

Buzzy and Doc had driven down to visit their chieftain, crashing for three nights on our floor, playing five-card stud, drinking beer, and sharing Homestead gossip for three days at our small table. "Prissy spoilsport," Doc had called me when I'd banished his black bag from the place. But Kit had replied, "Not cool, man. Do as she says and apologize." Now it was Kit who circled want ads.

"We'll get something month to month, no lease," he said, still denying the wisdom of living near his foot doctor.

Kit ultimately rented a rambling, two-story former frat house on Fourth Street in Dinkytown, affordable only because it had seen far better days.

"Why on earth do we need such a monstrosity?" I asked.

"Handy to have a guest room," Kit said.

"But it's got *four*, and as many bathrooms."

"Now when your brothers visit, they can each have a room. And we'll still have our privacy. The main bedroom downstairs has its own wing."

The Fourth Street house didn't come with furniture, or even appliances. We acquired those at a used-furniture store and a going-out-of-business flophouse.

Though we were late in transferring, we were allowed to enroll at the U because of good grades and Kit's situation. But because we were late and Kit was still on crutches, we agreed to make it a light term. Kit registered for Political Science, I for Theatre History.

By mid-October, most of the Tribe, flush with the profits of the Homestead's harvest, had journeyed to Minneapolis for a visit, and

Buzzy—who wasn't an IJC student—and Doc—who claimed a break from premed would help his grades—hadn't left. Doc, of course, had brought Tink.

And by mid-October, though we had plenty of room, Woodstock's spirit of togetherness was starting to lose its luster. "What the hell, Kit. Are those two users hitched to you by an invisible rope?"

A look of bewilderment crossed his face.

"Consider them my family, Joey. I wasn't blessed with siblings like you, but Buzzy's a Nam brother I owe a big debt to. And Doc depends on my help right now, same as your brothers depend on yours."

He had me there. If Kit's right foot was also mine, I owed Buzzy as much as he did. And Kit had always welcomed my family.

And so, with old baggage, new worries, but a sense of excitement about the future, I was finally Elsewhere by a few hundred miles, determined to succeed at the U's well-regarded theatre department, and as Kit's recommitted partner. Our new place was soon called the Hotel.

Living in Dinkytown made Kit's antiwar mission both easier and harder. There was now an abundance of places he could speak his mind about Vietnam. The campus had Coffman Memorial Union—the big student hall—and other gathering spots. And clustered around the hub of Fourteenth Avenue and Fourth Street were coffee houses, pizza shops, cafés, restaurants, a bookstore, and an ice cream parlor. But the quantity and nearness of venues kept Kit on his feet more nights than not, and nothing I said made a difference.

"*Please* give your foot a rest tonight," I would beg.

"The doctor said to use my crutches and avoid pressure, and I'm doing that," he would counter. "If I can prevent one person from becoming a Nam gimp, it'll be worth my small effort. I can't do nothing, Joey."

It didn't take Kit to tell me the antiwar movement was growing. I could feel a new intensity in the chatter on campus, stories in the newspaper, and reports on the television, which was always on and blaring at six o'clock. More and more brave rebels like him were pointing an angry finger at the war.

The first major protest against President Nixon's handling of the war—The Moratorium to End the War in Vietnam—was held in the country's major cities in October, and Kit wouldn't have missed the Student Mobilization Committee gathering at Northrop Auditorium if I'd handcuffed him to the Hotel's scarred-but-sturdy mahogany banister.

Peace Now was the event's theme, and Kit cut class to attend, urging me to join him. But knowing how the Elizabethan political scene influenced Shakespeare's plots and dialogue, for a coming exam, was my personal mission, though I admired Kit's. He returned home weary and limping, having forgone crutches, but as exuberant as I'd seen him since Woodstock.

"We can do it, Joey. I believe we can end this insane war if enough of us dare stand up to the liars and hypocrites in our government."

Nothing was as magnetic as Kit in high spirits, nothing as heartening as his unique brand of joie de vivre. I wanted him to always be this happy and hopeful, and pushed aside the old gnawing jealousy that it wasn't me who'd caused his good mood. I embraced Kit's aspiration so he would do likewise.

"Was there a good turnout?" I said.

"A strong turnout." He sagged to the bed, pulled his right leg onto the mattress. "A meaningful turnout and inspiring speeches, most of them."

"Speeches." Of course there'd been speeches. "Was one of them yours?"

Kit peeled off his socks and began rubbing salve on his right foot, his back to me.

"Yup. Not sure how inspiring it was, though. Just one grunt trying to talk common sense and spread the idea of common humanity."

He hadn't mentioned his speech beforehand, of course. And though I'd heard many versions since its Easter debut, I felt a wave of regret. By pursuing my own goals, I'd missed seeing him shine, be part of something important to him.

"That's great. Wish I could have been there."

"Me too, baby. It was an uplifting day."

He was clearly hiding his foot, and I couldn't resist a bit of nagging. "I hope you were careful, Kit. All those people. No one stepped on it, did they?"

"No, little girl. Not a soul rammed this leaky old boat."

Like a willful child or a selfish mate, Kit's foot had entirely its own agenda. It was healing at a frustrating pace, and I felt a cold stab whenever I caught a peek of it, especially the day Kit plucked a jagged black object from an oozing red sore. "Just a little NVA souvenir," he said, handing me back my tweezers.

November blew in grim and gray, as it usually did, and Kit's doctor still wouldn't let Kit go. We were eating pizza at Vescio's—delightfully without company—the night Kit shared his doctor's recent opinion.

"He thinks I should undergo a skin graft."

Kit was the only person I knew who ate pizza with a knife and fork. "You mean surgery?"

"Yes."

"As in hospital?"

He didn't bother to look up from his plate.

"That's where, Joey."

For me, surgery would always mean slashing blades, pulsing scars, midnight moans, and men in white coats. Surgery meant the mutilation of someone you loved and their departure from your life. It was that old horror flick, and I was too stunned for tears.

"Is surgery the only option?" I wanted to run out of the restaurant and scream at the heavens. Not again.

Kit was reaching for another slice of pizza. "No. The infection's pretty much under control, and the foot is relatively stable. For now anyway."

I rubbed my thumbs over my eyes, heedless of smeared mascara, hating how Kit talked about his foot as if it didn't belong to him. I opened my mouth, wanting to say the right thing at this wrong moment, but nothing came out.

He picked up his fork. "I think I might go through with it."

I pushed my plate away. "When?"

"No sense waiting." He shrugged in that noncommittal way of his.

"What about school?"

Another goddamn shrug.

"I withdrew today. I'll re-up next term."

This discussion was clearly just a formality. I choked back resentment. What happened to Kit's foot affected my life almost as much as his.

"What about your parents? I thought staying in school was part of the bargain."

Kit gave me a wry look. "You've convinced me that what they don't know won't hurt them. Or me."

I'd shot myself in the foot on that argument, so to speak.

"Where will they place the skin graft?" I wanted to know, and yet I didn't.

"Where the flimsy skin is."

"Right over the top?" I was ignorant about this brand-new topic.

"They'll take the flimsy skin off first. It's called debridement."

I stared at him, now out of words, trying to push bloody images from my mind. But he must have seen the question in my eyes. He set down his fork.

"It's so hard to concentrate sometimes, Joey. And I have things I need to focus on."

That was the answer I was afraid of, which I'd known even without his roundabout admission. Kit was hoping the surgeon's knife would remove his pain.

୪ଟ

Kit had omitted a few details when he'd explained his skin graft procedure. But even a life-sized full-color illustration wouldn't have prepared me for the moment when a nurse with a clipboard and a starchy manner finally let me into his hospital room.

He hadn't mentioned the splints—made of white plaster and wrapping each leg nearly to his groin, held in place by wooden struts, only the stitched red flesh of the graft site exposed.

Nor had he enlightened me about the graft itself—a large flap of skin cut from his left calf and sewed onto the top of his right foot, but still attached to its source by way of a bent knee.

Which meant that two days after watching him walk rebelliously without crutches into the hospital, I found him flat on his back, legs cemented into a hideous triangle that left him completely immobile from the waist down. The densest grove of trees couldn't have made me want to run for open sky more than seeing him so confined. So helpless, so humbled. I wanted to vomit. Instead, I smiled.

"Quite a contraption you've got there," I said.

The pallor of his face said he was in pain. The glaze of his eyes said the hospital staff had done what they could to help him. His lips were cold when I kissed him, his breath hot and sour.

"Probably kinder than the rack," he said, attempting a wink. "Only a little crueler than a thumb crusher." His words took obvious effort.

"How long do they plan on keeping you mummified?" It wasn't very funny, but it was better than sobbing.

"Until the graft is stable enough to be fully detached. *If* the graft takes, that is, which it seems to be doing so far. Three weeks is the doc's best guess."

Three weeks was twenty-one days, two-thirds of a month.

"Twenty-one days," I said calmly. Twenty-one days, I shrieked in my head, cursing the entire universe.

"Give or take," he said.

"It'll be over before you know it." Oh my god. Twenty-one days. I didn't think I could endure it. And if *I* couldn't endure it, how could *he*?

"Blink of an eye," he said.

I was running my fingers across the freckles of his damp brow the way a blind person might do across a page of Braille. "So, what can I do, King Tut?"

The twitch of his lips was maybe an attempt at a smile. "Scratch the itch on my right knee."

"Ha ha," I said, trying to match my tone to my words. "Anything else, your royal highness?"

I kissed his brow and licked the salt of his perspiration from my lips, finding the taste of him somehow calming.

"Brandy," he said.

🕊

I sneaked Kit's flask into his room each of the hospital days after his skin graft. But it wasn't enough. The doctor increased his morphine the day Kit threw a bedpan and cracked the TV screen during a news story about a place called My Lai. The starchy nurse told me Kit had kept shouting, "There's no volume knob on institutionalized murder," until the hypo finally kicked in. "He'll be fine," she said, softening a little when she saw my face. "Morphine can do that sometimes." The doctor also had the television removed from Kit's room.

— TWENTY-SEVEN —

Bingo

"Looks like a New Year's Eve party," Kit said, almost hiding the tremor in his voice. "Don't know how I rate such a reception. All I did was lie on my back for a month and daydream."

"Yeah, we know you've been lollygagging all this time, bro, but we fucking missed you anyway." Buzzy reached up, as if to twist his moustache, but dropped his hand. "Scuse my French."

Both the starchy nurse and Kit had forbidden any hospital room visitors but me, and though I hadn't discussed his ordeal with the Tribe, one look at him that homecoming day revealed what he'd been through.

By some combination of Kit's determination to heal quickly, his doctor's belief in the recuperative benefits of home, and the angel of mercy's compassion, Kit was released from the hospital on Thanksgiving Day. On crutches, fifteen pounds lighter, and visibly weak—despite daily physical therapy after removal of his cast and full detachment of his skin graft—he was clearly pleased to be upright on his own turf. He smiled at Tink and Boo's decorations, made from pressed autumn leaves and orange crepe paper, then gave Buzzy a thumbs-up.

"Who's that pretty young thing next to your hulking old self?"

Buzzy actually blushed as he slid his arm around his new girl, a music major he'd literally bumped into in Gray's Campus Drug store while shopping for moustache wax.

"Georgianna, an Iowa girl who plays the flute like a fairy princess."

Gazing up at Buzzy with stars in her eyes, Georgianna literally curtsied. "Pleased to meet you."

"Our home is yours, Gigi," Kit said, nicknaming her then and there. "Maybe you can keep this wayward leatherneck on the straight and narrow. He's a renowned zigzagger."

That got a laugh. More than a year with Kit had taught me his easy way with people took plenty of effort. I now knew he considered bringing people together and making them feel comfortable his job.

"Smells like someone's been cooking," Kit said.

"Just a little," I replied.

I'd put the turkey and pies into the oven at four-thirty that morning, right after composing an essay on Christopher Marlowe. Which I'd done after boiling giblets and cranberries and assembling a vegetable casserole. Except for a quick nap near dawn, I'd been up all night. But having Kit on his feet and smiling in his secondhand castle made my weariness melt like basting butter.

"Hey, we all gotta eat," Doc said, looking sleepier than usual, which said he'd already celebrated Kit's homecoming with a few tokes. He'd pled a headache during my search for a potato peeler, slinking off like a weasel when Boo had volunteered.

Tink swished into the center of the room, hair floating behind her. "We're so thankful for our blessings today," she said, kissing Kit's cheek. "Welcome home, chief."

"Thanks, Tink." Kit gave her a one-armed hug. "You smell even better than the turkey. New perfume?"

That got another laugh. Patchouli oil, preceding Tink's every move, was as much a part of her as her airy giggle.

Boo, now sporting a waist-length braid, proffered an ink-stained hand. Balancing on his crutches, bandaged foot well off the ground, Kit gave it a firm shake.

"When you're feeling up to it, I'd welcome your thoughts on my latest poetry collection," Boo said. "I think I've finally landed a publisher."

"I'm no expert on poetry, but I'm always glad to read your work, man." Kit and Boo had spent many a midnight hour discussing the merits of various writers, particularly the beat poets that Boo loved.

"You're a poet in your own way, my friend," Boo said. Having watched Kit captivate a group of strangers several times since our move to Minneapolis, I had to agree.

We'd just turned toward our bedroom when the front door opened. Following an icy gust were Pancho and girlfriend Kate. Behind them, windblown and red-cheeked, were my brothers.

"Look who tagged along." Pancho nudged them into the room. "They say their sister isn't much of a cook, but she does make a mean turkey sandwich."

The boys burst out laughing when Jimmy handed me a jar of Miracle Whip. Their surprise, passably decent clothes, and almost tidy hair greatly pleased me, and only the appearance of wings on Kit's crutches could have improved that moment.

We finally arrived at our bedroom. I hadn't lain beside Kit in a month, and the relief I felt when I nestled against him, arm across his chest, was like rain washing away desert dust. "I'm glad to be home," he said. "With you." Life was again as it should be.

Just before dark, Tink and Kate knocked on the door and began transforming our room into a makeshift café, using every type of table they could squeeze inside it. I'd turned the finishing touches of Thanksgiving dinner over to them, assuming the Tribe would dine at the big table we'd bought for a song due to its scratches and missing leg, while Kit and I ate from a tray in our room.

But now that we were all together again, the Tribe was bent on fellowship. As Kit and I sat in bed like royalty on a throne, my red candles aglow on the dresser, Jimmy carved the turkey on a card table like a master and Jeff filled the wine glasses like a pro. I would remember Thanksgiving of 1969 with great gratitude.

Kit clashed with another television four nights later, after hobbling from our bedroom to investigate the hubbub in our family room—called the Cave for its dim lighting and wall-to-wall black-light posters. The drawing for the first draft lottery since World War II was being televised, and not even a Vikings-Packers Super Bowl game could have filled the room so fully—or caused a yell louder than Pancho's when his birth date was pulled from capsule number six.

Pancho was now huddled in a corner sobbing, "I'm too young to die, I'm too young to die," as numbers droned from two somber old men in business suits, holding the rest of us rapt, if rather vocal. Though I'd tried to shush everyone, there was no honest way to hide the historic telecast from Kit, who clearly grasped the gist of the scene with a single scan of the room.

The television was a color console with a twenty-three-inch screen that Kit had bought brand new. Most of the Tribe had never experienced the technological wonder of color TV, let alone on such a big screen, and Kit had been proud of his cutting-edge contribution. So it shocked even me when, after making his way through the transfixed gathering, he raised a crutch and rammed it through the middle of the glass tube, killing the broadcast with a sizzling crash.

The room instantly went still, and Kit settled his crutch back under his armpit. He turned and pointed at Pancho, hand trembling, flush obliterating his freckles.

"It's just a *number*," he shouted. "And you have *options*, man."

Pancho just stared, mouth agape, tears shiny on his face. I'd never seen Kit so angry, or so hurt.

"You can go to Canada. You can go to jail. You can join the goddamn weekend warriors or convince them you're queer." He ran a hand through his sleep-mussed hair. "You can even shoot yourself in the fucking foot, which would be a smarter choice than the one I made. You have options, Pancho. If you haven't learned that from me by now, I've fucking failed."

He was breathing heavily, nearly choking on his words. "And whatever you decide, I'll help you every way I can."

Kit was the only one in the room not sitting, and all eyes were raised, locked on him.

"They don't own your *conscience*," he said, voice cracking, as he glared and pointed a finger at each male. "You don't want to live with the things I live with. You don't want to dream the dreams I dream." He turned back to the TV, prodding the hole with his crutch, as if confirming the defeat of a foe.

"It's just a fucking number," he said. Then he left the room and went back to bed.

No one felt like playing cards, listening to music, or engaging in conversation that night, and within minutes the Cave was dark and silent except for the soft hiss of the dying TV.

The doctor had been right about the healing benefits of home. Surrounded by his handpicked family and inside the house he'd chosen, Kit regained his strength quickly. The new patch of flesh covering his mangled foot, though still red at the seams, was soon a healthy pale pink dotted with amber freckles.

Though I was grateful for the return of Kit's vigor, that vigor had its downside. No sooner was Kit feeling like his old self—and probably better for the lack of internal infection—than he was back to writing letters, making telephone calls, printing fliers, and reading antiwar publications.

Then came the blustery December morning when Kit's new boots—purchased after Woodstock—slid on with no discomfort or pressure. From that day on, Kit hit the world with the energy of a wild animal that had been caged too long. He had a revolution to win, and he had a refurbished foot to help him do it. There was no stopping him, and I soon learned not to try. He'd paid steep dues for his mobility, and any attempt to curtail it was met by sharp words.

"You wanted us off the Homestead, Joey. Well, here we are in the big city. You wanted me to have a goal, and I got a worthy one. Don't expect to put a fence around the garden you planted."

By the end of fall term, Boo and Pancho had transferred to the U and moved to the Hotel full time. Pancho naturally brought Kate with him, and Boo soon found that his blond-Chippewa-John-Lennon look was more appealing to city girls than it had been to country girls. He began rotating his nights between Barbara—a pretty black girl Kit soon dubbed Babe—and Genevieve—a lanky blonde who became Gyp, probably for her jangling gaggle of bangles and beads. Boo brought home a guy once, a fellow with green eyes who already had a nickname. And something in Boo's voice when he said, "Hey, gang, this is my friend Jade," told me it wasn't Babe or Gyp he really loved. Up north, he'd have been branded a faggot. At the Hotel, no one cared.

The Tribe and its followers kept expanding. But the Hotel's five bedrooms, big front parlor, Cave, and various crannies offered plenty of sleeping and hanging-out space. Which meant I never knew how many to expect for supper or Sunday dinner. Between Kit's meetings, guests of residents, drop-ins, and my brothers' occasional visits, twenty souls often sat at our table. Using Kit's meal-in-a-pot concept, I'd narrowed my menu to spaghetti with bread and butter, vegetable soup with bread and butter, and lentils with bread and butter—calling the mixed leftovers Fourth Street goulash. But even the Hog Farm hadn't fed a horde for more than three days. When I complained to Kit, he said, "You should delegate more, Joey."

"I delegate what I can, Kit. But I'm not a restaurateur with a paid staff."

"No, you're the lady of the house. If it's too much for you, just say."

Lady of the house. My dad had called me that too. "I have classes, homework, and goals, same as you, Kit."

I found three cases each of Dinty Moore stew, Chef Boyardee spaghetti, and Hormel chili in the pantry the next day, along with an assortment of meatless Campbell's soups. An electric can opener sat on the counter. Only Doc complained about the new menu. "Some women wouldn't serve that to their dog," he said from the kitchen doorway as I stirred pots of store-bought fare.

"If you want a plate tomorrow night, Fido, be here at five to open the cans."

At school, essays on Sophocles, William Shakespeare, Molière, George Bernard Shaw, and Lillian Hellman came and went, keeping me clacking on our old Underwood many nights after meal cleanup, which everyone now did on a rotating schedule. My class readings of scenes from *Arms and the Man* and *The Children's Hour* brought my Theatre History grade up to an A-minus, and I felt I'd added to my acting repertoire, if only a bit. Come the middle of December, I was impatiently awaiting the New Year and new school term, when I'd be able to get back on a stage and resume learning my craft. Like Kit, I was ready to be sprung.

Christmas was reaching for our doorbell the day I took the city bus downtown for some serious shopping at Dayton's, where anything you might want to buy someone was available for a price. Kit hadn't decreed homespun presents this year, and I was happy to save my dwindling free time by spending some of my dwindling savings.

Day was slipping into dusk by the time my shopping bags were full and every name on my list was checkmarked. I'd really splurged on Kit's gift. A snapshot of him strolling down the bus depot alley in matching blue was forever tacked to the bulletin board of my memory. When I saw the blue cashmere sweater on the mannequin in the men's department, the clerk made a sale without looking up from his paperback.

My last stop was Dayton's basement level, where the candy counter resided. I had another splurge in mind. The boys would be visiting for Christmas, and every Hotel resident was fond of sweets. I'd just raised my hand to hail the clerk when another shopper rounded the corner, doing the same.

"A box of ribbon candy, please," we both said.

I giggled, startled by the odd coincidence, then glanced at the shopper, a woman outfitted in the coat, heels, hat, and scarf of a Northwest Orient Airlines stewardess.

"Oh my god. It's you, Dee Dee."

It had been more than a year since I'd seen my old friend, and I felt instantly guilty for not having sought her out in my four months in the city. Though her last postcard had been mailed from San Francisco, it had included her Minneapolis address, and I owned a map of the city and a key to Rosie. But those four months had been so full ....

"It certainly is," Dee Dee said, cocking her hip and her hat. "And unless you have a twin sister you haven't told me about, it's you, Joey Dean."

Shopping bags and all, we were suddenly hugging, dancing, crying, and laughing as the candy clerk waited by her cash register, a baffled look on her face and a box of ribbon candy in each hand.

At our booth in Dayton's chic café, Dee Dee had removed the top of her BLT on toast, extra mayonnaise, to inspect its four strips of bacon, which rippled with greasy symmetry. She slapped the top back on her sandwich. "Absolutely wavy," she said. "You get what you pay for when it comes to restaurants."

Dee Dee had eaten at exactly two restaurants before leaving our hometown, and her air of worldliness caused a lump in my throat that I quickly dislodged with talk.

"So, sky queen. How do you like jetting around the country in a fancy uniform and being admired by planeloads of strange men?" It was a question I was obliged to ask, though I wasn't sure I wanted to hear the answer.

Dee Dee's laugh verged on a scoff. She took a sip of her coffee, which she'd cooled with an ice cube fished from her water glass.

"Let's get one thing straight, Joey. I'm a glorified waitress who gets pinched, pawed, ogled, and bossed while my legs ache, my toes hurt, and my constant smile makes my cheeks sore."

She chomped into her sandwich, continued as she chewed. "But, I'm having a ball. I didn't realize how much I'd enjoy life beyond our hometown, despite horny old men, demanding prima donnas, and screaming babies. Workdays are exhausting and my paycheck isn't big, but I get plenty of time off, some of it in interesting places."

I smiled, jealousy in check. "And your folks," I said, ready to change the subject. "They're doing okay?"

Dee Dee was applying ketchup to a french fry. "As okay as ever. Dad's a hypochondriac addicted to complaining, and Mom's a doter addicted to suffering in silence. They miss me, but they have each other, in their nutty way. How about *your* family? They managing without you?"

I pushed away a wave of guilt. "They seem to be. The boys visit as often as possible, and Kit is very kind to them. Daddy's still doing his thing, as they say. We don't talk or see each other much, but that's nothing new."

"Right. And how about you? Why aren't you in Pasadena?"

I'd been waiting for that one.

"The U has a distinguished theatre department and I changed my mind," I said, completely bypassing my summer of misery.

"That's great, Joey. And what about Mr. Griffith? He still the man of your dreams?"

I was ready to pounce on any hint of criticism, but her question seemed sincere.

"He's still the man I love."

"And your life with him makes you happy?"

There was no way to avoid Dee Dee's question, or her eyes, which held only honest concern. I suppose my pause said more than I wanted it to. I reached for the cream pitcher. My coffee was almost white when I answered.

"My life with Kit makes me happier than I would be without him."

The Tribe had finally trickled off to bed, following a lively evening spent decorating the tree Kit had purchased at a sidewalk vendor, where there'd been no wounded jack pine to rescue. This year we'd hung our popcorn, cranberries, cutouts, and tinsel on a plump six-foot blue spruce. By midnight the job was finished, along with the wine, and Kit and I were at last alone in our room, just enough energy left for a few private words.

"You'll never guess who I ran into today at Dayton's," I said, slipping into the yellow flannel nightgown that had finally replaced my raggedy pink one.

"I'm sure I never will." Kit was apparently too weary for guessing games. I glanced at him. He slept nude no matter the time of year, and was already sitting in bed, covers pulled eagle high. No hint of a smile followed his words. He was indeed very tired.

"My old friend Dee Dee Perpich." I climbed in beside him and lay close. "It's hard to believe I haven't seen her in more than a year. She's a stewardess, stationed right here in the Cities. I'm sure I've mentioned her. Been pals since we were kids."

I was expecting Kit to slide down beside me, but he remained sitting, head so far back on his pillow, he had a view of the ceiling.

"Any friend of yours is a friend of mine. Why don't you invite her for Christmas Eve or Christmas Day, or both," he said.

"I've already done that. She's coming on Christmas Eve and staying over. Doesn't have to fly out until Christmas night. Isn't that great?"

"That's just great, Joey."

Something was wrong. I'd learned every nuance of Kit's moods, and there was a heavy wool blanket hovering over our bed.

"You'll never guess who *I* ran into today on the sidewalk outside of Gray's," Kit said, mocking me without humor.

"Santa Claus?" My quip didn't dispel my unease. The sidewalk outside of Gray's was one of Kit's favorite corners for handing out antiwar fliers.

"My mother."

If he'd said the Ghost of Christmas Past, I wouldn't have been more surprised. Or more alarmed.

I sat up. "Jesus. What was your mother doing in Dinkytown?" Dinkytown was far more bohemian and youthful than my image of Kit's mother, and not the place a lady of means would likely have a reason to visit.

Kit's laugh was so out of place, I shivered.

"She was meeting an old sorority sister for lunch at Bridgeman's. Sort of a walk down memory lane, you might say."

"Your mother attended the University of Minnesota?" It was a dumb question, but I was dumbfounded.

"For a year. Before Vassar."

"Oh." He made me ask, though he damn well knew my next question. "How did things go?"

His pause might have been for dramatic effect, but more likely he didn't want to talk about what was always a sore subject.

"About the way I expected them to," he said.

"And how was that?" For a man not in the mood to play guessing games, he was playing irritatingly well.

"Fucking badly. It was one shitty encounter." My breath caught in my throat. This wasn't the way Kit usually talked to me.

"Meaning?"

His sigh was testy, his thoughts clearly not on my question.

232

"Goddamn it, Kit. Spit it out before I get an ulcer right here and now. What the hell happened with your mother, for christsake?"

He turned to me, eyes so dull and brow crease so deep, goosebumps rose on my neck.

"The checkbook is now closed, little girl. I broke the rules—as usual—and the ties that bind have been fully severed because of my selfishness, intransigence, irresponsibility, and unconscionable lack of consideration. I'm now all on my own in the big bad world. That's what happened with my mother."

"She disowned you?" My family was certainly no model of mutual devotion, but I couldn't imagine cutting any of them out of my life. I wrote to my father monthly, and spoke to him whenever I caught him at home when I phoned the boys, though that was rare. Family was family, and that couldn't be changed.

"*They* did. My mother and father are of one mind on this matter, I can assure you. No consultation between them necessary."

I scrambled for words that would revive Kit's normal optimism and good humor.

"C'est la vie and what the heck," I said. "We don't need those mean old fogies and their tacky checks. After all, money's only money, and there's always Uncle Sam. We'll do just fine without those envelopes."

Kit looked at me as if I'd misplaced my sanity, and I felt like burying my head in the covers.

"Uncle Sam's contribution doesn't begin to pay the expenses of our household, Joey."

I looked down, trying to avoid his hard stare, and noticed that I was hugging a pillow in front of my chest. In front of my heart.

"We'll just have to cut those expenses, Kit. I'll make a list of things we can do to save money. I learned from an expert how to stretch a buck to pay the bar tab."

Kit nodded. "Well, you'd better get out your pencil and pad, little girl, because the rent is due in ten days, and I can't cover it without that little slip of paper from Edina."

There was anger in his voice, and he was aiming it my way. I shot it right back at him. "Then our *household* will just have to help out. Last I checked, they were all able bodied, not one of them in the hospital or on crutches."

I hated using Kit's injury as a point of argument, but he'd asked for it.

Kit scoffed. "What do they have to contribute financially, Joey? Most are students without resources."

"Then let them find another sucker to carry them. This one's tapped out."

"*No*. Not an option."

"Jesus Christ, Kit. You *don't* have to help everyone you meet. What made you such a fucking martyr?"

That faraway look of his came and went in an instant.

"My guilty conscience."

"About what?"

A long moment passed.

"Believe me, little girl, you don't want to know."

His tone convinced me I didn't.

"So what now?"

He was staring at the ceiling again.

"I'll figure out something," he muttered, as if speaking to himself. "Don't worry."

But *he* was worried, and I wanted to erase the frown from that face I couldn't help loving, to change the subject that made him able to hurt my feelings. I pulled back the covers, lifted my nightgown to my waist, and straddled him, wrapping my arms around his neck.

"I'm not worried," I said. "I'm lonely."

Without bothering to look at me, Kit reached behind his neck, unclasped my fingers, pulled my hands to my thighs. He turned his head toward the wall and closed his eyes.

"Shut off the light, Joey. It's getting late."

— TWENTY-EIGHT —

Take What You Need and Leave the Rest

I returned my Christmas purchases to Dayton's the next morning, including Kit's blue cashmere sweater, then returned the money to the savings account I'd opened four months back at a University Avenue bank. Maybe it was an overreaction, but Kit wasn't a man to exaggerate a problem. And I'd been running a household long enough to calculate the cost of supporting the dozen-plus souls who lived full or part time at the Hotel.

I spent the afternoon making needlework vouchers from construction paper, hoping they'd please the Tribe again this year. Embroidery had been the task most requested at cash-in, and assorted Hotel denim now displayed my artwork.

Canned meals were now beyond our budget. I bought a sack of rice and served cooked rice with the night's lentils, plates dished up before going on the table, bread and butter absent. Using Daddy's old trick, I poured powdered milk, replacing large glasses with small. And I didn't bring out the Boone's Farm until I spotted yawns during the usual post-supper activities. Dessert was now reserved for Sundays and holidays, and I began planning a backyard vegetable garden for the spring.

I instituted new Hotel rules and taped them on the refrigerator, where no one would miss them. The heat thermostat was now off limits, fixed at a slightly chilly number with tape. The water heater's dial—turned from hot to just warm enough—was also hands off. Each bed now required two blankets, neither electric, hot-water bottles being available for cold feet. Leaving the light on in an empty room now incurred a one-dollar fine. Wasting anything—food, toiletries, household products—also meant a fine. Remembering Woodstock's

235

announcers and newspaper, I wrote Be Cool, Be Groovy, Don't Be Piggish, Share What We Have in bold letters at the bottom of my list.

No one questioned or complained about my rules, not even weasel Doc, which made sense. The Tribe considered Kit their leader. His generous and genial nature had touched them all, and his recent foul mood could not have gone unnoticed. It took only a list posted by his first mate for them to know the ship was being threatened.

Kit didn't hand out fifty-dollar bills that Christmas. His gift for all was a crate of Florida oranges, which caused a pleased hum among the Tribe when he carried it in from Rosie, no crutches in sight.

The Tribe was wise enough to keep their own gifts handmade or edible. The only thing I didn't return to Dayton's was the candy, which I set out in a dish on Christmas Eve. Dee Dee did the same with hers after Christmas dinner. You'd have thought it was frankincense and myrrh by the reception it received.

I should have known Dee Dee and Kit would hit it off, despite all her past harsh words. His easygoing charm and low-key wit were perfect counterpoints to her zippy barbs and bluff tongue. Within an hour, he had her laughing out loud. I could feel her watching us from across the room, and when Kit kissed me and whispered, "Ho ho ho, baby" just before bedtime, her nod said she finally understood.

Kit pulled off a miracle on New Year's Eve, paying our landlord a day early and bringing home three cases of champagne for a spur-of-the-moment party, to which he'd invited half the known world. Aware of every nickel in my cigar box, now serving as our household kitty, I knew he hadn't gotten the money there. He was filling the refrigerator with thick green bottles when my curiosity commandeered my tongue.

"Did you rob a bank, discover a rich relative, or just trip over a bag of gold on the sidewalk?"

Bubbly all stowed, Kit shut the refrigerator door, face flushed from physical exertion, expression mighty close to carefree.

"None of the above." He swiped a hand across his sweaty brow and down his pants leg, a maneuver only Kit could accomplish with grace. "I sold Lola."

That caught me by surprise. Though she hadn't come to mind in a while, I'd never forgotten Kit's motorcycle.

"I thought Lola was out of commission."

Kit's wink was especially feisty. "I'm mechanically handier than I look."

"I can't believe your parents actually let you on their property."

Kit hoisted a big bag from the counter and set it on the kitchen table. "As it turns out, my parents are in Tahiti. The maid took pity on me and unlocked the garage."

Another surprise, and another reason for despising two people I'd never even met. Tahiti was in their budget. Kit was not. "Lucky break."

"Most certainly."

"You were brave to go there, Kit."

He laughed. "Desperate is more accurate."

"I hope you found Lola a good home. I have fond memories of that particular girlfriend of yours."

"Her new owner is a Triumph lover of the first degree, with a tattoo on his arm to prove it. Lola will be well cared for in her dotage."

"Good to know."

"I also found a job."

He was pulling plastic champagne glasses from the bag and arranging them in rows on the table.

"Do tell," I said.

The table was by the window, and I could see a blue jay perched at the birdfeeder Kit had hung from our lilac bush.

"The new term is starting soon," he said. "And we both know it's hard to have a job and go to school at the same time."

The jay peered nervously over its shoulder each time it took a seed, and I understood why.

"But your high school days proved it's possible, Joey. And this is a night job, so I won't miss any classes." He raised an empty glass in a mock toast. "You're now looking at Vescio's new bartender."

"*Bartender.*" I suddenly felt sick. "But bartenders are always on their feet."

He was pulling various snacks from the bag. "True. And I have two fine feet to stand on, one somewhat finer than the other."

I shoved the bag to the floor, where it landed with a crunch. "You can't take a job like that, Kit. It's lunacy."

"I can and I have." He faced me with a look that didn't match his light tone. "Vescio's is close to home, pays a decent wage plus tips, and is a great place to meet people and spread my message. I'm fully healed, Joey, and I have things to accomplish with this one life I've got."

I wanted to bash those plastic glasses with a rolling pin.

"Goddamn it, Kit. You're tempting fate by taking a job like that." Bile had crept all the way to my tongue.

But the conversation was clearly over. He stepped over the bag and took my hand. "Come with me, little girl. I have a feeling we won't see our bed again until tomorrow, and I have a New Year's Eve present just for you."

Kit's New Year's Eve party was a smash. The entire Tribe and their mates attended, all in high spirits and happy to see their leader feeling the same. A large portion of the Twin Cities antiwar activists— sometimes called peaceniks, doves, student protestors, filthy longhairs, or hippie radicals bent on tearing down the establishment—also came to greet 1970 at the Hotel. As guests poured in our door, it became clear that, while I'd been studying Molière and Arthur Miller, Kit had been doing his own type of homework, getting to know the local players of the antiwar movement. Pursuing his aspiration. Advancing his cause.

Kit was in full Kit mode that night, putting everyone at ease without seeming to try, coolly melding a collection of disparate characters with his agile magnetism. Our party spilled out onto Fourth Street when the countdown hit the magic hour. "Happy New Year" and "no more war" echoed through the frigid night. Lennon's "Give Peace a Chance" followed "Auld Lang Syne," people weeping as they chanted the refrain over and over, softening the stark darkness with the mist of their breath and one simple desire. Peace.

As Kit predicted, we didn't make it to our bed until well past dawn. And even then, stragglers chatted and sipped in quiet corners, or searched for places to let revelry fade into slumber, while the stereo played on.

Kit worked his first shift at Vescio's the second night of the newborn year. Despite a host of roommates and a flock of droppers-in to keep me company, I felt oddly abandoned, that another "cause" was pulling him away from me. Each hour trudged by like an uphill climber carrying a backpack full of rocks.

I finally retrieved my embroidery bag, pulled my denim maxiskirt from the closet, took out my needle. By the time Kit walked through the door, long after midnight, looking weary but pleased with himself and not limping, the lower half of the skirt had become a flower garden. In the morning, Tink's friend Chrissy saw the skirt lying on the chair I'd tossed it on before accompanying Kit to bed.

"Far out, Joey," she said, stroking my work. "I just love this."

The skirt was a thrift-shop find I had no special attachment to. "Consider it yours."

Chrissy was studying my stitches. "Oh no. This is too beautiful to give away. How much will you take for it?"

That was the moment it hit me that Kit's bartender job wouldn't cover our expenses, no matter how much I cut the budget or the Tribe tried to conserve. That was the moment a hobby became a business. "Whatever it's worth to you."

Chrissy pulled a twenty from her jeans pocket and slipped it into my hand. "Hope it's enough. This skirt is a work of art."

Twenty dollars for an evening's effort was damn good money. I thanked her and said, "I take custom orders and I'm quick. Please spread the word."

☙

Afraid to spend more on tuition and books, I'd enrolled in only two courses that term—Creating a Role and Beginning Spanish. Kit had also registered for two courses, but dropped out in time to receive a refund. There were just too many venues to speak at about the war, too many rallies to attend, too many people to organize for his cause, and too many nights when he didn't get to bed until early morning.

"The University of Minnesota isn't going anywhere, and people are dying for no defensible reason," he said. "*Now* is when I have to do this,

Joey. The only way to change tomorrow is to take a new direction through it."

So, Kit and I went our separate ways each school day. And five nights a week, he opened Chianti bottles at Vescio's while I ran the house, did homework, and embroidered jeans and other garments for a growing number of customers. Most nights when we met in our bedroom, we were both exhausted, just enough energy left for a catch-up chat and a good-night kiss. But between our efforts and scattered contributions from other Tribe members, there was now enough money for rent, food, heat, and electricity.

The highlight of those early weeks of 1970 was my acting class, where I was chosen to play Martha in Edward Albee's *Who's Afraid of Virginia Woolf?* in a class production. Immortalized on film by Elizabeth Taylor, my role was meaty, one that could spread my name through the campus acting community and bolster me at an audition for a theatre department production if I did well.

Kit, as ever, was supportive. "Way to go, little girl. You're now in the bigs, and I know you'll hit it out of the ballpark."

I couldn't fault his words or tone. His sincerity and positivity rang true. But I was missing him greatly, though we shared the same house and bed. I was thrilled to again be onstage, but I was frustrated. The universe seemed bent on denying me one or the other of my two life passions.

ॐ

It started as a touchy red spot at the edge of the scar. I caught Kit fingering it one night after he'd removed his socks.

"What's that?" His foot was my business, and that's all there was to it.

"A bit of stitching in my boot rubs me here." He slid his foot under the covers. "I'll file it down and wear thicker socks. Nothing to worry about."

I didn't worry until he got home from work especially late one night and didn't know I was awake.

"You're limping," I murmured, not wanting to startle him as he undressed in the streetlight beam that shone through our window. But startle him I did, and his right boot thudded to the floor.

"Long night," he said. "Old habit when I'm tired."

I switched on the bedside lamp. "Let me see your foot."

"It's nothing." He shot a frown at the lamp as he slipped off his pants but not his socks. "Please douse that, little girl, and let me have your warm spot. It's the North Pole out there tonight."

"Show me your foot."

"Let it go, Joey. This old foot is ready for rest, that's all. Move over and let a weary man sleep."

"I mean it, Kit."

Kit switched off the light himself, slid in next to me, gave my cheek a peck. "Sleep tight, baby."

Come morning, I cornered him in the bathroom, where he was shaving nude after his shower. I could see the inflammation from the hallway. One side of the skin graft was swollen and angry red.

"You need to see your doctor, Kit. And I mean *today*."

"I suppose so," he mumbled as he kept shaving, his lack of protest saying his foot felt as bad as it looked.

Shots, salves, pills, footbaths, debridement, crutches, time off from work, bed rest. Nothing the doctor ordered did any good. The infection spread like a flame in a field of dry grass, devouring the patch of flesh that had been so carefully, painfully, and hopefully donated by Kit's left leg to his needy right foot. Kit's skin graft had gone bad, and the badness had turned on the whole vulnerable foot.

Still, the seriousness of Kit's situation—the reality of what that stubborn infection meant—never entered my mind until the day he spoke the worst word I'd ever heard him utter. It was early on a Sunday morning, the household yet to stir, when I opened my eyes and found Kit sitting up in bed, holding his naked foot like a treasured memento. He just blurted it out, no morning pleasantries or lead-in to slow the bullet.

"Amputation. The doctor thinks it's my best recourse at this point. He says the circulation in my foot isn't good enough, and I'll always be fighting this battle."

His announcement was a point-blank blast. My breath left me in one gush, and I clutched my abdomen, unable to speak.

He was stroking his foot like a dying pet. "He wants to schedule the surgery soon to give me the best chance at a good result."

I simply couldn't move or talk, but by avoiding my eyes, Kit had put a wall between us anyway. So it was that old horror movie again, playing one more time as I stared across the room into our dresser mirror. *Carcasses, cleavers, and men in white coats.*

"He hopes to leave as much of my leg as he possibly can."

Switchblades and stilettos.

"He says there's no lag time. I'll be fitted with a temporary prosthesis and start learning to walk with it right after the surgery."

Bam. Bam. Chink. Chink

"He says the prostheses they make these days for below-knee amputations are excellent. I'll be able to walk without a limp someday if I put my mind to it and work real hard."

I had no tears to cry. They were all inside my chest, submerging my heart until it was puckered, pale, and floating like a bloated corpse.

❧

Dee Dee missed her next flight, faking illness, to come when I called. We met in a coffee shop not far from the Hotel.

"I don't think I can stand it, Dee Dee. I simply can't bear for this to happen to him."

"Why, of course you can. You're the toughest person I know, Joey. You've handled plenty of hard stuff, and you'll get through this just fine."

She was holding my hand across the table, speaking as if to a child, speaking like the mother whose moments of maternal comfort I'd almost forgotten. "This will pass. You'll be strong, Kit will heal, and the two of you will go on together. You'll be happy again, I promise."

But she wasn't my mother and I wasn't a child. "How can you promise that, Dee Dee? How can you possibly know that?"

She released my hand but held my eyes, not a tear between us. "Because it's the only option love gives you, Joey."

What I hadn't known about skin grafts was a grain of sand compared to the Sahara desert of what I didn't know about amputations. If my first sight of Kit after his skin graft had been a jolt of unpreparedness, my first sight of him after his amputation was an atom bomb. Of course I should have asked more questions beforehand. But then, how do you ask more questions of a man who doesn't want to answer them? A man who had made his decision and didn't see the point in discussing it.

The great blessing of that day remains the fact that Kit was asleep when I first saw him. From the foot of his bed, where I'd lurched to a halt, I backed out of the room and fell on the first official-looking person I encountered. Fortunately, she happened to be a seasoned RN with the presence of mind to scoot me to an empty room and sit me down, after I screamed to the far side of the hospital, "Where the *hell* is his fucking *leg*?"

"You're here to see Mr. Griffith, I suspect." The nurse didn't wait for my answer. "It would seem you didn't quite know what to expect after his surgery. That happens sometimes. Amputees don't always like to talk about their amputation. Acceptance sometimes comes slowly, in stages. Let me tell you few things Mr. Griffith perhaps didn't mention. Things maybe you didn't know."

Things I didn't know. A leg is a complicated apparatus, walking a complicated process requiring two legs. For optimum ambulatory outcome, most below-knee amputations are performed at the juncture of the shank's first and second third. When the foot is cut off, so is two-thirds of the lower leg. What's left is called the stump.

Things I didn't know. For function and comfort, a stump needs shaping. A cast-socket had gone right over Kit's sutures, and tomorrow he'd start walking with a temporary prosthesis. He'd get a new cast-socket when his stitches were removed, another for his permanent prosthesis. With training, he'd be able to walk without a cane, but due to body secretions, he couldn't wear his prosthesis continually. If it wasn't worn regularly, though, he'd need to wrap his stump to keep its shape. Diligent hygiene could help limit infections, abrasions, and cysts. Crutches would be necessary whenever he wasn't wearing his prosthesis.

"Amputation is forever," the teacherly RN said, patting my hand. "But with patience and grit, an amputee can live a fulfilling, though undeniably altered, life."

I didn't see Kit again until the following morning. The sedative the nurse gave me after our little chat put me to sleep, and I spent the night in the waiting room of Kit's hospital floor. By the time I went to visit him, I was calm enough to put on a face.

ॐ

He was propped up in bed with a tray in his lap.

"What's for breakfast, Mr. Griffith? Looks like you have enough there to feed a village, and I'm starving. Care to share some of that?"

"Help yourself, Miss Dean. Take what you need and leave the rest, as they say."

I gave him a quick glance. His smile was sleepy, easy. Completely under control.

"Muchas gracias, señor."

I took a piece of toast and bit into it with a crunch that made me jump.

"Es un placer, chica bonita." He was still smiling.

I stood there chewing and ogling the room as if it were an art gallery, avoiding his eyes and the obvious place to look. Which was also the obvious topic.

"Nice digs," I said. "You actually have a view." Two elms and a clear blue sky.

Kit leaned back against his pillow, and I could feel his eyes on my face.

"I've been in worse places, I must admit."

When the toast was gone, I bent over his tray, picked up his half-eaten bowl of oatmeal.

"Do you mind?"

"Not at all." He handed me the spoon. "Couldn't finish it. They don't make it the way you do."

I shoved a spoonful into my mouth, pretending to analyze it as I smacked my lips.

"No brown sugar and butter," I said. "That's my secret. Brown sugar and butter."

Kit nodded in exaggerated solemnity. "I promise I'll keep it to myself."

"Please do. I don't want anyone usurping my position in the Hotel kitchen."

He shook his head with great ceremony. "Don't worry. That could never happen. No one can top your cooking. Or your other special skills, for that matter."

"My my, but you're a charmer today, Mr. Griffith."

"Nah, just an honest man, Miss Dean."

My half of the clever repartee had run its course, and the time for me to sit down had more than come. Kit, rising to the occasion better than I, finally got me off my cement feet. "Please have a seat, Joey."

And I did, settling as gently as I could on the lower end of the bed and emitting a relieved sigh. Things were moving along pretty well, so far. He was in a good mood, faked or otherwise, and I wasn't sobbing.

"Jesus Christ! Not on my foot, Joey. *Not* on my *foot*."

The panic in Kit's voice was a brand-new sound in my lexicon of Kit sounds, nightmares notwithstanding. I jumped up, staring down at the empty spot on the mattress where I'd temporarily parked myself. "Oh my god, I'm so sorry."

Yesterday's informative nurse had not left out something called the phantom sensation—the feeling that a missing limb is still attached. A sensation that may decline or disappear with time, but is often very painful. And if *I* knew about this phenomenon, Kit surely did. I'd just sat on the foot that wasn't there.

I could still feel his eyes on my face, and there was nothing left to do but confront the truth of this day.

He was grinning inanely and his shoulders were shaking. With a guffaw, he burst out laughing, slapping the mattress beside him and doubling over, hilarity possessing him.

I couldn't help it. I started laughing too, cackling and snorting until I fell into the chair by Kit's bed. He looked at me, I looked at him, and we kept laughing. Laughing so hard, tears rolled down our faces. Laughing and laughing and laughing in each other's arms.

— TWENTY-NINE —

Yours, Mine, Ours

With the passion and persistence of a wrangler taming a wild stallion, Kit was hell-bent on mastering his new limb, and mastering it fast. Both in and out of his ambulation training, he pushed without mercy to make his prosthesis as functional as his God-given leg. He'd shed his tears. During those grueling weeks after surgery, he didn't whine, mope, complain, get angry, plead weariness, or slow his pace.

"I want to get this over with," he said. "To move forward."

The day his permanent prosthesis finally arrived, he was up at sunrise for strength and stretching exercises.

A primary goal in walking with an artificial leg is doing so with grace, making the fake leg seem real. Kit embraced that goal like a buoy in a raging sea. He worked not like a man overcoming an obstacle, but like a man refusing to have one.

"No mortars above me, no rats below," he said. "It could be worse."

And before March departed like a lamb with an attitude, he'd resumed his life as if nothing unusual had happened. Kit's gait had always been measured, and soon, even I couldn't tell that a man-made leg was strapped on under his pants.

Even in the bedroom, Kit became adept at appearing unchanged. Aesthetically, his prosthesis matched his left leg surprisingly well, and he took great care never to let me see him without it. He wore it even during sex, which he now reserved for night and a dimmed room. Though he made love with all the vigor and nearly all the agility he always had, when our interlude was over, he'd quickly withdraw to the bathroom for the nightly care of his stump and prosthesis.

"I'll just be a minute," he'd say. "Save my place, baby."

If health reasons hadn't required Kit to free his stump each night, I believe he would have slept wearing his artificial leg. In the morning, he somehow was always first awake, fully dressed with prosthesis in place by the time I opened my eyes.

Kit hid the phantom sensations that sometimes pained him, as he did the sore places and raw spots that plagued a patch of flesh not meant to bear a man's weight. A twitch or stifled groan were the only clues of his come-and-go misery. Amputation of a troubled body part, I learned, didn't end the trouble. Keeping his stump healthy would be a lifelong battle.

I admired Kit's determination to go on as normally as possible. And I appreciated his hiding the visual truth of his surgery. He let me examine his stump only once, and once was enough. From knee down, what had been the second most beautiful limb in my world now resembled a very short loaf of french bread. Not that it frightened or repelled me. Physically, spiritually, emotionally—if it belonged to Kit, I adored it. What bothered me was the cruelty of his loss, and the finality. Nothing was ever going to grow back in those long inches between his stump and the floor. That gap in his life was there until the end.

Kit conquered his new appendage like a soldier fighting to save his country. And I believe he saw his struggle as precisely that.

"If you don't expose the rot, you *are* the rot," he said.

Mere weeks after his surgery, he was back at his mission, working with the array of activists he'd so doggedly made it his business to know. He was once again staging antiwar rallies, giving antiwar talks, writing articles for antiwar publications, and standing on street corners handing those publications to any passerby who'd take them. When he returned home, he was understandably tired, but if he was pushing himself too hard, no limp betrayed him. Kit's recovery was a marvel of personal resolve.

Kit also quickly returned to work. Vescio's management did their best to accommodate him when he wisely chose to forgo bartending, assigning him the night audit and various bookkeeping duties. But the duties weren't full time and didn't include tips, which meant his income decreased noticeably.

My income, on the other hand, kept growing. I now carried business cards, and Tink had created some attractive promo fliers, which I'd tacked on bulletin boards around campus and Dinkytown, taped in several store windows. I called my business Joeyful Threads—a play on "glad rags" that Tink didn't get. She'd drawn samples of my embroidery designs on the fliers and printed the Hotel phone number in bold letters. I began receiving as many calls as Kit.

I fought internal battles over the success of my little enterprise as the weeks passed. I dearly wanted to reduce Kit's burdens. Between his skin graft and his amputation, he'd been harshly punished by the universe. Though my schedule grew heavy, I was glad to assist the cosmos in making it up to him. I believed in his cause, didn't want to unsettle him. But I couldn't sew hours onto the day, and my schoolwork suffered. Special requests now poured in, some especially elaborate and profitable by my pricing formula, and I dared not refuse them.

Our dresser top now served as station for my sketches, hoops, threads, needles, scissors, and in-progress projects. I'd incorporated loops, knots, fringe, beads, and small buttons into my designs, giving them a three-dimensional quality, gaining a reputation for cleverness. As always, Kit generously praised my work, but I caught him frowning at my cigar box, which now held more of my earnings than his.

"This is a temporary situation, Joey," he said.

Though Kit hadn't been in the student audience, I'd gotten an A for my role in *Who's Afraid of Virginia Woolf?* I'd practiced hard for that grade. In the hospital while Kit slept or worked with his therapist, in the Hotel kitchen while stirring dinner pots, in our bathroom so I wouldn't wake Kit, I'd studied the psyche of middle-aged, disillusioned, and bitter Martha, memorizing her words, tone, and movements until they were mine. On performance day, Martha, not I, walked onstage. She was another gold-starred name in my repertoire, my backstage pass to campus recognition.

I was earning an A in my acting class but a D in Spanish. Memorizing lines and learning a language both take time, and I didn't have enough. I dropped out of Spanish late in the term, losing my tuition but avoiding a failing grade, hoping Kit would pull off another save-the-day coup by spring term.

By mid-March our life had settled back into a routine, if our life could ever be called that. Kit's reduced work hours allowed him to be home more at night. But as usual, the Hotel was the evening meeting spot for not only his partners in the antiwar cause, but also the Dinkytown bohemian set and various souls drawn to Kit's charisma and world. And naturally, the Tribe and mates were around in some combination, sharing their usual nighttime amusements with our guests. I cut back even more at mealtime, making rice, noodles, or potatoes our mainstay, but Kit wouldn't let me abolish the Boone's Farm.

"Wine brings people together," he said. "And togetherness is everything."

"Togetherness is putting us in the goddamn poorhouse," I said.

"I've got a plan."

"Selling the Homestead?"

He shook his head. "Boo's family is living there for a while."

I just sighed.

"I'll fix things soon, Joey."

Kit and Doc seemed to grow closer after Kit's surgery, though they'd always been tight. Kit would often single out Doc for private discussions, which they'd hold in a quiet corner or empty room as they shared a joint or Kit's flask. Doc was Kit's first follower, a fellow alumnus of Chicago's police riot, and maybe that was why Kit turned to him after his great personal loss. I held my tongue when Kit loaned him Rosie for a trip to see his mother. But I let it loose when I looked in the cigar box.

"I'm not sewing my fingers raw to give that leech a fucking vacation."

"A vehicle with an empty gas tank is worthless," Kit said. "I'll make it up to you, Joey. Be patient. I've got a plan."

Though Kit was now home more in the evening, our time alone didn't increase. As always, the bedroom was the only place he was truly all mine. But nowadays he was often ready for sleep when we shut the door behind us. He'd sometimes nod off even before we made it to our room, falling asleep wherever he happened to be sitting. I attributed his loss of stamina to his surgery and his determined pace, believing he'd eventually recover that as well.

Kit didn't pull off another financial coup by spring term, and I didn't need an adding machine to know I couldn't slow my embroidery output. But my own stamina was sagging. Something had to give, and the solution seemed obvious. Telling myself I would attend summer classes, I skipped spring enrollment.

Dropping out of school seemed my only option. Kit's miraculous recovery had somehow hit a wall. He was looking gaunt, and dark circles now ringed his eyes. His head now drooped long before bedtime, and he was having trouble keeping down his food. I grew alarmed at how often I found him in the bathroom upchucking his supper, how often I fed him milk toast and dosed him with Pepto-Bismol. His body had been through hell, and he had pushed it too hard. By summer, my cigar box would afford tuition and Chef Boyardee. And by summer, Kit would be Kit again.

All Kit said when I told him I'd skipped registration was, "I promise this is temporary."

— THIRTY —

Gimme Shelter

The telephone sounded oddly urgent the night Dave Dellinger called, its ringer wailing through Led Zeppelin's "Whole Lotta Love" like Robert Plant's louder and lewder twin. Dee Dee, who was visiting for a few days, jumped in her seat near the phone before grabbing the receiver and covering her other ear to block the sounds of sex set to music.

"A guy named Dave Dellinger for Kit," she said, her hand over the mouthpiece as she caught my questioning look from across the room.

"Oh wow," I said. "Keep him on the line until I find Kit. Dellinger's a big kahuna in the antiwar scene."

I'd seen Kit and Doc wander into the Hotel's innards a while back. Dashing down a hallway, I tried the Cave first. No luck. Only Kate and her gang of yoga devotees. Kit and Doc weren't in the kitchen, the pantry, the porch, the dining room, or our bedroom either. I raced for the staircase, and took the steps two at a time. Dave Dellinger was holding. At the top of the stairs, I turned toward Doc and Tink's room.

Tink was standing outside their closed door, braiding her hair and looking bored. It was a peculiar place for grooming, but Tink never tended toward the ordinary, especially after a few tokes or sips of wine.

I hurried toward her. "Hey, Tink. Have you seen Kit and Doc?"

Tink dropped her thick plait and shook her head, eyes wide. "Nope, nope. Haven't seen them, Joey. Not in ages upon ages."

Her fingers were fidgeting in the gauzy depths of her skirt, and her head kept shaking. I knew she was lying, for some kooky reason that made sense only to her.

"Just let me check your bedroom. Kit has a really important call." I reached around her skirt for the doorknob.

"*No*," she said, blocking the knob with her body and giving my shoulder a surprisingly sharp shove with her palm. "You can't go in there."

By now Tink's eccentricity had strained my good humor. "Yes I can. Kit and I pay the rent here."

Tink didn't reply, and I elbowed her aside and threw open the door. "Dave Dellinger's on the line!" I said, erupting into the room.

Even in the dim light of the bedside lamp, Kit's inked eagle, dragon, and tiger stood out against his pale skin. He was sitting shirtless on the edge of the bed, and Doc was leaning over his arm, inspecting his Vietnam tattoo, which truly was a work of art. They both turned my way and froze. Tink and her patchouli were right behind me, and she emitted a squeak that made me wince.

I heard something tinkle onto the floor just before I said, "Don't worry, Doc, those critters won't bite you," glad to have found Kit and trying to be witty.

Then I saw the rubber tubing tied around Kit's bicep, the blackened spoon on the bed next to Kit's Zippo and a small packet of white powder.

"What's going on here?"

Kit yanked the tubing from his arm and turned away. The length of rubber plunked to the floor beside the syringe as he dropped his head into his hands.

Doc stood upright and looked me in the eye as directly as his saggy lids would let him.

"Hey there, Joey. I'm Kit's friend, and he needs his friends these days."

A thousand-watt chandelier couldn't have made it clearer what Kit and Doc had been doing, but it still took me several moments to believe my eyes. For all the reality-skewing substances that Kit and the Tribe dallied with, needles were in a class of their own. They crossed the shadowy street that separated lighthearted tripping, sensory exploration, and mind expansion from degeneracy. Needles equaled hard drugs, which equaled danger, addiction, and death. Hard drugs were what smelly lost souls in gutters used, what deranged rock stars did just before their obituaries hit the front page. They were for those who'd left the bright possibilities of the world for the hopeless realm of darkness.

"Shooting him up is friendship?" My voice sounded like a stranger's. "Jesus, what are you mainlining into him?"

The twitch of Doc's scrawny beard gave me the answer before he did.

"Smack's the only thing that helps, Joey." I was shaking badly, but my eyes were aimed at him like gun barrels. Doc refused to look away. "But I assure you, it's the cleanest horse out there."

I wanted to slap the calm confidence from his face and rip out his sickly whiskers. I wanted to strangle him with that rubber tubing, to scoop out his bowels with that charred spoon.

"Heroin." I was trembling so much I had to lean on Tink's pink wingback chair to keep from falling. "What kind of monster shoots *heroin* into the man who took him in when he was down?"

The righteousness of Doc's sleepy stare was gasoline tossed onto my flaming outrage.

"I'm giving him what kills the pain."

There was no remorse in Doc's words or his manner. No guilt. Kit was now hunched over so far, all I could see was his back. The bones of his spine looked fragile, exposed.

"You're making him a junkie."

Doc shook his head. "You don't know what he lives with, Joey."

I punched him then, right in his squishy gut, though my shaking fist didn't pack much force.

"I know what he lives with a hell of a lot better than you do." I was shouting now. "I *sleep* with him for christsake. I'm with him when the lights go out."

In that moment, I understood the term crime of passion, and the concept of wishing a fellow man dead. The peace-and-love vibe of Woodstock seemed a planet away. All those nightmares, sleepless nights, and long-distance stares. All those visits to Hill 881 South, the Mekong River, the Ho Chi Minh Trail, the rice-paddy villages, the snake-and-sniper infested jungle ....

I was choking on my words. "*You*, in your eternal pot haze, don't know what the fuck you're *talking* about."

By now Kit was on the floor, curled into a fetal ball, motionless and moaning. I didn't know if his misery came from physical need or shame or both, and in that moment, I didn't care.

"How long has this been going on?"

Gasping from my blow, Doc still held my stare. "If you know him so well, then you know when it became more than he could take."

That one threw me. It really did, though this wasn't the place for reviewing Kit's and my past and the signs I'd clearly missed or misinterpreted.

I swallowed, trying to reel in my rage, groping for calm. I had to know what I was up against. "How often?"

Doc shook his head slowly. Arrogantly. Shamelessly. "He's my friend. I don't keep track of when I give him my help."

"How *often?*" I was screaming again.

Just then Dee Dee walked through the door. "I couldn't keep that Dellinger guy on the phone any longer, but I got his number."

She halted just over the threshold, glancing from my face to Kit's body. The piece of paper she held in her hand fluttered to the floor, landing a few inches from the hypodermic needle.

Doc shrugged. "Two, three times a day. Depends."

Though my knowledge of heroin addiction was sketchy, his answer terrified me.

"Where did the money come from?"

The slightest rise of Doc's lip turned arrogance into a smirk. "You're a smart girl, Joey. I bet you can figure it out."

The evening powwows. The borrowed bus. Doc's trip to visit his "mother." Kit's desperation to increase our coffers. I was pretty smart, all right.

"Get out," I said, no longer shouting, beyond anger.

Doc's smirk had settled into an amused smile. "You forget. You're in *my* room."

I leaned in, stuck my finger in his face with eerie calm. "No, you're in *my house*. And unless you can produce rent receipts, get the hell out."

Doc suddenly had a new attitude. He blinked, looked down at Kit and back at me.

"Hey there, Joey. Come on." His tone was sickeningly close to a whine. "You're overreacting. Kit has a problem, and we're coping with it. You should be glad."

I spit in his face and watched my saliva run down his sad attempt at manliness. "Oh, you bet I'm glad. Glad you and your coping methods are finally out of our lives." I glanced at my watch. "You have until ten. A little less than half an hour."

"What!" He was swabbing his beard with his sleeve. "Let's talk this over, for godsake."

"Take your filthy black bag and whatever else you can carry. Mail me your new address for the rest. Just write Judas on the top of the envelope."

Tink finally stepped beyond her befuddlement. "Geez, Joey. You can't actually be kicking Doc out of the Hotel."

"You too, *partner*," I said. "Go."

Her hands were fluttering, feet shuffling. "Joey, you can't mean this …."

I turned my back on the sorry scene, headed for the door. "Ten o'clock. If you're not gone by then, you'll be whining to the cops."

I didn't lower my voice when I passed Dee Dee. "Please stay with Kit and keep these vultures *away*. I'll be back as soon as I put this house in order."

Once downstairs, I pulled one of Kit's crutches from our closet, holding it in front of me like a rifle as I stepped into the parlor's clutter of human beings. By midnight, everyone but Kit, Dee Dee, and me was gone. By midnight, no cops needed, I'd banished the Tribe to the wilderness. I finally had Kit to myself.

৵৵

I would have installed a padlock if it had come to that. But Dee Dee and I didn't need to lock the door to keep Kit in the room where he withdrew cold turkey from heroin. Minus his crutches and prosthesis, which I removed without guilt after we hoisted his anguished body into bed, he was my captive.

He argued at first. "Give me my goddamn leg," he snapped. "Not on your goddamn life," I snapped back. He eventually became too sick to go anywhere on his own anyway, during those dire days. On that slow crawl through agony, I postponed every Joeyful Threads project indefinitely, and Dee Dee took an emergency leave from Northwest Orient. We put a cot in the corner of the room, and the two of us split the eternity of Kit's journey to hell into four-hour shifts.

I suppose I could actually have killed Kit, denying him so abruptly what his body so deeply craved. But Doc was my only source of heroin, and he was the devil who'd led Kit to the other side. Short of calling in medical authorities, who'd be duty bound to get to the criminal bottom of things, cold turkey was the only option. Instinctively, I counted on my love to bolster Kit's body in its struggle, to augment his endurance, believing my devotion had more power than any drug. In my quest to heal him, I was an eagle with lethal talons, a tiger with killer teeth, a dragon with flaming breath. Kit Griffith was mine, the prophet of possibility I'd chosen to follow, not some lowly gutter junkie. He couldn't die.

🕊

Jesus hadn't said much during his three days to resurrection, and Kit was almost as tight-lipped in the ten days to his own rebirth.

"I'm scared, Joey," he said, squirming against the pillows in the early hours of that first morning, panting and yawning compulsively. His last fix had been botched by my interruption, and he couldn't hide the panic in his voice, the fear in his eyes.

I pulled the covers to his chin to ease his shudders. "I'll be right here for as long as it takes."

"I'm so ashamed," he muttered the first time the cramps came and we couldn't get him to the bathroom in time. Dee Dee, bless her quick tongue, had the reply. "Good God, will you look at that? Kit Griffith does it just like the rest of us." We soon learned to rig him with a towel and safety pins, diaper style, despite the humiliation in his eyes.

"I can't stand this," he said as the craving grew so strong, the hairs of his arms stood up like little amber blades of grass. By then his eyes, nose, and pores were spewing body fluids uncontrollably, his innards rejecting their contents without warning through whatever orifice would take them first.

257

"Yes you can," I said, stroking his scorching brow and thrashing legs with a wet cloth that never stayed cool for long. They didn't call it kicking the habit for no reason. The pain in Kit's legs overtook his muscular control like a madman with a whip, and the frenzied kicks of his whole and half limbs eventually shredded the sheets.

Three nights and days into his war with heroin, seventy-two hours without sleep or food, he said, "I'm going to die."

"The hell you are," I countered, squirting cool water onto his tongue with a turkey baster and rubbing brandy across his lips with a sponge, not sure he wasn't right. His body was now so weak from exhaustion, dehydration, and lack of food, I feared his heart would fail. I clutched his hand, silently ordering my pulse to strengthen his, willing the energy within me to cross that skin-and-bone divide.

The actress in me cooed and cajoled with pretend calm. "You need to eat something, Kit. Is there anything you could maybe keep down?"

On the fifth day he said, "Hungry . . . sweet."

Peanut butter cookies were his favorite confection, and within an hour, I'd pulled dozens from the Hotel's oven. Holding back almost a week's worth of tears, I watched crumbs tumble down Kit's beard and cling to his chest hairs as he ate what I held up to his mouth.

"Water . . . cold." he said, when he'd finished.

Our refrigerator held two trays of ice, but I ran to the market for more. Kit wanted *cold* water and, sobbing for joy, I made gallons of it.

By the seventh day, Kit's lack of sleep ended any words that made sense. Though the revolt of his body seemed to be subsiding, he was now only capable of sighs, moans, and grunts.

On the tenth day he finally fell fully asleep, and I crawled in naked beside him, both our bodies freshly washed, and did the same. Kit's life, and mine, began anew the following dawn.

In the middle of the night before that new morning, Kit woke and said, to me or maybe just the darkness, "My right foot hurts so bad." A mockingbird suddenly began to sing in the tree outside our window, chirping away as if the night didn't exist and the world had nary a care. Kit's right foot was the one he no longer had.

I stroked his face and ran the brandy-soaked sponge over his lips until his breathing slowed. "It's just saying it's sorry for leaving you, Kit. And you can live with that."

— THIRTY-ONE —

Oh-High-Oh

"How can I thank you for pulling me out of that pit, Joey?"

Kit was buttering the corners of his toast as if skipping a crumb would land him in jail. He hadn't looked me in the eye since the café waitress had left our corner booth with an empty tray. Actually, he hadn't looked me in the eye since the night I'd found him in Doc's bedroom.

"Why on earth are you still with me?" His hangdog shake of the head made me feel sick.

I don't know what I expected when we finally rose from the depths of Kit's addiction and returned to the everyday world. But of all the attitudes he might have taken toward me—wounded pride, nonchalance, false cheer, irritation, or even anger—abject humility was the one I was least prepared for. Kit shamed was not the Kit I'd been trying to achieve when I'd overseen his withdrawal from smack.

"I'm with you because I love you." I salted my eggs for a second time, searching for words that would lighten this scene. "We all lose our way now and then. I just helped you back onto the road."

His toast impeccably buttered, then forgotten, Kit stared out the window, where a heavy wind was shoving raindrops sideways, making them splat against the glass, then wriggle in flattened streams till they disappeared. "I let you down. I let everyone down."

I scraped the salt off my eggs with my coffee spoon, flicked it onto my saucer, where the granules clung together in a huddle, as if hiding.

"Everyone is better off for what you've given them," I said. "And you should be proud of that."

Still aimed at the window, his eyes were glistening. I reached across the table and took his hand. I couldn't endure his tears.

"You're the same man. It was just a slip."

He pulled his hand away, covered his eyes, and I knew we were on the edge of a dark and birdless forest. "I haven't been the same man for a very long time, Joey."

His sigh halted my protest. The window was now a rippling shroud of wet, and moments passed like a silent prayer for the departed.

He finally dropped his hand and turned to me, the haloes of his eyelashes shimmering. "Did you have to kick out *everyone*?"

I could only shrug. "You took on too much, Kit. You need a break, and they'll be fine."

"But what am I good for now?" he said in a cracked whisper. He might as well have roared.

"What do you mean?"

"I used to be a gimp with a monthly piece of paper to share. Now I'm just a peg leg and a junkie. I don't know what to do."

The window rattled, but it felt like my soul.

"Why, you keep doing what you've *been* doing. What you carefully *chose* to do. You keep working to end the war."

I was carving the yolk from an egg. A little yellow lake oozed to the base of my hash browns.

"And as long as you stay off the junk, Kit, I'll be right by your side."

I slid the yolk into my mouth. It was gritty with salt, and cold. I swallowed it whole.

"Is that true, Joey?" He was blinking hard.

I licked the corner of my mouth, where a clump of salt had clung on, and locked the door on his tears.

"Well, I can't be by your side if you're dead."

The Hotel phone had screamed in our parlor like an abandoned baby during Kit's illness. Dee Dee and I had let it ring, concerned with nothing beyond Kit. And in the early days of his return to the world and Dee Dee's return to her own life, Kit and I continued to let it ring, both too shaky to open ourselves to the needs of others. But strength and equilibrium slowly buttressed our existence, and the morning finally came when Kit shouted from the parlor as I stirred a pot of oatmeal in the kitchen, "I'll get it."

The outside world hadn't forgotten Kit in the days our telephone had shut it out. He'd become known in the upper echelon of antiwar folks, a fact I'd realized but quickly forgotten the night Dave Dellinger dialed our number. And something had happened during his hiatus from the antiwar movement that no one with an interest in the war could possibly ignore. President Nixon had announced the invasion of Cambodia by US and South Vietnamese troops. With a pretty map and a stack of notes as props, he'd explained to the nation on television that the purpose of the action was ending the war and winning a "just" peace. He'd asked for the country's support of its troops, who were fighting, he said, for a future world of peace, freedom, and justice.

"Convoluted thinking," Kit had said after the president's speech. "Ass-backward rationale for sustaining a flawed and fraudulent policy. I don't believe a word he read from those lily-white sheets of paper."

So it was no shock that Kit's first phone call was a call to action. We were eating our oatmeal at the dining table, which yawned faceless and silent before us, now just a long slab of wood, when he said, "Things are happening at a campus in Ohio. I'd like to show my support in person and help out if I can."

Ohio. That was a long way to stretch Kit's newfound health and stability. My breakfast sank in my belly like a bowlful of cooked gravel.

"What's going on in Ohio that isn't going on at campuses a lot closer to us?" The president's Cambodia announcement had set off student protests across the land, according to television and radio news reports.

"The authorities have declared a state of emergency and called in the National Guard. Maybe you remember them from a certain night in Chicago. They were the ones with rifles and fixed bayonets."

A wry half-smile spread across Kit's face, and I hadn't seen his eyes shine that way in months. Part of me felt overjoyed, part of me terrified. And part of me, as always, envious.

"You're going to Ohio just to be there?"

He nodded. "Strength in numbers, as they say. Solidarity. The National Guard has set up tents on the campus lawn, for godsake.

There's a rally scheduled for tomorrow, and it's my job to be there, Joey."

His eyes held mine, beseeching me to understand. The return of Kit's enthusiasm thrilled me. The reason behind it did not.

"It's something I can do," he said.

I didn't exactly march across the Rubicon, but I crossed it. "Then I'm coming with you." By choice, I'd made myself Kit's only Tribe member. "And *this* time I'm not sitting things out in Rosie or a ladies' room."

Kit's face fell.

"Joey. They're using tear gas again. They've got rifles again. The ROTC building has been torched, store windows smashed. And someone was actually stabbed with a bayonet. It's a heavy scene."

I just looked at him. Chicago was a million miles behind us.

A moment passed before he shrugged his acquiescence, but I saw a hint of gratitude alongside the resignation. "We have to leave right away if we're going to get there in time. The demonstration is scheduled for noon tomorrow. We'll have to drive straight through."

"Fine." My life with Kit had always involved blacktop and speed. "What should I pack?"

Kit was already out of his chair stacking our breakfast dishes. "A few changes of clothes, some food and wine. And plenty of cigarettes. Facing those blue shirts and weekend warriors without a smoke was the hardest part."

I had to laugh. If the memory of lighting cigarette butts in the back of Rosie wasn't exactly comedic, it was a bond with Kit forged through mutual distress.

I looked down the length of the empty table, refusing to feel nostalgic. It was time to remove the extra leaves. "So, which campus are we going to?"

Kit was halfway to the kitchen, dishes rattling in his arms. "Kent State University."

I picked up the spoons and pitcher of powdered milk. "Never heard of it."

After a lunch of cheese and tomatoes on rye at a rest stop on the far side of Chicago, Kit was at the wheel. "The Hotel feels so empty now," he said. "It actually echoes when we talk."

Refusing to sell his cherished red bus, Kit had doggedly taught himself to push its pedals with his prosthesis, practicing hour upon hour in an empty parking lot to sync the movements of his fake foot with those of his stump. I felt uneasy when he drove Rosie these days, but not because I didn't trust his driving ability. If any amputee could handle an accelerator and a brake, it was Kit. But during his turn at the wheel, sweat drops gathered on his brow, betraying the effort it now took him to do what once was effortless, reminding me of what he had to live with. Or, rather, without.

"I think it feels quiet and peaceful for a change," I replied. "I like having you to myself, and I don't mind admitting it. To me, it feels romantic."

Kit didn't take his eyes from the road. "Your perspective is understandably different from mine. While you were growing up in a small house filled with siblings, I was in an oversized showpiece, left alone with the maid most of the time. And in Nam, living and sharing with others you counted on is what kept you alive. I like having people around, sharing what I can." He slowed for a bird, which barely missed the windshield. "You never understood that, Joey."

I wondered if his need to share himself would always make his love for me feel unequal to mine for him. "I tried," I said.

I checked my watch. We'd been sixteen hours on the road, trading off every two. It was my turn to drive.

I glanced at the speedometer. Kit was pushing Rosie hard. I had no doubt we'd make it to Kent, Ohio, in plenty of time for the rally, if the old girl held up under the pressure.

"Well, I've got an idea," he said.

I smiled. Kit with an idea was the Kit of old, the Kit I'd been longing for.

"Let's hear it."

"I think it would be nice if your brothers came to live with us until they're through school. I've always felt bad about taking you away from them."

My smile went the way of a ladybug on the side mirror. I felt a rush of guilt followed by a rush of resistance. "It was my doing, not yours. I've served my time as Daddy's babysitter."

Kit reached over and squeezed my leg. "Of course you have. But that doesn't change the fact that your brothers lost their only real parent when you left. We both know your father isn't around much."

I moved his hand back to the steering wheel. "We spend time with them."

"Holidays and an occasional weekend."

"I talk to them on the phone, send money when I can."

"It's not the same, Joey."

"Jeff is now as old as I was when Mamma died, and Jack is actually older."

"They're still too young to be on their own. Just as you were."

"So what's your plan, Kit?"

He swerved around a large pothole before answering. "Invite them for a visit when school's out and ask them. If they like the idea, I doubt your dad will put up a fuss."

"How will we support them, pray tell?" I hadn't touched my embroidery needle and Kit hadn't seen the inside of Vescio's in many days. House virtually empty, our household expenses had decreased, but not our rent. I'd been waiting for the right moment to suggest a smaller place. I hadn't given the boys money since Christmas.

"I'll figure out something," Kit said.

A billboard for Bulova whizzed by, a giant watch perpetually declaring it was three o'clock.

"You always do."

Kit lifted his foot from the gas pedal, momentarily reversing the speedometer.

"Something legal, Joey. I know I'm a washout, but there's gotta be a way I can make a difference somehow."

His self-deprecation hurt my ears. I resisted the urge to stroke his hair. "You make a difference for me. Can't that be enough, at least for a while?"

"But we have that big house." His eyes were hard on the road. "Maybe we could get married. Make it a real family."

"Married!"

A stunning suggestion, a sweet dream I'd carefully stowed in an internal cigar box. A just-you-and-me union of two people in love. But it was too late for such innocent simplicity between us. That possibility had died somewhere between a dark cemetery and an overcrowded hill.

I stared at the centerline, an endless divide rolling past us, and fought back tears. Of course I wanted to be Kit's wife. It just didn't come out that way.

"I'll think it over," I said as he swerved around another pothole.

We were on a curve, and the oncoming car on the far side of it screeched left as Kit tried to brake, clutch, downshift, and yank us back to our own lane all at once. The car missed us by inches. Kit pulled to the shoulder and cut Rosie's motor as the car honked its anger for five hundred yards behind us.

He turned to me and shook his head. He opened his door. In that moment, the click it made sounded like a gunshot.

"I think you should do the driving from now on. I just can't get where I'm trying to go. I can't find the way."

🕊

The scene we found at Kent State University made me wonder why recurring dreams were always the scary ones, why the most vivid memories were always the bad ones. Why did Kit still dream about Khe Sanh instead of Woodstock? Why did Mamma always appear in my mind as a too-naked reflection in a mirror instead of a snapshot in time when she'd been beautiful and happy?

Not that everything at Kent was the same as Chicago. The location was a small town college campus, not a big city lakeside park. The crowd was maybe two thousand students and youthful onlookers instead of a sprawling collection of Americans. The face-off between protestors and National Guard was in daytime rather than at night.

But the essence of the situation was exactly the way it had been almost two years past. People against the war standing up to members of the government. The antiwar folks—dressed in jeans, khakis, button-downs, and tie-dye T-shirts—were armed with slogans, curse words, hand gestures, and an occasional stone. The government folks—dressed in helmets, gas masks, and combat gear—were armed with pistols, M-1 rifles, bayonets, and tear gas launchers. Maybe I should have been afraid, but my instant anger at the David-Goliath makeup of the scene, and my proximity to Kit, made me feel safe enough to join the chanting.

"One, two, three, four. We don't want your fucking war!" I shouted from our spot on the campus commons near the big brass victory bell that had chimed the rally's start. "Pigs off campus!" I bellowed at the policeman in the Jeep who was ordering us to disperse.

I didn't like calling any human being a pig, but he really was acting hoggish with that bullhorn. I didn't like the rocks being thrown at his vehicle either, but he had a vehicle and we were on foot. And why couldn't the rally's first speaker say what everyone had a right to say? Whatever he felt like saying. Kit was right. Something had gone seriously wrong in the land where everyone was supposed to be equal and free. These days, all we had to do to lose our rights and become the enemy was speak out against the war. I could finally relate to the internal turmoil Kit's aspiration had caused him.

"Pigs go home!" I hollered.

Then came the tear gas, the panic, the cries. *Gas! Run! Cover up! Head down!* Bodies running in front of me and behind me, a grassy hill below me, Kit pulling me with an iron grip. Marching after us with guns, blades, and chemicals were uniformed men, their gas masks making them truly look like swine. Stumbling at the crest of the hill, I hit the dirt, ripping my pants and cutting my brow before Kit jerked me back up. Clutching his shirt, I glanced back as I staggered on. Someone not fast enough was being clubbed in that familiar old way. Acrid fumes snaked around us, burning my nostrils, searing my tear ducts. I kept going, down the hill, gasping, weeping, bleeding. *Run! Run!* It was all insanely déjà vu. Chicago, Illinois, had transformed across space and time into Kent, Ohio.

We were in a parking lot when we finally stopped. Kit whirled around, whirling me with him. Our group had splintered, making us now just three or four dozen souls. But it was another face-off. The guards glared at us from a grassy area down below. "Pigs off campus!" we countered. Minutes passed like a funeral procession in a midnight rainstorm. "Fucking pigs off campus!" A brave comrade out front waved a black flag at the bullies.

Their response was to kneel and point their rifles at us. Kit yanked me behind him as someone said, "Scare tactics," and someone else said, "They've only got blanks," and someone else said, "Or rubber bullets, same as Saturday night." Those long guns aimed straight at us made me concerned, for the third surreal time since I'd known Kit, that I was going to wet my pants.

But the guardsmen finally gave up their game, rising to their feet, forming a haphazard huddle. They were up against a fence with two choices—advance or retreat. Some in our "troop" threw rocks at the masked green horde. They naturally fell short. Others tried to toss back the tear gas canisters that had been fired at us. They didn't go far. Still others flipped their middle fingers at the guardsmen and took up our chant. "One, two, three, four. We don't want your fucking war! Pigs off campus!" We were a force to be reckoned with, no doubt.

"Stay behind me," Kit shouted, and I followed his instructions, same as before, peeking around his body, expecting the moment to shatter into shards, as it had in Chicago. Expecting the day to explode into bloody chaos.

But the moment passed and then another, then another. The afternoon simply halted as the wind lifted the tear gas into the sky, as the powers that be mulled over their options. Then suddenly, they about-faced and began marching back up the hill, snouts pointing away from us, war livery and implements in retreat.

I waited for a cautious moment, then scooted in front of Kit, wrapped my arms around his waist. I'd been right by his side, as I'd insisted, but I was relieved, even elated, that the altercation had ended. I'd proven my loyalty and bravery, but I was ready to head home. "It's over," I said. "Let's go back to Rosie and open a bottle of—"

A loud crack broke the calm, and something whizzed past my ear. Then came the explosion, and I was on the ground, Kit on top of me, my back pricked by broken glass, once again. And the day just kept exploding. *Bam Bam. Bam Bam. Chink Chink. Chink Chink.* Oh Jesus, I knew that sound. It was the sound of human misery. It went on and on.

And then there was nothing.

"Stay down," Kit whispered as he lifted his head into the silence that rushed at us from every direction. Eerie mute moments passed. And then came the first scream, then the second, then the chaos.

Kit had me pinned hard to the ground and I struggled to rise. "What is it? What is it?" His body was a rock that wouldn't roll away.

Immobilized, I could hear a helicopter chop-chopping overhead. I could hear a siren wailing in the distance. I could hear Kit breathing like a long-distance runner near the end of his race.

"Close your eyes, Joey." His voice came from the far side of the Pacific. "They weren't shooting blanks."

We spent the night in a motel just outside of Toledo. Kit had phone calls to make, my nerves badly needed a warm bath, and Rosie had developed a nasty cough. I was shakily setting out our dinner—cheese, pickles, and apples—when Kit clicked on the six o'clock news. The anchorman didn't take the scenic route to the situation.

"Four dead in Ohio."

— THIRTY-TWO —

Forward, March

Kit and I holed up in Ohio for two days while he tried to cure what ailed Rosie. To conserve our waning cash, we checked out of the motel and made a wayside rest stop our home, not sure what the van needed. Engine exposed, shirt off, tool kit open, Kit checked the possibilities as I switched Rosie's ignition on and off to the point of his thumb.

Air filter. Spark plugs. Points. Carburetor. Fuel line. Kit borrowed my nail file to clean a little gizmo he called the points, which spoiled the file but made me feel useful. A clogged hose turned out to be the culprit, probably the result of some bad Indiana gas.

"Good thing you're so full of hot air," I said in an attempt at humor when Kit tried to blow out the hose. "Your kisses will be positively flammable tonight." Kisses. The past few weeks hadn't seen many.

I was relieved when, face the color of his beard, he finally changed tactics, using an unbent wire hanger and some twine to snake the hose. That eventually did the trick, and we decided to splurge on another night at the motel, where a bath could only lift our mood.

We were in no condition to share the tub. Grime had turned Kit's tattoos into modern art, and the May sun had left me as soggy as his bandana. I made Kit go first, grateful for his mechanical talents and worried about his stump. As he bathed, I reached for the television dial but changed my mind, savoring our refuge from the racket of traffic, never keen to see Dan Rather or Morley Safer crouching over a microphone amidst gunfire and explosions. Instead, I picked up the newspaper someone had left behind on the nightstand.

The headline read "4 Kent State Students Killed by Troops." Beneath it was a photo of a boy lying prone in the grass, a young woman

270

kneeling over him, her arms spread and mouth open. I knew she was screaming because I'd heard her. I knew the boy was dead from seeing his blood. Besides the four fatalities, nine had been wounded, some badly. There was also a photo of the troops and tear gas we'd faced two days back.

I scanned the other front-page articles. Almost all of them had to do with the war. I opened the door and shoved the newspaper behind the rosebush budding beneath our window.

But there was no hiding anything from Kit. During my bath, I heard him dial the phone several times, speak in low tones, and I knew he was keeping current in his own way.

"Why don't we go out for a pizza?" I said when I emerged from the bathroom a clean woman if not a new one. "There's not much food left in the bus."

"You go ahead," Kit said. "I'm not hungry enough to put my leg back on." He was under the covers already, studying the atlas he kept under Rosie's front seat and absently rubbing his stump. "And I'm waiting for a phone call."

Damn that leg. It had no mercy. "There's some peanut butter and a few crackers left. I'll manage something."

Kit didn't reply, and I flinched when the phone rang, even though I knew it was going to. I threw on some clothes, slipped out the door to inspect Rosie's stores.

I set our dinner on a towel on the bed so Kit didn't have to move. We'd polished off every morsel, including the Fritos and M&M's I'd gotten from a machine by the motel office, when he finally put down the atlas.

"We're in the middle of a second civil war, Joey. Protests about Kent are going on at half the country's campuses, and hundreds of campuses have shut down altogether."

I sat on the edge of the bed, trying to absorb his words.

"That's heavy," I said. "But do you think it'll do any good? Does anyone really care if some students cut class?"

"Colleges are major commerce, Joey. They employ a lot of people, make a lot of money."

"So those kids didn't die for nothing?" I closed my eyes, trying to block out the images, but they just became more vivid.

The deep crease in Kit's brow had been there for two days. "Like you, a lot of folks turn the channel when the war reports come on. But this story is everywhere, and it's too hideous to ignore. This happened right here in America. I think Kent might be the blizzard that blows down the door and exposes the decay inside."

I wanted to believe that, but feared another letdown in Kit's life.

"Yeah, but a lot of people think the war is a noble undertaking," I countered. "A righteous cause. Root out the commies, spread freedom, all that."

Kit held his ground. "After a closeup view, I'm of the opinion most South Vietnamese just want to be left alone to grow their rice. That's their concept of freedom."

"Most people don't know that, Kit. Most people haven't been to Vietnam and aren't very interested in hearing from those who have. To the average American, it's all about the red threat to democracy."

Kit shook his head.

"But that threat has always been on the other side of the planet, Joey. It was just a color on a TV map. The whole red mess could be ignored by simply switching to Red Skelton. Dropping bombs in the name of peace didn't need to make sense. But the fight came home on Monday. Unarmed school kids got shot dead. I don't think that's going to just fade away. Insanity has transpired, not democracy. I mean, you don't kill a kid for saying fuck."

"So what now? Is the U of M involved in the rebellion?"

Kit stared at me. "It's gone beyond Minnesota, Joey. At least for me. And beyond pamphlets, slogans, speeches. Our own soldiers declared war on us when they pulled those triggers, and I'm not waiting around for a draft notice."

I just nodded, waiting for the upshot, already knowing he'd made a decision.

"It's time to get involved at a higher level. Rot always starts at the top, and that's the place you have to go if you really want to eradicate it. We need to be more proactive. The brass have to be shown—close up—

how far we're prepared to go to end this war. It's a revolution, Joey. And for the sake of everything that matters, we have to win at all costs."

I just waited.

"There's a demonstration scheduled for Saturday in Washington, DC. I plan to be there. If you don't feel like coming with me, I have enough scratch for a bus ticket to Minneapolis."

I felt hurt that he wasn't certain, by now, that I'd want to share his journey. But he was giving me an option, a way out of a third clash with soldiers. "Of course I feel like coming with you. I'm with you all the way, Kit."

He reached for his flask, a faint smile on his face. "Okay, little girl."

He hadn't used that intimate endearment in a while. "Okay," I said, smiling back.

I rose from the bed, knelt by our duffel bag. I'd packed for the unexpected, but visiting Washington, DC, was beyond unexpected. God knew who we might run into there. Maybe Woodstock's elusive Oscar. Maybe Tom Hayden. Maybe even Dave Dellinger. I pulled out my blue floral blouse and Kit's white tunic, which I'd embroidered with a blue floral border. We were a synchronized duo at last.

Kit drank brandy that night for the first time in many nights. For the first time since he'd been off heroin, to be exact. And maybe the brandy brought on the nightmare. Khe Sanh again. Rats again. Thrashing and moaning, he kicked at them with his lone foot, occasionally shouting "Get away from me, goddamn it!" or "Incoming!" as he ducked his head into his arms and I lay there powerless to save him.

Kit wasn't into conversation the next morning. He hadn't driven Rosie since the pothole incident, and stared silently out the side window as miles passed like fleeting memories of days gone by. We'd just crossed the Pennsylvania border when he ordered me to pull over. The moment Rosie skidded to a stop on the shoulder, he was out the door, vomiting into the ditch.

"Maybe Christian Brothers has changed its recipe," I said as I pulled back onto the road, hating the rueful look on his face and trying to defuse the awkwardness.

273

"It's not the brandy. It's my foot. The old guy is really missing me this morning."

At times like this, there was a small part of me that didn't hate Doc for what he'd done. For the haven he'd provided Kit. "Maybe that phantom pain will go away someday."

Kit lit a cigarette and cracked Rosie's window before he exhaled. "Maybe." The wind whistled like a harmonica stuck on one note as he closed his eyes. "Maybe not."

We stopped for gas at a station in Pittsburgh. The attendant was about Kit's age, and Kit struck up a conversation that grew animated. In minutes, the two were laughing and slapping each other on the back like old pals. When Kit poked his head in the car door and asked for the checkbook, I gave it to him with a raised eyebrow. He'd clearly talked the fellow into taking our out-of-state check.

Back on the road, I couldn't help asking, "Won't he get in trouble when that bounces?"

Kit gave me a cool look. "I postdated it. I'll get it covered."

"Might I ask how?" The words just came out, and I would have braved another line of National Guard rifles to retrieve them.

His face instantly flushed, but he stared at the road. A long moment later he said, "Is your faith in me completely gone, Joey? Isn't my word good enough for you anymore? I said I'll cover the check, and I will. I want to be prudent with our cash right now. Maybe you know something I don't, but I'm not sure what to expect when we get to DC."

"I'm sorry. It was an asinine question. I'm sorry, Kit."

"Forget it," he said, so softly that the thump-thump of the road almost obscured his words. "Just forget it."

— THIRTY-THREE —

One Too Many Mornings

I'd never been to our capital, but I was pretty sure it didn't normally look the way it did when we arrived late Friday afternoon, taxiing into the center of things from Rosie's parking spot. Whether you called them college kids, long-hairs, hippies, the younger generation, or bums, as Nixon did, they were everywhere—outfitted in colorfully rebellious duds, making the city of stately white buildings, famous monuments, and reflecting pools look like a carnival-colored refugee camp.

"Seems the bums have laid siege to the place," I said as Kit paid the cabbie and picked up our sleeping bag, into which I'd stuffed cigs and edibles. Under no illusions this time, we'd prepared better than we had for Chicago.

"Let's just say those who live or work here are no longer in their comfort zone," Kit said, stepping alongside me. "And that's good. As Woody put it, this land is also ours, and it's time everyone gets that." The closer we'd gotten to DC on the drive east, the more Kit's mood had lifted. To my delight, he was now in sparkling form.

It was a pretty May day, I'd brought my camera, and for the first time since Woodstock, I felt like recording my surroundings.

I caught Kit in a picture-perfect smile, a smile that said he was finally feeling well, happy, and in his element. "When are you supposed to meet your friend?"

"A few hours yet."

"Up for some sightseeing?" I'd done all the driving, and Kit, gazing about from a ready-for-action stance, seemed strong on his feet.

"You bet. Looks like one interesting town."

"Should we go see if the White House is really white?"

"Groovy idea. Lead on, lovely tour guide."

I snapped tourist landmarks as we meandered away the time till our meet-up. The White House barricaded by a string of district buses. The Washington Monument surrounded by antiwar signs and black flags. The Capitol Building steps swarmed by slogan chanters with more signs. Pennsylvania Avenue dotted by small mobs with a mission. The National Mall turned into a picnic zone, the Reflecting Pool into a swimming hole.

"This is where it's at," Kit said, eyes bright. "*This* is the place to make a difference. To get their attention in a sensational way. To show how committed we are."

He pointed at a sign, held high by a boy whose blonde ponytail didn't go with his striped button-down. THEY CAN'T KILL US ALL, it read.

"It's always been a matter of life and death, Joey. Kent State just brought that home."

ॐ

I heard a tour guide say Abraham Lincoln's face depicts two periods of time, in the mammoth marble statue that honors him in the city where he was shot dead by a fellow American. One profile shows him at the beginning of his presidency—before war had ravaged both the country and the man. The other profile shows a weary leader made old by strife, anguish, and worry. The theory appealed to the romantic as well as the realist in me, and I chose to believe it. As I framed and snapped Lincoln's stone visage onto film, camera aimed high, I felt sure I saw the difference between his two sides. War, I knew as well as any sculptor, could change a man forever, could crush the spark of youth right out of him.

Kit's long-distance friend introduced himself to me as "a Pittsburgh peace freak," allowing Kit to instantly dub him Freako, and I never did learn his real name. We shook hands at the designated place—Lincoln Memorial, top of the steps, inside the huge Doric pillars, just left of the great man's feet. Freako, a nice-looking fellow without being memorable, was certainly no freak in appearance. By rebel-student standards his hair and clothes were prep-school conservative. His language, however, was positively renegade.

"There's an internal debate going on over tomorrow's locale. Some of the organizers want to set us free on H Street. Others want to corral us behind the White House in the Ellipse field, where there's less chance of confrontation with the authorities. I'm for the *streets.*"

Freako threw up his hands. "I mean, what kind of message can a herd of hippies in the grass send to anyone?" he scoffed. "We're hoping for a hundred thousand kids, but what kind of power will we have without *movement?* Where is the opportunity for civil disobedience? Hell, if we let them coop us up in a field, we'll be sitting *ducks.*"

He leaned in and lowered his voice. "Rumor has it the Eighty-Second Airborne is camped out in the basement of the Executive Office Building. They could drop a net over us from a chopper. They could spray us with tear gas or agent orange. They could cut loose with their pistols and M-1s. We gotta be out there in the open with options for action, ahead of the pigs and in front of the cameras."

Kit's bright countenance had darkened. "The field idea is definitely bad. Sitting in the grass is how you have a picnic, how you listen to music, not how you end a war. A dramatic face-off is the only way to get the attention of those who need to know what this is really about. We need something visual—a moral explosion to force the public out of their sheep mentality."

"I vote no on the field," I said, remembering my panicked moments at Woodstock. "But whatever we do, our numbers will surely make an impression."

"Maybe," Kit said, as if to himself. "Maybe not."

When nightfall came, talk of tomorrow's protest eventually gave way to the need for sleep. By then the three of us had grown into a small tribe of eight or ten, waiting for dawn with no place better to lay our heads. We bedded down right there near Mr. Lincoln, Kit and I taking a private spot by one of the great pillars, in sight of the lighted Reflecting Pool. Inside a sleeping bag with him once again, I didn't turn Kit down when he said, "You soothe my soul and feed my spirit, Joey Dean." It was the most beautiful place we ever made love.

☙

Sometime well after midnight but before dawn, the sound of footsteps and voices woke me. Kit was already sitting up, looking toward the statue. I followed his gaze.

Two men in business suits were viewing the great sculpture, one talking, one nodding. Other members of our current tribe were stirring in their sleeping bags or rising. The talkative fellow walked over to one of them and held out his hand. He looked tired, oddly sweaty, and badly in need of a shave. His deep under-eye circles and dark whisker shadows made me think of a boxer who'd just lost a big match. He began speaking in a low mumble.

"Oh my god, it's the president," I whispered.

Kit was reaching for his brandy flask, which he'd tucked inside our sleeping bag. "Or Lincoln's ghost on the way home from a costume party."

Despite his quip, I knew Kit was as surprised as I was, when he spilt brandy all down the front of his white tunic.

"I think we should get in on the conversation," he said, tossing the empty flask onto our bag, unable to shake a drop into his mouth.

By now several others had joined the group around Richard Nixon, including four or five men I took to be Secret Service agents. The students looked sleepy and startled. The agents looked tense and uneasy. Kit didn't hang back, maneuvering us within earshot of the man who embodied the war we so despised.

The president—still mumbling, eyes averted from anyone's face—was talking about the Syracuse football team. Football seemed a strange subject, given the time of night and the fact that we'd hijacked his town for the purpose of defying him.

Kit whispered to me, "Maybe that limo is really a spaceship." I wondered if the president might actually be sleepwalking.

But as he rambled from subject to subject with no apparent direction, swallowing many of his words, staring at nothing, I eventually decided he was indeed awake, but in some sort of strange mental state.

He reminded me of Doc after he'd toked one too many. In fact, if I hadn't known better, I'd have said Richard Nixon had smoked a big joint without passing it around.

He spoke of his press conference, apparently broadcast earlier that night, and most of us just stared. Press conference. A staged charade. An inadequate gesture. Nothing he said to news reporters could justify murder, or erase it. Words wouldn't bring back the dead that were on his head.

"I'm sorry you missed it," he said. "I tried to explain that my goals in Vietnam are the same as yours. Stop the killing . . . end the war . . . peace . . . Cambodia . . . out of Vietnam."

"Please speak up, Mr. President," someone said. "We can't hear you."

Kit was shifting from foot to foot, more agitated than I'd ever seen him be.

"Yes, let us all hear what you have to say," he said politely but loudly.

"Probably most of you think I'm an SOB," the president went on. "But I want you to know that I understand just how you feel."

It was such an absurd statement, tears filled my eyes. This was the man in charge of the National Guard. This was the current boss of the Vietnam War. This was one of the thieves who'd stolen Kit's leg.

He began talking about his Quaker youth, when he'd leaned toward pacifism and admired Neville Chamberlain. "I thought Churchill was a madman. In retrospect, I now realize I was wrong," he said. He called Churchill the wiser man, and seemed to be connecting us to his younger self, Churchill to his older one. But the Vietnam War was not World War II, and the comparison suddenly made me feel sick to my stomach.

Maybe the president felt he was treading on dangerous terrain—discussing the war in the middle of the night with our scruffy little tribe, which was growing by the minute. Maybe his thoughts simply shifted. He abruptly changed the subject.

"You must travel when you're young," he said. "If you wait until you can afford it, you will be too old to enjoy it."

What followed, as we stood there mutely listening, was a meandering travelogue of the world, parts of it too muffled or low for me to catch. Europe. China. India. Malaysia. Russia. Prague. Warsaw. Haiti. The president droned on and on about foreign locations. "Europe," I heard him say, "is really an older version of America." He said Asia was the place we would particularly enjoy visiting.

Asia. What was the matter with the man? Vietnam was in Asia. The Ho Chi Minh Trail was in Asia. Hill 881 South was in Asia. Was he mocking us or just talking down?

"Some of us have already been there," Kit said back to him, breathing hard, leaning forward.

If the president heard Kit, he didn't let on. He kept rambling. He said he hoped mainland China would be opened in our lifetime, if not during his presidency. China. Wasn't China supplying North Vietnam with weapons? Wasn't China a bad guy? Why would we want to go *there*? Or anywhere else but *here*, where the heart of the war was beating a few feet away?

"We're not interested in what Prague looks like," someone said. "We're interested in what kind of life we build in the United States."

The president caught that remark, looking startled, even wounded by the challenge. "The whole purpose of my discussing Prague and other places was not to discuss the city, but the people," he replied.

The people. Dead soldiers were the people. Dead students were the people. Dead *American* soldiers and students. They were the reason we'd traveled to this particular foreign land.

"Christ," Kit muttered. "The man is retarded or mad." I could feel the tension in his body without touching him. He was electric with passion and frustration.

The president zigzagged between other subjects—the "Negro problem" and slavery, the destruction of the American Indians, Mexican American poverty, the environment. Kit was now biting his lip, fingering his beard. I wanted to take him away from this place, to squeeze the brandy from his soaked shirt back into his flask so he could swallow his way to calm. I looked around me. I saw blank stares and quizzical glances. We were at a hopeless impasse with a zombie from a different universe. A zombie who just happened to be the leader of the free world.

The president was fairly babbling now. "Ending the war and cleaning up the city streets and the air and the water is not going to solve the spiritual hunger which all of us have, which of course has been the great mystery of life from the beginning of time." He said we were searching for the same answer he'd searched for forty years ago.

"Jesus," Kit hissed. "He actually doesn't see the difference." He was flicking the top of his Zippo with a frenzy. We'd left our cigarettes in the sleeping bag. I wanted to sit by the Reflecting Pool and share a smoke. I wanted the war to magically disappear from our life. I wanted this loony old man to go back to bed.

"I hope you realize that we're willing to die for what we believe in," someone behind us piped up, maybe Freako. I heard a bird frantically chirping in the distance. A wren, maybe.

"I certainly realize that," the president said. "Do you realize that many of us, when we were your age, were also willing to die for what we believed in and are willing to do so today? The point is that we are trying to build a world in which you will not have to die for what you believe in, in which you're able to live for it."

"No one *his* age is dying in Vietnam," Kit murmured. "Or getting shot in the middle of a schoolyard."

The president folded his arms and looked thoughtfully toward Mr. Lincoln. "You must remember that something that is completely clean can also be completely sterile, without spirit. What we all must think about is why we are here."

Kit raised his hand, then let it drop. "We're *here* to address the war, Mr. President, and there's nothing clean about it, let alone sterile," he said, voice loud and clear. "You must understand what an immoral cause it is. How dedicated we are to ending it. That there is blood on your hands. People are dying for no justifiable reason in terrible ways. Soldiers, women, children. Babies. We shoot them, torch their villages,

281

burn them with napalm. And they fight back."

The president's gaze seemed to land somewhere vaguely in Kit's direction. He still wasn't looking anyone in the eye.

"I know you want to get the war over," the man said. "Sure you came here to demonstrate and shout your slogans on the Ellipse. That's all right. Just keep it peaceful. Have a good time in Washington, and don't go away bitter."

Kit looked at me, clearly dismayed. Clearly stunned. "He doesn't get it, Joey. The human price of this war isn't real to him. He hasn't been there. He can't visualize what death in war means. He can't see the blood, hear the screams, see the fire." Kit was breathing too fast, blinking too fast, trembling. I tried to take his hands, but he yanked them away. He looked down at his Zippo, which he was still clutching. The open top was clinking, and he cocked his head, as if the sound was telling him something. "I've got to show him what war means."

Then he backed away from me, away from everyone in our small huddle, not looking where he was going, but smiling at me as he receded into the retreating night. Smiling a strange and radiant smile that said I love you and forgive me and farewell and hallelujah all at the same time. Kit was still smiling, his hair shimmering in the hint of a new day, when he shouted, "Mr. President!" Then he flicked his Zippo and turned into a newborn star—a star so bright it blurred my vision, so hot it singed my brow, so potent it shriveled my nostril hairs.

They tried to keep him unconscious because of the pain, which no amount of morphine could stop. It was the only humane thing to do, and he opened his eyes just once in those final three days.

There was no bit of him I dared to touch, as he lay wrapped in dressings and drugs, but his eyes were all I needed to reach. Without the haloes of his lashes, they were even more intensely the blue-green of a foreign sea. I stared into them, unable to look away, seeing a reflection so mysterious and deep I wanted to drown in it, but knowing I couldn't, that he'd left me with a duty I couldn't shirk.

I touched my belly as a house sparrow carefully interwove her collection of twigs out on Kit's window ledge, and I said what Kit needed to hear and I needed to say.

"I'm so proud of you. It's been all over the news. You made the president understand. The government brass are having meetings, rethinking their war policy. They finally get it, Kit."

A single newspaper had noted the "unfortunate accident" of an unnamed student on the eve of the march, the night Nixon came calling. And Secret Service agents had blocked the momentary unpleasantness from presidential view. Nixon had been whisked away in his limo with only the fledgling sunrise in his eyes.

I dared not touch Kit as I recited those rehearsed lines, but I kissed the air and blew it his way. And he nodded at me, I know he did.

"Wait for me," I said, nodding back. "I'll be there as soon as I can."

— THIRTY-FOUR —

Someday, Baby

The applause had dwindled to the coughers and stray clappers, cuing me that my moment for expressing gratitude had begun. I slid my borrowed gold shoes close to the podium, gazed out at the crowd. A flashbulb exploded, capturing the look on my face for posterity, or a dented file cabinet at the back of some dusty closet. Capturing a moment of validation I'd yearned and worked for since age seventeen, thirteen long years ago. Maybe it was the flash that disoriented me, made my breath catch as I realized how long I'd hung on.

I cleared my throat as I slipped my list from beneath the rhinestone bracelet that could almost pass for diamonds in the spotlight. I unfolded the bit of paper, but it fell from my hand. At the edge of my vision, I saw it drift to the floor like a playbill insert announcing a stand-in. From far up in the rafters, I heard the flutter of wings.

He was right there front row center, hair and beard especially ablaze that well-lit evening, twinkling smile the one I remembered so well—the smile that sustained me daily, always promised sun when clouds hovered.

I should have known he'd show up when I least expected him. When I most needed reassurance he approved of the path I'd chosen, a path so different from his, yet ultimately with a shared destination. In that moment our eyes met for the first time in a decade, I relived it all, all that had gone down since he'd gone ahead.

I relived the drive across half of America, his ashes in a cardboard box on the seat beside me. As I'd once driven home from Chicago and upstate New York, I drove home from Washington, DC. I made it all the way to the Hotel without losing my mind or the child I instinctively knew we'd created that last time. It was all I could manage in those first days after.

Once home, I did what he'd suggested. I invited my brothers to stay. But to say I took care of them again wouldn't be quite the truth. They gave me meals to cook, lucky socks to wash, torn pants to mend. They gave me three reasons to get up in the morning, until the fourth reason pushed its way into what remained of my existence. They kept the abyss I flickered inside of for many months, like the last ember in the cosmos, from going dark.

The Tribe paid their respects, even Doc, leaving small tributes and sharing stories that made their leader come to life, if only for a moment. Tommy sent a tasteful sympathy card containing three twenties but no note. Daddy just sent a card, but he signed it with love.

A cosmic sister came to help. When black waters flooded my days and acrid flames burned my nights, when birth pains racked my bones and death almost snatched my boy one bitter winter, Dee Dee was there.

People did what they could as my years of perdition passed. Even Kit.

His birthday camera paid the rent after Boo praised my Woodstock photographs to a writer friend who'd landed a publishing contract for a book about the legendary event. His insurance policy—dated the day before his amputation and folded neatly in the bottom of my cigar box—covered tuition and books almost to my graduation. Joeyful Threads did the heavy lifting, though, even when an acting role with a paycheck finally came along. An acting role in the city where treading the boards is a laudable aspiration and a three-room East Village walk-up is home to my boy and me. Where my needle and thread still sustain us. It's not Elsewhere by a million miles, but it feels elsewhere enough anymore.

My boy grew big and strong, a love child at the core of every smile and caress I still own. On summer days, the sun shoots amber beams through his hair, turns his eyes the color of an exotic sea. I plodded on toward my chosen goal, but he is my only cause. On a full-moon night last June, we spread his father's ashes in the Homestead's long-abandoned garden, the weeds stroking his face, the moonlight shimmering off the silver bracelet on his slender, freckled wrist.

Did I understand why Kit did what he did? Eventually. He tried to make a difference. To end the pain he'd seen, felt, and caused in a time of chaos, conflict, and carnage. In a time of blazing hope. He gave all he had to give, as he saw it. And who was I to complain or judge? Sixteen aspirins might have prevented us from ever meeting. How could I not be grateful for a lifetime in three years and a purpose on this earth? In his way, Kit saved me from my fate. The war he'd fought in and against finally flickered to an end five years after his death.

☙

In the split second of recognition, I relived it all, every tick-tock since our last exchange. And then he pulled me back into my reality, winking at me in that old way, silently urging me to go on with my speech. I leaned toward the microphone. Of all the emotions vying for control of that moment, regret and longing stepped aside so I could say my piece. I'd finally taught them how to yield the stage.

"Thank you to the *Village Voice*, the Obie committee, and everyone involved in this production. Though longevity wasn't the fate of this off-Broadway run, participating in it was the most rewarding episode of my acting career. For a short time we were family, a tribe with a sweet shared goal."

I glanced at the rafters, no tears threatening, finally accepting that death is the only certainty in this temporal place, that even heartache is a gift.

"Thank you to my mother for her ever watchful eye. And thank you to my brothers—Jack, Jeff, and Jim—and my dear friend Dee Dee. You all know why. And many thanks to my son Gabriel. You're the man I live for, Gabe.

"Thank you also to Peter for finding value in my snapshots of some idealistic rebels. Another tribe I once belonged to, with a dream too big and bright for this world.

"And finally, I'd like to dedicate this award to my son's father, who's here tonight. He bought the camera that gave me a different view of the trees and a glimpse of that peaceful beach beyond the sorrow. I'll love you always, Kit. And when it's time, I'll meet you where the ocean joins the sand."

My deepest and everlasting thanks to—

My Rollins College professors Lezlie Laws, Maurice J. O'Sullivan, Philip F. Deaver, and Connie May Fowler for their unwavering wisdom, inspiration, dedication, and encouragement along my writing journey.

My Spalding University MFA in Writing program professors Roy Hoffman, K. L. Cook, and Rachel Harper for their many wise, insightful, and constructive contributions to the growth of my creative writing, and Sena Jeter Naslund, Kathleen Driskell, Karen Mann, and Katy Yocom for an incomparably enlightened, uplifting, and life-altering writing program.

My beta readers, Katherine Vaccaro, Kay Mullally, Lynette Christensen, and Carol Swartz, for their gracious and untiring efforts and support.

My publisher, Joan Leggitt, for believing in Joey and Kit's story, and for her consummate expertise.

About the Author

Renée Anduze holds an MFA in Writing from Spalding University and a BA in English from Rollins College (summa cum laude). She has worked as a professional writer and editor for nearly 20 years—five of them at Rollins College. Her work has appeared in national magazines, newspapers, newsletters, and online. She has won several writing awards, including three Royal Palm Literary Awards. Her poetry is published in *Rollins Book of Verse 1885–2010*. Renée has taught and tutored upper-level English and participated in Bread Loaf and many other major workshop conferences. She is a member of the Association of Writers & Writing Programs, Florida Writers Association, Sigma Tau Delta International English Honor Society, and Alpha Sigma Lambda National Honor Society.